CW01025271

IMPERFECT CURSE

A DARKLY FUNNY SUPERNATURAL SUSPENSE MYSTERY - BOOK 2 OF THE IMPERFECT CATHAR

C.N. ROWAN

MAIN ROCK PUBLISHING

Copyright © 2023 by C.N.Rowan and Main Rock Publishing.

Cover design and artwork by Nick Jones.

All rights reserved.

No portion of this book may be reproduced in any form without written permission from the publisher or author, except as permitted by U.S. copyright law.

Any resemblance to real persons or other real-life entities is purely coincidental. All characters and other entities appearing here are fictitious. Any resemblance to real persons, dead or alive, or other real-life entities, past or present, is purely coincidental.

To Najla, Ilyas and Lyanna.
Three points that form the whole of my heart.
Every word is always for you.

FOREWORD

Welcome to the second book in The imPerfect Cathar series!

A warning which I'm sure you're aware of, if you have read the first one –
and if not, you really should before diving into this merry tale of havoc and
death – that there is plenty of language that isn't just profane. It does in fact
stick two fingers up at profane and insult profane's mother. All apologies
to my own mother. She did raise me better. The fault is entirely my own.

British English is the order of the day in a 'pie and chips, Sunday roast
with a pint of stout, cor blimey guv'nor' kind of way. That also means
expect S's for Z's and RE's for ER's. And not in a 'regarding the hospital'
sense.

We have – as a collective entity
called WRITER-EDITOR-PROOFREADER-EVERY-LIVING-PER-
SON-I-CAN-GET-TO-LAY-EYES-ON-IT (catchy title for a gestalt monster, no?) - tried our absolute damndest to catch every one of the grammar
and spelling mistakes. Nevertheless, and despite our attempt to pull off
a 'We Are Legion' impression, we remain human, and mistakes may slip
through. If you come across something please do let me know by dropping
me an email at chris@cnrowan.com. It's always a pleasure to hear from you
anyhow.

There's a special free short story available by signing up to my newsletter at the end, but as it revolves around one of the characters we meet in this book, I advise you to wait until we get to the end before diving after the freebies. It'll still be there when you finish. Promise.

Anyhow, enough of my precursory ramblings. Let's get onto the main ramblings themselves.

Onwards to shenaniganary!

CONTENTS

GLOSSARY

Mec – Modern French slang for a male friend.

Cadorna – Ancient Languedoc insult, literal meaning old cow.

Saabi – Arabic slang for friend

Laguna – Old Occitan/Basque slang for friend

Ami – Modern French word for friend.

CHAPTER ONE
TOULOUSE, 8 APRIL, PRESENT DAY

Approaching burnout at a rate of knots. Painfully aware that the odds of me slowing down before crashing into that particular iceberg are minimal.

There's nothing like coming home to find a kid bleeding out on your doorstep.

I'm worn out. Exhausted. Done in. Ready to slump in front of some mind-numbing eye-candy of a TV series with my own bodyweight of sugary goodness for company due to recent escapades involving torture, betrayal, dying (three times), and more twists and turns than a waterslide designed by M C Escher.

So you can picture my ecstatic joy when, on parking outside my humble terraced house in central Toulouse, just up from the Canal De Brienne, I see one of Franc's people sitting on my doorstep. Nobody knows what Franc is, but we can all agree on one thing. He's *powerful*, absolutely radiant with destructive *talent* and magic; even stranger than that, he uses it to connect him to his "lovely lads and lasses" — the homeless and desperate who swear allegiance for a magical blessing that keeps them alive, although not protected from misery and suffering. In exchange, Franc feeds off said emotional distress and uses them as a network of spies, encasing a tiny tendril of his putrid essence in their brains. We made an accord when I got back to Toulouse in the nineteenth century and found him, a monster, living in my beloved river, polluting it with his presence. I wanted to kill him on the spot. Problem was, I wasn't sure the city would be left standing if I tried.

He met me under a flag of parlay –a dirty rag stained with unnamed bodily fluids, but a "flag" nonetheless– and I was too broken, too worn down by misery to think clearly.

So we have an agreement, one sealed with oaths on our power. It's served me well many times, and I've regretted it bitterly even more often. It's pretty straightforward really. Franc reports any Talented who manage to sneak past my borders surrounding Toulouse –hard but not impossible– and I don't try to kill him.

But if this kid's pitiable state is Franc's fault, if he did this deliberately? That renders our agreement null and void, and I'll be more than happy to skip some much needed sleep to get to murdering him.

Well, to try, at least.

The kid is so young, it hurts to imagine they know anything of the unfair vitriol of life, let alone that they've lived the harshest it has to offer. Lank yellow hair curtains the kid's closed expression, layer upon layer providing a hiding place. A hood pulled up corrals the strands to cover as much as possible. Grease and dirt obscure all but the striking cut of cheekbones. That and the blood I can see. Their hands, crossed over their body, unconsciously push up the sleeves of their T-shirt, scratching at scabbed sores that speak of dingy squats and dirty needles. Their loose sleeveless hoodie and their lack of three square meals make their form androgynous, so as I can't tell if they identify as male or female, if either. When they raise their head, it doesn't matter. I'm looking Franc straight in his white eggshell eyes.

Normally, he's happy enough just to ride along in the backseat, voyeuristically watching from behind their conscious mind. But when he needs to, he can grab the wheel and hijack their physical form. It's all part of his deal with them. All part of what I despise about the deal I made with him.

'I calls upon our treaty-teasings and all promise forms, little lordling,' he says, but there is none of the usual bantering menace, the good-natured promise of waiting death for all and sundry — me, him, the whole damn world. The words wheeze out as crimson tears spill down the wretched shell's cheeks. Then they vomit blood.

CHAPTER TWO

TOULOUSE, 8 APRIL, PRESENT DAY

What can top off a shitty day better than being covered in vomit? Being covered in blood and vomit, of course.

Had I not exsanguinated more than a few people (and that's a phrase most don't foresee themselves saying when they're young, looking towards a hopeful future), I would find it hard to believe this tiny child could contain such a stomach full of claret. It soaks my T-shirt, plastering the fabric to my midriff and pools at my feet like a player select icon from a video game. Jesus Christ. *What have you done, Franc? What the fuck have you done?*

'Franc, what the hell is going on? Why are you bringing this bullshit to my front door?' I hope my words convey just how pissed off I am even though I'm now propping up the kid, trying to stabilise them with my healing magic. Jade energy rolls down my hands as I *push* them into the kid, trying to force the power to take control, to stem the flow of blood pouring from his nose, gushing down his chin, and soaking through the already encrusted T-shirt. But it's doing nothing. I don't know why, but it's like water off a duck's back, just sliding off the kid, falling to the floor like the burgundy rivulets from his face. The kid feels *wrong*, even more so than Franc's chosen ones normally do, than even Franc himself does. It's making me feel distinctly nervous, the grainy tiredness to my eyes taking those worries and stepping them up a notch. Nothing's gone right since I died in the shit wizard's basement a few days and multiple bodies ago. Right now, it feels like things might be about to take a turn for the worse.

'Our promisings, our pledges and pray-thees, brightling. All accords a-calling, demands due.' Franc hisses from the borrowed, bloodied mouth. 'No time nor forcings found to beg or bind. Come with my little peck-pecking startled starling now, whether at your inconveniencing or no.'

The eyes flash and fade, turning back to brown haunted by suffering. The kid's breath hitches, startled, then they bolt from my door and my gaze. Once they establish a safe distance, the street's hard-learned lessons to keep out of reach now instinctive, they turn and make a swift one-handed beckon, then stumble up the road towards the Boulevard Lacrosses.

The Good God damn it, I don't need this. I really don't. All I want is to rest, some serious continuous, unbroken sleep. Eight hours would be good. Eight days even better right now. Then some whisky, some fine dining perhaps. Franc can wait. Whatever he wants can't be that fucking important. Not more than sleep and booze. Except...

Except I keep seeing the blood pouring from an innocent face. And I don't know if it's because of Franc or by Franc. Either way, I have to know. I have to do something about it.

The Good God damn it.

Cursing the names of the many gods I've encountered across the world, I follow Franc's emissary, blood drops like breadcrumbs spilling from the poor, twisted Hansel/Gretel stumbling lost through an urban forest.

To say I'm on edge is an understatement. I'm balancing on the thinnest crack between plunging into exhausted paranoia on the one side and blind panic on the other. It's like the world's shittiest tightrope made of my strung-out nerves, and it's not at all what I had in mind on the drive home. Franc's kid passes the shopping centres and neon lights, diving down the side road, Rue de la Paix.

They're like a rabbit, turning, their foot twitching like Thumper, constantly reassuring themselves I'm just behind them as I hurry as fast as a body crying out for a bit of downtime can manage. I've not seen Franc, not since he went into hiding after Ben, my best friend and student from my first life turned psychopathic destroyer of worlds, carved up some of his people as a warning to stop feeding me any information I might use against him. I feel my chest tighten at the thought. Ben's gone, no longer stuck in a cycle of reincarnation thanks to Jakob's incredible capacity for forgiveness. That's something I can't manage. To forgive. Not Ben, for what he put us through. Not myself, because there's a part of me that feels his descent into madness was my fault. And that loss, his loss that haunted me through a hundred lifetimes is all the fresher once again, like a picked-off scab on an old war wound. Even if the man he became was a monster, I can't help mourning the brother I lost, bleeding out on the stone flags in the castle of Lavaur.

And that's the thing, of course. I can't shake that thought as I rush after this bleeding, broken street orphan. If *Ben* could turn like that, a man I considered the best of us when he lived the first time, then what might happen with a monster like Franc? Not to mention that I believed myself the only person in the world to be gifted –or cursed– with this continuous reincarnating. Now we know Ben got his own terrible, twisted version of it because he caught a few drops of the essence from the Holy Grail as it broke. And he wasn't the only one in the room.

That Arnaud Almeric, a madman who sacrificed hundreds of my people to corrupt the Grail in an attempt to bring forth the devil, might be alive has woken me up every night since in cold sweats. And now Franc, a monster I made a foolish deal with centuries ago, sends a bleeding wreck of a child to bring me to him?

Nothing good is coming. That much I'm sure of.

The runner slips in through a set of half-open red-painted gates just as I clock our destination. In the nineties, a group of left-wing activists found out La Chapelle, the old abandoned chapel in front of me, was going to be sold to developers. They mobilised and squatted in it, occupying public space to keep it in public hands. It became a centre for various associations, as well as a social hub. Concerts, debates, charitable collections, and shared collective meals made it into an institution. It earned the label of the longest continuous squat in France. Eventually, the local government caved in to its popularity and achievements, and in recent years, they gave it recognised status, intending to sell the building directly to the associations that use and maintain it. It was a fait accompli for people power.

But Franc isn't a people person. Not unless they're his people. As in, owned by him, body and soul.

I don't like this. On the one hand, this is definitely edging towards Franc's terrain. Squats and doss houses are the homes where his people survive, permanently severed from society's cold-hearted embrace, where you're only welcomed as long as you conform, fit in, and contribute without being a burden. But this place isn't his. No. This is the people who fight for more, who demand a better world for the unvalued and unloved. Here's somewhere that would save Franc's people from him. If that were possible.

But surely Franc can't be inside? He lives in the dark, in the shadows, under the water's surface, in the lightless depths of the Garonne River.

When he surfaces, it's on abandoned pathways, in half-forgotten sewers. Anywhere away from any human he doesn't own entirely. But if I'm here to meet one of his emissaries, why not just talk to me through the poor youth he had staking out my doorway? Half of me's worried this is all one of his grand gestures, a massive waste of time.

The other half of me is far more worried that it's not.

I wonder how closely the flaking paint on the entrance gate resembles the colour of the metal underneath. How much ruin has penetrated underneath the once-glossy surface. Pushing the gate further back, wincing at the accompanying screech, I step onto the grounds of La Chapelle. The place is eerily quiet for the time of day. Normally this is when one would expect to see members of the association getting things ready for whatever was happening this evening or else just tending to the shrubs and trees pushed up against the main building or the outhouse, away from the concrete centre that is used for communal meals and meetings on warmer days. But now it's empty. And that can't signal anything good. Dread creeps its way through my system as I make my way towards the main entrance of the old once-church.

I approach the doorway leading off a large brightly painted concrete shelter that's used as a stage for open air jams and concerts. The panelled wooden door looks timeworn, but it carries its original quality in its grain — it's solid and expertly carved. There's a half-open gap that the kid slips through, but I'm not about to squeeze through that tiny opening. I push the door fully open, allowing myself inside.

Within, a makeshift bar runs along the left-hand side, ready to serve drinks or food depending on the event. The walls are white-washed and plain. This is that rarest of things — a humble French church. Sure, it has a vaulted ceiling, and there are arches and pillars. Still, it lacks the usual ostentatious calling cards of such buildings throughout the country.

It seems an entirely appropriate setting for the association who normally occupy it. Effective without needing to be showy. Getting the job done. But it's not them sitting in the former nave today.

The collective are all elsewhere, undoubtedly persuaded to be otherwise engaged by Franc's magic or by his minions. At least, that better be the case. If Franc did anything to them, we're about to go to war. This building probably won't be standing afterwards.

Perhaps Toulouse won't be, either.

Groups of homeless sit huddled against the walls, all of them looking sickly. Bloodstains are in evidence on any light-shaded clothing, and many of them have fresh or dried patches painted under their eyes or around their ears. Skin tints range from an unhealthy greying to a far more worrisome jaundiced yellow, speaking of organs close to failure or bloodstreams awash with toxins. The place carries that odour that lurks in hospices and old folks' homes, obscured under bleach and bonhomie. It is the smell of dying from the inside out, the frustrated incontinence of the deteriorating form. It smells of Franc's failed promises to each of these people, and it makes me furious.

My eyes sweep around them as my rage builds. This is unacceptable. They may have chosen to go to Franc, but only the driving jaws of sheer desperation pushed them there. And they made a deal when they did. A deal where he would protect them. They don't look protected right now. They look drawn, broken. Ruined. And if Franc has broken his deal with them, then ours is through too. Yet, he's not hiding this, not keeping it under wraps away from my attention but summoning me to meet him here, to stand witness to their appalling state. My brain whirs away, trying to come up with a good reason for it. I can't think of any reason at all.

The largest gathering is at the far end, where they press themselves against the legs of a battered red velvet chaise longue on which Franc reclines. I would've normally laughed at the image of Franc at rest like some tawdry Roman emperor wannabe surrounded by his dispossessed court, but he looks on Death's door himself. His skin has darkened, his normal Mariana Trench luminescence giving way to a putrid green that glistens under sweat, soaking every inch of him. Dark ichor, black and thick, oozes from his nose, his eyes, his ears, his lips. He shivers and shakes, and I realise that the surrounding people are pressing themselves against him as a human blanket to ease the chill. I wonder how a creature who lives in the murky depths of the Atlantic-fed Garonne, the cold waters of Toulouse's river, can feel cold. Is he sick? I've never known a magical being to get sick, but there's always a first time.

I stalk forward. 'Franc, what the fuck is going on? What have you done to these poor bastards?'

He pushes himself up onto one giant elbow with considerable difficulty and looks at me. His usually waving frond-locks hang limp, and even his cloak, which normally billows with his power, lies still, wrapped tight around his inconceivably colossal frame. His eyes, normally empty white holes, now wear cracks of criss-crossing lines, their black the same shade as the essence leaking from his orifices. If I wasn't relatively confident he's immortal, I'd say he is dying.

He tries to pull his lips back into his trademark inhuman, intimidatory grin, but his heart isn't in it. I can see the points and jags of his ruined mouth, but the expression is too close to human to be usual for Franc. He nods, well aware of how he looks, and gestures outwards expansively, a flat hand sweeping round to encompass the church and his disciples.

'A-welcoming I'd be making, all pretty curtseysings and bow-wow bobbing, but for my stationary state, loungers left a-lying, all mangered like a mangy cur. Still, make your welcomed self to a claimed dome for a kingdom, for a king done in, poor I.'

He stops for a moment, coughing more inky liquid down his coal-black, threadbare coat. Drawing ragged breaths, he looks set to start once more into his florid phrasing. I cut through, in no mood for his nonsense.

'What's going on, Franc? What happened here? What's happened to you and to these people? Cut out the mannerisms and give me some actual information.'

Franc draws himself up as though about to rise, indignant at my insolence. He breaks down into another coughing fit and deflates. A woman, her face-lines mirrored by the erratic arrangement of half-formed dreads, rushes to him, mopping at his brow with a towel rigid with black encrustations. Her efforts add scarlet into the mix as she ignores her own bleeding features to wipe at his. He briefly allows her tending, then shoves her back towards the masses. They catch her stumbling form, and she merges back into the safety of their collective. I pull my attention back to Franc as he speaks.

'Cursings, long living, little boyo. Cursings all thrusting, twisty deep onto old Franc.'

CHAPTER THREE
APPROACHING MIREPOIX, 28 FEBRUARY, 1244

I t's hard learning magic. It's even harder when you're travelling through terrain that was once homely but is now hostile, where threats lurk on each side.

It's harder still when the last of your faith — or former faith, as I have to keep reminding myself — is about to die.

'Concentrate, lad,' Isaac says, his tone patient and tiresomely calm. The flame flickers in my hand, then burns viciously, my flesh instantly reddening underneath. A moment later, it extinguishes as I shake my hand furiously, my aforementioned concentration breaking entirely under the pain.

Isaac presses his cool palm over the top of my rapidly reddening one, and the blazing pain recedes, diminishing, backing away under the force of his magic. Of course, it doesn't do anything for the sense of mounting frustration.

We've been making our way through a land much changed over the past two weeks. Doors once open to strangers are now firmly shut, and inns aren't welcoming to Jews anymore, no matter the colour of one's gold. Forty years of encamped northern troops, quick to use any excuse to rob the locals, particularly accusations of accommodating either the Israelites

—like my mentor of the past thirty years, Isaac— or Good Christians —as I was prior to breaking my Perfection by embracing magic— has made any landlord wary of robed strangers and loath to offer much in the way of hospitality. An occasional hay bale out the back, like now, is the most comfortable our nights have been.

But through it all, Isaac has remained unflappable. Still smiling his greeting to faces more closed than their doors, averting his gaze from rambunctious soldiers who sneer and spit at us. Even though he can swat them like the flies buzzing endlessly around the smoking pyres of what might be slaughtered livestock or just those slaughtered alive in a land now rife with bandits — deserting conscripts choosing to rob and steal rather than march to war. The local lords may be weakened, but there's still death to be found in service of the northern king. Easier pickings can be found among a terrorised, traumatised populace marked by decades of murderous war.

"Why are we even practising?' The Good God knows just making our way across the country is fraught enough. Not to mention my fear for those I seek to help.

'Because, lad.' Isaac straightens his back, stretches, and cracks his neck. 'We're here at your insistence, against my advice, and you are still in my debt to the tune of another seven decades of apprenticeship. If, despite the foolishness of this venture, we are gifted with time, then that is time I will insist we use to learn to master the *talent* you still have far from grasped.'

He's right, of course. As per usual. But I'm not feeling in the mood to accommodate that. 'I still don't understand why we're going to Mirepoix instead of straight to Montsegur.'

Montsegur. The last stronghold of the few remaining Good Christians. Word reached my ears that they had all gathered there under the leadership of the Lady Esclarmonde. A formidable woman, a friend of sorts, and a

Perfect, as well as the sister of the Lord of Foix. There, troops have rallied to defend the last remaining Perfects.

And the Frankish troops have it besieged. Time is limited. It will fall soon.

Now it is Isaac's turn to shake his head. 'I'll not come with you to Montsegur, lad. I've told you before. For the love I bear for you, I'll try to find you help up the mountain, but you're on your own after. There are a people, the Cagots, who know the hidden paths through that region. If they will provide you with guidance, then so be it.'

I flex my hand, now fully healed, the flesh calmed, pink once more. It doesn't feel right. I should be marked. Scarred. Disfigured by all I've been through. But it doesn't take. No, if Isaac isn't there to heal me, I come back again, reborn in a dead form, taking it over and gaining new life. A grave-robbing reincarnation. It happened after that first life, when I destroyed the Holy Grail and stopped Papa Nicetas from bringing some unspeakable evil through to our world by sacrificing hundreds of Perfects. It happened both times I've died since. Each time due to my impatience and inability to control this new power flowing through my body. This magic. Isaac assures me it's no curse. A lifetime of beliefs and my inability to die have left me unconvinced.

'Who are these Cagots then?' I ask sullenly.

'A strange group. Outcasts, though no one knows why. Ostracised for hundreds of years, their presence stretches throughout the Basque country and up as far as Bordeaux. Held apart from the general population, though they've no unique beliefs and you'd be hard pressed to pick one out in a crowd. They're shunned. Refused baptisms, turned away from hallowed ground — though it does them no harm if they enter it. Never allowed to work with metal under pain of death. Kept to the outskirts of society, never allowed to mingle with anyone else. And all of it for no apparent reason.

Ask their neighbours why they treat them like that, and they'll shrug, tell you a hundred different tales about witch ancestors or ancient curses or else not have an answer at all. Suggest they change their behaviour? The vehement responses are a sight to see. It's a mystery I'd seek to unravel if not for the respect I hold for their leader and her request that I leave their secrets be.'

If I were not so downcast between the wearying travelling and Isaac's refusal to intervene directly, I might be more intrigued. As it is, it's the latter point that weighs more on me than the former.

'Why won't you help me properly, man?' The plaintive tone is only an inch above begging, but by the Good God, he shares his body with an *angel*. He could storm the gates of Montsegur and force the Frankish troops aside with a thought. My frustration at the misery he allows to be wreaked through Languedoc, France, is boiling over.

I finally see some frustration on Isaac's expression at being forced to rehash this discussion. He draws breath to answer despite that, but then stops, cocks his head, and listens intently.

I hear it too. A woman's sob.

It's muffled, constrained, either by terror or force, a hand wrapped across the mouth or fear striking at the senses. Either way, it speaks of ill intent, and we're both on our feet in a moment, away from our bales of hay and around the other side of the barn where scuffling sounds carry.

It's dark, the half-crescent moon shaded by cloud, and my eyes struggle to make out the scene at first, still night-blinded by my recent attempts at mastering fire. But Isaac doesn't hesitate, and a second later, everything is illuminated in blinding silver light emanating out of him, picking out the details in clear contrast.

Three brigands, soldiers perhaps — or at least formerly so — are in various states of undress, their manhoods shrivelling back from previous pride as fear replaces lust's fancies. Below them, a young wench from the tavern lies, with her clothes torn, her face tear-stained, and one rough paw wrapped over her mouth from the bastard holding her from behind.

Their intents are clear, though I believe we've arrived in time. Small mercies.

'*Begone!*' Isaac's voice thunders out like a storm washing all away before it, and the three ruffians turn tail, their removed clothing left strewn in their path. I wonder what they'll think — whether they'll recognise an angel threatened them with retribution or whether they'll consider it the devil's work of magic. Both are correct in a sense.

Isaac checks the girl, then looks up. 'She's passed out, but she's fine.' His relief is palpable as he ensures her dignity, making sure she's covered properly. 'We'll make sure she's found, but we'd best be on our way before then.'

'Us? Why?'

'Who do you think they'll blame, lad, other than the Hebrew and his companion for such actions as these?' His words are firm but still calm, but it's not good enough. None of this is good enough. And apparently the last remaining of my creed aren't good enough either.

'Why did you let them go? They should have paid for their actions!' My indignation is rife. That such men should walk free while the Good Christians sit trapped up in their rocky fortress with naught but the bonfires awaiting them in their future.

'What would you have me do, lad?' Isaac looks up, and for a moment, his age is clear, the years he carries beyond those shown physically. There is a weariness, a worn aspect that suggests this is not the first time he's had this conversation.

'Punish them! Make them pay!' It seems so obvious to me. I can't understand what he finds so difficult.

'Aye. I could have. Though Nithael would have had none of it, I could have used my own *talent* to bring them down. We could have punished them. What would have been fitting, lad? Hot iron pokers in their eyeballs? A slit throat like the pigs they are?'

'Yes. Both.' I know he's trying to shock me, but I remain belligerent. I'm no longer Perfect, no longer tied to the peaceful inaction contained in my creed. I would see the bastards pay for what they wanted to do to that young girl.

'Of course. And then perhaps I should step up in judgement on their commanding officer, eh, lad? For letting them run loose to terrorise the countryside? And why stop there? Why not up to the lords who they stand in service for? The king himself? Why don't I storm the gates of his palace and bring him to justice for his people's crimes?'

'Yes! Why don't you?' My frustration is clear. I don't understand why there is such power, and yet, evil is allowed free rein, unchecked.

'Because who would replace him? Me? You?' He laughs bitterly. 'And once I started to use my powers in such a way, where would I stop? Nithael wouldn't work with me anymore. I don't know if he can abandon me, but I'd stand alone. And once magic was exposed, categorically, once I seized power from a Christian king, do you think the other rulers would stand for it? Not to speak of all the Talented now revealed who'd want my head? They'd all come for me, and I would fail and fall.'

He pauses as he rubs the back of his neck. 'Or I'd succeed. Drenched in blood, having marched down the most monstrous of paths for the most righteous of causes. The sort of paths you can never walk back up. The ones that only lead deeper into the dark.'

He looks at me, and there is that resolute man, the goodness, the honesty, all that I admire as much as it may frustrate me at times. 'I am not the judge, not the jury. I'll not send them to the pyres or the hangman's noose as they do to your people or mine. Adonai's role is not mine to assume. So, I'll protect, I'll save where I can. And I'll not go marching up to the foot of the mountain of Montsegur, wrapped in my righteousness to save your people, Paul. Their choices are their own. They're not even yours anymore. And yet you insist on this attempted rescue. So I'll try to find you a guide, but I'll go no further than the Cagot camp. If you walk this path, you walk it without me. But until we get there?'

He shrugs and pushes himself back to standing from where he crouched by the girl's side. 'You're still my apprentice. And you'll practise in the hours of rest to make up for the days lost by this misadventure. Now go break camp while I lay a trail to bring those inside to the girl's aid.'

He turns his back on me, and I have to bite my lip not to argue, not to demand that he's wrong, that we must and should act. Because I recognise my own want in that. My desire for vengeance on those who are murdering my people and my religion. And I cannot, hand on heart, find fault with his logic however deeply I might wish to.

So instead, I walk back to our meagre bedding to fold it up, ready for a forced march through the night, running from the judgement of those who were once my fellow Languedocians, for actions not our own. It's a bleak outcome, and only the saving of the girl brings me any comfort.

CHAPTER FOUR

TOULOUSE, 8 APRIL, PRESENT DAY

Pretty confident he doesn't mean cursed in the, "Fuck Franc. He's an absolute arsehole" kind of way. Seeing as how I do that every time I ever think of him.

'You've been cursed?' I'm not sure what Franc is exactly, whether part-fae, part-god, or just some other incomprehensible spawn of coupling monsters, but his magic is intrinsic. Most magical beings are, the magic providing them with a level of innate protection against human-wielded spellwork. I can still set him on fire with a fireball or crush him with a thrown boulder (in theory; I suspect such attacks are more than likely to just bounce off him). Hitting him with a curse and making it stick is no simple matter. It requires considerable brute force and magical knowhow. I suspect it'll also cost the caster dearly. Curses like this on powerful targets don't come cheap.

He tries to growl, but it comes out more like a groaning mewl. 'Wyrdings by Hekate's she-dogs, manling, by my oath. All slipsy gliding through my floatsome flotsam it came, but my own tidings no longer glad. Now treacherous ripperies that slicked up my glimmering province, carrying cursings. Taken from me, all know-me-nots and back-turned banks. My Garonne, gone, adrifted.'

Bloody Franc. Half of what he says is affectation, I'm sure. The other half? Just a representation of the weird way his fucked-up brain works. Furrowing my brow, I try to work it through. 'Hekate's she-dogs? Are you talking about the Sistren of Bordeaux?' *Own tidings no longer glad...* 'And she cursed you in the water? Or cursed all the water?' A river-borne plague descending on the populace sounds like exactly my kind of luck. I desperately wish I had time to relax before all this. I pinch my nose, feeling a headache coming on. It's a common occurrence when I have to speak to Franc.

He hisses and flaps his hand in anger. 'Would you gift them so freely, all package-wrappings of poor old I? They holds the water, hurts the wearer, worn and weary. Knew always I should never have been a-settling here, their presence at the yawning mouthery of mine own soaking bed always a danger, ever a "here's a bladed landing, sail no more" in its possibles, count them off.'

I stare hard at Franc as he flops backwards in misery, pawing and pulling at his cheek with the hand he isn't gesturing with. *I'll take that as a yes, and it's targeted directly at him.* 'What did you do, Franc?'

Don't get me wrong, the Sistren aren't some sort of holy order despite the name. They're witches, and a major Power in their own right, holding Bordeaux with the usual mixture of politics and raw power. But they play the game, and they don't look for trouble unless it comes knocking at their door. Plus Franc is Franc. If I'm going to believe anyone is in the wrong, I'm going to assume it's him. I doubt it will turn out that I was unnecessarily harsh on the fucker.

He shoots back up, indignant, but the sudden movement sets him off coughing again, undermining the dramatic moment. He composes himself before answering.

'Done? Done in and doomed in dome and demandings is he of our doings.' He pauses, then exhales, and some pretentious posturing leaves as he deflates. 'Don't know, does I, manling? No, my pretty boy, I never dids nothing that I knows of to bring offence to that Lady's sororitous assemblage. Kepts me here, far enough away, thought I, all giddy-headed by the warm-bodied packery, clamped in tight. Easy to find my pretty little ones, simple swap-sings of gifts for goods, all fair trading, no harms doings. Paragonic is I, all virtues and tellings. No known wronging brought, no offence offered, all bright stringed and glorious.'

'So you've no idea why they've targeted you?'

The wretched monster shakes his head, sending tar-like globules splattering across the crowded, assembled bodies.

The Good God damn it, I just don't want to know how Franc's offended the Sistren. Why they expended so much power *to bring this misery down on his head. All I want is to crawl home and drag my sorry hide into bed. Except I can't. Because over two hundred years ago, I made a deal that made my life easier in the short term. And now I'm bound by those accursed words that were sworn on my* talent.

Doesn't mean I have to beat around the bush though. 'What is it you want me to do?'

'Straight-dealings I has always offered, my tellings all true and never with a "thank 'ee kindly' asked or answered. Now 'tis time for testings of treaties and their truths-tastes, is it not? Promises made, compacted. All alliances in our bandyings, back and forth. Need you to seek 'em out, the moon dancers, Undyer. Find what poor old Franc could have done, all privacy privy, kept myselfing only wrapped in my rivery reverie's embraces.'

My expression hardens. 'That seems outside the remit of our accord, Franc. I don't remember you ever riding into battle by my side when my life was in danger.' And that's happened often enough. 'Where were you when we got bushwhacked by Hastingues? Hiding, refusing to help me any further.'

'Did my part and playings, all truths and troths fullfilleried.' The monster coughs again, hacks, gargles. 'Hads to be protectings of my lovely lads and lasses, and that was always in accorderies and wordings.'

'You did the minimum, then ran off to protect you and yours. Now you're asking me to risk my own neck by finding out how you pissed the Sistren off?'

'Always loyalness was I, all at your service, by your pleasing,' Franc whines, a begging tone to his voice. 'Who gave you their tellings, a-whispered in your pretty lugs, straight-pointing with their truths and trusts of trysts and threatenings? Kept you safe, kept *here* safed up and secure, forsooth.'

He leans on his side to bring his pock-scarred, misshapen face closer, a more familiar cunning returning to his gaze. 'No requirings of your doing deeds on account of I, not alone, not simple singular. Binded tyings are all quick-twist woven across my lovely boys and girls, are they not? Knows you how many sits in service, all safety-offered by poor I, poor I? More than this meagre gathered grim faces, many times, many ties. Would it be doom that you'd be presenting in your no's and not I's? More kindly to be gizzard slicer, chop chop and done, drawn, quartered, 'ey, my little lord? If old Franc does dance his last quick shufflestep into the fingery beckons of twilighting, their lingerings will be sad, so sad. Then gone, in pricey pain, and who will pay that? Ask those of Hamlin if their pridery was the wot of what was lost.'

The threat is transparent even if his words, as usual, aren't. If he dies, so does his congregation. I look around me and know that the aroma and aura of terminal illness isn't Franc's alone. I hold no love for Franc, no illusions that he is anything other than a definitely-not-plain-speaking villain, but his captured, captivated wretches deserve a chance to change, to live. He organised this meeting with all his usual cleverness, arranging his people just so to remind me that there are stakes I might care about.

I look the creature up and down contemptuously. 'I don't doubt you could free them if you wanted to.'

'Free them? They're all fine, free and fettle. Choosings they made, we all makes, now and next and never ending 'til our skip-beats are silenced off. Prices paid are promises kept or cut or chomped up, swallowed down belly rocks.'

I'm not going to get anywhere arguing with him, and he knows me well enough to know he has me. If he was about to run amok, I might take the risk and end him. Or leave him to his ending and let those who threw in their lot with him take their chances. I won't do that to them when he isn't an actual threat. At least no more than he's always been, and given his sorry state, a lot less than usual.

I rub my forehead where I feel a headache building up to an ice-burn above the bridge of my nose. I really need to stash some Ibuprofen in my etheric storage for times like this.

'Okay, Franc, I'll talk to the Sistren for you, find out what's going on. You're going to owe me for this one though. More than our usual accord, I mean.'

'All debted and due dates draped o'er our days ahead, little Lordling, all honour bounded outside all boundaries, upon my power. No questions posery, all "meanings of meat in meeting" meanery. Concordulant in gratitude, the doffery and dotage passed in perpetuem, is it not?'

I take a moment to work out what he means. *Meanings of meat in meeting* — who knows. But *upon my power* sounds good, like I'll get eternal gratitude from an over-*talented* bottom feeder. It must be my birthday. 'It better bloody be, Franc. It better bloody be.'

CHAPTER FIVE

TOULOUSE, 8 APRIL, PRESENT DAY

Looking forward to updating Aicha on what I just agreed to about as much as I want to pull my toenails off with a pair of needle-nose pliers. Actually, I might prefer the latter.

I heave in a huge gasp of air as I step out of the old church. The sweet allure of spring flowers is like a medieval nosegay against the Plague. It banishes that cloying, malingering odour, but it does nothing to stop its impact on me personally. Still, I'm happy for its placebo effect, even momentarily. The absence of the smell of decline and Franc's twisted headfuckery of a turn of phrase helps to make my brain feel less like it's been pulled out of my nose, embalmed in candyfloss, and then shoved back in upside down. It allows me to regain a grip on my common sense and do what I should have done the moment I saw the street kid on my doorstep. I pull out my phone and call Aicha.

She's going to kill me, is my first thought. Aicha Kandicha, Druze Queen, the undying warrior guardian of the Aab-Al-Hayaat, the Waters of Life.

My best friend — currently in the running for "person most likely to tear me a new arsehole for having agreed to help Franc".

The phone rings. I'm already marshalling my thoughts, trying to put together my argument. At least it's not as bad as it could be. I could do without the trip to Bordeaux — or anywhere further than my mattress and duvet– but the way I see it, we rock over there, deliver the message, discuss terms so Franc can appease the Sistren, undoing whatever fuckery he's pulled off to upset them, and then we head home and grab a pint for a job well done. Simple. I hope.

The click of the answerphone pulls me from my reverie.

'You're through to my phone line — obviously, as you can hear my voice. Paul, don't even think about fucking getting us involved in any more bullshit. We've got enough to deal with.'

Beep.

'Hey, Aicha... guess what? You're gonna be so damned pleased to hear who I just talked to... Give me a ring back when you get a minute, preferably a minute you've got several minutes prior to this minute, where I'm calling you. Yeah, um. I'm not sure that was entirely clear, but basically just call me back ASAP — or sooner. Go Team Bonhomme!'

I hang up and start walking back towards my house. The phone in my pocket vibrates as I'm close to home. I pull it out and answer it.

'Are you out of your fucking tiny mind, Paul?' The voice on the other end sounds exactly as happy as I expected. Which is not even slightly.

'Nice to speak to you too, Aicha! How is everything? "Oh, fantastic, Paul, thanks! What fun adventures have you got for me today?" So glad you asked, Aicha. We've got a doozy on —'

'Fuck your adventures, Paul. You've finally clocked on to the idea of a team name, and you come up with Team Bonhomme? Fuck my life.'

I stare blankly at my front door, feeling the cogs trying to turn. It takes me a minute to replay the answerphone message I left her. 'Okay, fair. In hindsight, maybe calling the entire team after my last name was a bit dumb.'

'Don't forget egotistical. And narcissistic and — '

'I take it you have a better idea?'

'I have unlimited better ideas, mainly because Team Fucking Incapable is better than Team Bonhomme. The opportunities, the endless opportunities! How about The Urban Achievers?'

I groan. '*Big Lebowski* references, really? Dude!'

'Not just Dude — *The* Dude! If we're going to use names, how about The B Team? Keeps with your letter, cult reference, and sums up how much you drag down the rest of us in terms of capability.'

'Let's stick that one on the back furnace,' I reply dryly. 'Any others?'

'How about King Gizzard and The Shitty Wizard?'

'Pass.'

'Missing an opportunity to nod the head to Cheech Wizard is a terrible mistake, Paul. On the same theme though, how about Shizzard Killers?'

'Shizzard?'

'Shizzard — shit wizard. It wasn't a bad first attempt from you, shit wizard. Mad props, et cetera. Needs refreshing though. I give you shizzard.'

'You're giving me a headache. Or at least further aggravating the one Franc gave me.'

There is a momentary pause.

'I'm on my way. Don't charge off and do something stupid. Don't get yourself killed. Wait exactly where you are for me. Otherwise, I'll kill you.'

There is a click.

I crack out the tension in my neck with a quick left-right twist, unlock my door, and finally, *finally* manage to get into my house and just be home for a moment. I sink into my plush faux-leather sofa and decide to studiously ignore reality's existence. Until Aicha brings it barging back through my door with her arrival.

As pleased as I always am to see Aicha, it doesn't seem like I had anywhere near long enough to just sit down. She sweeps in, kicks my feet off the coffee table, pivoting me to a sitting position as she passes, and perches on the facing armchair's edge, her eyes locked on me. Her intensity level normally stays stuck at eleven, but regarding Franc, she's ready to kick it up a notch — *bam*!

The warrior facing me is a study in elegant deadliness. Her cheekbones are almost as sharp as the various bladed implements she keeps stashed around her person. She'll cut you to the quick just as fast with her burning gaze, the kohl whorls underlining her coal-hard irises. The siyala facial tattoo on her chin represents personal growth. I had to catch her wrist mid-jab last time someone asked if Post Malone had inspired it. I guess there's always room for further growth.

The Aicha I see now, the one I had on the phone, isn't the Aicha most people get to see. This is Aicha at her most relaxed. Which is frankly terrifying, and I'm pretty sure her general physical state of constant readied tension is enough to give a chiropractor mental trauma. She's a coiled spring on a hair trigger, and for all her complaining about the antics I drag her into, I don't doubt that she appreciates the distraction. It keeps at least some of her nightmares at bay.

The problem with being a regenerative immortal is if some sick fucko gets hold of you, they might decide to test exactly how far that stretches. Nazis definitely count as sick fuckos, and five years of her captivity and experimentation led to a plethora of issues and PTSD. Sadly, there aren't many psychiatrists equipped to hear about how they chopped your tongue out, then timed how fast you grew things back when they carved another piece off every half hour. Adding to that, she got locked inside her own unending bonfire by Ben only a couple of weeks back, burning continuously for hours. Yet, she still found the resolve to come and save the day even as every inch of her flesh turned to charcoal repeatedly…

But getting her help isn't easy, even if she was willing to trust anyone with her intimate secrets. If a psychiatrist didn't try to get her committed (and boy, wouldn't that be an interesting exchange!), they'd be seeking counselling themselves after she offloaded the teensiest amount of her suffering. After I rescued her, I let her get on with healing in her own way, making myself available as a sympathetic ear, as did Isaac — angel-bearer, father of Kabbalah, and the closest thing to one for me since my first death. Hunting down Nazis and kicking the shit out of bad guys (or mediocre guys or, in fact, just vaguely annoying chauvinistic guys) seems to help her out. It also does me a solid (and the world in general), so I'm not complaining.

'So what did the river wretch want with you, *saabi*?' she asks.

I scratch the back of my neck, searching for how to sell this to her. I decide to just get to it. 'Franc looks like he's dying.'

'Oh. No. What. A. Pity.' She stretches out every inch of intonation to make her intent one hundred percent clear. Saying Aicha isn't his biggest fan is like saying sticking red-hot pokers in your eyes doesn't help you see the TV more clearly. Which, incidentally, is exactly what she wants to do to him. And I'm not talking about sitting down to catch up on the latest hit telly series. Although, I do sometimes get the feeling Franc would be down for a little Netflix'n'chill. It's a thought that is beyond nauseating, and I have to scrub it from my brain as soon as it pops up.

'It's not that straightforward, Aicha.'

'If it's overly complicated, I'm thrilled to make it really, really simple for him. Can you say euthanise? Say it with me now.'

'If he dies, so do all his "pretty boys and girls" throughout the city.'

She mulls that over. 'Any idea how many we're talking?'

I don't need to fake the look of shock on my face. 'Jesus Christ! What are you talking about?'

She holds my gaze coolly, completely unfazed by my reaction. 'It's simple maths, Paul. Someday, eventually, you're going to have to go toe to toe with him. When you do, there's going to be a fall-out, probably casualties. Maybe better it's his reserve forces rather than actual civilians?'

I stare her down as hard as I can, but she doesn't blink from her position. 'Those are innocent people, victims even. They took up with him 'cos society had nothing to offer them except excuses and slow deaths in doorways and shooting galleries. They are not going down with him.'

She inclines her head, conceding the point, although I don't get the impression she agrees with it. 'Fine, we'll kick that problem further down the road for now. What does the overgrown reptile want us to do?'

'We need to go to Bordeaux. The curse is apparently a weaving of the Sistren, sent down through the waters of the Garonne. Or at least, that's what I think I deciphered from his ramblings.'

'Who's going? Just the two of us, or are we taking the other twofer with us?'

I shake my head. It is a gentle joke at Isaac's expense, but I'm not playing along, unable to serve her the normal banter she's expecting. She really knocked me off balance with her willingness to sacrifice the street-folk who serve Franc to see him taken out. 'I think there's no need to drag them into bargaining with the Bordeaux Coven.'

'Bordeauven?'

I try to keep the stern look on my face, but I can't hold it, and I crack into a grin. 'Fine, when negotiating with the Bordeauven, *although I seriously suggest*—' —I fix her with my hardest look, hoping it can equal hers— 'that

you don't call them that. I think we can give Isaac and Jakob — *Do not!*'
I wag a finger at her. 'Call them Isakob or Jakac, please. They're still two
distinct people. They just happen to be locked in one body...'

'With two angels.'

That was the only tasty part of the whole shit-sandwich that was our
recent dealing with Ben. He captured Jakob and his body-sharing angel
Nanael in a super powerful skull, whose previous owner had been an
arsehole religious extremist from my first death called Arnaud Almeric. In
order to get them out of the prison skull, Isaac invited them into his own
head instead, meaning there's now four souls –two human, two angel–
riding around in that big old brain of his.

I struggle my way back to what I was saying. '... with two angels, yes,
thank you. They're brothers, not lovers. They don't need some Brangelina
tagline. Thanks very much.'

I pause, pushing my curls towards the back of my head as I try to regain
my equilibrium. 'What was I talking about again?'

'Isakob.'

'*Isaac* and *Jakob* will be more use here. Perhaps they can work out a way
we can protect Franc's chosen ones if he dies. I reckon you and I should
go find out what's going on, how Franc's pissed them off, and whether
there's anything we can do about it. They can work on Plan B in case it's
unavoidably terminal.'

Aicha claps her hands together like an anime schoolgirl. 'Oh, please let
it be terminal. Yay, terminal!'

I massage my eyes with a thumb and forefinger. 'Look, let's get Isaac and
Jakob...'

'Cough. Isakob. Cough.'

'... Isaac and Jakob to meet us for a drink. We can fill them in, find out
if they have any insider info about the coven, and then we can even think

about heading out if you're up for it? We've no idea how long negotiations might take, and we'll have to present ourselves directly. They'll probably accommodate us.'

She hits me with the one-eye sardonic brow manoeuvre. 'Probably?'

'Well, they might decide we're an invading Power and try to fuck us up like...' My mind goes blank.

'Like a shizzard?'

This trend better not last long for the sake of my few remaining strands of sanity. 'Fine, like a shizzard. The only thing in our favour is that they must have spent, and this is the official measurement, hella loads of power cursing Franc. I don't think they'll be too keen to get all up in our grille. Let's go grab a drink, then we can hit the road.'

'Yeahhh bwoooooooyyyyyyyyyy.' Aicha's Flava Flav impression is several decibels too loud for my aching head.

I roll my eyes, fishing my phone out of my pocket as we head for the front door. If I'm lucky, we can get this wrapped up in a day, and I can get my head down for some rest.

I try not to think about how rarely I get lucky.

CHAPTER SIX

TOULOUSE, 8 APRIL, PRESENT DAY

Oh, Danny Boy, the pints, the pints are calling...

We head to the Garonne, dropping down onto the lower modern promenade keeping it company as it meanders through the city centre. Dog walkers and pushchair families stroll casually down the sun-warmed pathways that still hold their heat despite the advancing hour. Evening's radiant chill is giving way to the promise of summer. Only brighter days lie ahead. I wish I can feel it is a metaphor for our future, but I am not about to sucker myself by entertaining such a viewpoint. Storm clouds feel more likely on my personal horizon.

A group of twenty-somethings pass beers and other bottles back and forth as a tiny speaker, worn from overuse, bangs out a mix of afrodance and amapiano. One or two take turns showing off dance moves, and as we near, two of the guys, their cornrow braids immaculately woven and their clothing casually box-fresh, step forward into a syncopated pre-planned routine, mile-wide grins plastered on in the sheer pleasure of movement. The rest of the group mirrors it, the whole assembly constantly shifting rhythmically; even the bottle being passed keep step with the four-four timing. The joy of uninhibited expression is an innocent delight even as the first signs of lengthening shadows come, the sun dipping behind the high-rises and hospitals.

As we approach the bridge, a sole red figure lurks in one of its maw-like circular brick passages that were created to let flood water pass without pulling the bridge down. If I didn't know better, I might believe the figure is a Nain Rouge, a nasty little trickster faerie the colour of sunburnt salami.

But I know it's a sculpture carved by a fellow called James Colomina, who has a penchant for making these strange little red figures. This isn't the only one in Toulouse, although it was the first, causing quite a stir when it appeared apparently out of nowhere. Also, no Nain Rouge is going to waltz into the city. The last one who tried still owes me a favour for the favour I did for him...which was me not letting Aicha see if his insides were as red as his outsides. Pretty big favour.

We reach the Rue Saint-Michel. Ahead stands a repurposed fountain I first saw installed in the Jardin des Plantes, a striking building-sized wall leading to where the "grand" rue narrows to a single lane in each direction. Neoclassical, the frieze shows the Garonne, a strong feminine celebrant, tearing the flowing spring from the rocks above her while a subservient but nubile Ariege accepts her pouring water into her jug. It is both beautiful and Freudian and about as subtle in its suggestions as a seventies bawdy comedy. I wonder if deities actually possess the Garonne or the river Ariege. I can't help thinking about how the Garonne would feel about Franc having taken up residence. This, coupled with the not very subtle suggestiveness of the carving, leads to thoughts of Franc being *in* the Garonne, which makes me feel like I might need to bleach my brain and then sandpaper off the parts capable of conscious thought. I hurry us on away from the nightmare factory the arty fountain has become, down a few doors more, to the O'Bohem.

The O'Bohem fully lives up to its name, bohemian in all aspects. It is dark and homely and overflowing with artistic vibes often accompanied by the artists themselves, who are more often overflowing with the reasonably priced and generously served drinks. The walls hang with street art-inspired paintings for sale, with all money going to the artist. This is another "solidaire" bar, like L'Astronef, where it looks after the people who need it before looking to make money. There are few places left like that in the world, so they always get my custom when I have the chance.

Isaac's already there, waiting, thankfully. I order a Nikka Coffey Grain single malt and receive an overly generous double that I'm really not complaining about. Isaac gets a pint of something dark, although not Irish-stout dark, and Aicha is carrying what looks like fresh orange juice when she plonks herself down. She broods internally for a moment and then visibly perks up as she speaks.

'So a Cathar, a Druze, and a Kabbalist walk into a bar,' she says.

The seconds drag by as I wait for some witty punchline about me, her, and Isaac.

Eventually, I feel it necessary to prompt the punchline. 'Do go on?'

'I dunno, that's all I got. Erm, the Cathar almost certainly poked his nose somewhere he shouldn't, meaning the Druze and the Kabbalist are going to have to work their arses off extricating him out of the shit he got himself into? Instead of enjoying their drinks peacefully. 'Cos he's a twat.' She punctuates her statement with a dainty sip of her drink and a middle finger.

'Hey, this one isn't my fault.' I pause, remembering it *is* because of my original peace treaty with Franc. 'Okay, it sort of is my fault, but from hundreds of years ago. That makes it sort of not-current-me's fault, right?'

'The whole shitshow with Ben was also due to stuff you did hundreds of years ago. Still holding you responsible for me *being continuously on fire for several hours.*'

Isaac jumps in before I can apologise. 'A fair point, lass, and I think there's none of us who don't regret what happened to you. It got me back my brother though, so I'm bloody glad it did.'

There is a change of expression that, had I not spent a good while in the brothers' company prior to heading to Hastingues, inspecting the mystical skulls of terrifying power before stashing them, I might not have noticed. When they speak next, the vocal timbre is lightened slightly. It is a subtlety most will miss, but one I know means Jakob is now at the metaphorical wheel.

'And it led to my freedom, finally. It's been a terrible, terrible time. So many acts he forced us to do, so contrary to our natures. Poor lost soul that he was, I find it a terrible burden to remember all our doings and an immeasurable relief to be out of his clutches.'

Aicha squints hard at Isaac/Jakob.

'Jakob, is that you now?' she asks suspiciously.

'It is indeed, my dear lady, and again I apologise profusely for the suffering you underwent on my part. It grieves me greatly.'

The switch happens again, and Isaac replies to his brother, 'It wasn't your fault, old boy. You never acted for aught but love.'

'I rest a simple fool, Isaac, to be tricked so easily by his behaviour. He felt so familiar the second time, so much like home, I should have recognised him. I wanted so much to believe I could have another chance.'

It's bizarre, watching the brothers discuss the problem from a single mouth. Aicha's brow screws up as she stares at them with a level of concentration so intense I suspect it's only because they're protected by two angels that they don't burst into flames. She focuses on their facial changes as the two of them flick back and forth, like an umpire at a tennis match.

For me, it's hard hearing the blame Jakob heaps on himself too. Ben tricked him by making him fall in love with him repeatedly, reincarnating in different bodies and presenting himself as different lovers. Pushing his thoughts in a certain direction, killing himself to torment Jakob with guilt over his death. It's still a hard thing to reconcile with the man I once considered closer than family, as the best of men. To see what he did to someone actually worthy of that title? Honestly, it hurts. It makes my soul ache.

Isaac's no happier with Jak's interpretation of events. 'You weren't wrong to want to give yourself another shot at happiness, Jakob. Ben played us all for fools. He just started in on you earlier, is all.'

Aicha coughs, interrupting, and holds up her hand for silence. 'I swear, next birthday, I'm getting the pair of you Clark Kent glasses. You can fight it out between yourselves who gets to be Superman.' She pauses. 'When is your birthday again?'

'Aug-May-ust-The-Twel-Four-Th-Teenth.'

Watching the two brothers trying to talk at the same time is like watching an epileptic getting hit mid-seizure with a taser. I grin.

Aicha takes it entirely in her stride. 'Well, I have no fucking clue when Augmayust the Twelfourtheteenth is, so I'll just get some the next time opportunity comes along, all right, boys?'

Isaac/Jakob (and I am really, really having to fight the urge to label them Isakob; Aicha will not win) draw breath, then realise what is about to happen and settle for nodding sheepishly instead.

I get into the nitty-gritty of what happened between Franc and myself over at La Chapelle. There is no sympathy in Aicha's expression when I describe just how sickly Franc looks. She wears a darkly satisfied smile, but

Isaac (I am pretty much certain he is in the driving seat) looks considerably more concerned.

'Franc may be a sleazy character,' he starts, but a snort from Aicha cuts him off. He tries again. 'Franc *is* a sleazy character, but he's also incredibly *talented* and naturally so, by my estimation. It's not learned; it's an integral part of him. To curse him so effectively and through his own affiliated medium...' He breaks off again as he sees my confused expression. 'Water, my boy. He's a water creature. His magic is tied to the water. He lives in the water. I have no doubt his bonding rituals with his chosen ones involve exchanging liquids. To hit him so hard and turn his own element against him so effectively...' He pauses, grim-faced. 'I would have said such power was beyond the Sistren, but if they did it, it will have cost them greatly to cast. This is no minor attack on another power. This is a major declaration of war.'

I nod in agreement. 'I'd say nail on the head. Maybe if Nith and Nan got on board, we could manage something similar, but it'd be a major undertaking. I've never felt outmatched by the Sistren. So they've either moved up a weight class, which we must know because it means we need to be on our toes in case they come after us, or they've paid dearly to go after dear old Franc. Either way, I want to know what's going on, so looks like we're heading to Bordeaux.'

'Fan-fucking-tastic. Did I mention the Cathar is a twat?' Aicha says, slamming back her juice like a prairie-dusted cowboy slugging whisky in a two-bit saloon.

'It might have come up, yes,' I reply, knocking back the rest of my drink as well. Seeing as how mine actually *is* whisky, I wonder how Aicha still looks like more of a badass. It seems distinctly unfair.

CHAPTER SEVEN

TOULOUSE, 8 APRIL, PRESENT DAY

Feeling much better for some alcoholic lubrication; although I'm about three bottles of whisky and a whole bar-load of tequila shots away from being ready to tangle with the Sistren.

I start setting up the required ritual material to place a scrying mirror call to the Sistren when we get back to mine from the bar. Aicha lets me go as far as pressing the athame point into my wrist before she pulls her phone out, rolling her eyes. Apparently, she has a direct line to one of the Sistren. How she came to have it, I have no idea. The oceans of mysteries surrounding Aicha are unfathomably deep. And she gets far too smug when I question her on stuff like this, so I just let it go. However much it makes my brain feel like it is full of hyperactive monkeys covered in itching powder.

After her call, we follow the road that hugs the banks of the Canal du Midi. There's a gentle slope allowing access to the towpath of the canal. On our right, the departmental building offers shelter to La Chapelle from the noise and hubbub, protecting it from the principal route. I contemplate heading over there and dragging Franc along with us by his earlobe. I worry, though, that the Sistren will simply strike him down on sight. It is my instinctive reaction every time I see him, after all. Instead, we trek up along the canal to Matabiau, Toulouse's train station. Heading down into the underpass leading to the platforms, we find waiting employees lurking like under-stimulated bouncers for a strange platform-based rave. I've got to say, the station itself, minus the rails, reminds me of a few warehouse parties I went to back in the day. The wedge-shaped roof is supposed to be an architectural wonder, but with its time-worn air, the darker edges giving way to lightening translucent sections, all balanced across substantial black metal struts, it makes me think of nothing so much as an immense cat-tle-shed. It feels industrial and functional but not beautiful. A bit like my soul.

Aicha doesn't have much to say along the way. I don't mind. It isn't unusual for her to be taciturn, and I need the space to think. As the four-note musical signature of the rail company calls out over the tannoy to draw attention to an almost incomprehensibly tinny announcement, she nudges my arm. The TGV fast train we are due to catch is pulling in.

'Looks like the tanker from *Mad Max 2*,' she says, lifting her chin, indicating the arriving cab.

She isn't wrong. I don't know if the train is going to take us to Bordeaux or smash its way through a horde of cannibalistic wasteland fashion vic-tims. The cattle guard on the front looks like it would pick up a Hummer and toss it over its shoulder like a superstitious pinch of salt. Maybe that is the point. People aren't very good at following rules at the best of times. When said rules are there to save their lives, they are even worse at it.

So things like flashing lights meant to show, "Stop here, you fuck-ing idiot; there's a hundred tonnes of impossibly durable steel about to come through at hundreds of kilometres per hour", become interpreted as meaning, "Everyone else should stop here but *you* — you should speed up. You'll definitely make it through in time". Better they get shoved aside than the whole train goes off the rails, literally. I guess I can understand the post-apocalyptic vibe for the leading cars after all.

Once we get on board, the train is much more standard. The seats are roomy with grey as the main motif and a gun-metal blue picking out the overhead storage to break up the monotony of colour. Outside, the clouds are multi-layered cotton-candy swirls, their tops so luminescent, they are hard to look at, their underneath dark and threatening, promising cleansing rains whether wanted or not. The fields are uniformly green, crops pushed high, ready for harvesting, while trees stand proud, individual in size and style at irregular locations, refusing to be subsumed into the homogeneity of the surrounding farmland.

We slow as we enter towns, where simple cottages, lime-wash cracking with time and tectonic movement, stand next to sprawling renovated farmhouses and spartan crisp-lined new builds without letting their heads droop. These are lived-in lands, and the principle of equality runs deep. At least in lip service. Words said behind closed doors or behind the cover of a clutched pint are another story entirely.

'How did you get the Sistren's number?' I ask suddenly. It's been a constant annoying mental itch. A mosquito bite of a question. I've been steadily trying to ignore it, but it just keeps getting more and more irritating.

Aicha regards me laconically. 'Seriously?'

'What?' The defensive tone of my voice says I know exactly what.

She heaves a sigh and turns to look at me properly, patting my leg. 'Much as I know you believe you are the centre of the known universe, I have a life outside of you, Paul. You're my friend. Not my guardian. Not my dad, thank fuck, because I already have enough deep-seated trauma as is, thanks. Believe it or not, I know other people than you and Isaac.'

I feel embarrassed, so I do that typical thing we males do after being calmly and correctly put in our place by a woman — I push on insistently despite the obvious fact it's a stupid thing to do. 'Come on, you can tell me.'

'I know I can,' Aicha says. She blinks, then returns to the copy of 'Afropean — Notes From Black Europe' that she was reading, effectively dismissing me. I go back to staring out the window and stewing in my own impotent nosiness.

Hasty black-and-white graffiti dub plates welcome us into the St Jean train station, with occasional flashes of colour in between startling the attention, dragging it in. We step off the platform and into the lobby; the place feels cavernous and palatial after the illusory interior of Matabiau.

A couple standing in the expansive central entrance of the station are easy for me to identify as coven members. They look like a power couple, both dressed in the smart casual that speaks of exquisitely expensive labels. She comes styled to within an inch of her life — hair carefully coiffured, her naturally tight curls confined with artfully deployed clips and pins. He looks like he spent even more time on styling his beard. Their *talented* glow is a murky turquoise, like the glowering menace of a storm-tossed sea as the waters calm temporarily. They obviously have no problem picking us out either as they slide into position on either side, escorting without talking. I turn to Aicha.

'Is your loquaciousness infectious?' I say, inclining my head at our silent accompaniers.

'Nope, but I heard rude people often catch a severe case of the beat downs.'

A muscle twitches under our right guard's eye. Bingo.

'Okay, so you're in charge,' I say, turning to the guard. 'You're trying to make an impression. *You're on our territory, we're hard as nails, don't fuck with us, et cetera.* Got it. But your chief invited us here, so how about you stop being a pair of arseholes and fill us in on what's going on?'

The man stills, slowing. You can see when he decides to stop being a dick. He turns, giving us a shallow bow. 'My apologies, Lord Cathar. You are right. It is inexcusable, but we are all somewhat on edge at the moment.'

I guess the reason probably has something to do with why we are here. I am equally sure we will find out when the time is right. For now, it is better to be magnanimous in my politicking. 'No need for the lord bullshit. Just Paul will do.'

'Or Lord Dickhead, to give him his full title.'

'Thanks, Aich. Love you too.'

She blows me a kiss, and the tension in the area ratchets down a few notches.

'So are we driving or hoofing it?' I ask.

'We will proceed on foot if that is acceptable, sir,' he says, and I notice his inability to use my name. Still, sir is better than lord. Even Lord Dickhead.

'No problem for me. It's been a long time since I've been in Bordeaux,' I say.

It has been a long time. Bordeaux has been Sistren territory for as long as I have known about them. One doesn't simply wander into another Power's territory in much the same way as one does not simply walk into Mordor. Both are liable to lead to a swift and agonisingly painful demise, One True Ring or no. That does not mean never though. Meetings and parleys happen; invitations are occasionally offered. Politics is politics, whether demonic or democratic. Only difference is, demons are more honest than politicians.

The area around the train station is a strange amalgamation of old and modern. The two styles seem to play tag as we walk up the large boulevard, heading west. One moment the right-hand side will be eighteenth-century façades while the left of the road is a rotund, brutalist monstrosity. Then that will give way to a late nineteenth-century schoolhouse, originally only for boys, named after Gustave Eiffel. Meanwhile, the right becomes seventies builds crammed together, cafés and takeaways pressed up close to the other, the air rich with the smell of the big three C's of North African cooking — cumin, coriander, and cinnamon. I would love to grab something, but the escorts are hustling. I get the feeling they are under orders to take a little while to get back (thus walking instead of driving) but not too much time (thus them striding off like a group of middle-aged women wielding walking poles and can-do attitudes).

We arrive at an expansive roundabout, the road widening to fit in with the rapid enlargement. The right opens into a large square with cafés staking claim to sections of the space. A four-storey eighteenth-century stone arch, reminiscent of the one in Saint Cyprien in Toulouse, acts as a symbolic gate to the city proper, as it was in the eighteenth century. As we beeline for it, we pass a large metallic statue of a tortoise with its young. I have to slow and take a closer look when something catches my eye. What looked like strange bumps on the shell at first are, on better inspection, bizarre faces pushing their way out through the carapace. A tiny pixie-sized figure is riding the neck of the mother. It gives me strange chills after seeming to be such a tranquil familial scene. I shake it from my mind and head after the two witches.

We make quick work of the last ten-minute stretch, with the Place De La Comedie quickly becoming visible straight ahead. Peculiar lampposts shaped like wheat sheaves and embedded with clock-tower-style watch faces around head height separate the roads. The elegiac buildings look like someone has pinched them directly from Paris, although in reality it is their architects who were snaffled. On the right, the Grand Theatre stands dominant, like a proud proprietor surveying all it owns.

It isn't a subtle building. Corinthian columns hold up the outer façade, providing a shaded colonnade where various people shelter, either awaiting company or just loitering aimlessly. The top of the walkway is as intricately decorated as the tops of the columns, the stone carved with an expertise that speaks of talent and high prices regardless of the era. On the top of the arcade are many statues that almost seem to lean out over the edge to regard the plebeian masses below. Officially, they are supposed to represent the nine muses.

Unofficially? I've heard they are carvings of each of the Mothers who previously guided the coven. When the current one passes, a new statue will appear, perhaps. No one will notice this impossible arrival –the joys of magic- and the tale will simply adapt to incorporate the additional statue. This is the stronghold of the Sistren of Bordeaux, and the world will bend and bow before them here to incorporate their whims and desires.

We head in, and the lack of restraint continues. I can imagine the client brief for the architect went something like this:

'Do you want columns?'

'Oh yes! Lots and lots of columns. Endless columns. More columns than the goddamn Parthenon.'

'Okay. Well, we've got Corinthian, Ionic, and Doric columns.'

'Yes, please.'

'No, which one?'

'All of them. *All the columns.*'

There is no delicacy. They just put as much exaggerated detailing on everything as they possibly could. It's overwrought and busy enough architecturally to have the same effect on easily overwhelmed visitors. The real understanding of the place –illumination, if you will– strikes you like the sunrays that pour down, focused from overhead, when you reach the central dome, a few steps up, the floor set below it like a raised dais.

Then you see.

This isn't just a theatre. Nor is it a palace.

No. This is a temple.

There was once a Cardinal Richelieu who went down in history for being a bit of a knob to D'Artagnan. He had no connection to Bordeaux, but he had a nephew who loved the city and wanted it to be the rival of Paris in all things. So Louis-Armand, Richelieu's nephew, hired the prestigious Parisian architect, Victor Louis, to the disgust of the Bordelais, as the Bordeaux locals call themselves, who wanted nothing to do with imported talent. There was, therefore, plenty of sniggering when Victor's work got held up for almost eight years.

The reason for that was twofold. First, political — the city council kept fucking him about for their own amusement. Then, when he was finally ready to get started, they discovered the remnants of a Roman temple underground, underneath the building they'd demolished.

I say remnants because that was the official story. Actually, it was an almost intact place of worship pre-dating Christianity. A more suspicious, less frustrated man might have wondered at how it had come to be in such perfect condition. Almost like it was still in regular use. Louis, though, had little time for further delay, so once he wangled permission to build the theatre from the local authorities, he just covered it back up and built his enormous neoclassical love letter to pillars on top of it. Or so he thought. The Sistren had made sure they could still get access.

We head through the main foyer and weave down several of the side corridors, walking around the back of the stage. A door that no unTalented or unwelcome individual will ever notice opens, and we descend into the long-forgotten world below.

The earthen walls surrounding the original Roman temple practically crackle with the Sistren's collected power. Cardinal Richelieu wasn't a friend of witches or, indeed, clever womenfolk in general. It must have amused the Mother greatly at the time to get the man's idiot nephew to pay for their new base of operations. For the building above, just as the building below, belongs in truth to the Sistren, and it channels the energy of devotion back down to their base. People come here to bask in the power of art and expression. There's a form of worship in the experience of high level stagecraft — an exchange of energies that builds and multiplies for both performer and audience. All of that is a form of magic, one the Grand Theatre channels downwards to the priestesses below its feet. In the day, the sun streams through the dome. At night, the moon bears witness to the Sistren's devotions.

On a great gothic chair, its points and crenelations reminiscent of a pre-fire Notre Dame, sits the Mother, her back ramrod straight and her fingers wrapped over the whorled ends of the wooden armrests. Swirled robes of black and purple obscure her form, but you can tell she carries no excess in anything, either physical or otherwise. Her face mirrors her throne, the flesh taut over pronounced structure, the myriad wrinkles all accentuations, seeming deliberate in their placements, reflective of the woman who wears them without bowing under their weight. Perfect white hair contrasts her walnut complexion; a single anchor of a dreadlock wrapped into a rounded crown, perilous in height, sits atop her head. Her imperial eyes are sharper than any sacrificial blade and used to cutting through any bullshit brought before her. I feel them fix on me, although I am equally certain she is keeping a careful watch on Aicha as well. She isn't one to let danger go unmonitored in her presence.

The silence holds the weight of a van full of gold balanced half-over the edge of a sheer drop. I'd love to have said, 'Hang on a minute, lads; I've got a great idea,' but, honestly, I have no idea *what* I've found myself in the middle of. I am rapidly starting to wonder if walking straight into the heart of another Power's dominion was the smartest move, especially to stand up for a P.O.S. like Franc.

After the oppressive silence continues for several more moments, after I am relatively sure that the Mother has trepanned my skull with her laser beam regard, I crack. It isn't my finest moment — I've stood solid under a plethora of torture techniques both physical and psychological before, but the force of the leashed emotions boiling behind her eyes is too much to stand. Especially when I have no idea what is actually going on and have little actual skin in the game.

'I don't know if you know why we're here, reverend Mother,' I begin, but she whip-flips her wrist up, her hand flat out to stop me speaking.

I quiet.

Several more moments pass. She continues to bore into me with her gaze, then she speaks. 'There was a Daughter of the Sistren,' she says.

'There was a Daughter of the Sistren,' she repeats, 'much loved and mollycoddled. There was *talent* there, young and naïve but with so much *potential*. There was an education provided, a world of playmates and promises of wondrous futures. There were...' She stops, and the emotional furnace seems to flicker, dimming for a moment behind her eyes. 'There were perhaps too many limits. Too much attempting to pass on lessons hard learned with no accompanying suffering with the acquisition. There were mistakes.'

The Mother stops, seemingly lost in thought, perhaps searching for those mistakes in her memories, when what the Coven hoped for in a young Daughter failed, when optimism turned out to be misplaced. When she raises her head again, her eyes burn as brightly as ever, fixing me in place with their intensity.

'There was a man. There always is. There was a man with a honeyed tongue and a carefully crafted careless charm. There were promises made that could never be kept. There was a foolish love, all the more powerful for the warnings issued. And there were warnings. There were threats and admonishments. There were tales told of young love's promises and their dust-ground endings. Always the young know best; always the old tales are nothing but Fear's tremulous tongue. So there were the beginning of weavings to drive the man away.' The woman stops, and a fleeting ironic grin flashes up the right side of her mouth, peeling lip over canine. 'Or that it was claimed would drive him away. There was perhaps worse in store for him in the Sistrens' plans.'

Again, the spiel halts momentarily. The elderly woman peels her gaze away from me, and I have to use all my willpower to stop myself gasping in relief, allowing myself to breathe easily again. She searches the shadows, locking on to whomever she's searching for and makes a gesture. She turns that piercing regard on me once more, and had I not been ready (and were this not round two), I think it would have knocked me back a step or two. This woman is intense to a frightening degree; either that or something really unpleasant has awoken that intensity. If that is the case, I'd love for someone to swing by, sing it a lullaby, and send it back to sleep before she looks at me like that any longer, please.

She waves her hand, and an image of a young girl appears in front of me. I can't suppress a groan, giving away my recognition of her. The green hair of her mohawk drooping over her eyes doesn't disguise the broody glare peering up from underneath them. I last saw her a month ago, as I made my way from the shizzard's house to find Franc for a chat. She'd been hanging around the centre of Toulouse with one of Franc's "lovely lads". I judged the girl not to belong to him then, but it seems she took the plunge after all.

'There was an... absconding. In rosy language, an eloping, although there are always thorns prickling beneath linguistic blooms. This girl and boy ran, him giving her promises of safety together. Come, come, away and up and over and out into a world drabber than any imagined, where the tinting of love's lens can only keep the colour so long. There were other offerings to keep the world brightened up. First love, then liquor. Then a rock smouldering in a pipe's embrace. A glittering needle to bring back the comforting haze of deniability. Then there was another offering. Offerings of service for safety, for protection. Protection exchanged for servitude.'

She leans slowly forward with great deliberation, and I realise who she reminds me of. It is Aicha at her most furious, her most righteous, about to dish out well-deserved justice, and for the first time, I start to feel afraid.

'There was a monster lurking under the water's surface. Contracts existed between the boy and the monster, for he belonged more fully to that creature than he could ever to love. There was safety there in those waters, in the storm-walls that stood like fortifications because there was an *alliance*.'

I wouldn't have believed it possible, but she stares at me harder still, and I know without a doubt that she holds me responsible — if not as much as Franc, then enough to be ready to pass judgement on me. I feel Aicha change subtly to full readiness. She doesn't move beside me, but I know she is running over her catalogue of hidden weaponry, mentally rehearsing movements in relation to the placement of parties around the room's shadowy edges. She's also detected the subtext. This conversation, which was supposed to be with me as a neutral party acting under the flag of parley, suddenly feels on a knife's edge of explosive confrontation.

'There was a deal between the monster and the boy. A higher priority, a right-hand seat at the table, a level of protection not offered to all the other little lost lambs. No pain when the drugs were scarce, no cold when shelters were full and winter came calling. But it was a deal, and deals always have a price to pay, especially with those of lost origin. There is so much truth in all the old tales. Never make deals with those who make you promises based on the misery of others.

'There was something the monster sought, that he wanted more than anything else in those who would bargain with him for his largesse. There is a spark carried in the breast of some that lies dormant for long years. There are ways of guessing the size, of seeing it when it opens up, unfurling its petals, but it is still asleep. There are many of those whose *talent* stays dormant throughout their lives and who never know it is there. And after all, if it is never known of, then it can never be missed, can it? This was what the monster wanted more than anything and what he gifted the boy to see pre-blossom, ready for his picking, sending him out into the world to gather those he could find back to his service.'

I feel sick to my stomach, and I am almost glad that she has me locked into her vice-like stare, keeping me standing when my legs want to give way. I feel too ashamed to look over at Aicha, too afraid of what I might see reflected back at me out of her eyes.

'There was a monster.' She cannot hide the sneer in her voice, but the pain underneath it makes me wonder if she isn't sneering at herself. 'There was a *monster*, and he ate her magic.'

I want to stammer out excuses, to explain why I made the deal with Franc, why I was prepared to accept peace rather than wiping him from Earth's face. I want to give self-exculpatory justifications, but they will do nothing to help that girl, and I see in the Mother's face what any words on my part will bring to pass, so I keep my mouth closed. She briefly studies me again, letting me see the rigidly constrained fury so I know it is only her will of iron keeping us from a smackdown right now.

'There was a rescue and a breaking of bonds that held her. Returned to the bosom of the Sistren, there was a time of healing, time to recuperate and regenerate. But there was no regenerating. The girl waned even as the addictions were burnt from her bloodstream, even as the sustenance put meat back on her bones. There was a fading, as though the girl pined away, though whether for love or loss was unknown. Then there was the discovery that her magic was gone.

'For a normal person who is *gifted* but unaware, the loss would still be a hideous violation but one they never know of, their life forever changed but not realised. For the girl, the Mother invested in her the breath of the coven, readying her to become the leader. Her energy and her magic were inextricably linked through to the coven itself. The Sistren's power also started fluctuating, becoming unpredictable. There was an investing in the girl that will lead to an augmentation of the coven. If the girl fails or falls — there will be a lessening for all.'

Still, she holds me captured by the emotion carried in her regard, and now the fury gives up centre stage, allowing terrible, tender pain to take a bow.

'There is a girl, but because she fell in love, she is dying. There is a Mother. There is a Daughter.'

She stops speaking, and something about what she just said bothers me enough that I have to replay it in my head to understand it properly. Then it clicks. There wasn't any capitalisation of the words. She didn't say there is a Mother, a Mother of the Sistren. That there is a Daughter of the Sistren.

She said there is a mother. There is a daughter.

I look at the image she made appear, all moody, rebellious teenager, and back at the aged witch facing me, who burns with rage and pain, and I make the connection.

We are totally and utterly screwed.

Chapter Eight

BORDEAUX, 9 APRIL, PRESENT DAY

Realising I've got two chances of playing the disinterested, neutral party here — a hellbound snowball's chance and no chance whatsoever.

The regal Mother, the grieving mother, the crux of power on the South Atlantic coast, lets two tears run down her cheek. I tremble because I know that if they come fully, if the dam of her self-control breaks and the flood pours forth, there will be no going back. It will submerge her, reason drowned by suffering, and the time for talk will be over. She closes her eyes and breathes deeply for a few seconds. When she reopens them, she is back in control, and I am infinitely glad. The Sistren have done me no wrong, and I feel more than a little responsible for what has happened to them. If we throw down in these conditions, only one of us will walk away. However desperately sorry I feel for the woman in front of me, I will still do everything I can to make sure that is Aicha and me. I don't feel entirely confident of success though.

She searches my eyes, and the intensity in hers lowers; perhaps she pulled from my gaze all my resolve and sentiments towards her and what has happened. Whatever it is, I sense we've momentarily stepped back from the precipice again. She inclines her head slightly, coolly, and the Mother of the Sistren of Bordeaux is wholly back.

'There has been a wrong offered,' she says. 'There has been an injustice served. There are amends to be made.'

'I acknowledge the wrongs, good Mother,' I reply. 'I came here thinking myself outside of whatever was between you and Franc. I...I no longer feel that to be true.' I hang my head slightly. I don't need to take responsibility for this. It is Franc's doing, and my truce with him was a logical course of action. But my decision has led inextricably to where we are now. 'I accept my part in what has happened to your daughter and will see the wrong undone. So how do we sort this fucking shitheap of a situation out? Pardon my language.'

A half-hiss gets inhaled next to me at the same moment as, for the first time in this entire conversation, the Mother smiles at me. A sadness runs through that smile though, mirroring the shock in Aicha's inhalation. Aicha knows what I've just done by saying that, and what I just promised myself to as a course of action. I've acknowledged responsibility. Now, it's not just Franc who has to make amends. It's me as well. I'm in this now until the end, whatever the end might be.

'There was a curse placed on the head of the monster who tied himself to this girl and ate up her magic. If the monster can gift back his digested meal, then the curse will break, and the conversation between a Mother and a Good Man might be at an end. What conversation that Good Man might have with the monster is between them afterwards.'

Her gaze no longer freezes me in place, but it leaves me in no doubt about how she wishes that conversation to be completed. Pointedly, with the emphasis on the pointiest of points.

'What if he can't regurgitate her magic? What if it's already been totally digested?' My stupid brain starts working out how Franc would evacuate digested emotions and magic, how he might *excrete* waste products. It is the stuff of nightmares and exactly why I often hate the aforementioned brain. Unfortunately, I can vouch, as someone who's had it separated from the rest of my central nervous system more times than most, that it's not possible to live without it.

'There may be other options. If there are, then the Good Man must follow them to their end. If there are no others, then the water monster will die and the Sistren will languish, at least for a time. There will be no love lost between Bordeaux and Toulouse, but no vendetta will be held as long as the oaths that have been made by you now, Cathar, have not been broken.'

'I'm a man of my word. Maybe I was mistaken in giving it freely...' There is a cough that sounds suspiciously like 'dickhead' from Aicha that interrupts me. I pick up the thread of what I was saying again. 'Maybe I was rash, but I always knew there'd be a price to pay for that alliance. Looks like the piper has come demanding his due.'

The Mother looks at me now with a sadness that engraves itself into her facial wrinkles, pulling them tighter with a tenderness that hurts because it foresaw suffering and could not or would not act to stop it. 'There was a piper who led children into mountains and played tunes that made promises of pacts and powers shared. There were tears shed and darkness spread by the monsters that lived in the mountains when the piper led them to a cave hidden under falling waters.'

I blink, mainly to jump-start my brain, which appears to have stalled or backfired. 'Are you saying Franc was the Pied Piper?' I ask, mind blown.

'There are always origins of stories, and they are not all happily ever afters. There are truths in fables, and there are softening smudges applied to the sharp edges that prick at children's fears like spinning wheel needles, by parents too kindly, unaware that protection from a pinprick now might only leave space for a scalpel to slice out their heart later.'

That isn't really an answer — or not a complete, comprehensive one. Pretty par for the course when talking to a major Power, and the Mother is crafty and sharp enough herself to make little incisions that will let doubt into one's mind, serving her purpose later on. Still, the idea of Franc stealing children away doesn't seem outside of the realm of possibility; it only adds to my sense of responsibility for not having dealt with him more severely from the get-go.

'Well, it seems like I need to be having further discussions with the Pied-Bullshitter directly then, so if there's nothing further to discuss, we'll be on our way. We can still catch the evening train and be...'

I start to move, but the Mother raises her hand, and her expression is hard to bear again but for different reasons. Her gaze hurts once more but not for her this time. She seems to weep without tears for me, simply by an emotional outpouring from her eyes. I freeze, half out of my seat, and stop speaking.

'There must be a chaperone, a witness, to ensure our bargain is honoured and all efforts made to correct the wrong that has been done. Not one of the Sistren, no; there are rules and reasons why when one volunteers themselves as champion, there must be a separation, a sense of equality on the playing field. One who holds duties and connections to both sides. An observer, assessed as neutral, indebted to the Sistren but not of them, will go with you to verify your actions claimed after.'

I find my voice. Just about. 'Who?' It comes out as a croak, like the sudden prophetic terror is freezing my vocal cords. Something terrible is about to go down.

'There was one, protected by this court of the Night Weavers, Hekate's beloved daughters, from betrayals of her own court. Summer and Winter both,' the Mother continues. *The Sistren protecting one of the fae who betrayed both the Courts of Faerie?* Now I'm really baffled.

The Mother sees my confusion and smiles, but there's no real warmth there. Perhaps something else though. If I didn't know better, I'd say it was pity. 'Neither court are forgiving sorts, and their mercy is not known. Still, we managed to negotiate a peace, a place of safety here for them. There have been services rendered for that protection and for answers to other questions, questions about a certain immortal Cathar. There were prices paid for that knowledge too, and now all debts have been called due.'

A shadow I didn't notice until now, behind the throned chair, moves forward. The light illustrates features subtly changed since the last time I saw them. They were always bright and fine-formed, deliberate in their delicatesse, a graceful-looking beauty whose fragility dissipated when one looked in through the soul's window. Now they are uncanny in their exquisiteness, with a sharpness that cuts through the bandages that have held my broken heart together for two hundred years. There are two things she was the last time I saw her that she is not anymore. One is human. The other is dead.

My heart stops. I'm sure of it. It can't beat. It's as if it suddenly remembers it's been a shattered ruin for centuries. Like all the actions I took to coax it into carrying on are undone. As am I by the sight of her.

I take a step towards the woman I found butchered on our wedding bed. A mystery that tore me apart, that I never found an answer to, has been turned into a whole new incomprehensible enigma. Yet, she draws me still. Even changed, I recognise my wife Susane...

Then she turns her head, breaking eye contact. Refusing to look at me. The sharp points of her ear replace her gaze, and the other side of this impossibility hammers home into me. It's not just that my dead wife stands in front of me. She's not human anymore. Her razor-sharp features, their perfection and otherworldly beauty speaks of the Daoine Sidhe. Somehow, she's a fucking fae.

That sounds bad, that level of instantaneous judgement. It's the way a parent reacts to their kids coming home with a partner with a darker skin colour than their own, and believe you me, I'm the first to applaud vigorously when their offspring puts them in their place. Preferably with a swift uppercut. But this isn't a "judge them on their race" scenario. This is a "the so-called Fair Folk have spent hundreds of years delighting in stealing, subjugating, torturing, and murdering humans just on a whim" situation. There might be a good Faerie out there somewhere. Isaac's always spoken well of Leandre, the Lutin Prince. As a general rule, though, they're malicious, vicious, cold-hearted monsters. There's a reason we all nailed iron over our doorways until the metal became so embedded in our society, in our world, as to keep them and their dark games at bay. They tend to break their toys, and we're nothing more than disposable playthings for them.

Now I can feel it. The paranoia. The sheer-edge thin-line of reason I suddenly find myself walking on, knowing I can tumble off it and into terror at any moment. Ben came back. He was the best of men when alive and became the worst of monsters by being reborn. And now, my dead wife stands in front of me, unable to even look at me, wearing the form of a creature from our collective nightmares for thousands of years. A woman who I loved wildly. A woman who I now have to ask...

'Were you even human? Ever?' She doesn't even reply, just holds herself still. Haughty. Aloof. *Elven*. As if my questions as a mere human are beneath her attention, unworthy of response.

And then another thought strikes me, the image that's floated through my every dream and every waking moment, that's tainted every happy second I've ever passed since I found her gutted, an island of flesh in a claret sea, soaking into the straw mattress and out across a tiled floor as cold as her dead body. Her belly, previously distended by a blessing I thought nature could never give, torn open. And the foetus, never born, never to be born, torn from her. I assumed it was for dark magical purposes, perhaps even to be used against me –fruit of my loins, flesh of my flesh– but now...

Hope. For a moment, hope. If she lives again...

My mouth shapes the words, but no sound comes. No air can escape my terrified lungs, too wary of the hurt that the wrong answer could cause, too aware that it's still what I expect. I set my will against my treacherous, protective body, and force the words to form.

'Our... our son...' It's a croak, a toad's lament, a creaking prayer for an impossible answer.

'He died.' She turns her head, angling her body to close me out. 'It doesn't matter.'

It doesn't matter. Is that the answer? It. Doesn't. Matter? What happened to him, to her, to me? The pain I've carried? The crack that ran from soul to self, rending me in two, into a shadow puppet, hands miming life, heart emptied and ruined?

Doesn't matter. Apparently it doesn't matter.

The ring of footsteps, deliberate and dangerous, reverberating off the stone, rebounding from the temple walls, bring my head up. Just in time to see Aicha reach Susane and send her flying backwards with a savage right hook.

The crack rings through the rafters, echoing back on itself through the stunned silence. Susane's nose splatters across her face, her neck whiplashing back from the blow, and now claret floods from between fingers clasped, prayer-like, around her features.

'Don't look so haughty when you're pissing blood out of your nose, do you?' Aicha asks her, staring her straight in the eye.

'You dare thtrike a high fae, creature? When guest in these hallth?' Susane starts, but Aicha cuts her off, screwing her face up like a preteen mocking a classmate, prancing on the spot, ridiculing a spoiled brat who just got their comeuppance from a teacher or peer.

'Ooh, you dare strike a high fae, neeah. I'm a stuck-up bitch who talks like Lou Carcoilh when my nose is broken, meeeh.' She stops, all playfulness evaporating, and bends closer, bringing herself eye to eye with the bleeding faerie. 'You broke his heart. I broke your nose. Fuck around. Find out. Dickhead.' Then she stomps back over to stand by my side, readied for action.

Chapter Nine
MIREPOIX, 28 FEBRUARY 1244

I feel tiredness' teeth nipping at my heels as we finally make it into the town of Mirepoix. A sleepless night, the silent walk made all the heavier by the thoughts tearing through my mind — a debate I want to put to Isaac, the arguments I can't crystallise into words that will convince him. That will convince myself. Still, I'll not abandon Montsegur, however foolish he considers my reasoning. If I can save the Good Christian faith, even when my own faith lies broken, there is reason enough, by my oath.

We weave our way through the busy thoroughfare leading into Mirepoix, watching for worn or uneven cobbles in the bustle of arriving wares. Carts and cattle take precedence through sheer force of presence, their bulk dominating the road. While most head for the central marketplace where the overhanging houses are home to merchants and makers, we turn away. Down and round. We pass by smaller dwellings still proud in bearing. The pride of each building slowly diminishes as we progress. Now they are like ale-sodden barflies, propping up against another afore ending up face first in the muck and mire of the streets out front.

And even that begins to give, so that the leaning becomes lean-to's, material propped up and scarcely covered. Yet, there is something to them still. It takes some time before I realise that, though the sizes are shrinking and the quality of building materials speak of what they could harvest without enraging lord or neighbour, there is still a level of care. The wattle and daub of the walls was mixed and applied expertly, albeit with a subtlety that does not crow of expertise. This is a neighbourhood carrying pride with its poverty. But carefully, surreptitiously, not rubbing it in the faces of those who live nearby. Resentment has ever sharpened ploughshares to blades. Then buried said blades in the backs of people who refused to know their place.

We come to the largest of the dwellings, which is not to say much. The outbuilding Isaac has given me as lodgings back in Montpellier is considerably bigger, and that is to do naught but sleep in. This place contains a whole life. Multiple lives, no doubt. A tanned ox hide hangs in the doorway, providing a privacy that's absent elsewhere and marking the building as special, to dare display any form of ostentatious possession.

Isaac pushes his way in, and I follow. The inside is sparse but clean, a tidiness that speaks of good housekeeping and echoes the cached prideful impression of the exterior. Simple wooden stools sit neatly arranged around a central fire pit. Slung skins against the rear wall floor provide sleeping space, with small carven toys stacked in between. Another doorway leads into a second room, further evidence of luxury compared to most nearby. Another skin hangs over it, obscuring a view of what might be beyond.

Three young boys ranging from three to five play on the compact dirt floor, pushing strange figures at each other. I would have called the toys soldiers, and certainly, the play is such, children strategising at war, but they look unlike any army I have ever seen. Differing sizes and shapes, combinations of man and beast, walking trees and bipedal wolves. At our entrance, they scurry back, snatching at their precious playthings, and scramble for the other doorway, disappearing to supposed safety from an unknown potential threat.

A woman sits straight-backed at the fire and picks at threads between thumbs and forefingers. Her hair is a raven's coat with a single streak of silver, a moonbeam piercing the black of night. She looks ageless. Were you to tell me she's as ancient as fifty, I'd believe you. If you instead insisted her to be a woman of thirty, I'd not doubt it either. She sings as she works, a low rumbling harmony to her voice, the song entirely unfamiliar.

'... *through the wild and wavering,*
Through fell and glen, the fallen men,
Who fled away from graves therein,
A welcome held in court of fen...'

The singing stops, and she raises her head to look at us. There is an acuity there that makes me feel as though I am one of Isaac's tomes and she has just read each page. She looks fully at Isaac, and a smile breaks across her face.

'Ah, Isaac, welcome! May the horn never sound upon your watch,' she says, nodding her head on a slant.

'And may the hunt never run you down,' he replies, acknowledging her with the same gesture.

The woman attends to her wool-picking, carefully tidying it away. While she does so, I look askance at Isaac. The greeting is new to me. He gives a small shrug, a sign I take to mean it is particular to these people. I would have sworn our momentary exchange is imperceptible, and that the woman is otherwise engaged attention-wise, but when I turn my attention back to her, hers is fixed on me.

'Well, Good Man,' she says, a crooked smile upon her face. 'Have you ever heard the story of the dashingly handsome young noble who became obsessed with wanting to know how his face would look without his nose upon it?'

I'm startled at her notice and taken aback further by the question. Still, I've manners, so I find my voice with relative quickness. 'I have not, my lady,' I reply, bowing, my head angled to mirror the exchange between Isaac and herself.

She laughs delightedly and claps her now empty hands. 'Oh, a delight you have brought to our house, old Jew.' She leans forward, still focused on me. 'Well, one day, he could bear it no longer and cut it off so that he might finally know. Tell me, Good Man, do you think the knowledge brought him happiness?'

I shake my head. 'I cannot imagine so, although who could place themselves in the mind of fools who would act in such a manner?'

'Who indeed?' There is a strange quirk to her smile. I do not fully understand, but I feel I am perhaps the butt of some joke. Still, I am in no position to be taking offence. Isaac has been insistent that this woman is the sole person who might help me find a way up to the castle of Montsegur.

'So now, rabbi, what brings you to my door? Not that I am not delighted, for there will be tales and truths we can exchange, I doubt not. You are always an education and, thus, are eternally welcome here.'

'A feeling shared, Gwendolyne, and ever so. Still, I am not solely here upon a social call, truth be told, though nothing would delight me further. Nor indeed am I here upon my own behest. I seek aid for my friend here, newborn into our world and impetuous with the rectitude of youth.'

The woman raises an eyebrow at me and opens her mouth. I assume for further questionings or mockery, perhaps. Instead, she sings again.

'*Youth carries its pride like a pommel to draw,*
And raises its hand ne'er away,
Age learns there are lies same as honour in all,
And a weapon sheathed ne'er will stray,
There was ne'er a villain who ne'er did right,

No hero with heart clear of hate,

And never a victory gaining delight,

When esteem took to steering our fate.'

She has an eerie doubling to her voice, as though harmonising with herself. I have to shake myself free of the melody as it settles heavily upon me, like a hound after a cleansing river plunge. I regain myself and my impatience.

'Your song is as beautiful and as charming as you are, My Lady Gwendolyne, but I seek aid rather than entertainment. My people make their last stand at Montsegur and are about to fall. I would offer escape to those who would take it, and Isaac said you could help.'

She looks me over thoughtfully. 'Did you ever hear the tale of the team of sheepdogs who believed that protecting themselves from the wolves was of utmost import?'

I shake my head again, trying to rein in my frustration and keep it from my face. 'Never, my lady.'

'They kept themselves safe, 'tis true, but the wolves annihilated their flock, easy pickings. When their master could not replace his sheep, it left him destitute, and they all starved to death, for who would buy a pack of dogs who forgot their duty?'

I narrow my eyes. 'And the Good Christians are the hounds in this story?'

'"Tis not my place to say who is barking nor who is howling at an uncaring moon. So what service is it you think I can provide, Good Man?'

I look over at Isaac. 'I do not know. 'Twas his idea, not mine.'

Isaac tuts at me, shaking his head. 'You border upon loutishness now, lad. Have I ever led you astray? Cool your temper 'ere you say something regrettable.'

He turns towards Gwendolyne. 'The Good Christians have taken refuge upon Montsegur and are besieged. Paul would offer a chance to flee, and though he is Talented, such an undertaking is beyond him. I remember you told me of secret passages the Cagot have learned through the mountains. Private places where you might hide your secrets and honour your own. The mountain is close to here. Would you know of ways to the top to avoid the entrenched forces at the bottom?'

The woman rubs her chin, staring into the firepit. The swirling smoke neatly evacuates through a hole above, none of it fogging the room. I'll bet *talent* accomplishes this feat.

'In many ways, you are in luck, young man,' she says. 'Had they chosen Bugarach instead of Montsegur, we could not help. We will not go upon that place even for our own ends, certainly not for yours. The lesser mountain though, we know well, ours before your Good People came and will be ours again after they are gone. There are many ways through that mons. Ways you will never find without us.'

My heart leaps. 'Will you guide me? I will be in your debt.'

Isaac interrupts. 'You're already in my debt, lad. Do not be so quick to take on more. No, this will square things between us, Gwendolyne. I will take responsibility for him. He can owe me further rather than being torn between two duties.'

The lady nods, still looking into the crackling fire. 'I cannot leave. The world is unsettled right now, as well you know. The priests seek heathens and heretics, and the knights seek wealth and honour, and both seek to spill blood. Did you ever hear the story of the king who wanted to keep his kingdom safe from war forever?'

We both shake our heads. It is the start of many tales, but I suspect it goes nothing like those I've heard before.

'He sought a deal with a fae and offered his life and crown for the promise. They struck a deal, and he returned home to bid his farewells before giving himself over. On arriving at his land, he found nothing left, all had been razed to the ground. He returned weeping and furious to reap vengeance upon the fae but found himself unable to raise a hand against it. "I fulfilled our bargain," said the fae. "I have kept your kingdom safe from war forever. For who would attack a memory, a ghost?" Then he took the broken once-king and was gone.'

She settles herself back in her chair and picks up her wool again. 'I cannot leave. In helping fulfil a debt owed, I would risk my people's safety.'

I feel my hope being snatched away. 'So you will not help us then?' I ask bitterly.

She looks back up at me. 'I will not. Still, I think there is another who might help. Susane!' she calls out loudly, and the curtain twitches back, revealing a young woman who steals the breath from my lungs. Had our paths crossed before I took up the black robes, I would never have become Perfect.

She is darker than Gwendolyne, darker even than I, sun-drenched until her skin is closer to the Moors south of the Pyrenees. There are echoes of feathery sable in her hair, but a life outside has bleached her, turning it to golden flax in places, the ringlets changing in colour, a progression from root to tip. Her face makes a mockery of my first life's calling, for she is truly perfect, each angle of her visage another wonder that reveals itself in thrown-out firelight. Her eyes sparkle emerald green. I would have marched away to war or performed herculean tasks to see them glittering with anticipation for my return. Then she speaks, not even looking in our direction.

'I heard you telling tales, mother. Which one is the noseless noble then and which the foolish dog doomed to starve by his own actions?'

Her mother smiles fondly at her. 'Which would you think, my love?'

She studies us carefully before turning back to her mother. 'I would never wager that I could spot which were which, for an inquisitive fool might hide behind a wise regard, and a yapping mongrel could still hold its tongue from time to time. Still, I think an impetuous youth more likely than a wiser learned head. I think the student probably is both.' She turns and curtsies. 'A pleasure to meet you, master rabbi and your muzzle-less pup.'

I am, for the first time in any of my lives, in love. This is a complete disaster.

CHAPTER TEN

BORDEAUX, 9 APRIL, PRESENT DAY

'... and on the next episode of Paul Bonhomme's Shitty Life — see his centuries-dead dad resurrected just to kick him in the balls and then piss on his dreams.' Worryingly plausible, considering recent events.

Susane aims to stand like a bloodstained Jadis, a regal ice queen. She is shades paler than she was when I last saw her. The blood pissing down her face ruins her whole stately pose somewhat. She keeps trying to obscure the mess, pushing her hand up daintily to her nose as though she can outperform Canute and force the tide to turn back inwards. She's having his same amount of success.

And I'm still here but not. Because a part of me's back *there*, the last time I saw her. I'm still standing over her bloodied body, still breaking, turning animal as my fragile grip on what kept me human slips away, and rage swallows my mind whole. The bars of the beast's cage snap along with my heartstrings. All worth to my world is gone, and I'm ready to kill it, to destroy the universe, to make it pay for what happened to her, what happened to our child...

But that doesn't matter. She told me. It doesn't matter.

The Mother of the Sistren sighs a bedevilled sigh at Aicha's actions but not before I think I see amusement in the quirk of her mouth. She waves a weaving from her hand, aquamarine in its luminance, and the bleeding slows, then stops. Susane tries to parlay that into a haughtier stance, but the blood that has already dried in encrusting track marks on her chin undermines the effect.

I stare at her, realising that the foundations I rebuilt myself upon once I pulled myself out of the grief of her and our son's deaths, outside of the opium dens I once embraced, are constructed on nothing but shifting sand. Aicha's hand settles on my shoulder, a grip that lends me strength, keeping me from collapse.

'Don't give her any victory here, *saabi*,' she murmurs in my ear, making sure no one can hear. 'Game face on. Hide it behind a cutting smile.'

She's right. Of course, she's right. The Good God knows that's what I've learned. Cover it up with a quip. Hide a dead heart with a sardonic quirk of the lips. And never let them know they've got you beat. That, and hold onto the good you've got. Isaac kept me from going down the same path as Ben after I found her dead; he wrapped me in Nithael's wings until I wore myself out with rage and grief. This time it's my sister-soul who keeps me from breaking again as Trauma comes back around for a second helping of kicking me square in the balls, and Life stands by, watching and laughing.

I close my eyes, draw breath, and push it deep down inside. There'll be time and space to unpack this later, to grieve and rage and suffer all over again. Right now, Aicha's right. *Game face on, Paul.*

I open them back up and fix a smile that feels like a rictus on my face. But I'm not trying to fool myself, just the rest of the world.

'You're looking well for being dead for over two hundred years, Susane. Red always did suit you as a colour. Not sure about the whole pasty-white skin thing though. Maybe now that you've crawled back out of whatever hole you've been hiding in, since letting me think you were dead, you can catch a tan before you fuck off back there again.'

She draws breath to speak but falls silent at a sharp glance from the Mother that is weighted and purposeful. 'There are tales that must be told.' Alarm flashes onto Susane's face, but the Mother looks entirely determined. 'Tribute must be made with words. There is always a price to pay. Always.'

The Mother's intense gaze comes back to me. 'There was once a man from Bordeaux who wished to win a woman all had failed to woo and regain honour lost by battle won. His name was Huon, and he was proud of arms and hasty with youth's surety, but in all other aspects, wiser than most. He knew of the Sistren and heed and honour were paid. There was an encounter that raised tempers to fury. Hands reached for pommels upon a capital-bound road that led to blood-reddened dust scattered across the trail. Huon stood victor, but to engage in armed exchanges with a stranger, no matter the insult, means the price to pay might be more than known beforehand. The adversary he slew was more noble than had been realised — Charlot, son of Charlemagne. There was debt owed — gilt for guilt.' The Mother looks across at the closed features of the stranger who looks like my long-lost love with a genuine sorrow. 'There is always a price to pay.'

I don't want to listen to these damn stories. I want to know what happened. *'It doesn't matter.'* Empty words from a cold heart, or cold words from an empty one. I don't want this bit of meandering history. I want to know who this woman in front of me is. Want to know if I ever knew who she was.

But the Mother of the Sistren isn't one for wasting her breath or to gift it unnecessarily despite her griot delivery style. And now that I've got a grip on myself again, now that I've pushed the pain far enough down to allow myself to breathe, to think again without breaking down, I know there're other kids at risk. All Franc's lovely lads and lasses, youths as lost as I was after Susane was taken from me. And a price that hangs over their heads to pay for his actions, for my inaction in shaking hands on a deal with him. So I shut my mouth, clamp down on my tongue, and force myself to listen.

The Mother heaves in a breath. A half-annoyed nasal exhalation follows as she stands from her throne for the first time. Her dread coronet unwinds as she does and tumbles to the floor, strewn backwards, wedding train-like. Two young witches, black-garbed and fresh-faced, dash forward to port it as she walks slowly, poise perfect, to stand between Susane and I. She turns back and forth, her sweeping gaze like a lighthouse's beam piercing the fog.

'There was a choice to be made. Bordeaux was far from the court of Charlemagne, and Huon held riches enough that he could have hidden in safety or fled with his wealth if need be. France did not exist, and the Franks did not hold complete sway so far south. Charlemagne set Huon a traditionally impossible task to assuage his red-raw grief. Travel to Babylon, no small feat in and of itself. Purloin a handful of the Emir's hair and teeth, powerful spell elements he would guard fiercely. Slay the Emir's fiercest knight, a giant warrior never defeated in battle. And steal three kisses from his bewitching daughter Esclarmonde.'

I suck in a breath at the name, my eyes widening instinctively. It's not an unusual name, but the synchronicity is striking. My thoughts can't help but turn to the Lady Esclarmonde, who led the Good People in their last sanctuary of Montsegur. Who I last saw that first time I met Susane.

The name doesn't cause Susane to react like I do. Some of her composure has cracked a little, judging by the way she occasionally worries her bottom lip with her tongue, but there's no surprise there, only concern. This isn't a new story for her. She just doesn't want me to hear it. That just makes me all the more determined to hear it all.

The Mother continues, still looking between us. 'When mortals are faced by the impossible, there are three choices that are normally made. They quit, a sensible decision when pitched against insurmountable odds. They fail, a glorious and pointless death, their normal reward. Or they cheat. There was a man called Huon who, whilst too proud to walk away from the undoable, was wise enough to know he was outmatched, and so he sought the Sistren's help.'

This time, I audibly suck in breath. Charlemagne ruled the Franks at the end of the eighth century before becoming Holy Roman Emperor. I had no idea the Sistren has held sway on the south coast for over fourteen hundred years. To guard a territory for so long, in a time when magic was more rife, and when even the greatest of Talented tend to reach their end in that span of time? Incredible.

'There were limits to what could be done. The Sistren were not prepared to travel three months to another Power's heartland, placing themselves at such risk for any price or promises. Huon had need of a helping compan-ion, and the Sistren brokered a deal for him.'

The Mother quirks one eyebrow at me, queuing me up. I hate being so predictable, but she's hooked me with the story, and I take my cue.

'With who?' I ask.

'There was a hill, inland from Archachon, surrounded by a ring of age-bowed stone pines. Inside that, a circle was woven of foxgloves and forget-me-nots, purple bells ringing amid the bright blue blossom. There was a way there, a way that was still easily opened, though not so easily closed.'

And now we're close. I can feel it. Close to an answer. Why my dead wife is now a Fae creature, cold and callous. And why it's not a tale the Sistren would make widely known.

'You opened a gate to Faerie for him, didn't you?'

She smiles at me, and I feel like a star pupil who just received a gold star; albeit, I suspect I am still in the bottom set of the remedial class. 'There was an offering for an opening, and Oberon came to parley with young Huon.'

This time, Aicha interrupts, 'Oberon, as in King of the Faeries Oberon? Oberon and Titania? Don't like you, have a donkey head for a bit, Oberon?'

The Mother nods, the movement impressively matched by a quick advancing of her two hair-bearing handmaidens to make sure it doesn't tug at her locks. I don't imagine she'll take kindly to having her hair pulled. 'That was Oberon in a more playful mood. There has always been a darker side to the Fair Folk. There is an irony to that name, much as calling the Erinyes the kindly ones. The fae have never been fair in their dealings, except to themselves.'

I nod while Susane looks distinctly put out, almost personally insulted.

'So you made a deal with Oberon then?' I ask.

The Mother throws her head back, and a clarion peal of laughter echoes up into the elevated rafters crowning her throne room. 'The Sistren make a deal with the fae? There was never a Mother who was so foolish as to do that, Cathar!'

She chuckles and takes another look at each of us, particularly me and Aicha. I think she is checking to make sure we aren't about to launch ourselves at Susane again, which was why she put herself in the middle, I'm sure. I am now engrossed in this fascinating piece of hidden history and know Aicha's inquisitive nature enough to be sure she is the same. The Mother clearly draws the same conclusion. She turns slowly and regally and returns to her intricately wrought and incredibly uncomfortable looking seat. She sits, her attendants splitting to the left and right and arranging her train of dreadlocks in two halves over the tallest spire-point of the chair-back on each side.

'There was a Mother then, as there has always been a Mother, and the Mother then *brokered* a deal between Oberon and Huon. A deal that allowed Huon to achieve all his aims and even steal away an additional treasure, the heart of Esclarmonde, which was followed back to Bordeaux by the lady herself.'

She looks hard at me, but still some of that humour from a moment ago lingers around her eyes. 'What did that mean then, Lord Cathar?'

I nod, knowing what she wants to hear. I've picked up on the theme. 'There was a price to pay.'

She matches my nod slowly, never letting go of my gaze. 'There is always a price to pay.'

CHAPTER ELEVEN
BORDEAUX, 9 APRIL, PRESENT DAY

Huon earth would make a deal with the fae? Huon of Bordeaux, apparently. Fucking eedjit.

The Mother of the Sistren of Bordeaux treats me to a dazzling beam of a smile for a moment, and I again feel like the class swot who remembered some impossibly obscure date or piece of trivia. 'There was a faerie king who was asked to travel the mortal realm and deliver the impossible for a proud young lord. There was the weighted load on one side of the scale and a deal to be struck. What do the fae always want when given access to human lands to frolic and filch?'

The blood drains from my face. I hope I've misunderstood, desperately hope I've misunderstood. My eyes drop to Susane's belly. 'They want children. Human children.'

I break. That ironclad resolve I borrowed from Aicha, to wrap around the pottery shards of my shattered ceramic heart snaps. But not for grief. For rage. For fury that flies through my extremities, that rides me like Franc rides his lovely lads and lasses. My sword is in my hand, pulled from my etheric storage before I can even think. My feet carry me across the narrow distance, and I press it tight, so very damnably tight to the throat of the only woman I have ever loved so that a single ruby pearl of blood wells out where it pushes through the first layer of her skin. *The fae bleed red at least*, I think inanely to myself. Those stupid thoughts, when our brain fixates on the most meaningless of trivia when the terrible truths of reality become too much to comprehend. Maybe I'm about to die a final death right here at the hands of the Sistren for breaking the treaty and striking down Susane. It all depends on the next words my dead wife speaks. If she was never anything but a fae glamour cast over my eyes to make me believe in her perfection. Whether there was ever a woman or if it was just a monster wearing beautiful skin.

'Did you give the fae our unborn child in exchange for' –I wave my free hand up and down her changed inhuman form– 'this?' The sword trembles in my hand, mirroring the tremors passing through my arm from the weight of pain rather than the steel itself.

The horror and grief that come to her expression finally humanises her again, and for a moment, I see my lovely Susane surface from under the cold flawlessness of her new form.

'Never!' she cries, and I hear the truth in the word. I let the blade's tip drop downwards before letting my sword disappear. Hunched over, I feel drained, drowning in old miseries all over again. I look over at the Mother, who did not move to intervene. Her expression carries a knowing and forgiving understanding. I guess she understands better than most, my reaction. It is why we are here, after all.

'There has been a Sistren in Bordeaux since Hekate ran with wise women for the first time through the wilding woods and laughed and danced and drew power from that communion. There has always been a Mother to guide them, since the Lady of the Moon first laid her hand in blessing upon a guide to shepherd her daughters. There has always been a Mother.

Children would never be offered in tribute, though Huon might have accepted such a deal.'

Now the understanding erases itself from her expression. She becomes more pensive, almost brooding.

'There was a reason the fae wanted human children. The Fair Folk had long understood the potential for danger as well as delight amongst mortals. They saw in the blossoming petal spread of iron forges across all lands an ever-present danger for them when they chose to come and dance on Earth's green hills. Oberon wanted a source of information, to keep abreast of the risks, to know when and where they might still come and if the day might arrive when they themselves would wish to seal the circles and close the mounds. There was a deal struck by an arrogant man and a fae noble, that his children would have two lives. Not just his children, but those of his most loyal men, who stood by his side and nodded their eager agreement. There was mirth and joy amongst them all over a second life for their offspring. And not just any second life, no. A second life as immortal fae, where they would go and dance forever beneath the barrows, bringing updates on time's ravages to the anachronistic fae. There was a compact reached, witnessed by the Sistren, and Huon set out with Oberon by his side, ready to carve out a place for himself amongst the notes of the troubadours' songs.

'There were illustrious victories and adventures and, eventually, a return to Bordeaux in glory, with even Charlemagne acknowledging a settled debt and heroic status. There was love and laughter, and Oberon did tap his antlers in acknowledgement and disappear from land and thought. For a while.'

The old woman sighs, and there is real pain in it, for the foolishness of men who think themselves equal to the bargains of fae and for those who have to pay the price.

'There came a time when Huon's young man-son, just come of age and glorious in attire and appearance, was laid low in a hunt by a wild sharp-tusked boar. There was grief spread throughout the people at his death, and Huon and Esclarmonde wept over his body laid out on the bier, empty as the heat had fled the form. They had forgotten in their pain, the promise of Oberon, so that even they were startled when, two days into the mourning, their son sat up and looked about him. Except, of course, he was no longer their bright-eyed boy, a noble human lord in training. Now his eyes were as sharp as his ear points and teeth, and he was as inhuman as he was perfect.

'The parents, of course, cared for little but that their child had come back to them. The masses who had gathered to grieve with them felt somewhat differently.'

I look closely at the creature in front of me who is wearing a form so close to the woman I gave my heart to long ago. I try to force myself to look past the haughty façade, to see it as a protective construct, a one-way permeable shell with pain going in but no emotions getting out, nothing writing itself on her face. I wonder if I can detect a tremble to her hand, whether the fist clenched over the hankie shakes from pain, and whether it's physical or emotional. Whether a momentary darting of eyes in my direction, breaking away from the magnetic presence of the Mother in mid-story, is her assessing a potential enemy or whether she is also searching for something in my face, some other emotion besides rage and disgust. I wonder how good her now fae-made eyes are, if they can detect anything else below my own carefully constructed exterior. If they can read the pain that's filled my emptied chest. If I am betraying myself all over again.

The Mother continues, 'There was not much subtlety or humility to Huon, and they did not keep the reborn young lord from the public eye. The strangeness of the boy was displayed for all and sundry, and the family's passing was now greeted by half-hidden gestures or mumbled prayers to ward off evil. The boy could no longer wear hammer-beaten armour or wield a steel sword, hissing at it if it came too close. Nor did it escape comment that the children of all Huon's companions gathered by the lad, following him with a fascination that marked him out as their leader. Now comments were made about each of them, how there was something just so about their elegant poise or the brightness of their eyes or the length of their incisors, that suggested more than plain humanity.

'There is a way that rumours grow that is both natural and monstrous, a tumour that consumes a community's cells. A failure of a crop here, a spreading sickness amongst a herd there. A bowl of milk that had curdled blamed upon the boy even in the turning heat of mid-summer. As was ever the case, the strangeness of the child was placed, its full-weight upon the mother. The superstitious and simply suspicious alike attributed all woes, real or imagined, to her corrupting influence upon the bloodline, easily aided by her skin being as golden as the sands of Babylon.

'There was a laying of plans, an ambush laid on paths that the lady walked through dappled forest glades, singing songs of her faraway childhood. There were hands, seizing and grasping, and iron spikes driven in hard, with cries of pain taken as signs of corruption. There was baying and blood and the worst of humanity displayed in the savagery of a group feeding fuel to that wildness just as they stoked the pyre they made. There was a burning, and it did nothing to allay their fury.

'The group swept on, driven by their rage, through the woods to where they heard the ringing of laughter through the glens. They found Huon's boy and his companions, and they slew his companions first with sharp steel, then after with their fingers, tearing apart the frail forms. Then they used the same piercing spikes they'd pulled from the mother's charred form to fix the eerie boy in place. They laughed as he whimpered and wailed at the touch even before they drove them home and danced to his uncanny ululations of agony until he died.

'There was a burning that swallowed up the bodies, and studs of iron driven into shards of bones broken under the pummelling onslaught. The people held them high above their heads and howled their victory against the unnatural as red dripped from their matted hair and their clothes clung to them like they'd run through a storm of blood.

'There was a moment. When the madness abated and realisation crept in. That they had killed the children of men trained in war. That their scythes and knives were no match to swords wielded with a father's grief. Fear took root in their hearts as the anger drained away. Hastily grabbed weapons tumbled from fingers suddenly numbed, not by horror for what they had done but by fear of retribution already saddling up to ride down upon them and their own offspring when their actions were revealed.

'They fled, but they were not crafty in their panic, and they had not been quiet in their crimes. It was not long before Huon and his men sought their missing offspring, not long before they found the flame-charred bones, not long before they realised what was lost and howled it at the obscured sky. The villagers heard it echoing back through the forest's twisting boughs, and dread consumed their every thought. naught remained but to flee from the growing thunder of the horses' hooves and the thunderous ire that rode in search of them.'

There is a sadness to the Mother's face that I think for a moment is because of her own situation. I look again though and realise she is looking at Susane, and this time I see the pain in the fae's eyes even as she keeps her gaze downcast, listening to a story I am sure she knows well but one that is no more comfortable for the re-telling. The inconsistency in the story suddenly occurs to me.

'Hold on,' I say, confused now. 'If Huon and his companions' children were all iron-staked, they wouldn't be able to be reborn as fae. Iron and faeries have never mixed, and I can't imagine iron-studded bones could take on a new life. So how does that tie in to Susane's Lazarus impression?'

'That is a question that has already been answered several times, Good Man.' The Mother smooths down her robe where it pleats across her legs before raising her eyes to mine. 'There is always a price to pay.'

Chapter Twelve
LEAVING MIREPOIX, 4 MARCH 1244

It's going to take a few days for us to be on our way to Montsegur. Susane is not able, or at least not willing, to drop all her own responsibilities in order to escort me up and through the mountain.

Susane, like her mother, is Talented, although I will consider it no boast to say I hold more potential than she. What she does possess, however, is imagination and finesse, and both seem to be more useful than my brute *talent* might be. As she dances through the Cagot territory with me following after her, she makes minor workings, aiding and healing, cleaning and sealing, distracting and guarding. Her presence sets her people at ease and protects them simultaneously. Her efficacy awes me, and I cannot help comparing it to Isaac's tendency to leave dust to gather and lose rare texts. She is a whirlwind of activity, doing all she can to help her community, both physically and magically.

I am of little use, except to occasionally let her borrow power or to carry such items that need moving. She speaks to me enough to direct my actions, but her tone is short, her time precious. My prattling will not distract or divert her, sad to say. And prattle I do. I have never found myself in so miserable a situation, where I want so badly to repress my tongue, to share only the most precious of considerations. Yet I find my mouth almost endlessly running, babbling nonsense like an over-eager child desperate for parental attention. I lose count of the number of times I repeat that the weather is unseasonable and how many times I insist it is exactly as one might expect. Each time, I feel like a failing Fool unable to stir the court to mirth, undeserving of his capitalisation. The only small mercy is, as time wears on, she starts giving me small smiles, though I am not so blind nor blinded that I do not see the pity heavily present.

Now, both at last and far too soon, we are ready to go. She packs us knapsacks replete with rope, candles, provisions, and water.

'How long do you expect us to be in the mountain?' I ask, confused.

'It's not a mountain; it's a pog,' she replies absent-mindedly, verifying our supplies once again.

Her reply takes me aback. It is a longer reply than I have extricated from her in many of the days previous. I know the word "pog", of course, a local dialect rending of "mount", whereas I am speaking in the Frankish dialect Isaac insists we use as cover. When weary or in one's cup, it is still necessary to pass for other than we are.

'So be it, my lady. How long would you envision us being inside the pog?' I correct my question.

She sighs and turns to look at me directly. Another much longed for rarity. 'To make your way up the pog by the path would take little more than an hour, Good Man. Mind, I think the encamped troops might have words to say at your passing. Inside the pog, now...'

She looks away, returning her attention to the meticulous inspection of the packing. 'There is more to the pog of Montsegur, more to the pogs of that region, than is known or seen by most. I am not most, and despite your endless jawing, I do not believe you are either. Those tunnels are ours, and they welcome us, but there are other tunnels that are not and do not. Sometimes, they can surprise us, replace our tunnels or add on to them if we allow ourselves to get distracted. People turned around have ended up lost for days in a few feet of rocky corridors. Some have gone in and never come out. I hope our tunnels lead us up in not much longer than the time it takes to stroll the pog path. Indeed, much quicker, without interrogation or arrest to fear. Still, I respect the Iron Pogs. I will not do them the disservice of underestimation.'

She looks up at me, a challenge in her eyes. 'Not all of us are heroes, Good Man. Some of us stay alive much longer and are more able to look after our people by not being. I will not see my kingdom razed, all things being equal.'

That was more words than she has said to me in all the previous days combined, and it is enough to close my mouth-hole, to think and give due consideration prior to speech.

'I think,' I say slowly, 'there is heroism there, within. I think, mayhap, that you are the sort to be drawn towards action and accomplishment. That perhaps staying here and guarding your people stands at odds against a natural want to head outwards and away. Perhaps that is your heroics.'

She nods, pulling tight the cords binding the bag. 'Not just a pretty face, are you, Good Man? Not all of us can head off from our duty in search of destiny instead.'

She falls silent, and I sense an end to the conversation for the time being. I mind little though as I have plenty to consider. Not least that she considers my face attractive. That is a heroic victory in my accounting.

As the sun rises, we take our leave early. With a day of travel ahead of us to reach the mountain, we have only what we can carry. There is no desire to risk being conspicuous on the roads leading towards the army's campsite. Little of the traffic will be friendly to the likes of us. Less so if they know our motives.

As we walk, the sun drives the worst of the chill from the air, and the walk drives the last of it from our limbs. While the silence is still there, it has a more companionable feel to it. Perhaps that is only in my head, but it is enough to still my jabbering tongue and keep me from any further buffoonery, for now.

We walk, our capes drawn up, our eyes alert, ready for danger. Although I know the Church has Talented, I believe them to be the exception rather than the rule. I doubt many of the ruffians, royally approved or otherwise, that we might encounter en route will be much of a threat to two magic wielders such as ourselves. Still, we don't seek to draw attention to ourselves.

Susane hums a tune that worms its way into my ear so that, even when she stops, it seems to resonate inside my brain. It is both simple and haunting and seems almost familiar, like a face in a crowd that makes you look again, sure of shared cause or history.

'What was that song?' I ask in the end, unable to think of much else.

'Hmm? What song?' she replies, starting out of her own trance-like state. I think she was entirely unaware that she was making any noise.

I do my best to replicate the melody and hum it back to her. Her eyes widen as I do so, and I conclude perhaps she did not intend to share it. She sucks in her cheeks, and for a long time, silence reigns. I have just concluded that it is best left alone when she throws back her head and sings out loudly:

'*When the dooms are due and the truths are told,*

And Bugarach cast in ruthless gold,
When tombs outgrew anew unfold,
The patterning of cracking bones.
When pain is gained and hardships done,
Woven force drawn from harnessed sun,
The Lady will unmark our tongues,
The scattered will at last come home.'

I bow my head, surprised to find tears threatening appearance at the simplistic beauty of parole and melody. 'That was truly wondrous. Tell me, what does it mean?'

She shrugs, withdrawing back into herself somewhat. 'Who can say? Some say it is a prophecy of our people. Some say an image of our lives' courses. Others? A pretty song.'

We walk farther before she speaks again.

'All people have their ways. Nobles have their troubadours to bring them songs to inspire their troops and justify their actions. The Church has pomp and ceremony, the mystery of Latin as almost a hidden language. What does that leave for a people such as ours, except stories and songs to store up hope? When you are allowed nothing –no place, no status, no possessions, nor position– what would you value higher than what they cannot take away?'

I nod in acknowledgement, for the truth in that is clear to see. A noise gathering from behind draws my attention as I am about to reply. Engrossed in both the song and discussion (and indeed, in the company), I failed to notice the score of horsemen now galloping up the road behind us.

I turn and draw my buckled sword, ready to stand and defend Susane with my life for I can see that these are a party of Frankish horsemen riding either to join or return to the siege. The thunder of hooves becomes almost deafening as they draw closer and closer to me, their speed and presence monstrous as they arrive...and then pass me by, streaking to each side, missing me by inches as I stand stock-still, my sword aloft, belatedly clamping my mouth closed as the dust flies up from them charging past.

By the time they are gone, I look like a stone statue carved in memoriam to a glorious soldier, the road dust having liberally coated both me and my sword so that it clings to me and turns me to a rocky grey. I lower my arm and turn to see Susane bent over. For a moment, my heart stops, fearing the errant knights harmed her until my ears clear of the clattering hoof-caused ringing, and I realise she is clutching her belly, laughing until tears stream down her cheeks.

'Did...did you mean...to fight...ten knights on horseback...with a sword?' She gasps and then shrieks with laughter again, fighting to draw breath. 'You truly are both a hero...and a fool...Good Man. Where was...your magic?'

I realise she cast a spell around us, keeping their attention from us while I was posturing and readying myself to lose this current body. I am also aware that I mainly did so in order to impress her with my bravery. I flush with embarrassment, then chuckle at my stupidity. I cannot deny her point. Raising my sword again, I invest it with my *talent* so that the blade crackles with green balefire energy.

'Would that have been better?' I ask. We look at each other for a moment and then the pair of us collapse into uproarious fits of merriment. It looks like my buffoonery has at last broken the ice between us, albeit unintentionally.

CHAPTER THIRTEEN

BORDEAUX, 9 APRIL, PRESENT DAY

Can't help noticing Susane has been silent for a while. Guess it's a case of "the Cagot her tongue". Heh.

The pale-skinned fae who was once my blushing bride keeps her eyes on the Mother, almost motionless. The only thing that betrays her internal state is an unconscious light tapping of her little finger against her side, rapid enough it almost seems to vibrate. I don't think she expected this story to be relayed, but she isn't about to overrule the witch-queen in her chambers. The imperious façade of the storyteller is now very much locked in place — the Mother is completely in control of her emotions. The weaving of the tale has allowed her to regain her equilibrium, and she is regal in her poise once more.

'There was a reckoning. Huon and his men, enrobed in grievous suffering, hunted down the murderers, pushing their horses hard, their spittle-flecked heaving breaths and wild-ridden eyes matching their masters'. They pursued them through gnarled trunks that snatched at faces with knot-jointed finger branches, scratching and slowing. Whether by chance or design, the rallying horns encircled the villagers in a net that tightened to draw them together in a glade complete with a flower-picked circle. As they stumbled, terrified and quivering in tree-rent clothing, into the clearing, with the hunting knights slowly advancing at a menacing canter, they crossed the wildflower markers and huddled in fear. The horsemen pulled short at the crossing, even Huon, though he shook with rage that threatened to tip into the berserk madness of the doubly bereft. The killers, who had been without mercy a short time previously, knelt, weeping and begging for a clemency that a father would never give.

'As they knelt there surrounded by sword points and sharper anguish, they realised they were no longer alone inside the circle. An unearthly king, replete in spiderweb cloaking and yellowed-bone antlers, arose out of the ground, and there was now another bereaved progenitor in their midst, his form crackling with fury and uncanny force.

'There were pleas and promises for mercy and mitigation to desolate fathers, both human and fae. Perhaps if they had been outside of the faerie circle, the traumatised and vengeful hunting party would simply have ridden them down. No matter their grief-driven anguish though, none of them were foolish enough to cross the ring. The murdering villagers were safe from them. They were not, though, from Oberon.

'He spoke with a voice that chilled their marrow as he proclaimed judgement. They had stolen his eyes in the human world and fresh blood from the fae world, and so he would steal their own young, claiming them as faerie for a second life. They would not be raised up as lords and nobles in this world though but would be marked for their stealing of the treasured gifts of Huon and his knights. They would carry the weaknesses of their fae side with none of the gifts — iron would burn them, and they would tell the truth no matter what harm might befall them for it. When they rose again as fae, they would not be elevated in the courts but stay as servants and subordinates. They were wyrded and would stand as such in both worlds, outside of the known and noble, they and their own offspring ever after, cast out like wild dogs.

'Huon and his men protested, seeking a blood vengeance, but Oberon stood insistent, and as the villagers had stolen his part of the bargain, there was little Huon and his men could say. There were beatings and breaks that would take long to heal as they stepped from the fairy ring, but all was done under Oberon's intimidating, watchful regard and limited. Huon named them *ladres*, meaning thieves, and they wept as they were driven from their homes. Their inability to comfortably touch or work iron marked them out wherever they went, and at first, they wandered through the Occitane, stealing and hunting to survive, using crude wooden and stone weapons, dressed in torn furs, so they became known as the wild hunters, the Ca-got. The edict of Huon that none were to help or harm them carried along the wind to mark their passage through the land.

'As each died, Oberon claimed them, but stories of their resurrections, along with their weakness in the face of the Church's heavy-wrought iron crosses hanging in naves and pulpits brought them a vampiric reputation. Some say Bram Stoker encountered a far-flung tribe in the east of Europe that gave rise to his tales of Dracula. Eventually, they settled on the outskirts of communities and became accepted, if never welcomed. Taking the roles of bakers and woodsmen and taking communion outside of the churches, they were neither embraced with open arms nor entirely shunned. They remained apart, weird-marked, just as Oberon had said. And so the Cagots came to be. They carried their secret and made a pact that none outside of their number would know of their second life and their carried curses nor the true reason.

'There was a rising reborn after death kept hidden from a grieving outsider husband by requirement of the Cagot culture. There was a woman forbidden by her elders to speak to her love, who mourned, or to seek him out in the limited time before they shepherded her to her new life in another realm. There were eyes that watched both her and him to ensure their separation. The woman knew the history of her people and their origins. She knew who had negotiated the first agreement between Huon and Oberon, so she sought the Sistren of Bordeaux. There was a supplicant filled with tales of torn, red-soaked wedding night finery, who knelt and offered her tears and begged for intervention between her and the Lord of the Fae.'

And there, in my heart, that ruined, shattered mass that's dead weight inside my hollowed out chest, for a moment, I feel a beat. A pulse, a single bass drum thump as hope kicks in. And I hate myself for it, of course. I know what this sort of hope is. The Good God knows I've seen it time after time, across lifetimes. It's that tiny little whispering voice that's desperate to believe those who've hurt you meant you no harm. That same thud a woman feels as she cradles a phone, hiding blackened eyes behind hair curtains as he promises that, 'This time it'll be different, babe, I'll change.'

Because, maybe, just maybe, this isn't Susane's fault. If she had no choice, if her people had their tongues sealed by Oberon's magic, by Huon's bargain, by their ancestors' murderous errors...then maybe she couldn't tell me.

Maybe this isn't her fault.

'Was it...' I wave my hands half-expansively, half-helplessly, trying to encompass *this*, all of this. The story, the legend, the curse on her people. 'Was it magic?' A simple question loaded with dishonesty. What I really mean is, 'Was it not your choice?' 'Could...could you have come to me?' Could she have chosen me as her protector, ready to go in to bat for her, ready to go to *war* for her instead of the Sistren?

She looks at me with those piercing, perfect eyes that are almost hers, yet somehow aren't. 'No. Not magic. Honour. I could have. I chose the Sistren.'

And just like that, my heart's last foundation crumbles away as the ground swallows it whole. She didn't have to go to the Mother. She didn't have to keep her secrets. Those were choices. She trusted them more than me.

The truth? She never trusted me.

Aicha steps forward with a malicious grin on her lips. 'So if she can do the whole Jedi "Strike me down and I shall become more powerful than you imagine" business, nobody's going to mind if I go a bit Roberto, right? I need to stab someone. Where's my stabbing knife? Ah, here it is.' She pulls an enormous blade from a thigh holster I've never seen before, rust-red and yet still wickedly sharp. Susane turns paler still, stumbling backwards. Aicha advances, humming the "Imperial March" as she does so, swinging the blade expertly, slicing the air in time to the rhythmical *dums*.

'Peace, Druze,' says the Mother, raising her hand and throwing up a barrier between the two women. 'There is still more to know.'

Aicha looks unblinkingly at the Mother while still making random cuts at the barrier, as though testing to see if it's dropped yet. 'There's always more to know. Doesn't mean it's worth knowing. Or worth changing course over. Sometimes it's best just to stab them in the face first, ask questions later. Right now, I'm feeling a bit stabby.'

I walk over and lay my hand on her shoulder. 'Appreciate the stabbiness, *laguna,* but we need to finish this story.' Aicha looks at me, then makes a last half-hearted slash at the petrified-looking Susane.

'Ah, fuck it. There's always later,' she says and walks back to where she stood, flipping and catching the knife's blade carelessly, still whistling Darth Vader's theme song.

The older woman lowers her time-creased fingers only once Aicha slips the knife back into her holster; she clearly hadn't put it past Aicha to make a final thrown attempt, and to be honest, that was entirely wise. Once the Mother is happy that the immediate danger of Susane catching a thrown blade with her face is gone, she starts speaking again.

'There was a deal made between the woman and the two parties. She would first serve two hundred years in Faerie, taking the lowliest and most despised of roles. Then she would be allowed to return to the keep of the Sistren in our service until such time as the investment made by interceding was judged fulfilled. So she will accompany you as an agent for the Sistren to ensure completion of our deal is made as satisfactory. Then there will be freedom.'

Freedom. What a strange term. I don't think I really understand the concept anymore. I've never been free. Not of the weight of what happened at my first death. The fall of the Good Christians. Ben's death. Susane... Our child... I thought I put them behind me, but there they are, still buried in my heart like a knife shaft, the muscle regrown, misshapen around what can never be pulled out. What does freedom mean for Susane? What does she want to be free of? Or of who? Me? Because she didn't come back. Didn't trust me to save her, to keep her safe from her people's past sins coming for her. She let me think her dead forever, let me be destroyed. It's only her duty, her oath to the Sistren that's brought her back to me, and only to serve them. Only paying her debts. Now we're forced to partner up, for her to act as their agent in this fucked up mess I've found myself drawn into. And it hurts so damned much.

And through it all, I'm still tied up by ancient promises made through pain's lens and the prices to pay for them.

And from those, it seems, I'll never be free.

CHAPTER FOURTEEN

BORDEAUX, 9 APRIL, PRESENT DAY

Wondering if the selkies are the origin of the name of the Summer Court because they're kind of seal-y. Sealy. Seelie. No? My comedy genius is wasted.

I t is not a convivial train ride back to Toulouse.

Aicha takes immense pleasure in spending the entirety of the journey sharpening each of her blades, and when I say the entire journey, I really mean it. The woman carries an inordinate amount of cutting implements, both great and small.

And I am lost.

I've been lost since the moment I staggered from that room painted viscerally in the ruins of my wife and son, the morgue made of our wedding bed, when Isaac wrapped me up in Nithael's power to save me from destroying every living thing in reach of my magic as I screamed and raged, a howling, mindless thing. When I came back to reality, reclaiming my shattered self from grief's clutches, I found the Cagots gone, their doors closed on me, the room cleaned of blood and body with no explanation offered, no chance to investigate, to hunt down a culprit and burn them in the fires of my loss. Even the finest opium purchased with a hundred lifetimes of savings squandered without thinking could hardly dent that rending of my soul that left me a shredded shade. I was a scarecrow of a man, the wind blowing through the tattered rags of my humanity, my emptiness poking through at the grief-split seams.

And I wallowed.

Sank into the sucking black tar pits because I'd lost her, and nothing else mattered. Rode the sweet pipe smoke down into oblivion to get away from all I'd thought I might finally hold and own.

When all I had to do...

Well. "All". All I had to do was smash my way into another land full of clinically insane monsters filled to the brim with magic down to an atomic level and fight my way through them all to rescue the woman I loved.

But I would have tried. And if I'd died trying, there'd have been a peace in that I've never known since.

Except I never had the chance. She never gave me the chance. Never wanted me to have the chance. She went to strangers, to another Power, and made deals with them to leave me drowning in the dark.

And I don't know how to feel. If I hate her for living and what that makes me if I do. The Good God knows I've always hated myself for it. Living without her. And now she sits, in a strange little porcelain package, all prim inhuman perfection, and I don't know who she is. Or who I am now, when the man I was got eaten by grief, and the man I am is face to face with his past self's failure.

But I've been hollow for a long time. Lost my humanity and learned to fake it till you'd never know there was only pain and loss behind the easy smile. So I pin that sardonic grin back across my features as though I don't feel a thing. There's a part of me that prays it becomes true. And a part of me that hopes Aicha will kill me once and for all if it ever really does. Meantime, a meaningless smile and a light word, a careless, heartless joke, lets me hide while I hold on by my fingertips to sanity's crumbling dust edge.

'How is Isaac these days?' she ventures quietly, the same desperate tilt to her tone that once coloured mine when I first tried to get her to talk to me, when I followed her around, making a fool of myself just to gain the honour of her attention. The memories cut deep, pulling up my love for her after centuries of it being buried, making it as strong as it once was while somehow still breaking it even more than it'd ever been broken.

'Alive. Invested,' I reply, unable to say more in my grief, and the heavy silence settles once more, broken only by the rasping grate of whetstone against edge.

'Did you ever find any trace of his brother?' she tries again a few minutes after.

I chuckle, pointing gun fingers at her in acknowledgement. 'Funny story that. Turns out he was captured by my previous acolyte and best friend. Who I'd thought dead. And turned up to...' I mime scanning back through a book, putting my finger in the imagined correct spot. 'Fuck me over completely?' I ask Aicha inquiringly.

'Bing-bada-bing-bing-bing. Popcorn,' she replies, shooting the same gesture to me with a spin of the blades around her digits. Gun-knife fingers? Gunife fingers? I sigh inwardly, my heart not in this linguistic game. She's better than I am at it anyway.

The seconds tick by in time with the sweeping stone strokes.

'So what have you been up to recently, Paul?' Susane asks, determined not to give up. Or maybe she's just uncomfortable in the silence stretched taut between us. I can't decide if I love it or hate it myself.

Guess I hate it too given I answer her.

'I mean, how recently are we talking? Recently after I found my dead pregnant wife and nobody would talk to me about what had happened? Sent me on a bit of a downward spiral for a bit, that one, can't imagine why. Opium addiction, shady deals with water monsters that are causing me a fuckload of issues now.' I click my fingers and point at her again. 'I know. Misunderstanding said water monster's abilities and letting him eat a load of poor fuckers' magic. That's been my latest and greatest discovery of how I've spectacularly fucked up in the time since you died, Susane.'

She leans forward, intent, her eyes fixed on mine. With the glamour she wears softening the unnatural edge, she almost resembles the woman I fell head over heels for hundreds of years ago. The eyes give her away though. Hers were a soft grass-green in our life together, as warm as her hands as they wrapped around my waist, as her breath pressed into my neck. Now they are a cold stone jade, pretty and perfect and not right in the slightest. I wonder why she was reborn with pale skin and features Caucasianised. Turns out the fae are massive racists. Who knew?

'I am sorry, Paul,' she starts, reaching out a hand to place on mine. I pull myself back immediately.

'Sorry doesn't really cut it, Suse. I mean, that's an understatement. Sorry is a kid's play-knife, covered in protective foam, and "it" is made of adamantium. Getting killed, eh, I'll give you that one. Happens to the best of us –'

'Happens to you, most of all,' Aicha throws in.

'As I said, happens to the best of us,' I reply automatically, though my heart's not really in it. Mind you, I don't really know where my heart is right now. Certainly not in the empty void inside my rib cage.

Aicha makes an obscene gesture over a cough-obscured, 'Wanker', then returns her concentration to her knives.

'Keeping secrets, sure,' I say, the words tumbling out, unstoppable like a river after heavy rains. 'I understand you were carrying societal responsibility. You were brought up with this "keep it secret, keep it safe" approach to your fae nature –'

'It's more than that,' Susane interrupts. 'We are all oath-bound never to reveal our secrets. They already counted me a betrayer for wanting to share my life and having shared my bed with you. I couldn't break faith entirely, betray my people completely. I gave up everything to be with you, Paul. Oh sure, the Cagot still acknowledged us. There was a wedding to be had, and people lifted their hands to help and greeted you, and I'm sure you felt like it was a big joyful homecoming for the charming eternal boy-child who'd stumbled lives later into adulthood and responsibility. Another group of outcasts you could dazzle with your smile and wit and power, and they would love you for it. Just like I did.'

She never looks away from me. 'You were never welcome, Paul. Never wanted. The wedding and the pleasantries were a parting gift to me before they exiled us. Oh, they'd have monitored us to know if our child took after you or me so they could know what would happen when he died. Outside of that though, they'd have shunned us.' She laughs, a sharp momentary crow's caw that stands in harsh contrast to her perfect beauty. 'The outcasts would have cast us out, Good Man. They'd planned to the day I chose not to conceal my pregnancy from you. The day I said, "I do" to your damned question and earned my kins' distrust. So I've paid and paid and paid again for ever having known you, Paul Bonhomme, for having helped you, for having held you, for having loved you and been lost to you. I am sorry I left you alone, never knowing I lived still. I've paid my weregild for it though, and I'll not pay now with extravagant displays of shame to massage your already over-inflated sense of self-importance. Go fuck yourself.'

There's a low whistle and a slow handclap from Aicha. 'Oh, I like this side of her more, at least. I wasn't really getting how the two of you ever bumped uglies. I mean, I'll still make your life a fucking Galadri-hell if you so much as look at me funny, but it makes more sense, at least.'

Groaning, I roll my eyes. 'That was dreadful, *laguna*. Please don't do that again.'

'Are you worried I'll hurt her fae-lings?'

'Jeez, Aicha, knock it off.'

'I can't promise it'll be the Lego-last, *saabi*.'

'Fuck my life.'

She fixes me with a look, gives me the most minute nod, then turns her attention to the window. Ah. She did that on purpose. And I can see why. The comfortable familiarity of the banter's grounded me, let me break the surface for a moment, long enough to take a breath, to get my bearings, a second's break from drowning in all of this. By the time I look back, Susane has transferred her attention deliberately to the world outside the window, the steadier distant greens only highlighting the closed-in fencing and walls, the similitude only broken by graffiti colours flashing by faster than the eye can decipher.

'That's not what I meant,' I say softly, 'when I said, "Sorry doesn't cut it".'

'Then what did you mean?' There's a pleading tone there, both to her voice and to her eyes. And I don't know what she wants. To understand or be understood.

'You...dying...' I feel like my lungs aren't working properly. Like they've collapsed, shrivelled up like they've been blade laced, unable to give me enough air. I've been stabbed often enough to know the sensation better than I know the woman standing in front of me. 'It broke me. All of me.

Not some part, my heart or something. Nothing made sense. The whole impossibility of you ever even being pregnant...'

The words fill my throat till I can't get past them. Not air. Not thought. They're a blockage that I can't overcome, that I've never been able to move past. Isaac told me, back when I first came to him as an apprentice, that the chances of me ever becoming a father were infinitesimally small, a side-effect of hijacking corpses to keep on breathing. And I didn't give a damn. Not until I met Susane. Not until hundreds of years later when we got together. Not until she told me she was pregnant, and suddenly it became the most important thing since my own first breath. Not until I found her cut open and emptied, all vibrance and colour scooped from life, along with the spark we'd made.

Susane leans forward, and if the eyes are truly the gates to the soul, then for a moment, I really think they swing wide open, that she's forcing every-thing that ever was her into them for me to see. And I do. There. Inside, refracted by half-formed tears, I can see the woman I waited centuries for a chance to woo. And who was worth every single second.

'Paul, I can't...' Her words trail off as she searches, pushing against something. A promise or a geas — a magical binding, I would guess. 'I can't tell you much, but know this. Justice was served. He was revenged.'

'The bastard who killed you both...'

'Dead.' She snaps off the end of the last syllable, her lips locking shut, and I'm certain that's all I'll get out of her on the subject. But it's enough. Not to assuage my sense of having failed her –that she sought help elsewhere shows me exactly how much confidence she had in me after that night– but that need, that parching thirst for unserved vengeance for my long-lost son. My momentary mirage of a family has been with me every second since she died. I'm not fool enough to trust her though, and she's shown me she never truly trusted me, but I saw her in that instant as she spoke. I know that was the truth. That particular tiny voiceless ghost can get laid to rest. Maybe now I'll be able to mourn him properly.

Susane sits back, and that impassive expression locks back into place. 'So what is your plan of action, Paul?' Her words are measured, neutral. This is her in role of the Mother's agent then.

I sigh, but strangely, it's easier to breathe than it was a moment ago, simpler to pull that breath in. 'Well, my instinct is to go and murder the fuck out of Franc –'

'Good plan. Well made. I vote for that.' Aicha underlines each syllable with a blade scrape.

'Thanks, *laguna*. But after I've gone and wrung every drop of information –'

'And blood.'

'And blood, thank you again, Aich –'

'And spinal fluid.'

I blink. 'Err, I guess?'

'Ooh, and I'm going to wring his stomach acid out into a little sack and then drip it into his eyeballs till they melt!'

'I think we're straying from the plan of action a little now and into flights of fancy.'

'Oh, I really fancy doing it. Don't need to go flying. In fact, it'll be far easier on the ground. Not much room to manoeuvre when disembowelling someone on an aircraft.'

The worrying thing is, the factual tone, speaking of actual experience, is probably warranted. I decide to just ignore her and press on. 'Anyhow, once that's done, I...'

Now it's my turn to break off. '...I don't really know what to do.' Good God, that hurts as a confession. 'And while my tendency is to go beat Franc to death, that's not going to save the Mother's daughter. So instead of just going off cockahoop, I'll gather as much information as possible, then bring it to wiser heads than mine. Namely Isaac, Jakob, and Aicha. Then I'm not only going to ask for advice, I'm going to try and actually listen when I'm given it too.'

The swiping, grinding noise of blades being cleaned ceases as Aicha's hand hangs in mid-air. The silence continues, as does her staring at me until I wonder if I've grown an extra head. Just as the moment moves up the comfortometer from "squirming in your seat" to "enough pressure to make Al Capone crack and plead for mercy", Aicha wipes an imaginary tear from her eye. She bends around me, looking down the cabin.

'George?' she calls out. 'George? Get in here. It's a miracle. It's a Christmas fucking miracle.' She checks her bare wrist as though inspecting an invisible watch. 'In April. Lordy lord.' She sits back hard in her grey-scale seat, fanning at her face with her hand like a faded Southern belle.

Susane looks baffled by the entire performance. I guess they don't have much in the way of TV channels or streaming services in Faerie. She looks askance at me. 'Is she always like this?'

'I mean, generally so, yeah,' I reply. 'She's either funny or murderous.'

'Or murderously funny,' Aicha adds.

'Or some combination of the two, so really, I'd pick which you prefer.'

Susane looks unbelievingly at the Druze warrior, who is now gripping a wickedly sharp, regularly used death-blessed blade as she continues to fan at her face with her free hand, as though at risk of passing out from the oppressive heat and atmosphere.

'And you're happy with this, are you?' she asks Aicha, looking from her to me. 'Not concerned about following him around, making jokes, and killing when needed? That's how you choose to allow yourself to be defined?'

Aicha stops dead and fixes Susane with a gaze reminiscent of a cobra eyeing up the world's juiciest little guinea pig. 'Are you questioning my decisions, little faeling? You know nothing of me or where I come from. I am Aicha Kandicha, renegade queen and guardian of the Aab Al Hayaat. I have wandered this world since before your ancestors were foolish enough to meddle in the affairs of fae-kin and have seen wonders and horrors that marvel and mar in equal measures. I've seen men and their obstinate attempts to either satisfy their egos' need for glory or even just do the right thing fuck it up time after time. I held power and authority for nearly a thousand years across a swathe of the world not famous for paying atten-tion to powerful women — negotiating and manipulating and charming and killing pig-headed men to protect a people I'd adopted.'

She sighs, picking at a nail's cuticle delicately with a point that could sever the whole finger with the tiniest slip. 'It gets...tiresome after a while. I set up my successor, formed them in the arts of both magic and –' She shudders. 'Politics. I wanted a simpler existence. To go exploring, to have adventures again without having the weight of expectations of a whole hidden nation upon my shoulders. I wanted some simplicity for a while.'

She reaches out her free hand and pats me on the cheek like a mother would a child who showed them they'd put their own trousers on for the first time. 'They don't come much simpler than Paul, bless him.'

She stretches languidly for a moment, wriggling her neck to click it, giving a small shiver of pleasure at the noise, smiling beatifically. 'I'd never fucked up before, never got myself captured before. Certainly never needed a fucking man to come and save me. Paul got to ride in on his white charger. I owe him for that. He's as good a man as it's possible to be, and I'm happy to help him with that. He's also my friend. That being said. I'll not be indebted to any fucking man, though and someone needs to save him from himself. May as well be me. Besides' —she reclines herself back into her fanning position— 'I have always depended upon the kindness of strangers.'

I roll my eyes. 'Yes, thank you, Blanche Dubois.'

'Most welcome, kind sir,' she murmurs back, batting her eyelashes and picking out another lethal weapon to hone.

I turn back to Susane, needing to explain. 'Your death broke me. If I'd been capable at that moment to become Perfect again, to unburden my soul of all its sins so as I could finally die forever, I think I would've been gone from existence there and then. Fortunately, though I might not have thought it so fortunate, I was about as incapable of selfless action at that moment as I was of resurrecting you both. Honestly, the thought of trying crossed my mind — Ow!'

Aicha leans over without even really looking and slaps me round the back of the head with enough force to cause cranial haemorrhaging in most people. Lucky I'm so hardheaded, I guess.

'That's for contemplating being such an utter wanker even two hundred years ago,' she says, her attention still on her back-and-forth strokes.

'Yeah, okay, first thing, use your words, not your hands –'

'I used both. I'm just that damn capable,' she interjects.

'But second,' I continue, ignoring her, 'I think you're right, but I was a total mess, no question. The Cagots probably did us both a favour when they moved your body. Good God knows what it would have done to your natural resurrection if I started casting spells about. Plus, it probably wouldn't have done my mental or spiritual wellbeing much good to mess around with necromancy either.'

'Plus, zombie babies, *saabi*, for fuck's sake.' Aicha shakes her head in disbelief. 'Have you never seen *Braindead*, man? Peter Jackson warned you.'

'I think that came out a bit after the eighteenth century, Aich,' I point out.

'Meh, any excuses, Paul,' she says, her eyes never raising up.

'Look, anyway, I can't help feeling we're straying away from the point here. Main thing is your death wrecked me, and I've never recovered. I don't think I'm going to shock anyone by pointing out that the juvenile humour and devil-may-care attitude towards physical wellbeing are all only masks for concealing that pain.'

'Incontheivable,' says Aicha in her best Vincini voice.

'Yes, thanks, Dr Fuckface, psychiatrist at large.' I sigh, massaging my temples. 'Do you remember me talking about Ben? The man who died when I died the first-time round?' I ask Susane.

She nods, her eyes wide as she watches me. I talked about him in my low moments, shared with her my pain but never went into the specifics.

'His death, his dying for me, my feeling that I failed him — that scarred me for a long time. It drove me forward to learn, to be better, to help people, to protect those I could. I felt I was on a continuation of the Perfect creed still, even if by doing so, I had to stick around, stay tied to the world. Then it turned out he hadn't truly died either. He'd been reincarnating differently and had turned into a seriously messed up puppy who came pretty damn close to destroying the world until someone got their flaming hands round his neck.'

Aicha starts whistling 'Ring of Fire' by Johnny Cash, backed by the timpani of knife scrapes.

'So one of the big motivational moments in my life, one thing that kept me pushing forward, striving to do better, to help people, to make things right, turned out to be based on a lie, and the person I'd put up on a pedestal was completely undeserving. Now you turn up.'

I look her over, both my Suse and not, the absence that occupied my insides for over two hundred years impossible to fill even with vengeance and violence and quippy non-sequiturs. I kept trying, but the eyes of a hollow man are just slammed doors. Nothing really gets through.

'I am not the Paul you knew, not even a shadow of him. I'm not the man trying to change the world or save people or species. I've tried doing what I knew to be right, and it's paid dividends.' I gesture at Aicha, who taps a pommel to her forehead in unseeing acknowledgement. 'That's part of the problem though. I did what I knew to be right, I never felt it. I carved out Toulouse as mine and even then, I did a half-arsed job, leaving Franc running loose and doing what he wanted. Isaac was always more theoretical than firebrand, however revolutionary in his research, and he's been happy to retire into anonymity. I've done little, achieved little. Just swam "round in my little pond, proud of my big shiny scales".'

'He's either working on the whole "big fish" metaphor, or else he's talking about his balls,' Aicha clarifies unnecessarily.

'Look, the point is I've done some stuff but only a fraction of what I should have done. Now we face a whole new cross-country convoy of trucks filled to the brim with shit that's going to dump itself at my door, and you rock up, a whole different fucking species, and I don't know what matters anymore or what any of it means, except things are almost certainly about to get done over in a way worthy of a Hans Zimmer orchestral score.'

Aicha stops suddenly and looks up, excitement written across her expression, her entire form trembling with anticipation. 'Paul,' she says, her tone unbelievably eager.

'What?' I ask, confused about what has grabbed her attention like this.

'Paul!' she says again.

'What?' I ask again, only getting more confused.

'*Paul!*' she practically yells at me.

'*What*?' I bellow back, no idea where this is leading.

She leans slowly forward, quivering, practically vibrating with whatever thought has her so animated.

'Paul,' she murmurs, husky-voiced, a tone of wonderment under her words. 'We could commission our own theme music. Our own fucking theme song!'

I blink as I look across at the deadly magical warrior practically bouncing in her train seat, then rapidly rewind through my heartfelt confession, looking for the missing link to make it all make sense. I fail miserably.

'Our...own...theme...song...' she practically hisses at me, as if unable to grasp why I, too, am not leaping from my seat to somersault down the aisle like "Joliet" Jake Blues in James Brown's church.

'You're a total fucking loony, Aicha,' I tell her, shaking my head in disbelief.

'But I could be a total fucking loony *with a theme song*, Paul,' she says, matching my headshake. Then she dismisses me with a regal hand wave and returns her attention to her sharpening. 'Make it so, Number One.'

'Hold on, how am I Number One?' I ask. 'I'm clearly the captain, not his first mate.'

Aicha looks up at me with compassion and pity for a moment, then pats my cheek again and turns her attention to Susane. 'And that level of delusion, along with all that other touchy-feely bullshit he just unloaded on us, is why I stick around. Someone needs to stop him from doing himself an injury, poor thing. Imagine him thinking he was in charge!' She snorts a very unladylike laugh and then puts her head back down.

The only thing that makes me feel even slightly better is that Susane looks even more baffled than I am. 'What just happened?' she mouths at me, and for a second, I am back on the climb up to Montsegur, and I can't stop myself from grinning through the confusion of the surreal exchange.

'I have no idea, but then again, I rarely do. I just go with the flow most of the time,' I say.

'And that's why you got upgraded from being a disposable red shirt. Keep up the good work, Number One,' Aicha says, her own wicked grin refracting in her back-and-forth inspection of the polished metal before she slides it away.

Chapter Fifteen
TOULOUSE, 9 APRIL, PRESENT DAY
About to have a very franc discussion. Badum tish.

We don't dally when we get off the train but head straight to La Chapelle. There are no assembled masses of the desperate this time around. Franc huddles alone on the centre dais, wrapped in a polyester blanket, grime-grey where it was once beige, covered by child-friendly renderings of fruit that look as faded as he does. I stop at the entrance, looking around.

I point at a corner by the door, looking at Susane. 'Stand there. Don't move. Stay quiet.' Her words on the train made sense, but they didn't make me trust her. There's still too many unanswered questions. And considering how things went the last time someone I cared about came back from the dead, I'm not about to just believe everything she says. I'm not an idiot. I think again about the situation we've found ourselves in. I'm not a total idiot, I amend and hope desperately I am correct.

'Not got your court with you this time, hey, Franc?' I ask, my tone neutral and controlled.

He raises his head feebly, his normally diseased colouring even more off than usual. He coughs, a phlegm-laden rattle that suggests he can hawk up a loogie the size and colour of his villainous heart. A weak smile splits his lips, toppling enamel obelisks peeking through the gap.

'The little lordling and the sword-singer, by my oath. Gladling am I, all jibber-jabbered and lung-rattlered to be seeings yous and your fine fecklings. Delightery in your gracings, is it not, and with accompanyings like oompah-pah.' Franc takes a better look at Susane, and his eyes narrow, the lip split turning snarl-like. 'Though I see a seelie I'd be Unseeing by preferentiations. No time nor tidings for the Fair Folklings, has I, nor sanctuaring, indeed. Though' —he turns his attention back to me and brightens his tone again— 'if she comes in your fine lordling's companion-ings, what choicery but warmings and welcomings in the offed and offered, is it not? As for your initial inquirings and questionary, I've not my lovely lasses nor lads with me at present momentaries, though they wish and wonder, all worryings for their loyal protectory, poor old I. Needs must, says the rumblings of bellies and pocketry, and so they goes, all hand-flaps and quick-steps, to seek out their needings and give me knowings. Weak I am, but not a jestery yet, floppy hatting and a-capering dancery. Nay, let them to their sustenancing, for all needs their fillings, by my oath.'

I walk forward, my eyes never breaking contact, and Franc's smile falters.

'Well,' I say with a smile so humourless it seems like it could annul all mirth within a seven-mile radius. 'We all have to feed, don't we, Franc?'

When I reach him, I grab hold of his moist, mildew-ridden lapel and watch his smile disappear. It draws immense satisfaction as I see, for the first time in our long acquaintance, uncertain panic in his expression.

Then I hit him.

I hit him so hard I feel the misshapen teeth splinter and fragment as I follow through, lifting and spinning the eight-foot monster from his hunched position to smash through the wooden table behind him. There are a lot of noises of breaking, and I have no idea how much of it is the wood disintegrating on contact and how much is Franc's bones. I don't really care, except to prefer the latter.

He spits out a wad of bloody matter the size of a normal man's lung and cowers, throwing up his huge bear-paw hands in suppliance as he mewls through popping crimson bubbles hiccupping on his lips. 'What, what, what?' he stammers, begging at me with his posture as he scutters backwards with the one leg that still works properly. 'What, manling? Betrayalery? All vicious blows and slap-two-threes upon the bonce of poor Franc, for shamings? Truthery in my talkings has I been at all times, and now when lowerings and ill-weakeneds, does you bring this, for shame? 'Tis unbecoming, Undyer!'

His voice raises towards a shriek at the end as I advance on him again. He tries to drag himself farther away from my violent fury. I pay no attention to his discomfort, only drawing pleasure from seeing him broken before me.

'We all need to eat, right, Franc? You told me all your dietary needs when we first made our deal, right? Told me what you would feed on? Told me all the ins and outs of your culinary peculiarities, isn't that so? You wouldn't have misled me, would you, Franc? Wouldn't have toned down some details that you thought might disagree with me? Perhaps thinking they might stick in my gullet?'

Aicha, who was following just behind, steps forward and presses her foot onto Franc's throat, looking ready to crush him on a whim. 'Not good when things stick in there. Can lead to choking, asphyxiation, et cetera.'

'And I don't think anyone's arms are long enough to give you the Heimlich manoeuvre, Franc. I've got to be honest. Ah, ah, ah.' I step on his wrist with an audible *crack* as he attempts to manifest his cutlass into an outflung hand. 'Naughty, naughty, Franc.'

'Whys, whereforings, Undyer? All honest at all timeries in my knowings was I, and ever I was! Why now, the betrayalings?' Franc whines through a half-closed throat and a half-broken jaw. I have the impression he is too panic-stricken, perhaps in too much pain for the subtleties of the way I am phrasing it. Ironic, considering the headache he's given me over the years, deciphering his bullshit.

I draw on my *talent*, and an image of the young woman appears, lithe and carefree, sinuously dancing, joy written large on her features. She stops, looks at Franc, and shrinks inwards, her colours fading, the life that imbued every element of her disappearing as she looks down on his monstrous form. I watch him, expecting a moment of realisation or horror as he clicks the gig is up. Instead, he glares indignantly and lets out a wheezing squawk through the boot pressure on his throat when she vanishes.

'Mine! Mine!' he cries out hoarsely, reaching out with an arm where the flaccid hand flops unnaturally, the breakage forgotten, at least momentarily. 'Mine by rights, by oath, she is. All gone, mirror trappings and bottomless boxes, ta-das and crowd confuselings. Felt the severings like red cold sawery, bitings on leather straplings, then lop lop, off with legs, off with anklings.' He tries to push himself up indignantly but falls back at a hard shove from Aicha's foot. 'She's mine by oathings, sworn and worn. Where is she, little manling?'

I sigh and crouch down, squatting on my heels. 'You really are a stupid bastard, Franc. When you and I struck our deal, you said you fed off their misery. Not all you feed on, is it?'

He looks indignant, trying to puff out his gigantic chest in his prone position, though his restricted oxygen supply undermines the effort. 'Never ates her; I didn't! Never even a nibbly nip on a toe or taken tongue, by my oath! If she was munchered or taken by murderings, 'twas not by my handlings, and I'll be wanting ear words that bends all breakery once fully fortifighting fittery again with those who hold that precise debtery, to bring them my strength and song-burstings of depths and deaths.'

I rub my fingers across my eyelids, trying to assuage some of the pressure building up behind them. 'She's not dead, Franc. She's safe and mostly sound, well away from your clutches. You're completely missing the point of what I'm saying. You didn't just eat her misery, did you? She had *talent*, you scheming fuck, and you ate that down as well.'

Franc blinks and shudders as wracking coughs shake his form. As they subside, he regains his composure slowly, sucking breaths in to calm little by little. He looks back at me. I thought to see shame or perhaps the arrogant indignation of a revealed villain at the meddling kids as they peel away his rubber face mask. Instead, he just looks confused, totally and utterly confused.

'Well, of coursings I did, my little lord, did I not?' he says. "Twas alwaysing such and suchlikery since our deal, forge-struck and stuck upon me, upon my oath. Why now the beatery and bloodletting when all infirm and frailings, floor flailings, poor I?'

I stop dead, and it feels for a moment like my heart has stopped simultaneously, like I have locked gazes with a gorgon, petrified in an instant. The moment stretches like a rubber band looped over a clock hand as I stare at the bewildered, terrible monster at my feet and try to remember what I agreed with him precisely all those many years ago. Then the elastic snaps. I draw a sharp breath, and time moves forward once more.

'Are you trying to tell me,' I ask the bleeding monstrosity so at odds with the bemusement written on his face like that of a child snapped at for taking a cookie he'd asked for, 'that this was a part of our original agreement? I never agreed to this!'

'Surety and certitudes upon it, my good lordling, troth and truth. I dids present, staking pains all bait-like and bleating, drawing your attentions 'pon the finessery and frillerings of our wordery forgings. Old Franc is pater of the pitterings in gloamered alleyways, all shield and staffings to the lost and lonerley. Their painings, shivering slow nappery on the road to long sleep's knavery beddings, are soothed by my songs and soakings, blade-dulled as I bite the bitings.'

'I'm aware you eat the edge of their suffering and keep them alive, Franc. What does that have to do with taking their *talent*?'

Aicha eases back on the pressure, and Franc props himself up on his elbows with a wheezing groan. 'Hard lives not hearts light is alley-dwellery, lost below society's surfacings, only seen in pretty little air bubblings a-pop popping up before gone agains with petty gainings. Cold and cruelry for even my lovely lads and lasses, no mind for the lost unfound by old Franc, poor they, poor they.'

He pushes himself further up, blood-flecks marring the eggshell uniformity of his eyes as they fix on mine despite the lack of pupils. 'You've danced the addictery horn-piping, felt them jaggery fingers of need, need, needling ice-fiery in your heartings clap-two-three, but easy enough for you with the quick two-step and oops-me-boys, a new fleshery to be playing happy housings in, is it not? Never walked the frightery of danger's shadelings when all weak and easy pickery for the rumbling strummers, target marked all red ringings, centring concentricity of circles. To *see*, my Undyer lordling, is to be *seen*. Them's is ravenatious that lingers in the darkery, all eyes and mouths open, devoted to their devourings. Those with enough *talentry see* but little for their shieldings, arm-strappings and all.' He grins his face-splitting grin, all the malformed shark teeth I didn't knock out of his mouth on display. 'Them's are the one's who get's whole-swallowed by the watchers in the darkery, is they not, my laddie? That's a bitter biting, indeed, and who's to keep them safe from that, if not old Franc, minding your pardonings? 'Tis covered by the deeds and detailery of our concordings, is it not?'

I scratch at the top of my head, partially to try to massage it into action to decipher Franc's "worderys" and partially because clawing my frontal lobe out might be the easiest escape from this conversation. I hold up a hand to pause the creature as he heaves breath in once again.

'Hold it there, Franc. I'll be right back.' I close my eyes and dive into my mind palace.

Walking through the mental hallway, I pass the door to the cinema room and head into my magnificent library. It always makes me feel like Ron Burgundy, in that it holds what appears to be innumerable leather-bound books and smells of rich mahogany, conjuring up a plethora of bibliophilic sanctuaries I've passed through over my many lifetimes. It simply being a representative store for all the essential long-term memories I hoard, filed away for future reference, I don't really need to search for the relevant tome, but I still take a moment to enjoy the sensation of running my fingers along the multiple spines, to profit from an instant of calm and serenity no matter how fleeting, when everything outside is chaotic and demanding in its urgency. Books always relax me, even when I don't have time to read them. Their very presence speaks of taking time out, separating from the weight and worry of the world, and I'll borrow a neighbourly spoonful of sugar from them if it's on offer before heading back out into the breach.

I don't allow myself too long to dally though; the stakes remain oppressively high. I pull out a port-red stained hide-bound memory book and open it instinctively to the correct page. It shows a woodcut-style image of myself and Franc at our first meeting, me with *talent*-fire burning round my sword raised to shoulder height, Franc with his white flag gripped in clawed hand and his signature grin slicing his face. If I want, the image will move, replay the memory — or as much of it as is intact, though I expect it to still be extremely accurate, considering the significance and comparatively short time frame since it happened. Today, however, I'm not looking to rewatch what happened on the banks of the Garonne just over two hundred years ago. I want to go through the text with a fine-toothed comb and refresh my conscious memory as to exactly what happened.

I pore over the lines that contain our back and forth, hammering out our agreement. I am looking for the precise wording of what we shook hands on. My head hurts from translating Franc's particular turns of phrases precisely as much as it did the first time, which, considering I am currently *inside* my own head, creates all sorts of sympathetic creaking and groaning from the structure, and makes me feel like setting a spinning top going, a la Cobb in *Inception.* It is doable, however, especially when I can look at it in written word form.

I reach the relevant final phrasing and read, then reread the entire section. Shutting the book with a sigh, I walk back down the corridor and out the front door, away from the quiet serenity and back into the batshit crazy of the waking world.

Aicha looks at me expectantly as I open my eyes, a throwing knife casually balanced across her palm in the perfect position to embed it through Franc's unnerving eyeball on a whim. I shake my head minutely, huffing as I do so.

'He's within the agreement, Aich,' I say, my frustration clear in my tone, although even I am unsure exactly who is the primary cause of said frustration. 'We agreed he could, and I quote, "Consume or draw sustenance from anything hurting or liable to cause hurt to those sworn to him". Despite what the creepy shithead implied, I've seen plenty of the young and Talented who've suffered through too much magic and not enough skill or protection.'

'We all have,' she replies, equally grimly, and I wonder who or what she is thinking of. It is a question for another time.

'So he's justified in his interpretation. Eating her magic, combined with his blessing, was probably likely to keep her safer on the street had she been a normal runaway. What it means for us –' I slump down with a groan, my back pressed to the cold bare wall, and rest my head on my hand that is balanced against my knee. 'What it means for us is that we are spectacularly and categorically fucked. I mean, you most of all Franc, but we'll be running a fairly close second behind you.'

Franc looks to have recovered somewhat from my (relatively restrained, all things considered) beatdown, or at least only looks as dreadfully unwell as he did the last time I was here. He drags himself backwards to prop up against the wall opposite, wiping at sweat and blood with the back of his dirty sleeve that clings tightly to his arm but would be big enough for me to wear as a dress in a Derelicte fashion show by Mugatu.

'Whys and whereforings am I all strumpeted, face paintery rouged and berry-crushed lippings then, Good Man?' he asks, still heaving for breath from his new position but looking more comfortable, at least.

'Because you're an abomination,' Aicha answers, picking either microscopic or imaginary dirt out from under her fingernails with the point of the throwing knife, her attention fixed on her nail care.

'I mean, yes, good point, well made,' I say, clicking a finger gun at Aicha. 'Top marks to the uber-violent Druze for brevity. It is indeed 'cos you're an abomination but mainly because you're a greedy and fucking lazy abomination, Franc.'

Franc growls darkly, placing his palms flat on the floor as though to push himself to standing. 'Prettyings of word foilery and fencings does nothing but rile and rise the wroth, all slumbery and sleep-tied in tidings. A plainer particulating of phrasery would be a wiser way away from wailings and weepery, little Undyer.'

I am too dumbfounded to speak. Aicha stops picking at her cuticles and raises her head up to look at me. 'Fucking hell, Paul, you just got told to speak more directly by fucking *Franc*. Shamed, *saabi*.'

'I...have no idea how to respond to that.' I scratch at the starting stubble growth on my cheek, taking a moment to recompose myself. 'In fact, I'm just going to place that on the "ignore and, by the way, go fuck yourself Franc" pile for now and deal with more pressing issues, like the fact you're almost certainly going to die, you big scaly wanker.'

It isn't my best effort when it comes to insults, but I am still reeling from Franc's demand for brevity and directness, which makes me feel like I've stepped into some sort of parallel dimension. Plus, unpleasant river monster or no, he still signed his own death warrant by the looks of things. That seems insult enough, to be honest.

Franc sighs, a phlegmy rattle I've heard often enough from my own chest, most recently when chained to a certain shizzard's wall. It isn't a good sign, put it that way.

'Wordsery's a-briefing, for we're all not spring-poppering into new flesheries when all sand-grain gainings are lost in the drip-dropping, on my oath.'

'Right, since we're all pressed for time, and I am apparently too flowery in my language for *fucking Franc*, then I'll make it clear. You got lazy, Franc. You decided about one of your candidates and did fuck-all investigation before you made a pretty major decision regarding their *talent*.'

Franc looks puzzled. 'How should I be investigatoring my lovelies before they are mine, all promisery given and gainsaided?'

I can't quite believe he is trying to play innocent yet again. 'You can't seriously be telling me that if you can borrow their bodies in order to talk to me or get information whilst they're walking the streets or begging for change, that you can't read their minds?'

Franc's eyes widen, his limescale-textured lips forming a perfect O. 'Investigatoring into their hidden mind stores and stories, all rummagery and tickling diggings, to read all ruminatings prior privy and private? Backstabbery and betrayalings that is, by my oath! Never from old Franc, not doings or delvings of such a wicked weaving, not I, not I!'

Franc's voice rises in both volume and indignance during the last part, and it is almost comical to see the gigantic river monster who feeds on misery looking like a perjured schoolboy accused of cheating.

'Congratulations, Franc,' Aicha says, giving him a slow clap. 'You're an evil fucking monster but less of an evil fucking monster than Facebook. Who knew?'

'Double congratulations, Franc,' I add wearily. 'One, for having any actual moral code at all, and two, for getting yourself killed by applying it. That girl whose magic you ate? That's the daughter of the Mother of the Sistren of Bordeaux and the appointed successor slash invested hope of their whole coven. Good work, top marks, you fucking idiot.'

Franc's expression loses its indignation but doesn't look any less shocked. If anything, the level of surprise has multiplied. Had he held any colour to his skin other than the sickly green pallor clinging to it like mould's first kiss on a fruit, it would have drained away entirely. Also, if his mouth opened any further, I am pretty sure it would result in the bottom half of his head just falling off entirely. He shuts it with some clear mental effort, then opens it as he takes a breath in to speak. He pauses, shuts it again, scratches the end of one eyebrow with a dragon's claw of a fingernail, gathers his thoughts, then draws breath again. 'Oh,' he says. 'Buggerations.'

I nod my agreement. 'Buggerations indeed, old boy. Buggerations indeed.'

CHAPTER SIXTEEN

TOULOUSE, 9 APRIL, PRESENT DAY

Really enjoying the whole "stunning Franc into silence" thing. Sadly, the effects are almost certainly temporary.

I turn my attention to Aicha, who allows the faintest trace of curiosity to pierce her usually stoic expression. 'Apparently, all it takes to get Franc to be succinct is for him to do something so monumentally stupid he is almost certain to die as a result. Live and learn.'

'How come you're suffering from such word diarrhoea all the time that even muggins over there has to tell you to fix up, look sharp, then?' she asks, a bored insolence to her tone that would give an over-pampered house cat a run for its money.

I act as per usual when Aicha gives me a verbal lacerating — externally ignoring her while whimpering inside, wishing I could come up with a comeback even approximately close in quality. 'So you've heard how spectacularly you've messed up, Franc, and we know exactly how deep the shit you're in is...'

Aicha stretches up a hand to approximately Franc's height. 'At least yay deep, I'd say?'

'At a minimum. Probably more shit even than that. A plethora of shit. A shitora if you will.'

Aicha shakes her head. 'Nah, no points for that one. *Trailer Park Boys* nailed that a million times better than you ever will.'

I stand up, carrying on as if I didn't even notice while cursing internally. 'The next question is the make or break though, Franc. Can you give the girl back her *talent* that you ate? You've only got two answers left on the board, and you can still phone a friend if you actually have any.'

We both watch as Franc thinks it through. I don't know if he is desperately searching for an implausible way to change the answer or if he has to work hard to translate everything we say in the same way we have to do with him, but it makes no difference. After a few tense seconds, he shakes his downcast head.

Aicha speaks first. 'Well, that's you fucked then. Couldn't have happened to a nicer piece-of-shit.' She heads for the door, whistling 'Fuck You' by Lily Allen, a jaunty swagger to her step.

I should feel relieved, I guess. Franc's inability to regurgitate the girl's power means I am off the hook. He will be considerably weakened, making him less of a potential threat for the foreseeable future. Then he'll die, releasing me from the stupendously naïve agreement I made with him. But that doesn't change the fact that an unknown number of people whose only sin was to be desperate and miserable enough to make a deal with Franc are about to pay for it by cashing out completely, all for his stupid error. I want to put all my hesitance to walk away on that, but there is something else — something about how completely defeated Franc looks slumped against the wall, clutching his drooping hat on his dipped head, as if forcing all the idiocy he released with his doings back into whatever parts of his brain deals with acts of terminal folly.

I'll be lying if I said I don't recognise myself in him, when I was at myriad points in my multitudinous existences, like when I stitched myself up like a kipper and often had just enough thread left to do some stitching for various people I cared for before hanging myself with the last bit. I'd wake up in another body, ready to stagger off into another massive clusterfuck. The people I left behind wouldn't, though, and had to carry the consequences for however long their lives were. I'm not a monster like Franc, a self-serving bottom feeder; my errors normally come from the best of intentions, but they are also the founding blocks for a major new infernal road, probably a triple lane motorway, actually.

Point is, none of us are perfect or innocent, and we are all capable of messing up in spectacular ways. The aftermath of many of my decisions was the equivalent of the floor of a spoiled kid's bedroom after opening all their Christmas presents. Littered with the unneeded discards. If I walk away, Franc will become just another thrown-off scrap from something I took responsibility for. This is, however, still likely to end badly. Good intentions, etc.

Aicha stops at the door, looking back over her shoulder. '*Ibn al Kalb*,' she swears, and I know she is furious because she only falls back into Arabic when I've really pissed her off. 'Don't do it, *saabi*. Just. Walk. Away.'

'I'm sorry, Dave. I can't do that,' I reply in an appropriate monotone, which makes me realise exactly how angry she is because the Kubrick reference doesn't even crack the radiant fury painted across her face. I try my best to ignore her attempts to make me spontaneously combust by the power of Glare^{TM} and look back over at the mountain of sickly self-pity taking up a large part of the facing wall.

'Is there any other way we can get her *talent* back, Franc?' I say, still not quite believing I am willingly putting myself back in the middle of this situation.

Aicha mutters something under her breath that might be, 'You just had to ask', or may equally have been, 'You're a massive arse'. Both are frighteningly appropriate.

Franc raises his head, and a smidgen of hope enters his face, visible despite his eerily expressionless eyes. 'There mayhap be a possibiling, my little lordling,' he says, and the excitement builds in his voice. 'Yes, yes, by my oath. There's a-one who could give such a gifting, even when all taken and tasted till naught but crumbs and crustlings. One who collects in her keepings but whose blesseries are power and potentry, yes indeed.'

Time seizes up, the moment forming ice in my veins that surely have stopped pumping, my heart now a frozen lump. I asked. Fuck me, I had to, didn't I? Couldn't just leave him to reap the consequences of his own actions. Now that the first inkling of where he wants to send us to sneaks into my brain, I want to take it back. The Good God knows I want to turn back time, the same time that seems to have stopped running in any direction, and undo what I said, let him alone to die with his fate. Because I don't want to go where his words point us. But I can't take it back, can't make the clock spin the other way. It was said. And time starts up again, though my heart still feels frozen solid with plain, simple terror.

'*Kol Khara*,' Aicha responds, her anger evidently not even slightly abated. 'You're suggesting to send us to the Lady of Lourdes, aren't you, monster?'

Franc nods, that pleading hopefulness still writ large across his craggy, ruined features. "Tis only herselfing who can take the dustings left and cause the cauteriserings to rise again in blossoming bloomery.'

'Son of a bitch,' I swear.

'I already said you were one for asking that stupid question, Paul,' Aicha answers.

'Good God fucking damn my stupid fucking mouth,' I say, groaning.

'Motion seconded. Carried with no objections.' Aicha still looks furious and disgusted at my stupidity.

I have made it a life mission to stay well, well away from Lourdes, but I have just committed myself, entirely unnecessarily, to either go there or else break my word with the Sistren. That will lead to an all-out war up and down the Garonne, and even with the coven weakened, it will still be a hard slog. All because I felt guilty for a poor decision I made hundreds of years ago. Talk about suckering myself. Good intentions, indeed. I upgrade the previously constructed triple-lane hell-bound motorway to an Elon Musk designed hyper-loop. I have a feeling I am probably travelling at top speed down it in the wrong direction.

CHAPTER SEVENTEEN

TOULOUSE, 9 APRIL, PRESENT DAY

Trust Franc to turn a bad situation into a shitstorm, the slimeball. Should have known — never mess with a reptilian when death is on the line.

I need to think. In fact, scrub that, I need someone far more intelligent than me to do some thinking for me. Based on recent acts, that list includes a lobotomised capybara, a magic eight ball, and half a brick. Luckily, I have a better option than that. I have Isakob. No, wait. Isaac and Jakob. I meant I have Isaac and Jakob. Goddammit.

'Can I still contact you through your usual intermediaries, Franc?' I ask the wretched creature in front of me, who is looking at me like I am his knight in shining armour. Considering it is Franc, I don't know if that means he is hoping I will rescue him or whether he is working out if he'll need a tin opener to eat me.

'Aye, can I, Lord Undyer, indeed, indeed,' he replies, nodding eagerly.

'Right, I need to have a serious bloody think about the whole matter. If — and this is a big if, a huge if, the Iffest if ever — if we go, could you come with us?'

Franc shakes his head. 'Can't even stand, toes-touchery to bring raining blow-for-blow of the blowing stormings with a little manling like yourself right now, can I? A pretty pacing all frolickery and fah-de-lahs to the ways and weightings along and away towards the mountainry.'

I expected that as an answer, but it is good to have it confirmed. 'Right, in which case, start thinking about who you might send along as proxy then. I'll get in contact with you once we have a better idea of what the hell we are doing.'

Aicha turns, an astounded look on her face. 'We sometimes know what the hell we are doing?'

'I mean, rarely, but it happens.'

'When?'

'Now, hopefully.'

'First time for everything.'

'Not helpful, Aich.'

'I know you're not, but what am I?'

'Right, as stimulating as this pass-pass comedy skit is, I think we can leave Franc to his busy schedule of bleeding everywhere and slowly dying...'

'I'll be here and hearing, my little lordling, will I not?'

'And we should go consult with the brains of the operation.'

'I'm right here, *saabi*.'

'Okay, the other brains of the operation.'

'So everyone apart from you then, Paul?'

I sigh. 'Yes, Aich. Everyone apart from me.'

This gets me the gun-fingers again. Susane, who was sensibly reserved during our entire exchange with Franc, watches all this with an aloof air, but I think I can see a tiny spark of amusement at our bantering flickering behind her jade eyes. I wonder if it is really there or whether it is just my desire to uncover the woman I knew in the fae standing before me. Certainly, my Susane would have jumped straight in, teasing until she left me tongue-tied, and I would then have had no choice but to sweep her off her feet and away to our room, the pair of us roaring with laughter and the weightlessness that new love instils in all life's burdens.

She always loved that I could laugh at myself, at her, at us. That we didn't have to take ourselves entirely seriously all the time. To be nigh on immortal and still have fun, to find joy in words shared comradely like broken bread was a big part of what first drew her to me. I wonder if that was why, when I remained, my heart powdered into crumbs by her death, I drew it up around me as a defining shell, guarding the hollow space left inside.

I call Isaac as we leave, and we agree to meet back at O'Bohem. We head south, towards the centre of town, initially along the reverse of the routing I followed with the first summons, the pavement still spotted with tiny blood spatters. The Hansel imagery comes back strongly, though I am not sure if I am heading out to safety or just deeper into the dark woods. I still can't decide whether Franc is the wicked witch in that metaphor, having fed me tasty titbits over the years, just fattening me up for the kill.

Or maybe I'm the monster. Maybe I always was one. Killing leaves me cold these days, not heated with guilt or shame. I would have beaten Franc to death with my fists, drenched myself in his blood and his last drops of life, then wiped myself down and gone on my merry way for more witty quips over a pint of lager without a moment's concern. It makes me think that perhaps this image of a person with morals and drive to do good, to be the Good Man I started out as always was entirely illusory. Like Patrick

Bateman, perhaps there is no real me. Peel away the jokes and *talent* and violence, and there's nothing left. I simply am not there.

Aicha jabs me in the side, her hooded gaze locked onto mine. 'Not too far down that rabbit hole, *saabi*. Still potentially a long time left to live with yourself. It's been...intense.' Her eyes flick across to Susane, who keeps pace with us, looking around tourist-like with her head on constant swivel, clearly unfamiliar with modern Toulouse. 'Be kind to yourself. Or I'll kick your ass. Dickhead.'

She gives me a quick shoulder pat and returns her attention outwards, assuming the protective bodyguard role again, alert and aware to all the passers-by. It isn't a bad idea, particularly with Franc at least partially out of action. I've come to rely on him to act as an early warning system for any potential threats assailing me in the city itself. Entirely too reliant, evidently. Thankfully, one of us is on the ball. We split away from the blood-crumb trail, down past Arnaud Bernard, and approach the Place du Capitole.

The Capitole building itself stands proud and prominent, cold in its neoclassical grandeur and beauty. The mixture of slabs of white stone and pink brickwork that defines the region is undeniably gorgeous. But its history, which I lived through, is just more blood and death. It got built by the Capitouls, merchant magistrates who ruled Toulouse for centuries after the previous lords were destroyed for sheltering the Cathars. Not long after it got built though, they fell too, disenfranchised of power by the king for the brutal execution of a Protestant merchant, shortly before the king got his head disenfranchised from his body by the French Revolution. Murderous religious intolerance once more led to an enforced change of leadership in the city. Which just goes to show how often history runs out of ideas and just recycles its greatest hits over and over.

We skirt along the western edge, weaving around tables protruding out from the over-priced cafés and restaurants crowded together to extract every last penny they can from tourists footsore from a busy day gawping at the monuments and architectural wonders that Toulouse hides around every corner. Today, the square feels oppressively full. The market stalls that fill the place are full of bric-à-brac with African flags and knock-off T-shirts featuring poor quality Bob Marley prints for sale next to a second-hand books and CD stall seemingly impervious to the movements of time that should have left its erratic hotchpotch selection of literary and musical styles trampled in the dust of the electrical revolution. There's a juxtaposition between the tat of the stalls and the snobbery of the eateries, and both reject us. It feels like the city itself is turning its back.

I wonder how much the deliberately unseen undercurrents of Franc's boys' and girls' diseased states are feeding back into the vibe of the city or whether it's me projecting. Then I realise I'm still spattered with blood from Franc's beatdown, and that my expression is probably matching in its grimness. If I were one of those working the stalls, I wouldn't be trying to entice us to take a look at some trinket or another, to crowd their tables with our grime. We'd be like scarecrows to all the flitting bird-like tourists, scaring them away to be drawn in by the next shiny thing to catch their attention.

I'm happy to get away from the open space, although even the normally welcoming embrace of the four- and five-story buildings around the narrow roads feels more claustrophobic today, their presence looming rather than enclosing. We walk by the mixture of brands and branches of known chains happy to pay the higher price for proximity to the Capitole and its accompanying footfall of passers-by.

As we wind our way farther down, the Rue Saint-Rome changes into the appropriately named Rue des Changes and so does the accompanying vibe. Individual clothes and comic bookstores become more the norm, and even the chain shops that are present tend towards art and craft or home deco that is at least nominally original or unique in output. A group of Franc's lads drink communally at the corner where the roads change over, pushing back the fear that lingers in their expressions with group bravado and a freely passed no-name bottle of spirits. Their eyes fix on us as we walk by, an uncanny symmetry in their head movements leaving me with no uncertainty that Franc is with us, via Beetlejuice-style body hijacking. Their dog –shaggy, wired hair clumping over patches of scabbed skin replete with red bite sores from either ticks or exceptionally vicious fleas– lifts his muzzle and issues a guttural warning to us, apparently responding to his master's sudden change of attention. I wonder if the dog can pledge itself to Franc as well. It certainly looks like a valid candidate.

We continue southwards, passing the bars and street-food eateries of Carmes, the crowded bustle easing, allowing me to breathe more easily. It feels beyond strange to be so out of synch with the city, like attempting to rekindle a long-abandoned friendship when lives have diverged beyond all measure. The awkward silence I feel in my little bubble is like that shared over half-drunk pints, each seeking to find the words necessary to bridge the gap while counting down the seconds until they can politely make their excuses and leave with a sigh of relief and no second thoughts. I have been absent for too long. I need to walk the streets and *invest* in them again, and I'm in neither the right head state or current company to be attempting such a thing.

A touch to my arm again startles me, this one more hesitant and gentler. I look over at Susane, whose demeanour matches her touch, holding back, seemingly unsure of what to say. Perhaps also seeking as she bites her lip, to pull wisdom from it like Finn McCool's thumb, to allow us to cross the yearning chasm that separates us. The gesture humanises her, pulling the essence of the woman I loved and married back out from under the alien fae nature, and it feels like someone pulled my heart out of my chest and let the Harlem Globetrotters do a two-hour warm-up session of tricks and shots with it before shoving it back into the empty cavity.

'I'm sorry,' she says finally as a decisiveness sweeps across her.

I laugh bitterly. 'And for what, exactly, is her ladyship apologising?' I ask, looking away to the street, at a young lad half a-pace behind two others, more confident, more at home, his expression of longing for full acceptance stressed by his quick, forcefully nonchalant laughter. At a woman unconsciously swishing her rucksack lower, instinctively covering a hardly immodest skirt as two drunk middle-aged men loudly and unwantedly compliment anyone they deem worthy to intimidate, full up on lunchtime wine and privilege. On the tracking eyes of a street youth barely older than the boy seeking his peers' approval, who fixes on us and never leaves us, even when muttering a thanks as a coin gets dropped, spinning like a rimshot around the edge of his paper cup before clattering down to join the minuscule hoard within. Anywhere at all, in fact, other than at the woman who broke me for too many lifetimes.

'Paul, stop it. Please.' Her hand is back, more determined, gripping now rather than touching, not pulling exactly but arresting the advance. I come to a stop and force myself to meet her eyes. Aicha stops a few paces ahead, attempting to hide her exasperation and failing miserably as the pedestrians wisely and instinctively alter their trajectories to flow around her.

'I don't know what you want me to say to you, Susane. I've been a broken shell for two hundred years, just going through the motions, following actions I thought might make your ghosts proud, might give you a peace I never could. And now you're standing in front of me, and I'm still haunted, and I don't know who you are.'

Something breaks in her composed demeanour, and she shakes. Her trembles pass up my arm, seeming to come to rest in my stomach like wing flutters. 'I'm your wife, Paul.'

'You're an impossibility, Susane. You always have been. You should never have been able to get pregnant, to carry my child, and yet, you did. You should never have died... You should never have...'

Now it is my voice that shakes, matching in sympathetic resonance, and I can feel the tears coursing down my cheeks.

'That. That's what I'm sorry for, Paul. So very, very sorry.' Her tears match mine as she pulls me into a hug and for a moment — just a moment — everything is as it should always have been. We stand and hold each other on the Place Du Parliament as Aicha positions herself to break the wave of people, splitting it around us.

I hold her and care nothing at all for Franc or for the girl or for what the future might hold. I pour out my grief for my lost child, for the man it made me into, for the joy it extinguished from my world. I weep for the woman who died before our life together ever began and for the years I didn't know she was still alive. For the opportunity lost to kick in the door of Faerie and bring her back, burning it down as I went if necessary. For a practical immortal to weep for the time lost seems ironic, but I do. I bawl out my outrage that the world took her from me when I could have been with her all this time. I cry for two hundred years alone.

Eventually, after what seems like another lifetime and yet entirely too short a moment, I calm down, getting back control. I look over at the translucent spectral reflection of the nearest window. My image looks washed out in the sun's glare but not enough to hide the splotchiness of my face, my swollen reddened eyes, and the tears produced spread liberally across my visage. In short, I look like a right catch.

We pull apart, and Susane looks entirely fine, completely composed, her features calm and as serenely perfect as an undisturbed mirror lake apart from two equally flawless tear trails that glitter silver over her pale cheeks. I wonder if they're the truth, the veracity carried through like dancing reflections on the seemingly still depths of the shimmering sea, shadows thrown up from underneath. Or whether they're just a meaningless gesture, a pretence at humanity. Whether the woman is there, underneath the fae polish. Or whether her death hollowed her out as it did me. Whether Faerie swallowed her whole.

Chapter Eighteen
Montsegur, 5 March 1244

On our way to the hidden tunnels of the mountain, Susane and I sleep the night in the woods not too far from the pog. She repeats the spell she used when the knights approached. It keeps us hidden from any intruders, deliberate or otherwise. She calls it a *do not look here* spell, and it makes us practically invisible. When I ask why we do not simply use it and progress directly past the army itself, she asks me how certain I am that there aren't any magic users or sensitives — those who can detect it but not use magic — in said army. She then enquires whether I like to back myself into a bolt hole when faced by an advancing armed horde without having previously scouted out the alternative exits. I have the feeling that she is being somewhat sarcastic. Still, the spell seems eminently useful, so I study it in order to better borrow the technique.

As the night breaks and dawn appears to add colour to the world, we proceed around to the far side of the mount, away from the major part of the invading forces, and in through a practically invisible cavern entrance, tiny and hidden by both rampant flora and overhanging escarpments. Susane leads us down tight paths, clambering through almost invisible breaks in the naturally formed ceiling, somehow always finding a way through and upwards. She is surefooted and deserving of her confidence.

'Who made these tunnels? Was it your people?' I say, attempting to make conversation. We have been inside the pog for close to two hours, and I am tired of the silence. Tired of the oppressive closeness of the narrow openings in the crags. I want to see the sky again.

'Are you calling me short?' She turns, visibly annoyed. The expression melts into amusement once I start blustering, trying to excuse myself. Her ability to play me like a lute will be the death of me.

'No, it wasn't my people. I believe it was the lutins.'

'The what?'

'Gnomes. Little People. Fair Folk who've chosen to live here rather than the demesne of Fairie. They've long known it wiser to travel away from the eyes of mortal men. Ignorant sensitives and Talented often believe squeezing them will cause them to spill the secret locations of riches.'

'Does it work?' I ask, curious. I am ever aware of my comparative ignorance of the world I now find myself in.

'I think it leads to them spilling up their last meal. Maybe their internal organs. Depends on how hard you squeeze them.' She makes a popping noise to demonstrate and then starts climbing upward again.

I curse my luck. If she was only beautiful and clever, my chances would be much higher to extricate myself from my feelings. That she is also witty is a terrible blow.

Distracted by such thoughts, I hardly notice when we come out onto a small crevice barely more than a man's width and long enough for three to stand. I can reach the top with a small leap. I pull myself up and over, then offer my hand down to help Susane, which she accepts gratefully.

Roofs stretch out just below us, expanding into the open space while a house stands to our left, its wood beams plastered on top of mortared stone. The village surrounding the castle is hodgepodge, each building constructed where there is sufficient flat terrain or where they can reclaim land by carving into the mountain. A path, little more than worn stone less steeply vertical than the surrounding cliffside, leads up the small ascent to the castle. The stone tower stands prominent, topped by wooden ramparts, the square covered by a triangular wooden roof. I hurry up the path, worry clear in both my manner and movement.

'What is wrong, Good Man?' Susane hurries along after me.

'What is wrong is that we may be too late,' I say, my brow furrowed at the weight of the dark thoughts. 'Roger of Mirepoix's flag no longer flies upon the flagpole. Montsegur may already have fallen.'

We crest the top, and I sigh with relief for there are still armed guards manning the entrance, replete in Mirepoix's yellow-and-black colours. A flag still hangs from the ramparts, the triple black arrow fletchings on a yellow background over the gateway. They see us at much the same time as we see them.

'Halt,' one shouts, lowering a halberd in our direction while the other two reach for their swords.

'Peace, man,' I cry and hold up my leather cord. It is as sure a marker of the faith as the traditional yellow-and-black garments themselves.

The men ease up a little, but the halberd is not completely lowered nor are hands lifted from hilts. 'What do you want? What foolhardiness drives you to seek this place at such a time if you are a Perfect, indeed?'

'We offer aid,' I say. 'A way out, an escape.'

The man snorts bitterly. 'A little late, Good Man,' he says. 'The truce is already struck and the surrender agreed. Montsegur has fallen. It is just that the stones themselves have not realised it yet.'

I look about, confused. The castle shows signs of damage. Walls crumbled in places, impacted and broken in others. I look around, trying to work out how the invaders might have managed such a feat. Hurling rocks so high up a mountain should have been impossible. I wonder if a Talented individual was at work.

'Look ye down there,' another says, seeing my confusion. He points backwards, past the rooftops, towards the furthest end of the land lived in by the Good Christian community. It is an area that should not need guarding. The sheer rock face at that end makes it impassable under normal circumstances. The siege is all based at the other side, where paths might lead you up to the castle. I blink, then rub my eyes in disbelief. At the far end, on the buff opposite, is a catapult.

'What magic is this?' I murmur. Luckily, the defenders do not realise how literal I am being.

'The magic of money, of course. The bastard Basque mercenaries had enough money thrown at them as to take leave of their senses. They scaled the cliff at night. Daresay the only way 'twere possible for in the day, no man could do it. If you could see the danger, would be impossible to continue. Still, they managed it, catapult parts and all, once they set up some pulley systems. Pounded us enough to weaken us for an attack that damned near broke us. It is clear to anyone that we are done for. A truce was negotiated but only for a few more days. Then we all surrender, and Montsegur is finished. The Good People too, the Good God curse the Francs' rotten hides.' The soldier turns his head slightly, trying to hide the wetness building around his eyes.

Susane's hand touches my arm. She looks at me with a sad sympathy in her eyes. 'I fear we may have arrived too late, Paul,' she says, and even to hear her at last calling me by my name cannot dull the sense of pain and failure that rings sharply in my heart at those words.

CHAPTER NINETEEN
TOULOUSE, 9 APRIL, PRESENT DAY

I do love walking into a
bar, tear-stained and covered
in snot; it makes a change
from bloodstained and covered
in viscera. Neither help you get
served quickly though.

We reach the O'Bohem at the same time as Isaac, who is walking towards the bar from farther down the street. He's been casually hiding whatever car he is driving, having needed to replace his 2CV (he *never* used his garage to park his car before, and suddenly, it is always mysteriously in storage when I call around). Part of me burns with curiosity to see what horrendous decision he made to replace the 'classic', as he labelled the 2CV. Most of me, though, is ready to burn down the rest of reality if it means I can grab a pint and a whisky to accompany it. Mocking Isaac can wait. For a little bit.

We walk up to the bar in uneasy silence, Isaac obviously ablaze with a million questions of his own regarding what is going on. But it is going to take a little while to fill him in on the catalogue of disasters that have befallen us since I completely failed to keep myself from getting involved in yet more bullshit, and I want a drink first. We put in our orders, and the bar-woman starts pouring all of our drinks apart from Susane's. The server's blonde wound dreadlocks flash me back to Bordeaux momentarily, even though her prominent piercings and colourful tattoos under her wife-beater aren't something I can see the coven leader getting down with. *Maybe her errant daughter would.* Meanwhile, back on the other side of the bar...

'Elderberry fucking wine?' Aicha asks Susane, her eyebrows raised in disbelief, which for her, is the equivalent of her eyes popping out and having to be picked back up off the floor like a Warner Bros. cartoon.

'I fear, dear lady, you may have mistaken the kind of establishment we are in,' Isaac inserts graciously.

'And the time period. And, I reckon, you also may have mistaken Toulouse for fucking Lothlórien.'

We persuade Susane to settle for a glass of the (pretty damn palatable) house white, and we sojourn to a nearby table. I fill in Isaac (and by extension both Jakob and their associate angels) on what went on in our absence. It takes a while. About three pints, which is the mathematically calculated limit for how long any one discussion can carry on before getting sidetracked by random tangents.

'So if Franc eats magic, do you think he shits fairy dust?' Aicha corners Susane, who despite having loosened up with a couple of glasses of wine in her, is looking like a fox trapped in what initially looked like car lights but has turned out to be a fire-breathing dragon wearing a headlamp.

'Um, no?' I think this conversation is making her more uncomfortable than being quizzed by the Mother made me.

'Ah, an incredibly erudite response. Can see why you two ended up together.' Aicha snorts and returns to poking at her alcohol-free cocktail with her straw, suspiciously trying to identify what the crushed pulp at the bottom identifies as fruit-wise. I suspect it might be genus-fluid.

'So I think we're getting a bit off track here. Isaac, Jakob...' *'Isakob' 'Isaac, Jakob*, anything that you didn't follow at all?'

'No, I think I'm fully up to date, lad. Me too, my dear boy.'

'So what about the whole "stopping every Franc-chained transient in town dying if he does" scenario?'

'I'll let you take this one, Jak,' Isaac says, and his face takes on the micro-changes meaning Jakob has taken the metaphorical steering wheel.

'I think, my boy, you will concur that I've had some...upfront experience of late with methods of confinement?'

I nod my assent. That is beyond a shadow of a doubt. Hundreds of years squeezed into a magical skull is not my idea of a good time. I have literally no idea how he hung onto his sanity, outside of the fact that he is a considerably better man than I.

'Well, I, or rather we, yes thank you Nan, were the architects of all of that design work. All a bit Daedelus-esque, really, shaping our own prison, et cetera. Keep on subject, Jak. Yes, thank you, Isaac, I shall indeed. Anyhow, the point I wanted to make is that we have some rather good ideas about how we might protect the poor souls in the unfortunate event of this Franc's demise.'

'Well, that sounds like brilliant news!' I say and then narrow my eyes at the less than exuberant expression on his face. 'Okay, spill. What's the catch?'

'They'll need to be gathered together in a rather limited surface area.'

My eyes narrow so far I am pretty sure their corners have become vanishing points that art students can study for mastery of drawing perspective. 'How limited?'

His face rearranges itself to show Isaac at the helm. 'About five metres squared, lad?'

I close my eyes and count to ten to calm down. In several languages. It doesn't make any real difference, but it does remind me that I need to brush up on my Aramaic.

'Okay, first point. We don't know how many people have sworn themselves into Franc's service, right?'

I open my eyes to general nods of agreement from around the table.

'Actually, that's it for points. Let's just get down to what that means we need to do. We need to find an unknown number of people, probably numbering in the hundreds, possibly scattered throughout the country, somehow gather them all together without the mind-sharing monster they've sworn allegiance to realising, bring them to one teeny, tiny room and then what? Get them to build a human fucking pyramid whilst you work your magic?'

I look across at Isakob. They deserve that title right now because the metaphysical daggers I am shooting out of my eyes like a medieval Cyclops are definitely aimed at both of them. They have the decency to look suitably embarrassed, to their credit. It doesn't help me with the situation, but it makes me feel better. It isn't me wearing that expression. For once.

'Look, lad, it's only been twenty-four hours so far. Main thing is, we've got some baseline theory to expand from. Today, five metres; tomorrow, the world and all that, eh?'

I nod wearily. I'll take that positivity right now like I'll take another pint. Anything to assuage the aching head and heart, even temporarily. The bar-woman does her magic, including a complementary round of some luminescent green shooters that are either magic or toxic or both. They are also free, a generous gesture from the server. Winner, winner, chicken dinner.

'Okay,' I say, settling back into my seat. 'Anything else you need regarding the research?'

'Well,' Isaac starts, but Jakob butts in. 'Maybe the skulls again? If we keep having difficulties, we might need to get them back from Lou Carc– Ow! Sorry about that, lad. Will we be all right to go get those from wherever they might be if needs be, do you think?'

I saw the point when Isaac apparently transcendentally clipped Jakob round the back of the head and took back control of the mouth that ran away with itself. I also saw his eyes dart towards Susane as he grabbed the reins. He is no fool, Isaac. To be fair, neither is Jakob, but he is overly trusting and naïve about a lot of things. It isn't a characteristic that always plays out in his favour either — see "several hundred years trapped in a skull" as exhibit A for that particular court case.

I move the conversation swiftly onwards. 'Right, so that's the backup plan in operation. Now we need to make a plan A for trying to get the stupid kid her *talent* back. Yes, Aich?'

She lowers her hand. 'If they've got the backup plan, does that make them team B?'

'I guess so?'

'So that means if we've got plan A, we're the A-Team? Bagsy, I get to be B A I pity the fool who tries to rock bling better than me.'

I sigh. 'That was spectacularly unhelpful. Thanks, Aich.'

'Any time, *saabi*.'

'Okay, now that Aicha's got that out of her system... So Lourdes and the Lady.'

Any lightheartedness seems to disappear out of the atmosphere simultaneously with any alcohol floating around in my system. The place and the person both have a pretty sobering effect.

The silence looms oppressively for a while. It is Susane who breaks it, mirroring Aicha's inane interjectory style by raising her hand. I point at her, acknowledging her and giving her the floor.

She clears her throat nervously, looking around at our gloomy faces. 'I mean, I've looked up Lourdes on the map, and I know where it is, but the last time I went that way, it was just small hamlets and farmland at the feet of the mountains. What's there now? And who is this Lady?'

I blink and see the same momentary surprise giving way to comprehension in the others' expressions. 'Of course, you would've been over in Faerie when all this was kicking off,' I say and wave my hand at Isaac. 'This sort of thing is much more up your alley, dude. Go for it.'

Isaac coughs, clearing his throat, and strikes what I think of as his lecturer pose. There is nothing the man loves more than to impart information, and I'm sure that, had he been able to come up with a believable excuse about why he never aged nor died, he would've sought tenure at one of the local universities. He'd have been wildly successful and massively popular with the students too, seeing how a couple of the student-aged population of the bar are looking at him, not just for his teaching style either. I wonder how that works with the whole twofer scenario. As far as I know, Isaac's taste runs solely to the female gender, and Jakob has shown a preference, at least, for men. Also, having sex with your brother as company or even tagging in seems creepy, verging on incestuous. I realise I've missed the start of Isaac's speech during my mentally scarring contemplation.

'... the girl went home and told her parents she'd met a beautiful lady in white robes at the stream, surrounded by shining lights. She was forbidden to visit again, which she paid about as much attention to as most young teenagers do the instruction of their parents. She returned, this time with her sister and some friends. When the vision arose, the young Bernadette knelt immediately. Those who'd accompanied her, though, didn't go unprepared, readied in case she was a demon. They flung some holy water at the apparition, which promptly disappeared. That didn't convince Bernadette she wasn't holy though.

'There were several more visions –or *aquerò* as the girl called them– of this Lady, happening practically every single day, and word spread. Her parents felt embarrassed and understandably so. Indeed, there were many of the village who said Bernadette was insane and murmured about locking her away in an institute, never to see the light of day. However, there were many more who believed that these were holy visitations. The regularity of them didn't hurt either. There was no TV in those days, and even books were a rarity in such small communities. A form of consecutive serial entertainment was as every bit appealing to them as it was to the modern-day soap opera or reality TV viewer.

'The official story afterwards, once the miracle was rubber-stamped by the Church, was that the vision revealed itself to be the Virgin Mary, claiming to be the "Immaculate Conception". We'll come back to that, but what is sure is that Bernadette wasn't playing around.

'On 25 February 1858, two weeks after her first vision, Bernadette calmly committed herself to an act of dedication to the Lady, vowing to drink from the stream, bathe in it, and to eat a "special herb" that grew there. Yes, grow up, please, Aicha, thank you. This caused some consternation for the villagers who actually gave a damn about her and worry for those who didn't all the same as they feared their entertainment might come to an abrupt end. The waters of the stream were little more than liquid mud, and whilst they might not have known about tetanus scientifically, they knew perfectly well what the probable outcomes of drinking non-boiled, dirty stream water were and what it would likely lead to. Dysentery would be a win in terms of outcome, and even that was likely to put her out of action for a considerable amount of time and could well be fatal. This was made even more likely by Bernadette's ill health, which she had battled with since being a small child. She remained half the size of other children her age and was constantly in and out of her sickbed. Surely, thought many, this would be the end of the strange little girl.

'Instead, to everyone's indescribable surprise, she didn't die or even get sick in the slightest. Indeed, the following day everyone was astounded to see that the water was flowing strongly and was crystal clear, all apparently from a fresh stream that had sprung up after Bernadette had dug on a specifically instructed spot. Even the most arduous of dissenters was silenced (meaning probably her parents), and the town declared it a miracle.

'What was even more miraculous was that the water appeared to have healing powers. Bernadette's own health improved dramatically, and the local priest, although initially suspicious, became convinced as inexplicable healings started being reported. Bernadette herself insisted the Lady wanted a sanctuary to be built there, and following multiple investigations by Church authorities, that's exactly what they started in 1863, completing three years later.

'What is perhaps strangest is that on the completion of the sanctuary, Bernadette abruptly left Lourdes, joining an order of nuns. When pressed on why she had left, she compared herself to a broom, set aside once the Lady had done her work. Away from Lourdes, her ill health returned, and the little woman died of tuberculosis, only thirty-five years old, pleading for forgiveness for her sins from the Virgin Mary on her deathbed.

'There were various details, almost certainly added in by Catholic officials over the years, like the thing about the immaculate conception. Rumour has it, amongst circles dedicated to the preservation of such esoteric knowledge, that the Lady simply claimed this was a chance for them both to be born again. Nothing was immaculate about it at all. They annotated details to bring similarities between the Lady and the Virgin

Mary as time went on, solidifying the Christian nature of the miracle. After all, Bernadette herself had said that the miracle only worked if you had faith. What she never said was *what* you had to have faith in.'

Isaac pauses, taking a swig of his beer. Much needed by my estimation. I can talk, but Isaac is in a class of his own once he gets into his groove. How he's not downing a whole horse-trough load of water after all that, I have no idea. If he ever gets tempted to the Dark Side, he'll be a natural for villainous monologuing.

Susane raises her hand again, although considering the collegiate feeling that Isaac speaking has inspired, it seems more appropriate this time. Isaac clearly feels so, acknowledging it with both a nod and a pleased smile on his face.

'This all sounds...peculiar. Fascinating even,' she adds hastily, seeing the smile fall from Isaac, which always feels akin to kicking a puppy. 'What I don't get is the...' She waves her hands in all our directions, to the hang-dog expressions and the assembled mood. 'This. The "it's the end of the world" atmosphere that seems to overhang our assembly. Isn't miraculous healing...' Again, she looks lost for words, searching for something appropriately expressive. Eventually, she gives up. 'Isn't it *nice*?'

There is a moment of silence, of looks exchanged. I am about to respond when, unexpectedly, Aicha leans forward, looking almost sympathetically at the bewildered Susane. 'Aren't you fae, woman? When was anything, especially magic, ever given for free?'

CHAPTER TWENTY

TOULOUSE, 9 APRIL, PRESENT DAY

I can't quite believe Susane thought some "nice" Talented might have just shown up in Lourdes to help people. That's not how the magical world works. Or any world I've ever come across.

S usane looks a touch upset by what Aicha said, but considering Aicha asked in as kindly a manner as she is capable of and did so without breaking Susane's nose again, she seems a bit on the judgemental side as far as I am concerned.

'I can give for giving's sake without strings attached,' she replies, a bit of that regal aloofness creeping in alongside the hurt tone.

Aicha goes blank again, emotionless as she examines the woman in front of her. 'Can you? Can you, indeed?'

'That'll be because you were human first,' Isaac interjects hurriedly, a palm outstretched in calming mode towards Aicha. 'And we've all known the genuinely open-handed and hearted over the years. But a magical healing spring powered by faith? Those don't come without some significant payment, either before or after.'

I take another large glug of my drink, then take up the telling. 'Initially, a lot of us Talented in the area thought maybe Bernadette was some prodigy using vast well springs of magic without even realising it, shaping the world to her childish viewpoint. It'd have been the best option.'

I shake my head and take another swig to steady myself. 'The woman I met at the convent when I went to investigate was Talentless. More than just that though; she was completely null. Everyone, even those unable to cast the simplest cantrip if instructed by an expert, has some traces of magical energy stuck to them, making them visible to the *sight*. When I *looked* at her –' I stop again. Pausing, thinking of it. 'It was like she wasn't there. No trace or outline of her.

'Not only that, but she didn't really seem to remember her time at Lourdes before joining the convent. Oh, sure, she could retell the events, perfect retellings, exactly as the official doctrine suggested once I got to her. Exactly. Have you ever watched any realistic police shows?' I realise who I am talking to and her relative isolation from most of such things; although, I have no idea how much access to modernity and modern media she had while serving the Sistren. I wave my question away.

'Never mind, look, the point is, all detectives say the same thing. If someone gives you a perfect, precise, word-for-word retelling of the same story each time they're asked to give it? Then that is exactly what it is. A story. Actual memories don't work like that. Sure, they crystallise when you keep telling them over and over, but even then little things will get left out or something forgotten gets remembered or the accent of the anecdote will fall on a distinct part of what happened compared to the previous time. What never happens is a repetitive word-for-word recounting. Yet, that's exactly what I got. I rode both train and horse to get to Nevers, halfway between Paris and Lyon, where the girl had moved to after joining the convent.

'Lourdes was sufficiently close to my territory that I wanted to know more, and provable miracles known to the public were unheard of in what we were all proudly thinking of as the modern era. I'd received a copy of a transcribed interview with Bernadette from a friend more closely situated, who had interviewed her personally some weeks prior to my arrival. After persuading the Mother Superior to allow me access, claiming journalistic credentials for a religious broadsheet, she repeated exactly what was written on the paper sent to me by my friend, ad verbatim. When I attempted to push her on a few details, to prompt her to deviate from her text, it made her physically unwell. She clutched at her temples and seemed overcome with a migraine, showing genuine distress. I attempted to use a small amount of *talent* on her.'

I focus on my beer as I remember that moment, the strangeness of it, the unnaturalness. 'It just...washed straight off her. Like it couldn't touch her. She was Teflon to magic. In fact, the attempt only seemed to make her worse. She had some sort of convulsive fit, and they hurried me out, journalist credentials or no.'

I can see the puzzlement on Susane's face, the lack of concern there by what I am recounting. None of this is making sense to her — or rather, it isn't making sense in terms of why we are all so deeply concerned by it. I decide we need to move the story onwards.

'We are curious as a species, humans, and when you've lived a long time, when boredom becomes the norm as far as mind states go, then anything new or different draws a lot of attention. People became intrigued, and whilst I headed north to speak to the young girl, two of my friends decided at the same time to head south.

I look over at Isaac. 'Did you ever meet Houdin?' I can't remember if their paths crossed.

'Briefly. Didn't really know him. Not like Ahmad, anyhow.' Isaac's brow furrows deeper than the ridges of the Mariana Trench. He knows where this story goes.

Aicha raises her hand. 'Hold up. I've heard you talk about Ahmad, assuming you mean al-Buni, the Algerian sorcerer. But did you meet Houdini? As in "the greatest escapologist of all time" Houdini?'

I shake my head. 'Nah. This was the original. This was the guy Houdini named himself after. He was the real deal. An unparalleled stage magician. And Talented too, though he didn't realise that till he met al-Buni.'

I can see the doubt on Aicha's face. 'Was he really that good?' she asks.

I nod. 'Good enough to convince the Algerian Marabouts to submit to French rule in fear of his terrible magics for Napoleon the Third. All of it trickery. Smoke and mirrors and sleight of hand. Ironic that it was the greatest Algerian sorcerer of all time who helped him learn what real magic is.'

Now Susane interrupts. 'I don't know who either of these people are. Who was this Ahmad?'

'Ahmad al-Buni,' I tell her. 'Arguably the greatest North African sorcerer of all time. First person I studied under after my apprenticeship with Isaac too.'

'A genius.' There is a misty-eyed quality to Isaac's regard. I know he is off in scholarly heaven, thinking about the technicalities of the esoteric works Ahmad produced. 'He revolutionised magic, both theoretical and practical.'

I nod heavily. 'He really was. More than that, he was my friend too. He edged further and further north over the centuries as authorities declared his studies heretical and his religion unwelcome — first to Andalucia from

Algeria and then later to the south of France. I helped him settle in Pau. He was a gentleman and a gentle man — eminently polite and integrally kind. Someone I was proud to call a friend, as well as a teacher.'

I stare into my drink glumly, thinking about the bright-eyed wizard, his amiable smile and inherent curiosity. He reminded me of Isaac and occupies a similar place in my esteem. 'He came across Jean-Eugéne Robert-Houdin in the twilight of his career, still treading the boards in Paris, still the toast of Parisian high society. Ahmad saw Houdin's *talent*, as well as his brilliance. He persuaded him as to the reality of *talent* and power, and took him on as a student.' I remember how excited Ahmad was, how proud and delighted to present Robert to me. 'He told me he believed Robert would be a great Talented, one who would surpass us both. Ahmad outclassed me considerably *talent*-wise. If he believed it, so did I. I still do. If only they hadn't gone to investigate the "miracle of Lourdes".

'We still don't know what happened there. Not really. I went searching for them when I'd heard nothing after some time. I found Jean leant up against a palisade at Ahmad's house, the one he'd bought in one of the nicer quarters of Pau. At first, I thought he was ill, seeing a glassiness to his eyes and an unhealthy greying of his pallor. He was feverishly incoherent. I was more disturbed initially by my old friend's absence and shook the man, demanding Ahmad's whereabouts. He just kept muttering and mumbling as he licked at the sweat pouring down his face when it touched his lips. All I could really get was something about service to the Lady, although whether it was in relation to himself or to Ahmad, it was far from clear.

'It was when I truly *looked* at him that the horror of what had happened became clear, and I understood the correlation between him and that tiny nun up in the north I'd visited. He was empty, stripped clean of all *talent*, nothing left whatsoever. This genius of sleight-of-hand, this potential future master of magic who would equal or better us all — he was gone. There was nothing left really but a shell.

'Eventually, he calmed down, healed somewhat from the physical symptoms he was presenting, the fever breaking, although he was a shadow of the showman who had wowed the whole of France. As the fever passed, it seemed to take all memories with it. He remembered nothing after arriving at the grotto at Lourdes side by side with Ahmad until he came to again in the bed I'd set him in at the house, weak but alive. He didn't even remember anything of what he'd been trying to tell me when I'd first found him in the courtyard, not even when I repeated back the fragments I'd gleaned. That parcel of time seemed taken away as completely as his magic had been.'

I stop, distracting myself momentarily with a one-two tapping of my fingers, poking spots of clarity into the fogging on the glass from the combination of cold beer and the warmth of the bar. It feels like I am trying to beat a retreat, to marshal back my emotions, regroup perhaps before sallying forth once more. I liked Jean as soon as I met him, all whim and wonder combined with prodigal talent. And *talent* — although he didn't have time to fully explore the intriguing new world he discovered before having it inexplicably ripped from him. It's hard, trying to distract myself from the sadness creeping back in before I speak again, thinking of his disappeared teacher. I still miss Ahmad, the boisterous, enthusiastic scholar, so eager to share the wonder he saw in every single fragment of existence.

'What happened to Ahmad then?' she asks, having physically crept forward, unconsciously leaning into the tale. I literally have her on the edge of her seat. Go, me. At least I know I'll have a possible secondary career as a storyteller if what happened to Jean happens to me.

I shrug. The heartache is heavier now than my constant desire to impress, and I no longer feel like carrying the story onto its unsatisfying conclusion.

'Nobody knows. He never came back.' I sit back moodily, doing my best impression of an eyelinered teenager whose parents just pulled out baby photos to share with his group of goth mates.

Isaac picks up both the prompt and the story. 'Basically, my dear, there was never hide nor hair discovered of him. And the problem is, it wasn't a one-off occurrence. There are always those either cat-like in their curiosity or confident in their abilities, perhaps overly so, who will poke a beehive to see if they will also get stung. Predictably, most stories tend towards exactly that happening.'

Aicha starts making sharp head movements, scanning back and forth between the conversation and the street visible through the large open wall-sized glass window at the front of the bar. It is as close as she comes to fidgeting and a clear sign that she's had enough of story time for now, thank you very much. I am not at all surprised when she interrupts.

'Basically, you go in, you don't come out. Or you come out like Robert-Houdin. Emptied out.'

I nod, still brooding. 'He died not long after, you know. Pneumonia officially. Many said it was a reaction to the loss of his son, killed in battle. The man I left behind in his family's care in Saint-Gervais...' I shrug. 'I don't think he could feel so deeply about anything, even his own son. I think he was already on the final countdown from the moment he got out of Lourdes again, away from the Lady.'

Susane perks up again, still hoping we are going to feed her own curiosity. 'So who is this Lady of Lourdes then?'

There is another uneasy silence. I'm starting to think it is something I could specialise in. I can see the advertising now: People coming round for dinner you never want to see again? Invite me, Paul Bonhomme, to ensure that they never want to spend another moment in your presence afterwards.

Isaac puts himself forward once again, the Good God love him. 'Nobody really knows. It's not as though anyone has returned with any... useful information, lass. Either they come back raving mad or broken or not at all. There are, as one would surmise, endless theories around the various potential possibilities. Some have put forward that she might be the White Lady of the Pyrenees as looks-wise, at least, she matches well to the description.'

I shake my head strongly. This isn't the first time we've had this discussion. 'No chance. The real White Lady is a strange creature, and I think there's more than a few who crossed her path who have disappeared because of it, but she's never harmed anyone like poor Jean. Never stripped them of everything. It's not her.'

It is Isaac's turn to shrug. 'The problem is everyone — or at least everyone I've ever discussed it with has recognised it as a purely theoretical exercise. It'd be impossible to confirm without paying Lourdes a visit.'

'And no one is in any hurry to do that,' Aicha adds sourly. 'Remind me, Paul, you complete and utter wankshaft. Where are we going thanks to your big fucking mouth?'

I don't respond. I just sit here glumly, swilling the last segments of my beer around the bottom of my glass, as though I can pull the future from them like a boozy version of tasseography. I can't really muster a comeback. I deserve that one entirely.

Suddenly, Susane springs to life, her eyes lighting up, which, considering all of our glum demeanours, makes her come over like a cheerleader at an emo convention. 'Have you thought to ask the Mother?'

I look up as though trying to see into my cranium to find the reason this is a bad idea. Fortunately, being a bear of little brain, it takes me hardly any time to realise I can't think of any.

'Do you really think she will give up information willingly?' I ask doubt-fully, the best I can muster in terms of a negative response to her buoyant intervention.

'It's in her self-interests too, isn't it? It seems like Franc is a dead end –'

'And liable to end up dead,' Aicha interjects.

'Quite possibly. Either way, this seems the only possible avenue left open to investigate. If you get your magic eaten or disappear, it does her no favours either. Surely, it's at least worth a try?' She looks at me imploringly. I get the feeling she wants to prove herself useful, although whether it is to me or to the rest of the team, I can't tell. Still, I can find no fault with her plan. Except one.

'I haven't got a clue how to go about reaching her,' I admit honestly. I am aware I can get Aicha to reach out to her "friend" in the coven, or I suppose I could jump back on the train over to Bordeaux, but that all seems a bit long-winded.

Susane rolls her eyes at me (what is it about me that makes everyone who ever cares for me do that regularly?). She fishes about in a jacket pocket before producing a battered antiquity — a Nokia mobile phone pulled from the primordial ages of portable telephones.

'Lucky for you then,' she says, smiling with that knowing look I learned early in our relationship to mean she isn't just sure she isn't wrong, she is even more sure I am. 'I have her on speed dial.'

She passes me the phone, and I can already hear the ringtone as it crosses the table.

'Speak,' comes the imperial tone of the Mother of the Sistren of Bor-deaux, as commanding across invisible airwaves as she is in person.

'Um, yes, it's me,' I start. Then because I am an incredibly awkward dickhead, I clarify, 'Paul Bonhomme, the, um, Cathar magician.' I wince as soon as I finish, trying to ignore the disbelief surrounding me that is going to transform into open mockery about half a second after I hang up the phone.

An earthy chuckle passes through the line. 'There is another Paul Bonhomme who might be contacting the Sistren through this particular telephone?' she queries, and I wince so hard it makes me grimace, grinding my teeth together till I'm sure I've taken a couple of millimetres of enamel off. A wincing grimace. A wimace? I decide I might try that one on Aicha later. After she comprehensively takes the piss out of me for the foreseeable future, of course. No point in trying to stop her before, but maybe it will help distract her from continuing. I am far from convinced.

'Look, I've got some good news and some bad news,' I say, still trying to regain my equilibrium after making a complete prat of myself on the introduction.

'There was bad news before. What new bad news is there to add?' she asks, any humour completely wiped from her voice now.

'The bad news is Franc is a write-off. He can't give your daughter back her powers.' I have to fight hard to suppress another wince, feeling like a disrespectful offspring about to catch a clip round the ear from an austere parent-figure despite the distance between us.

There is a lengthy silence. Finally, she speaks, 'That is bad news. There is always hope that the good news might outweigh it.'

I instinctively want to prevaricate, to hum and haw, to work my way up to the subject, but I realise it wouldn't be for *her*. It would be for me. The Mother won't really care if I disappear or if I get my magic eaten, except in the sense of not being able to help her or that my absence creates potential power vacuums in the southwest afterwards.

I simply don't want to say the words, don't really want to make it real. There is a moment of realisation, all of this happening in a fraction of a second as I compose both myself and what I want to say. I am really, truly scared. I don't want to go. I don't want to know who took my friend away from me. I don't want to go facing monsters who swallow up the Talented. And I don't want to end up like Jean, stripped of everything. All power, yes, but all personality too. All life, all joie de vivre with it, taken and gone. Words have always held power. Unfortunately, promises have too. I am far from perfect, but I still want to believe I'm not one to break a promise deliberately, and I made one to the Mother, of my own accord, in fact. I pull myself up by the metaphorical braces, give myself the spiritual equivalent of a clip around the ear, and make myself get on with it.

'There's still another possibility that Franc pointed us towards. It's not... It's not a *good* option, but it is an option. Thing is, we need further information. Susane suggested you might have some ideas for us.'

I feel like I've been pretty straightforward considering my desire to be as circumspect as possible, but there is a distinct tinge of impatience to the Mother's reply. 'Where did the monster suggest going?'

'He said the Lady of Lourdes can help us further,' I say, and it shocks me to hear an audible gasp from the other end of the line. That is the closest I've ever known the Mother to be caught off guard, to let something slip unintentionally. It looks like I am not the only one who is concerned by what lives in the grotto.

The silence stretches again, a putty ball of tension thinning at the strain as it pulls further and further apart from the moment before. It has to break; the only question is from which end. It is the Mother who speaks first, and she surprises me again with the hesitancy in her voice.

'And will you go?' she asks, almost a whisper, mainly a plea, and I realise she thinks I'm likely to abandon my promise. She expects I'd rather break my word and almost certainly start a war with Bordeaux than honour it and go there. I don't know if it reflects on how she thinks of me or how dangerous Lourdes is. Neither seem like pleasant options.

'I will go.' There is a cough on my right. '*We* will go, sorry. But we aren't going to go rushing in willy-nilly, getting ourselves killed in the process or worse. We need some proper information before we can go in there.'

Aicha makes a big charade of pinching herself to make sure she isn't dreaming, then mimes her head exploding. I guess it is a bit of a departure from our normal modus operandi, but this is another level of threat entirely to shizzards or rabies-infected sasquatches (which is a whole different story for another time). Even psycho, destroy the entire world, trap an angel in a skull Ben now seems a more normal kind of threat. Had he succeeded, I might have been sent to another plane, another life maybe, but I feel confident I'd have still been me. Despite him having dedicated hundreds of years to my downfall, this still somehow feels like a more personal risk. I could be stripped of my magic, end up mortal and Talentless. Don't get me wrong, there were times during my span of years when I might have jumped at the chance, but it isn't where I am now. And even those times, I would have reconsidered if I'd seen for myself the ineffable reduction of Jean-Eugène Robert-Houdin. That shade-state of being is a poor substitute for living. I've no desire to end up in the same condition.

'There is not much that can be told.' There is a deliberation to her words, even more so than usual, and I prick up. I can hear the sound of someone picking their way around what they can and cannot say. This is something subtle, and I'll need to unravel it.

'That sounds like you might know more than you can say. Like something might stop you, such as a promise. Or a geas.'

'There is not much that can be told.' There is frustration in there now, and the repetition is a key indicator. Now I have to approach this like a logic problem to solve. Breaking geases, or words on our power, carries consequences even more severe than the situation we've found ourselves in now. The key is that she said there is not *much* that can be told. That means there is something, some sort of hint or clue to point us in the right direction. Anything that can get us started will be a win right now.

'Right, got it. Hold on a moment.' I pull the phone away from my ear and look at the others. 'Did you clock that? Looks like the Mother knows something, but she's gagged magically. There's at least something she can give us, but we need to find out what it is. Batter up, team.'

I put the phone on speaker and place it in the middle of the table. I've already settled on the first question. We need to establish a baseline.

'Do you know who the Lady of Lourdes is?'

'There is not much that can be told.'

Okay, so that is a non-starter, but I was pretty sure it would be. Isaac clears his throat before speaking.

'Good day, good Mother. A veritable honour to speak to such an august matriarch...'

I cut him off with a neck-chopping "stop" hand movement. 'Top marks for effort, Isaac, but studies have shown sucking up is ineffective against geases.'

Isaac flushes slightly behind his glasses, and I hear a most plebeian snort through the speaker, most out of sorts with the Mother's normal mannerisms. Shame it is the geas we need to break rather than her poise. Isaac continues, flashing me a look that says he is distinctly put out.

'Ahem, excusing my cretinous friend's interruption over pure *politeness*, shall we to the matter at hand? Are we dealing perhaps with a French native?'

'There is not much that can be told.'

Damn. That was a good move. If we could narrow down the Lady's country of origin, we might find traces of her in folktales or fireside warnings. I go with something along the same lines.

'Did the brothers Grimm or Hans Christian Andersen ever mention them?'

'There is not much that can be told.'

Strike three. Luckily this isn't baseball — firstly as it means we aren't out and can keep guessing, and secondly because everything is already potentially perilous enough without me being bored to death on top of it. Susane unexpectedly chips in.

'Are they or were they once human?'

Good wording, and I like how she's playing to her own experience and strengths. It covers anyone who has ascended to a deity-level of power, as well as any other once-humans who might have changed species á la Cagots. The reply is the same –

'There is not much that can be told.'

But it seems to me as though there was just a momentary hesitation before she spoke, as though she was perhaps testing the limits of the geas, that perhaps we are in the right ballpark. The right ballpark being, in general, any one where they aren't playing baseball, but in this case, meaning where we might draw out some information. Isaac's brow furrows, meaning he has clocked on too and is almost certainly applying the enormous combined brain power of himself, his brother, and the two angels inside him. Like a Pentium quad-core brain processor. Pentecostium maybe. Shavuot-core. I just hope he doesn't overheat. He doesn't have an inbuilt cooling fan, and it is getting fairly toasty in the bar.

It is Jakob who asks next. 'My dear lady, she wouldn't be a water fae by any chance, would she?'

This is really great thinking and is worth him going slightly red in the face over. It never even crossed my mind, but the connection to the water for miracles would suggest that being a source of strength.

'There is not much that can be told.'

The answer is immediate but again with the level of frustration in the Mother's voice. It is impossible to tell if that is because it isn't true or because we've wandered back into the territory where the geas holds the greatest power.

I think back to what Susane asked and try again. 'Are they a shapeshifter?'

'There is not much that can be told.'

No change in hesitation nor in frustration-level. This is getting beyond irking for me, and I can see that Isaac/Jakob are about ready to tear their hair out as well. Susane looks lost in thought, obviously trying to carry on down the rabbit hole of her last question and find something else, anything else, that might start dragging us in the right direction. Aicha has just sat there stone-faced through all of it so far, but now she leans forward.

'Mother?'

'Yes, child?'

'What can you tell us?'

There is an audible sigh of relief from the other end of the line, and all the tension that was building flees like silhouette boogeymen at the flick of the light switch.

'There is one there who can ask the right questions, at least.'

Aicha pulls at a pair of imaginary britches, points at herself with both thumbs, and mouths, 'She means me,' at me smugly, then settles back into her emotionless state of attentive rest.

There is an elongated pause, long enough that initially I wonder if we have somehow got disconnected, although I realise when I think it through that the Mother is working out what she can say before saying it, trying to give us as much information as possible. After a few minutes, she speaks.

'There is not much that can be told. Nothing of the one you asked of originally. Only of the water. How it became.'

There is quiet again, and the breathing becomes harder, forced. The woman on the other end, the Talented powerhouse, is pushing as hard as she can up against the restraints encasing her. With heaving effort, she forces out one last word, sounding like every syllable is burning her mouth.

'Repetition.'

She hisses at the spent energy, and when she speaks again, she sounds wrung out, like she's run a marathon with a backpack full of boulders on. Magically speaking, I suppose that isn't a million miles away from the truth.

'There is always a way. This is the way.' Then the line goes dead.

Everyone is still radiating focus, centred on the now inert mobile on the tabletop. Looking over at Aicha, then Isaac, I scrub my hand back and forth across my face, rubbing the grit from my eyes and trying to get my head around the just finished conversation.

'That did not give us much to go on, my lad, and I have a feeling that is as much as we're liable to get anywhere.' Isaac settles back into his chair, his face set in worried thought as he takes a pensive swig of his pint.

'Hold on,' Aicha says, making a scene cut gesture with her hands. 'Wait, just hold on. Put that on the back burner a minute. More importantly, did the Mother of the Sistren of Bordeaux just hang up on a fucking *Mandalorian* quote?'

'Well, lookie see, seems like you aren't the only stoic pop culture addict up in these here parts, girlie,' I say, putting on my magnificent cowboy accent impression.

Aicha looks at me, dead-eyed, deadpan in her delivery. 'I'll slice you open and write, "dank ferrik" with sections of your intestines from here to the Capitole and do a painting of Grogu on the square with your remaining viscera if you ever call me "girlie" again.'

'Duly noted,' I reply, tipping her my pint and a wink, which is met with absolutely zero response.

Susane watched all this with the sort of horrified fascination reserved for watching someone spectacularly shorten their life expectancy unnecessarily by their inability to stop themselves from running off at the mouth. She leans sideways towards me, her eyes still fixed on Aicha's unmoving pose.

'Is she serious?' she asks me out of the side of her mouth.

'What do you think?' I reply, taking a cool, refreshing mouthful of beer. It always tastes better when you're living dangerously — like by riling up Aicha.

'Yes?' she answers, her voice rising on the end of the word, her disbelief showing that not only am I prepared to poke the sleeping bear, but I am also actually sharpening all the pointiest objects I can find, then taking it in turns to test which is the pokiest poker.

'Ah, it's all love, ain't it, Aich?' I say, still grinning at my friend, who radiates the icy stillness of a cobra about to strike.

'Keep telling yourself that, cowboy,' she replies. Lightning-fast, she whips both hands up from her sides, gun-fingers ready. I make to dive under the table, but it is too late. She releases her trigger thumbs with the accompanying *pow pow* sound, and I have no choice but to sprawl myself forward across the beer-crusted surface, dying moans and groans issuing from my mouth as she blows invisible smoke off her fingertips and doffs her imaginary hat with a grin.

Susane rolls her eyes in disgust. 'You are entirely ridiculous still, Paul Bonhomme.'

'Mamie, Mamie is that you?' I ask weakly, my hand shakily clasping hers as I peer through half-closed eyes. 'It's...it's getting dark, Mamie, so very dark, so very cold. I'm scared. I... I'm... urgh.'

I throw myself completely prone and then sit back up, picking up my pint, which I managed to incredibly skilfully avoid knocking over during my amateur dramatics. 'And...scene. Right, where were we?'

Isaac shakes his head in disapproving amusement. Aicha is still grinning, and Susane looks at us each, incomprehension clearly stamped into her expression.

'You're all a bunch of bloody loonies,' she opines in the end, obviously completely flabbergasted by exactly how good my acting chops are.

'Ooh, she can quote *Hitchhiker's Guide*. She can stay, after all,' Aicha says, beaming with pride.

'Quote what? I was saying you're a bunch of bloody loonies because you are. A bunch. Of bloody. Loonies,' she says, crossing her arms. Her body language says, "horrified encounter with dangerous insane people", but I know she is warming up to us really.

I turn to Aicha, horrified. 'Are *we* the Golgifrinchans?' I ask tentatively.

'You might well be, *saabi*,' she replies drily, settling back to darkly stab at the unidentified fruity mass at the bottom of her mocktail.

CHAPTER TWENTY-ONE

TOULOUSE, 9 APRIL, PRESENT DAY

Did you hear about the space elf bounty hunter? She was called Mandy Lorien.

I feel a lot better for a moment of communal lunacy, however much a certain fae might find it entirely incomprehensible. It has been a hell of an intense day with body blows landing from every direction, and we are all potentially about to go over the top in a big push that will work out about as well as the Somme did. I'll take a moment of fun between friends and any alleviation of the tension in a heartbeat.

'Right, let's recap,' I say, my head feeling clearer now, at least. 'The Mother couldn't tell us much. What exactly did she tell us?'

Isaac polishes his glasses on his sleeve as he thinks. When he speaks, it's slowly and deliberately as he tries to tease out the exact words while already doubtlessly racing ahead and trying to search out their meaning. 'She said she couldn't tell us about the lady, only about the water.'

Susane jumps in excitedly. 'About how it came to be, she said. The origins of the water.'

I nod. I can, of course, dive into my memory palace and replay the conversation word for word, but there is value in us pooling our viewpoints of what she said. Each person might have fixated on one aspect, even on one word. Someone else's input might just help trigger something additional in the others' thought patterns.

'And what was the last thing she added?' I ask, looking around at the assembled crew.

'Repetition,' Aicha says, still concentrating on the bottom of her glass.

'And what was the last thing she added?' I repeat, grinning.

Aicha looks up, utter disgust on her face. 'I said repetition, not repeat. That doesn't even work, dickhead.'

'Meh, close enough. Anyhow, yeah, repetition was the last word. So the Mother is under a strong enough geas that she cannot talk about the Lady at all nor anything that might point out who she is. That geas didn't cover the water itself though, luckily.'

Isaac picks up the thread of where I am going, and I can see the realisation energising him. He is ready to transform into Super Research Man, the scourge of knowledge hidden away in dusty tomes the world over. 'She believed that something in the story of how the water came to be was a repetition of a previous story about the Lady, that it was close enough for us to draw an identity of whoever the force may be by matching that.'

'I don't think it'll be easy,' I warn. 'I imagine the geas covers all the major elements of the tale. If the Lady was Nimuë for example, she wouldn't have been able to mention Excalibur.'

'More likely her favourite bedtime snack that got mentioned in passing by Geoffrey of Monmouth,' Isaac says, agreeing but with a steely-eyed determination that means he understands exactly what lies ahead in terms of digging through a million obscure sources and is hungry to get to work.

'Or talking about watery tarts,' Aicha says. Blank looks greet this one, and her expression of disgust returns rapidly to her face. '"You can't expect to wield supreme power just 'cos some watery tart threw a sword at you"? *Monty Python and the Holy Grail*? Honestly, I give up on the lot of you.'

'Actually, that's a more valid point than I think Aich realises,' I say, thinking back over the conversation.

'I know exactly how valid it is. I made it. Maximum validity, therefore. Add insulting name of your choice to end of phrase,' Aicha replies, cocking an eyebrow at my chutzpah in casting any aspersion on her input.

'Whatever. Point is, the Mother ended with a modern culture reference,' I say.

'Mandalorian,' Isaac and Aicha chorus in, although both look a bit abashed afterwards at being cued into playing support roles to my speech so easily.

'Exactly so. So maybe the point of reference isn't ancient literature or folklore but modern film or TV or something.'

I see the disappointment appear on Isaac's face and the excitement mount in equal measures on Aicha's. I raise my hand to calm them both. 'The fact is, we've got no idea. Both are possible; both need investigating. Let's play to our strengths. Isaac, get digging into, well, anything you can think of. Aich, the same goes for you with modern reference points. Just rehash what was the main point about the water, please, Isaac?'

'Of course, lad. Um, let's see. So the main thing, really, was Bernadette having said she had to drink from and bathe in the dirty stream, which should at least have made her pretty sick. After that, it was the stream running clean. Oh, and the new stream appearing from a spot where she said the Lady had told her to dig. It's the spring itself that is supposed to cause healing for those who believe in the Lady nowadays at Lourdes.'

'So we have three potential elements. First, someone drinking and bathing in dirty stream water and not getting ill. Second, a dirty stream purifying to become crystal clean overnight. Third, magically appearing springs popping up from a spot designated to dig at by the Lady.' I mull it over, thinking back over the conversation, trying to make sure there is nothing any of us might have missed that can be the point the Mother was trying to guide us towards. I come up blank.

'I think that's it. I'll replay the conversation a couple of times later, see if there's anything else — keywords, nuances of speech, et cetera that pop up. If so, I'll pass the message on, but for the moment...' I pause and look around at them all, the grave seriousness of the situation clear in my eyes. 'For the moment, nothing *springs* to mind.'

Assorted groans and the covering of eyes reward that pun around the table. Aicha flicks a piece of squashed fruit at me with the end of her straw, which I catch magnificently in my open maw, raising my arms triumphantly, imitating the cheers of the crowd out of the sides of my mouth. I'll take that as a win and draw on it as an augury of what is to come. We've had little enough other positive omens until now. I am more than ready to indulge in a little comforting superstition at this point.

'Right, let's call it a night then,' I say.

'It's a night,' Aicha answers.

'Thank you for that one, Frank Drebin,' I continue, not missing a beat. 'I think we've got as far as we can for now, and frankly, I'm knackered and need to get my head down. None of us are going to be more use today. Isaac, Jakob, for the moment, tracking down the solution to the Mother's cryptic conundrum is the priority. Once we've got a solution for that, then we can get back to working out how to undo Franc's literal deadman's hand switch concerning those in his service. Aich –' I realise I only have one spare room at my house, which Aicha has been occupying.

'She can have the room, *saabi*. I'm in no desperate hurry to sleep. Thought I might take the lounge. Streaming services and internet research.'

'Sounds like a plan. In which case, if you're happy in the lounge, Susane, there's a spare room at mine, where you can get some rest.' I'm not entirely sure if seelie fae need to sleep, but I am pretty much certain that all sentient beings need some downtime to recuperate, especially after high stress scenarios like the one we've been through today. I feel like I've been dragged multiple times through the emotional wringer, and while she might have been better prepared for today on the grounds of knowing I was alive, I have enough empathy left underneath my exhaustion to recognise it couldn't have been entirely easy on her either. I can't go digging too deeply into that right now though. Tear the Band-Aid off the wound, and I'll fall apart, and there's no time for that. But I can recognise it's been hard for her even if I'm still paying the price for her lack of faith in me, for keeping her second chance at life a secret. Doesn't mean I am ready to pull an Elsa and let it go, but I'm not going to leave her to freeze outside on the street alone either.

She smiles and nods her acquiescence, and I smile back at her without feeling as though someone has made an intricate voodoo doll of the various chambers of my heart and then used it as a pincushion. That's progress. I think.

We finish our drinks, thank Claire, the owner, who is now behind the bar, and head out into the light swirling motion of the litter caught as the evening's breeze picks up, bringing fresher air with it. Whether it is the cleaning movement of the winds or the sense of progress made over drinks, the pressure seems to have eased somewhat. It doesn't feel like that clean, crisp break after a storm though. It is more like when the squall line changes course and passes miles to the side, letting the built-up atmosphere slowly leak away, back towards a baseline normality without the dramatic sense of passage. The darkened streets feel more open again but still pregnant with the possibility of more storms on the horizon.

Isaac heads back to his while we wend our way back the way we took to O'Bohem the day previous. It proves for me the whole "Time is an illusion" thing by Douglas Adams because the thirty hours or so since we last walked this same path seem to have stretched out to hang across a week, like the wrong sized sheet on an oversized bed. Or maybe it is that a week's worth of happenings have got condensed down, shrunken like Rick Moranis to fit their busyness into such a few hours. Either way, there is a shared exhaustion between the three of us, meaning we meander back pretty much in silence.

'Paul?' Aicha breaks the silence as we pass underneath the Pont Neuf, skirting around the hectic edges of the central part of town. It may not never sleep a la The Big Apple, but it certainly always keeps one eye open when it does and is probably faking its snores most of the time too.

'Yes, *laguna*?' I reply, enjoying the feeling of breathing easy and even more so as the city seems to mirror it. It feels good that we are back in step, at least somewhat.

'What you said about people who come back from Lourdes coming back...lessened. Memories gone, *talent* gone.'

'Yes, Aich?'

'They don't get bitey at all, do they?'

I stop and check Aich out as well as I can see in the half-light mix of moon and streetlamp, but she looks serious.

'Aich, they're victims of magical savagery. They're not zombies.'

'Sounds quite a lot like zombies to me. Urgh.' She shudders.

I fight hard –valiantly so– to suppress the rising grin. I'm not convinced it worked based on the rapidity of her eyes narrowing.

'What?'

'Are you scared of zombies, Aich?'

'I don't know. Are you scared of me sticking this knife through both your cheeks and pinning you to your front door?'

'Um, yes? I guess so?'

'Well, there then.'

The conversation lapses, and we continue towards home. A few minutes later, Aicha pipes up again. 'Just so you know, Paul, if this does unleash magical zombies, you're on your own. I'm going to the pub, grabbing a pint, and waiting for it all to blow over.'

'You don't even drink, *laguna*.'

'I do when there are magical zombies, *saabi*.'

'Fair point, well made.'

We get in, and Aicha waves a hand backwards over her shoulder as she strides into the lounge, shutting the door deliberately behind her. She'll set up camp in there from now until we are ready to head down to Lourdes itself, and I am happy to leave her to it. She seems to have her own equivalent of the memory palace specifically for pop culture in all its glory and obscurity, and it's an impressively catalogued knowledge at that. I am sure she already has an idea or two about where to go hunting for information about the Lady, and she'll do a far superior job than I'll ever manage.

I head upstairs and strip off the bed in the guest room, remaking it with spare clean sheets from the cupboard. There isn't any need to worry about moving out any of Aicha's belongings — the room is as clean and as sterile as a monk's cell. She has her own storage room, keyed to her, out in the corridor, that she can use if she wants to, and she's more than capable of stashing her belongings if needed. A bedroom for her has only one use, and that is sleeping. She isn't interested in personalising or prettifying it and has clarified that I never need to worry about going in when she isn't in there. The bed will be used. The room will just be. She isn't about to put up posters of rock stars or movies on the wall. I once joked about putting up a picture of Edward from *Twilight*. She informed me she'd force-feed it to me if I did. And not through my mouth. I took the hint.

As I come out, Susane is waiting in the hallway, leaning back against the wall, her arms crossing her body in a self-hug. The body language alone tells me how uncomfortable she feels, how much she needs to reassure herself. What is even more interesting is how much the "high fae" schtick she tried to use as a starting note after getting her nose broken by Aicha has dropped away. The rigid self-control and composure she projected have disappeared, and her thoughts and emotions are peeking through like nosy kids finding a broken fence panel at a high-walled haunted house. Funnily enough, I feel like I am said house, and the hauntings that have been keeping me empty and walled off have suddenly taken on flesh and turned up with a realtor and a suitcase full of cash looking for a quick purchase. I am not sure I am ready to buy any of it. I certainly don't want to sell myself short. My metaphor feels about as confused and as fuzzy as the inside of my head does. I mean, it is just that the only woman I have ever truly loved has come back from the dead. Standard Thursday for me, really. Or whatever the hell of the day of the week it actually is now. One with a Y in it, I'm fairly confident.

The soft lighting I set in the corridor to provide a gentler mood glow for the evenings also reduces the harsh contrast between how she looks now and my memory of her, making more subtle the changed skin colour, the inhuman beauty, her ear-tips blending into her hair. For a moment, I can see us back in the candlelit halls of the Cagot, bare and basic, where I felt young for the first time in centuries, giddy with love, and where I was truly happy for the last time since.

She looks up at me, and I wonder if I am imagining a hopefulness to her regard, a desire for resolution, for reconciliation. A thought crosses my mind, whether I painted that into her expression, reading what I subconsciously hoped would be there beneath that changed physique. I want my wife back, just as I have for hundreds of years. I've never regretted more abandoning my black Cathar robes than in discovering the pain of lost love and of lost child.

'How are you holding up, Paul?' she asks, brushing her hair back behind her ear with her left hand, bringing her otherness to the forefront. I try to focus on that, to hold on to the differences rather than the similarities that call to me and tell me to drop my guard and do something entirely stupid.

'I'm holding. Problem is, I wonder if I'm just the same as those last daft bastard Perfects, sitting placidly with my doom at my doorstep. Holding the line, but what line? Just another arbitrary decision about what's right, what's wrong, a moral code that's as outdated as I am and just as meaningless.' I sigh. It has been a long day, but it wouldn't be a complete clusterfuck without ending on an existential crisis, after all.

She places her hand softly on my cheek, her thumb tracing the tension embedded in my jawline. 'Don't give up just yet, *cherie*. Perhaps you've been holding the right line all along, even if they are just drawn in the sand.'

I look at her sharply at that, wondering if she knows more than she's saying, but the soft sadness to her smile tells me she is remembering our previous conversations, when I told her about my initial visit to that strange grey shoreline and the inscribed message that appeared. The coincidence is something to think on though, and strangely, it seems to have given me a bit of an answer. I can feel a touch of pep entering my step again. I am exhausted, battered, and bruised by recent events and by the weight of responsibility I carry regarding decisions old and new. Still, I know in my heart of hearts that I'll always strive to do the right thing, to repay the extra turns of the hourglass that I keep getting.

I'm not really one for fate, but I can't help feeling there is a reason for it all, that someone higher up is in my corner. I'd love if they were more direct in their communication than a written two- or three-word message every eight hundred years, but we can't always get what we want. The fact that they are still helping me out in my direst hour so many centuries on suggests whatever they want from me hasn't yet been achieved. It also means they haven't given up on me yet. Maybe I shouldn't either.

'Thanks, Suze. I think you're right. It's been a tough few days.' I smile back. Concentrating on her eyes, I can see the woman I swore to hold in my arms every day for eternity, to find a path to immortality for once she gave birth to our son. I'd never have risked him, not for anything in the world, not even for her.

The thought brings the pain of his loss, of finding her mutilated and his body taken, and I wince, breaking eye contact, turning my head aside. She must have seen it or at least enough of it because she steps in, pressing herself against my body, not sexually but with that proximate sharing of presence that carries at least some alleviation in the moment, even to wounds that can never heal. She lays a chaste kiss on my cheek.

'I miss him too, Paul,' she murmurs, and we stay like that, her holding me almost as tightly as the grief does, paying no mind to my free-flowing tears streaking salt traces down her forehead. In the half-light, I can't be sure if her own join them in their journey downwards. In this moment, I don't really care. I'm so grateful for this second of communion I never thought I'd get ever again, even as the pain flows freely.

An unspecified amount of time later, which feels like both seconds and centuries, she releases me, pulling back to look at me, still wearing that same strange sad smile.

'It'll be okay, Paul. And it's okay to not be okay when it isn't, as well. You're doing your best, and it's better than most could ever manage.'

I think about doing my best Sean Connery impression with the, 'Only losers do their best,' line, but I recognise it'll probably be wasted on Susane. I'm guessing catching up on Michael Bay films wasn't high on her priority list since getting back to Earth. I also feel that, while it might help me keep my emotional protections in place often, right now, it'll just cheapen the moment. Also, explaining the joke would just ruin it, and I am too damn funny to want to ruin a single drop of my comedic genius. I'll just run with the latter as the main reason if anyone ever asks. Or I'll keep my mouth shut about the entire thing. Probably even better.

'Thanks, Suze. It's...hard to see you. I mean, Jesus, unbelievably hard, knife in my heart, crumble my life structure to dust level hard to see you. But it's good to see you even though it hurts so very fucking much.' I laugh. 'Apparently, I'm an emotional masochist. Who fucking knew?'

I didn't even realise she was holding my fingers in hers until she drops them, so gentle was her touch. 'I think you know yourself better than you think you do, Paul. There's a reason good people stick by you every single time. Give yourself a bit of credit now and then.' There is a mischievous glint in her eyes that makes me want to go full on Captain Caveman and swing her over my shoulder just like back in the old days, whisking her away to her boudoir. 'I let you ask me to marry you, after all. If you're ever unsure of your worth, just remember that.'

'I might just, at that,' I say, matching her grin for a moment. I then do the mental equivalent of a ten-gallon ice bucket challenge, reinstating my iron-willed self-control to stop me from doing anything monumentally stupid like trying to seduce my now-fae wife, who has just walked back into my life from beyond the grave. Emotions go brrrrrrrr.

'I think I'd better go get some rest.' And an actual proper cold shower.

She nods and moves away from me, pushing back against the wall to give me space to pass. 'I think we're all going to need it before this little adventure is done. Unfortunately, you do tend to draw trouble to you just as easily as good people, Good Man Bonhomme.'

I can't really dispute that, so I settle for a tip of my imaginary hat and force myself to walk on down the corridor, away from the only woman I've ever truly loved in eight hundred years and back to the relative safety of my empty bedroom.

CHAPTER TWENTY-TWO
TOULOUSE, 10 APRIL, PRESENT DAY

I never sleep 'cos sleep is the cousin of death. Actually, he's her brother, and my lack of sleeping probably has more to do with how often I run into her.

I wake up feeling like going to bed was a gross error of judgement. Considering the amount of tossing and turning I did, my subconscious is entirely in agreement as well. I slept in snatched moments of torturous dreams, reliving all the deaths I failed to stop and all those I caused too. You'd think as someone living in an eternal cycle of reincarnation I'd be used to the idea of death and life as cyclic, but seeing two other people break that expected cycle and for them both to be people who mattered deeply to me has apparently thrown a spanner in my psyche's works. Dragging myself out of bed, I stumble into my ensuite to verify that, yes, I do indeed look like shit warmed up. Thankfully, because of the miracle of indoor plumbing (and let me be categorically clear — fuck magic. When you've lived through the sights and sounds and *smells* of societal advancement, toilets and showers are the shiznits), I can at least make sure I don't carry the same odour.

After I scrub away the lingering touch of days on the road, if not quite the smell of a man stewing in his own self-pity, I stumble down the stairs before coming to a dead halt. Reality has clearly just ducked out, popping down the shop to pick up a packet of cigarettes and a strawberry Cornetto. Why? Because there are pancakes waiting for me at the breakfast table.

And when I say pancakes, I don't mean the little, easily churned out, American bite-size snacks packed with butter and sugar. I mean proper French pancakes — light and thin like little wedding veils draped across my blushing plate. There is lemon juice and sugar, and surely the gods have taken mercy on a poor, broken immortal for there is melted chocolate — a pot of fresh liquid gold smelted down to form the perfect ideal of what the cacao bean could be.

On the other side, plate piled high, Aicha feeds pancakes into her mouth as if they're dead bodies into a wood chipper, and she's desperate to dispose of the evidence. She drops her fork as I draw breath, shutting forefinger and thumb, instructions for what to do with my mouth.

'Zpt.' she says.

'Bu–'

'Dftt.'

'Ai–'

'Nyheuh, zippit, eat.'

'Where did these come from?'

Susane comes round the corner, carrying a fresh batch. 'Paul! I hope you don't mind. I don't really sleep these days, and I was at a bit of a loose end — lost up in all sorts of thoughts. I needed something to do with my hands.'

I may not have turned bright red at those words, but that is simply because of my blood stream being about as awake and reactive as the rest of me. My imagination, on the other hand, has already chugged five or six coffees and is more than happy to throw up a mixture of memories and desires. Thoughts of breaking our fast together, then diving back upstairs to stay in bed till hunger drove us out again, still giggling like school kids.

They almost, *almost* distract me from the food on the table.

Aicha jabs at us furiously with her fork. 'You — thank you. Shut up. You — just shut up. Sit. Eat. Or else...' And there is no doubt as to the veracity of what she is saying. 'I. Will. Eat. Them. All.'

This is clearly a plethora of syllables more than she wanted to say. In fact, she is now entirely excluding anything that will distract her from the presence of food and will probably forcibly eradicate anything foolish enough to interrupt the flowing tidal wave of pancakes heading into her mouth.

I am precisely that foolish. 'It's like witnessing Shai Hulud arriving to swallow a thumper whole. Nononoononononoooo...'

I intercept her fork as it heads to impale the entire stack left on the table by hastily grabbing my own utensil. A swift back-and-forth battle ensues that switches between Bonetti's Defence before her Thibault cancels out my Capa Ferro. At last, I flick the implement across to my left hand and skewer some of the delectable breakfast treats. I set up a defensive perimeter around my plate, sending out cautious sorties to procure the chocolate sauce while protecting my ill-gotten gains.

The next half hour passes in one of those silences when the pleasures being delivered to taste buds are only surpassed by the gluttonous excesses available. I stuff myself with all the pancakes I can, and luckily Aicha's early start means she is more carb loaded already than I am, meaning her reactions have slowed, allowing me to gather more of the deliciousness into my greedy clutches. Coffee appears miraculously in due course, and thus the morning becomes inscribed in the annals of history as the perfect morning, incarnated for one fleeting breakfast time in April. I feel fuller than I can ever remember feeling and am blissed out on a sugar high that is neatly underlined with the caffeine hit. I am up and running and ready to take on the world. Or at least, a mysterious *talent*-devouring Lady, who is probably going to swallow me whole and not in the good way.

That thought puts a damper on my mood that even excessive sweet intake can't get rid of. Apparently, my brain can sabotage even patisserie-induced states of bliss. I shake my mental fist at my grey matter like a curmudgeonly astral traveller who has discovered out-of-body experiences at exactly the same moment when all he really wants is to read the paper and drink a cup of tea, thank you very much.

The vibration of my phone saves me from the insanity of my imagination. A quick look shows me it is Isaac calling, so I accept and pop it on speakerphone.

'Paul, I think I've got something!' Isaac's voice is trembling with an excitement that indicates he almost certainly hasn't slept in the preceding twelve hours, lost in the inconceivable joys of hunting through endless manuscripts and weighty tomes. I am aware he'll be running on dregs and also that he'll be entirely incapable of recognising that fact. I know what needs to be done.

'Isaac...' I reply.

'Yes?'

'I've got *pancakes*, Isaac. *Really, really good* pancakes, Isaac.' I drop my voice further into a conspiratorial murmur. 'Really, really good pancakes *with homemade chocolate sauce*, Isaac.'

'Oh, my word! Isaac, I haven't eaten pancakes in hundreds of years. Tell him we'll come to his straight away. You just told him yourself, Jak. You just took control of our mouth. I'm so sorry, Isaac, how unforgivably rude of me not to seek permission prior, just swept away by the moment. I get that you're excited, don't worry. Paul, apparently, you've sold Jak on it anyhow...'

'I picked that up,' I say drily.

'And I'll admit, a bite to eat after a hard night's graft wouldn't go amiss. I'll head on over now, and we'll be there shortly.'

'Perfect,' I say brightly. 'I can see there's a parking space free right outside.'

There is a momentary pause. 'Well, maybe it'll be gone by the time we get there.'

'I can save it for you if you'd like?'

'No, no need. If it's gone, we'll park elsewhere. Sure we'll find plenty of options this time of the morning. See you shortly, lad.'

The line goes dead as Susane pokes her head out of the kitchen, and I realise I've made one of the classic blunders, and it isn't by starting a land war in central Asia.

'Um, Suse...' I start, and I watch her display that sudden alert stillness that women get when they know a man has volunteered them to do something stupid or time-consuming or probably both without asking them first.

'You wouldn't mind making another batch of those pancakes for Isaac and Jak, would you? Umm, you see, they're coming round, and I think they've been up all night, and...'

'You've already told them I will, haven't you?'

'I mean, not precisely. I told them that there were pancakes — incredible pancakes,' I add hurriedly, 'and that they are available here at this present moment in time. That might mean that they are coming over, expecting to eat said incredible pancakes, but I never specifically said those wondrous creations of culinary genius would still be available on their arrival. So, technically, no, I haven't volunteered you for the job yet.' I finish with a hopeful smile that is half intended as an underlining of my flattering charm, half as a kneeling beg on behalf of my good friends for her to provide them with her manna from heaven.

She rolls her eyes at my display, but I see the corner quirk of her mouth, no matter how much she tries to hold it in place. I am still the charming dog I believe myself to be. Woof.

When the knock at the door comes less than half an hour later, I can't help noticing that the parking space is still there and that the car is not. I give the space a two-handed Khaby Lame-style indication, and the faintest tinge of red appears on Isaac's cheeks.

'Aye, I came across some parking further up and didn't want to risk this one not being there, what with pancakes on offer and hungry bellies to fill. Please tell me there are still pancakes, Paul? Of course there are. He'd not play such mean tricks. I am so excited! I picked up on that, Jak. If you remember, I had to tell you to stop shouting in my head while I was driving so as not to wrap the car round a tree at each corner. Rather, sorry, old chap. Just, I really am rather partial to pancakes. I'm your brother, Jak; I remember well, and I'm sorry I haven't sorted it out until now.'

'Look,' I interrupt. 'As much as I enjoy watching this one body ventriloquist show — and just to be absolutely clear, Isaac, you're definitely the dummy — the table is laid and ready, and the pancakes aren't going to get any more fucking mind-blowingly awesome, so I suggest you stow the words and hit the serve.'

That is all the encouragement either of them needs. Isaac shoots past me, although he kicks off his loafers en route, showing that his mind still holds some mastery over the insistences of both his brother and his belly. Once he sits down, I surreptitiously top up his coffee cup while marvelling at how well he can incorporate manners with speed, clearing through the stacked dough-nations to the good cause of rejuvenating his energy levels. Dough-nations. Ha. I look over at Aicha to share that one with her, but the intensity of the concentration she's fixing on Isaac makes me pause. She truly cares about him. She wants to know what he knows, but she's letting him eat first rather than extricating it from him at the business end of the nearest pointy thing. As I once watched her disembowel a mountain troll with a disposable plastic spork, a breakfast spread holds a glut of suitable options. Her self-restraint is to be applauded. It is not, however, to be tested by my mesmerising wordplay. Turns out I have a self-preservation instinct sometimes, after all.

Once Isaac manages the impossible task of effectively inhaling the pancakes and doing so with style and finesse simultaneously, he looks up, startled to find three pairs of eyes fixed on him expectantly, having watched him lost in mastication until this point.

'What?' he asks, clearly panicking that he has sinned beyond all measure and left a crumb of food or a smudge of chocolate on his face.

I resist the urge to shake him. Even more impressively, so does Aicha.

'What did you find out, man?' I ask, feeling like the impatience has to be pouring out of my ears and forming a cloud over my head like an angry Dick Dastardly.

'Oh, right, of course. Ahem. Well, I may have an idea about who it is that you're dealing with. An idea only, mind you. It all started with the clue we extracted from the Mother in Bordeaux. You see, I knew the idea of a spring appearing as a signifier of a compact and an ascendance to power rang some bell in the back of this dusty old grey matter. Well, I dug through a number of poems and classical retellings, but it wasn't until I stumbled onto the classic text by Jean D'Arras that I –'

'Skip. To. The. End,' Aicha grinds out.

'Ah, yes, well, sorry. I think, and only think, mind you, that the Lady of Lourdes may be Melusine herself.'

'Ah,' I say.

'Right,' I say.

'Bugger,' I say.

There is a significant silence. Then Susane holds her hand up. 'Sorry, who?' she asks.

I think Isaac's eyes are going to pop out of his head, which only adds to my sense of having got transported somehow into a seventies cartoon.

'All right, calm down, Doctor Honeydew. Not everyone gets their rocks off from ancient mythology or considers translating ancient languages as foreplay, okay? Life for the Cagots was spectacularly unfriendly back when she was human, so there weren't many copies of courtly tales circulating amongst the population. Since then, she's been living in a fucking fairy tale, literally, so she might have been more preoccupied with surviving Oberon's court than with what happened a thousand years ago.'

'More than a thousand years ago, actually, lad. About twelve hundred from what I can work out from the texts I've studied. What?'

'Hold on just a minute,' I say and get up from the table. I head over to the desk in the study and rummage around until I find a marker and a blank piece of paper. I draw a huge positive checkmark on it and then hand it over to Isaac, who looks totally lost.

'What's this?' he asks, his brow furrowed.

'It's your pedant tick. You've earned it. Use it wisely,' I say as Aicha groans behind me.

'Paul, you're hilarious. Isaac, could you please, concisely, tell me who Melusine is?'. There is a definite strain in the way Susane says *please* that carries an amount of suppressed frustration that can make an IED out of a pressure cooker.

'Okay, let me explain,' Isaac starts, but I interrupt.

'No, there's too much. Let me sum up.' Aicha gives me a high five for that one, so it was worth it. I know Isaac's knowledge is a million times more in-depth than mine, but that means it'll take him a million times longer to get to the fucking point, which might well lead to Susane pulling a Michael Douglas in *Falling Down* manoeuvre on us.

'Right, Melusine is a faerie, according to legend, rocking around near Poitou in around about the ninth century, *give or take a hundred years. Yes, thank you, Isaac.* She is supposedly responsible for the founding of most of the major royal families of Europe through her offspring with a local lord, with various members of various ruling lineages claiming descendancy. In fact, correct me if I'm wrong, Isaac, albeit succinctly, please, but wasn't she herself only supposed to be half-fae? Right, I thought so. If I remember, the King of Scotland wooed her mother. She married him on the condition that he never enter her chamber whilst she was giving birth. Now most men would have jumped at this condition, especially back in those days, but the eedjit still messed it up and went in, at which point she fled, heading back to one of the fae realms with her kids.

'Anyhow, she proceeded to bad mouth their dad to the three girls, so when they grew up, they decided to go all Park Chan-wook and seek some serious vengeance on him. They tricked him and sealed him in a mountain, then headed back, eager for mum's approval.

'Well, mum turned out to be erratic in her angst and anger, basically immediately siding with dear old dad and condemning them all as terrible, disloyal daughters despite having spent their childhood slagging him off. Not only condemning them but cursing them all as well in a variety of ways I can't remember entirely, mainly 'cos all the stories were about Melusine rather than her sisters.

'Anyhow, Melusine decides that the whole family scenario is a bust, so does one by heading over to France, where she sets up with a local noble who isn't a king but promises him the moon on a stick –power, riches, legacy, the whole shebang– as long as he never comes into her bedchamber on a Saturday. He doesn't seem to ask questions about any of this, although by all the accounts, she is both mind-blowingly beautiful and very sharp too. I suspect it's probably because of the former rather than the latter that he just accepts all this. Anyhow, she somehow makes an entire castle appear, including servants and courtiers, which this apparently god-fearing man doesn't seem to think is even slightly suss, and — Yes, Isaac, what is it before you actually burst?'

'That's where I found the reference! It all started with her creating a spring out of thin air! If that's the causal link, I think it makes sense.'

'Isaac, you are a certified genius or, at the very least, should be certified. Either way, we bow before you and are not worthy of being in your presence. Getting back to the story at hand. The couple in question have multiple children, which is the most hilarious part of it all if I remember right. These are all the progenitors of the royal houses throughout Europe, and the guy writing this epic poem is doing so at the demand of one of the houses of Lusignan, claiming direct descent, but all the kids have, like, weird deformities. So the writer is like, "Oh, Geoffrey was noted for being the most handsome man that any human has ever seen, except for having one tooth as long as your fucking arm". No jokes. The kid was actually called Geoffrey Bigtooth. The others all have only one eye or are covered in fur or have one ear twice the size of the other, and the writer is constantly saying how everyone agrees that they are the very model of physical perfection, then mentions their physical deformity and skips straight on to the rest of the story. But I digress.

'Anyhow, everything is going pretty well. According to the story, several of the children fuck off to fight the terrible Moors in Jerusalem, but that was all standard pro-Crusade propaganda — drumming up support for bloody wars, covering the supposed Holy Land in death and misery. Not what I call respectful, but then Cathars never did see eye to eye with Mother Church, I suppose. The main point is that, would you believe it, at some point, the hubby finally decides there's something weird going on, mainly when other nobles ask questions about the whole "never being seen on a Saturday" thing. He goes to have a goosey, and lo-and-behold, his super devout wife turns into a fucking Naga-style thing every weekend. She's there, lying in a bath, and her bottom half is a snake or serpent of some kind. Anyhow, he's then broken the contract, and I've got to admit it all gets a bit murky in my memory from hereon in. I think she gets thoroughly pissed off and maybe transforms into a dragon? Either way, she fucks off, and the rest of the story follows the various offsprings' lordly adventures, I think. The legend got passed around and picked up by other countries. Both Germany and Britain claimed her as well, but the signs were that it all started in France, and certainly there's still a castle at Poitou that locals insist is the one she made appear out of nowhere. How did I do, Isaac?'

He nods slowly, thinking it over. 'Pretty good, actually. It's like someone tried to teach you the importance of study once upon a time. You're right about the dragon, and indeed, she's supposed to have returned to the castle in serpentine form at various times, but yes, otherwise, after that, she disappears from legend for, well, forever, until now if we've got this right.'

'So why the Pyrenees? Why Lourdes?'

'Well, I can answer that,' he says, looking slightly smug as he reseats his glasses on his nose. 'One of her sisters, Palatyne, got cursed to guard her father's treasure, which was fabled to be powerful enough to win back the

Holy Land for the Crusaders if they could find it. Well, that mountain was Mount Canigou, and can you guess where it's located?'

'The Pyrenees?' I ask, not really hesitating, but, hey, he did all the grunt work. I am happy to play patsy to his big reveal, especially as I've already stolen some of his thunder by telling the story of Melusine in less than a gazillion years.

'The Pyrenees,' he confirms, nodding sagely.

'Okay, so what? Husband fucks up, she fucks off and goes and bunks up with her sister for a thousand years before deciding to create a place of supposed healing where she eats people's magic?'

Isaac looks less sure. 'Yes?' he says doubtfully.

Susane raises her hand. 'I've got a couple of questions.'

'I think we've all got more than a couple, but go for it,' I say.

'So, I guess, number one, why were you so worried when Isaac said he thought it might be Melusine?' Susane looks genuinely puzzled, and I guess my ability to impart subtext to my storytelling isn't as good as I thought it was.

'Right, so I guess you missed the whole bit where she *materialised an entire fucking castle and court from thin air*? Don't get me wrong, courtier storytellers weren't known for restraint in terms of their flights of fancy, but if that's even vaguely close to true, then we're talking minor deity levels of *talent* at least. Also, I'm not sure if you missed the bit where she can shapeshift into a fucking dragon? As in, ginormous lizard with impenetrable scales, likes shiny things, seriously deadly form of halitosis? That's bad news. Dragons are tough as nails as a rule of thumb. Fae shapeshifting dragons –'

'Who eat magic.'

'– who — yes, thanks for the reminder, Aich, eat magic is some next level of toughness. Toughness squared or something. I guess it's not incredibly shocking that whoever captured or killed Ahmad is a certified badass, but the whole dragon thing is just the cherry on the piece of shit-cake that this complete debacle promises to be. Dragons can be quite reasonable as long as you're not trying to steal their horde –'

'Except for the Tarrasque,' Isaac interjects.

'Yeah, true, he's a proper arsehole. Fuck the Tarrasque all day, every day. Point is though, we aren't dealing with a dragon, where if we could produce appropriately valuable objects then we might barter for whatever we want. We're dealing with a god-like fae being who sired a large part of the ruling classes of Europe and then happily disappeared off into obscurity for a thousand years just because her husband saw her true form. That isn't really what I'd call reasonable behaviour.'

'If it's true.'

'Good point, Suse, if it's true. This is stuff from the depths of known history. How much is real and how much is rumour is bloody hard to sort out.'

'You brought me nicely to my second point, though, Paul. You said she sired the royal houses of Europe, right?'

'Yep, or so they all fell over themselves to claim afterwards, anyhow.'

'So if she was half-fae, then they were at least a quarter-fae. So how come all the royals over the last few hundred years haven't been seriously Talented or have fae-like beauty? How come they didn't end up coming back as fae once they died, like we do?'

I stop, stunned. 'That...is a fantastic point. I literally never even thought of that. Isaac?'

His expression mirrors mine. 'Well, we can't know if they come back as fae given how tight-lipped they are, but the rest...never even thought of it either. Bloody hell, lass. That makes no sense.'

'None,' I agree. 'I mean, it's not like they didn't keep it in the family enough inbreeding-wise to ensure that *talent* would grow instead of diminishing. I'd think Louis XVI might have been less easily led to the guillotine if he could set every dickhead on fire with a single thought.'

'Latter part might be true still,' Aicha says nonchalantly.

I swivel in her direction. 'What?'

'Latter part might be true. Royals as fae. Resurrecting after death. Makes more sense than them being blood-drinking, shapeshifting lizard aliens, and lots of people believe that.'

'Lots of people shouldn't be allowed to tie their shoelaces or leave the house unaccompanied either, Aich.'

'Still might be true. Maybe royals all resurrect as fae nobility after death.'

I look over at Isaac for help, but he looks completely blank.

'It's a reasonable suggestion, I guess?' he offers.

'I know it's a reasonable suggestion,' I snap back. 'We are being completely outclassed here in terms of suggestions. Get your head back in the game.'

Aicha turns her attention towards me lazily, like a predator that has already done all the mental maths and knows you've got precisely zero chance of getting outside their strike range. 'Are you really trying to make this a boys versus girls scenario, *saabi*? Are you really that stoopid?'

Once again, Isaac is there, carrying a whole barrel-load of salt, ready to rub it all into the wound grain by grain. 'Indeed, lad, hardly fair. With Jak, that makes three versus two.'

'Isaac, you're about as helpful as a paper oven glove dipped in ethanol. Look, all of this is dragging us away from the main point. Resurrecting royal fae might make for an interesting side quest someday, but right now I want us to get on to the next checkpoint, if that's okay. Susane, I'll explain what all of that meant and what video games are later. Please, put your hand down. It's bloody strange, I'll admit, but I don't think it's got a huge amount of bearing on what needs to be done now. Now, Franc told us...'

I stop, the words trailing off as realisation catches up with my mouth, and I look across at Aicha, who nods. 'You are, indeed, a total fucking dumbass, Paul.'

For a moment all I can do is gape at her. *She knew.* She fucking knew and didn't say anything. There's a second of fury that she kept it from me, not giving a rat's arse what happens to Franc. But she's made her point clear, and I've not been in any danger. This is Aicha's equivalent of giving me a right talking to. She doesn't think I should have got involved the way I have, and this is the "I told you so". With added "you're a fucking idiot". I'm sure if push had come to shove, she'd have told me. Eventually. Definitely that I'm a fucking idiot.

I can't even argue. I groan and put my head between my hands and then start banging it on the table. I am operating on the principle that it might kickstart my brain into working properly, but it certainly can't make it do a shittier job than it has been.

'What's going on?' Susane asks, looking concerned, whether for my physical or mental wellbeing, I am unsure.

'He didn't ask Franc. Franc told us to go there, and he didn't think to ask him who the Lady is. Made the same mistake last time. Told him then. Wasn't going to tell him again. Can't wipe his bum for him every time,' Aicha answers, shaking her head in rhythm with the banging of mine. 'Men, am I right?'

She is most certainly, indubitably, absolutely right. Bugger.

Chapter Twenty-Three
TOULOUSE, 10 APRIL, PRESENT DAY

Missing — one brain. Not much used but still somewhat damaged. If found, please return to Paul Bonhomme.

Our next course of action is clear. I check to make sure no one has any further information or ideas (they don't). We are tidying away the breakfast, ready to head out to find Franc or one of his affiliates when Susane's phone rings.

She answers the video call, and as soon as I see the streak marks of tears down the cheeks of the Mother of the Sistren of Bordeaux, I know this isn't going to be a pleasant chat about the weather.

'There is no more time,' she croaks, her voice cracking from grief carried in salt. 'There is no more time, and there are those who made promises still sat in their homes.'

'We have a lead, and we think we have a name, Mother. Melusine. We just need to check a few more things and then...'

'*She is dying now!*'

The silence carries in it that purest form of sorrow, the breaking of a heart at that most unbearable of prospects, a parent outliving a child. It is the robbing of life, of joy, of colour, of taste, a reduction of everything to ashes, kindling made of meaning as it burns away to nothingness. It is uncontaminated pain, untainted misery, a vibrant agony that leeches away the hope that still just clings on. And it is my fault. Not alone, but it is my fault.

'How long?' I whisper eventually, although it takes a few swallows to wet my throat enough to make words, as though her tears have drawn my moisture out as well with their potency.

The woman on the other end no longer looks like a proud witch queen, a noble dignitary, a powerhouse who wields more *talent* through her assembled flock than most can ever dream of. She looks like a mother who has carried fears from that first moment when a fist wrapped in instinct round a proffered finger and a new life wrapped itself around an old heart, and sheer, pure terror at all the possibilities for harm or misfortune became a constant boon companion. To have them proven true is a burden more terrible than anyone should ever have to bear.

'Two days, maybe three.' Her voice is paper thin, so that her very breath might puncture the words and they will drain away. All energy is gone; a tiredness is settling into her bones that will never leave again, not truly, if we don't achieve the impossible within the next forty-eight hours.

'I... We're leaving. We're going to gather one of Franc's boys and try to drag any information out of him, but then we're going, Mother,' I say, decided. I can see the alarm on Isaac's face, and the sad certainty on Aicha's. Of course, no one else sees it. It is a sign of how well I know her. Just like that certainty is a sign of how well she knows me. It's the look of the commanding officer in the trenches when word comes down from on high to prepare to go over the top. We're leading the charge, and me saying we'll go is the same as shouting to fix bayonets as we step into the firing line of the machine guns. We're nowhere near ready for this confrontation. She knows it. I know it. And it makes no difference. We've run out of time.

'There will be a need for an exchange on neutral ground where tricks cannot be played, and where a certain monster cannot seek instantaneous revenge when regaining his powers. There is transport organised to get to Narbonne and the Null Zone. Magic does not stick to her nor help her, so there's no reason to wait.' There is a bitterness to her words. Those of a woman used to commanding fate finding magic has failed her when she most needs it. It is something I am more than aware of. Thinking about that, I come close to missing her next and final words.

'Please. Please save my child.' I almost can't hear her. A chimney-whistling wind expels from her lungs, carrying a last pleading hope, and then the line goes dead. I know I've committed myself not only to a course of action but also a dramatically tightened up timeframe.

'Right, Franc's. Now,' I say grimly, and we head out of the door.

We pull up at La Chapelle and pile out just as Isaac pulls up behind us. The car he's been so embarrassed about? It is only a sodding Tesla Model S.

'This? This is what you've been trying to hide from us?' I ask disbelievingly.

He shuffles, looking at his feet as he pushes the batwing door down. 'Aye, well, it's a bit showy, ain't it, lad? Not really my style, but...'

He stops shuffling, and his head lifts purposefully. 'I was the one who asked. I missed out on the entire period of the combustion engine, outside of when Ben ported me from place to place in a bag or the like, my dear boy. I've seen what they can do, and I wanted to skip the whole petrol part and go electric, and honestly...' There is a wistfulness forming in his borrowed eyes as Jakob speaks. 'It's like something out of a far-flung dream even now, so impossibly fast, so of the future brought to the now. I've been stuck long enough away. I want to live a little even if the body isn't really mine.'

'It is so yours, Jak. "Mine is yours" was always more than just words between us. We'll share it till one of us breaks it. Or,' Isaac says with a grin to show me he is at least half-joking as he nods at me. 'More likely he does.'

I shrug. The possibility is present; I can't deny it.

We push into the building where Franc reclines on the chaise longue, like they've made Arthur Daley emperor of a crumbling Roman empire. A man, barely more than a boy, stands next to him, one I've not seen before. He's a handsome youth, and the wear of the street still doesn't mark him, although he's seen enough misery for that to be carried in his face — from before his new life roaming if I were any judge. I guess that's the reason he ended up coming to Franc. His features are sharp — defined, prominent cheekbones, but the most surprising thing is an innocence that still hangs about in his eyes. It speaks of faith. Unless I miss my mark, despite everything he's stood witness to in his short life, he still believes in people. Then I see him look down, just for a moment, at the gigantic, reclined form, and see almost reverence in that glance, and I groan internally. It is even worse. He still believes in Franc.

The monster raises his head. Bruise marks surround his eyes from my fists' earlier impacts and around his throat from the push of Aicha's boot. Those should have long healed. It looks like the Mother's daughter isn't the only one running short on time.

'Well, the little lordling, the delecicious sword-swinger and the wisery one...' He peers, then spits to his side. 'Now the wisery four, and all feathery flitterings for the halvery, upon my oath. Ready to be taking your leaverings, are you, boyo?'

'A couple of questions first, Franc, if you please. Do you know who the Lady is? Is it Melusine?' I ask first, ready to get to the point.

'But of course 'tis her and her alone, all quick to smilings and crunchings, she is, she is. Did you not know then? Why didn't you ask old Franc when here all hand-crackerings and pain-dealery?'

I try to ignore the quiet, 'Because he's a knob head,' from Aicha and focus on the situation at hand. 'Do you know how she manages to bespell the Talented, Franc?'

The creature gurgles a phlegmy chuckle and looks me in the eye, his face-splitting grin showing razors where broken dentures normally lurk. His glamour is cracking, crumbling away as he does. 'How does a pretty thing ever manage such a trapsering, all flutteries of lashings and lascivious of lookings, is it not? Had your heart a-picked by snappy stringings, hasn't you, my boy? Well, she and her will pluck a melodious meddling of medleys that will fill your eyes like the little cherubing's arrows, my word, my life.'

It matches with my thoughts on the whole matter. The story we drew upon for Melusine's origins will be a mixture of fact and fiction, but I don't doubt that she did some pretty major magic in front of a Christian Lord, and he and his companions paid it no mind while he went ahead and married her. The fae are well known for their ability to bewitch a mortal man and blind him to everything but their beauty. Looks like that is a major part of her arsenal of abilities we'll be running up against. It also makes me wonder if the Mother didn't have an inkling of where this might lead to even before I visited Franc. The fact she sent the only woman to ever steal my heart away along with us suddenly seems like a mighty convenient coincidence.

'What about her granting of miracles?' Aicha asks, and I am thankful for her ability to stay focused while I am off chasing another train of thought.

'A thingery-me-bobbing, upon my oath, all bounded bonery that channels her largessings as I does hear, and I does hear, is it not? Still thinks herself a queenling, bountiful in her generouses, so she is. Just takes from them that strays too close to her chasse reverse turnery and whirls them off and away till they're offed and away, I believes. Not of my knowings, though, just of my thinkings, they are, they are.'

'We're going now, Franc. Is this who you're sending with us?' I ask, looking again at the young man, who still seems only to have eyes for the dying monstrosity.

'Aye, the loveliest of all my lovely ones, he is, new but no mewling pettifoggery to the miserings and moanings of the sufferers, no indeed. A brave boy, a brightling, that I'll have returned safe and securings by your leave upon your leavings.'

'We'll do our best to bring him back safe, Franc. I'd worry about yourself in the meantime. Will you be able to reach us through the boy?'

'Aye, though my time may be belittlinged and brokery, no length or longings, no matter wish or wherefores.'

'It'll have to do.' I turn my attention to the youngster, who meets my eyes with a determination that speaks of courage or naivety or most likely, a healthy mixture of the two. 'What's your name, kid?'

'Gil,' he replies and hesitantly offers me his hand. He straightens his back as he does so, aware of his position and posture, trying to radiate capability and confidence. 'Gil, sir,' he repeats.

I shake his hand and give him a gentle smile, trying to set him at ease rather than disarm him. 'I'm no sir, and this isn't the army, Gil. Has Franc told you where we're going?'

'Yes, sir. I mean yes,' he replies. Nothing else comes, and I get the impression he was a boy of few words before meeting Franc and probably a young man of even fewer words since.

'Fine, as long as you know what you're signing up for. I haven't got time to brief you further. Time is a-wasting, and we need to go.'

Isaac turns to me as we head back outside. 'How do you want to divide up the people? I can take Franc's lad with me if you want?'

I slow and turn to look at him. 'Isaac, you can't come. You're needed here.'

His hands ball up, not because he is ready to lash out at me but in sheer frustration. 'Don't do this to me, Paul. You can't leave us out on this one. It's too dangerous. For goodness' sake, man, we're the most powerful one here, at least on the defensive. And you might well need defending this time, my boy.'

I put my hand on his shoulder, making the physical connection that is sometimes so damn necessary when circumstances start forcing a divide between two people as close as it's possible to be without a blood bond, perhaps even more so. 'Isaac, Jak too, I know you want nothing but the best for me, to look out for me, same as you've always done. And I'd give my left arm to have you next to me for this one. I'm not going to lie. I'm pretty freaked out by this. There's a damn good reason Lourdes has become the equivalent of a no-fly zone for us all. I don't want to disappear, and I want even less to end up like Jean did. But I might do. I really might, man. I think the odds are against us winning this one, and if we lose...' I swallow hard. 'If I lose, then that's it. The girl will die, Franc will die, and if you don't do something, every one of Franc's people will die too. You've got the base theory sorted. Now you just have to up the range. Go back in there, borrow one of Franc's people and send them to Hastingues.'

I reach into my etheric storage and pull out a blank business card that I imbue with *talent*, scrawling the magical equivalent of a signature across it. 'Give this to whoever he's sending, and Lou won't eat them. More importantly, he'll give them the skulls. Franc's too weak to fuck us over, and it's against all his self-interest. If we need to find a different stash spot afterwards, fine. Let's cross that bridge when we come to it. Meanwhile, get those people saved. Be on call to help us solve any magical conundrums we encounter. See if you can divert a part of your combined brain-power to work out the equivalent of lashing Odysseus to the mast with beeswax in the ears to get us past her siren song if you can. But you've got...' I pause and think through how long the trip is going to take. 'A bit over two hours, which will give us time to park and come up with at least a basic plan to get ourselves in there. Anything that springs to mind in that time, brill, call us and shoot it over. After that, concentrate on the matter at hand. Save the people you can. Make what we're trying to do count if we don't succeed.'

Isaac paws at his glistening eyes. 'Bloody hell, making an old man tear up, you bugger. I'd say don't get yourself killed, but odds on that are precisely zero, but Paul...' The intensity is strong, and I feel like a son heading off to war after a father can't turn his boy away from the spit shine and ceremony. 'Make sure you hot-wire a body afterwards and come back, lad. Make sure you come back.'

'I'll try. That's all I can say, man,' I whisper.

'Do or do not; there is no try,' Isaac answers in a squeaky voice, and we both collapse into that sort of heaving, gasping laughter that edges towards hysterics but simultaneously plays the role of a much-needed pressure valve.

'Crying out loud, 'Zac,' I say when I can finally draw breath again. 'That was literally the worst Yoda impression I've ever heard. I'm amazed Aicha didn't gut you on the spot.'

'Still considering it,' is her wry interjection.

'Ah, well, I'll leave the funnies up to you two bloody clowns in the future. Get out of here and get back ASAP. I'll be absolutely ruddy delighted when it turns out the forthcoming hours of mind-breaking magical theory are all for naught, and you've saved the day all by yourselves again.'

'See what we can do. Jak, look after him for me, will you?'

'Of course, my dear boy. Consider it done.'

'See you on the flip-side.'

We climb into the sleek Alpine that I decide Aicha has developed deep and intense feelings for and is probably mapping out a whole life together involving growing old with little half-human, half-car monstrous hybrid grandkids honking their horns around their feet-slash-tyres. My imagination is terrifying. Point is I've never known her to hold on to a form of transport for so long. It reminds me I've been doing a whole host of selfless actions and paying attention to my moral code. It doesn't feel like my soul is reaching Perfection again just yet, but it is something I am going to have to watch out for if I keep putting myself into considerable danger for others. Be too good, and I might not come back next time I die. Of course, I could just spend awhile being a selfish arsehole for a bit once we got this out of the way. Yeah, that sounds like a really tempting idea.

We head out of Toulouse, down the motorway, mirroring my recent runs both with Aicha and solo to do business with Lou Carcoilh over in Hastingues. Doubtless it'll be muggins here doing it again when the skulls have to be run back to Lou. Still, a more mundane concern for a less fraught-with-risk-of-imminent-destruction time. We need to survive this trip first.

It is amazing what difference a couple of weeks can make. The sky is a glorious unbroken blue, and the mountains are clear and visible on both sides before we get past Muret. They don't seem inviting in the slightest though, looming like a young tough's backup, ready to ensure the shakedown goes according to plan, ending with them taking everything in your pockets and probably your self-respect as well. They remind me of Samwise looking at Mount Doom. The one place we don't want to see any closer and the one place we are trying to get to. Normally, I love heading towards the freedom of the Pyrenees. Today, their quick appearance when I'd rather be heading anywhere else feels like deliberate mockery.

The world seems almost post-apocalyptic outside of the normality of the flowing traffic on both sides, with the presence of humanity clear via buildings and industry but with a sense of decay and an absence of people themselves. It's like we're in a protected time tunnel, taking us through a view of the future after the downfall of man. An enormous hypermarket sits next to the other side of the route, apparently in the middle of nowhere, cars parked outside but nothing moving. Greenery overtakes graffiti on half-broken brick walls that flash past us as we keep moving forward against all our better instincts. Similarly painted farm buildings are closed up, seemingly abandoned. Red rotted iron skeletons of lean-to's in the middle of fields look liable to collapse from a strong gust of wind, as industrial unmanned sprinklers pour reclaimed water over crops that can take to self-seeding in an unpopulated world.

There isn't much in the way of banter. Every time someone strikes up a conversation, we pass another sign showing the countdown in distance –150km to Lourdes, 100km to Lourdes– that might as well also be painted in blood: ABANDON HOPE ALL YE WHO ENTER. Whoever is talking then falters or gets no reply, and silence reigns once again, a heavy weight pressing down on all our heads.

The moment we see our world re-impress itself on the natural one is in a moment of startle and conflict. A dark-blue helicopter zips across the road, sending an off-guard flock of birds fleeing away from the noisy metal beast and its presumed terrible jaws. The helicopter hovers over a nearby field as though lurking, waiting for their return to feast upon them or else like a hawk waiting to spot a field mouse fleeing through the wheat before diving to bring it death in a clawed embrace.

The mountains themselves bring feelings of closing talons, their jagged points clear, with a sharpness both to how they stand out from the sky and to the crags themselves. The lone summit, which we seem to point at, is like a middle finger aimed right at us. Looks like the mountains themselves want us to fuck off. They aren't the only ones. I want us to as well.

We take the turning off for Lourdes as the city of Tarbes pops into view over the crest of the hill we wound up. It makes it all the harder for us to peel off at the next turn, away from calm, peaceful civilisations, into the wild world of the Lady of Lourdes.

The run in to the town itself is bucolic to a degree that it sets my teeth on edge. Bubbling craters should accompany the road, geysers spouting boiling acid-laced waters that eat away at the few shrubs hardy enough to survive in a bloated wasteland. Instead, verdant greenery, alpine and peaceful, span each side of the route that winds through the foothills towards the town itself.

The presence of people edges its way in gently, the power of religion less so. One of the first sights on the outskirts is a miniature chapel, undoubtedly initially a place of rest for footsore pilgrims, now with a low-price hotel attached to the side. Christian symbols glow in neon over storefronts that hawk the more upmarket items for the discerning believer. The town itself is a hodgepodge of architectural styles. There are whitewashed apartment buildings with the red roof tiles more common in the area, but other houses have the heavy black slate with long sloping roofs more common in the north of France. Much of it looks thrown up in a rapid expansion, driven by a miracle-based gold rush.

The closer we get, the busier it gets, the more buildings press in and signs direct us to a myriad of museums around holy items, articles, and reliquary. We ignore them all, following the Sat Nav for the parking closest to the Basilica and Sanctuary of Notre-Dame. Notre-Dame meaning Our Lady.

We walk down from the parking, weaving around pilgrims and plastic life-sized Mary figurines trying to tempt people in to buy miniature mass-manufactured religious trinkets. The area is a mixture of tat and tack with posters advertising '*Bernadette — The Musical*', and everything being religiously themed but capitalistically driven.

The gates leading in are Pearly-esque and thrown wide open in invitation to all the devoted and desperate. Many of the pilgrims wear orange neckties; I have no idea what they are supposed to symbolise. It makes them look like a Dutch faction of the Boy Scouts on a day trip.

I walk through, my head on swivel, trying to take in the sights while also being alert to potential threats. Sadly, that same alert state doesn't keep track of my colleagues' presence, which I realise when Aicha hails me with a high-frequency whistle that brings disapproving stares from the passing visitors.

I stop, wondering why they haven't followed me, and start walking back. Aicha taps on the air between the two gates, looking like she is performing a one-woman mime show, flattening her palm on and leaning into an invisible barrier. I stop where I nominally consider the other side to be and cautiously stretch out a hand.

Sure enough, I feel a force blocking my passage. I spool up my *talent* in my hands and watch Aicha do the same, then we both *push*. The force field separating us disperses our power easily, leaving us looking like we are performing amateur street theatre in the hallowed doorway. An elderly matron pushing a wheelchair fixes me with a stare that would have had Jeffrey Dahmer repenting his sins and saying his rosaries, and I disengage, equal measures abashed and annoyed by how easily the normal visitors progress through while we are stuck, separated.

'It's no use, Aich,' I say, shaking my head. 'This is the seat of her power, so we've basically just tripped the equivalent of her threshold wards. We're never going to manage to Hulk smash these.'

'Right,' Aicha says, then, 'Right,' again. 'Don't like this one little bit. Gonna go find either another way in or else ingest some more gamma rays to supercharge my transformation. Any chance you'll stay here, right here, whilst we get past the barrier?'

'I would, Aich,' I start as she rolls her eyes, 'but we haven't got time. Who knows if you'll find another way in or how long it might take you to get the barrier down? Trust me, I'd rather have you with me on this one, but I might have to go take her on myself or at least do an Obi Wan and power down the tractor beam.'

'Obi Wan got chopped in half by Vader coming back from that mission.'

'Okay, so not an Obi Wan. More like an Obi One-Two. Look, don't worry. Concentrate on getting in here, and I'll see if I can come up with a way to get out.'

She isn't happy about it, but there isn't much in the way of alternative options. We fist-bump through the barrier. I give Susane and Gil a nod, then I turn to walk into the Lady Melusine's lair with no definite backup. Bloody marvellous.

Heading down, the path opens onto a square at the end of a pedestrian boulevard to my right, leading down from the river. To my left stands the church and basilica that the Lady instructed Bernadette to tell the priests to build. It is...impressive.

I've had my differences with the Catholic faith over the centuries, what with them hunting down and exterminating my entire creed, but you must give them credit — they have always invested in nurturing architectural talent. The building is on two levels, with the bottom crowned by an indented ovular arch, each of the beautiful white stones carved with 3D reliefs that repeat their intricate detailing in bands surrounding the door. The architect decorated the doors themselves and the side panels with fabulous and incredibly original mosaic pieces depicting Jesus in a style that looks like they were designed by the guy who drew Samurai Jack. Curving steps either side of these doors lead up to the next level, as do two sweepingly wide bulls-horn-style sets of steps that reach out all the way to the central square. Archways in the right-hand side lead down to the grotto and the healing baths, and sculpted masterpieces in white marble are symmetrically placed along the balustrades. The second level... Well...

The second level is a church. I know it is a church. So I am not sure why my brain keeps insisting it is a palace — and the palace of a princess at that.

Then it hits me. The stunningly elegant spires, the central, sky-reaching, Gothically-intricate turret, the wide, sweeping ballroom like staircases leading up. I know there is a commonly credited German fairytale castle, but I can't help wondering whether Walt got some inspiration for Sleeping Beauty's castle from here too.

Thinking about that helps me make sense of why I find the place so weird. I'm in the religious equivalent of Disneyland, where someone found a magical mute button to silence the screaming children. Don't get me wrong, I know the Catholic Church has always appreciated a bit of razzle dazzle and glamour with their penitence and perdition, but this is something else. It feels...fake. Unreal, maybe. A cut-out cotton-candy church to allow you to swallow down your miracle more easily. The bells sound for the quarter hour, a four-note sequence that sounds vaguely familiar but that I can't place at first. Then it clicks. It is the second half of the first line of 'Three Blind Mice'.

See how they run, I think to myself. That*'s not incredibly ominous or anything at all.*

I don't know where to start looking. Normally, I'd love to take the time to soak in the sure and certain opulent beauty of the interior of the different levels, even though I still find Christians' fascination with the cross uncomfortable all these centuries later. But my gut tells me that isn't where I'll find the Lady. Fae aren't sensitive to religious iconography in the way folktales seem to suggest. I'm personally of the opinion that image of them cowering from the cross is allegorical, regarding the replacement of pagan faiths with monotheistic dominance. Still, I don't feel I'll find the answers here, at least not the ones I need.

I just decide to head down towards the grotto where Bernadette first made the miracle, causing the spring to appear from the rocks, when reality...*glitches.*

There is a moment where it feels like all movement stutters while the sound keeps going, like a streaming video bugging and then lagging the audio. My foot falls out of rhythm with my thoughts, and I almost stumble over, losing my balance momentarily as I go to put it down, finding myself suddenly entirely alone. In the square's centre, facing the church, there was previously a statue of the Virgin Mary, the pure white of the stone picked out by a brilliant blue cape and bright gold crown. There's still a statue there, a white Lady statue, but now it is not the mother of Jesus. This crowned figure is voluptuous with robes that flow and cling to very specific areas that would get religious carvers excommunicated for such a representation of the holy Mother. The statue's head moves, grinding stone on stone, and winks coquettishly at me. As it does so, a honeyed voice dripping with promise and promiscuity speaks into my head.

'*Welcome, my lord,*' it says and then everything glitches again.

I am suddenly back in the square with the meek and virtuous Mary statue, surrounded by believers and tourists. I know something strange just happened. Problem is, I can't think about it properly as my head feels like someone has carefully lifted my brain out, then wrapped it in cotton wool before snuggling it back into place. Something is different, but what, I can't say.

I look around, once again appreciating how perfect the place is, how truly awe-inspiring and holy it feels. I walk, embracing a sense of communion with all the truth-seekers and acolytes who walk with me, breathing in an air purified by the very nature of the place itself. The path leads my feet down by the riverside towards the grotto, and I line up patiently, contentedly waiting in the queue for the chance to touch the rocks surrounding the glass-protected spring that the Lady brought into being for the blessed Bernadette.

Wait, a part of me thinks. *She wasn't blessed. What happened to her here broke her.* But the thought disappears like stroking dewy threads of a spider's web. I don't think much of anything after that, just wait in line to touch the damp miraculous rock.

As my turn arrives and I stretch out my hand to touch the surface, which has been smoothed down by a million prayer-filled touches pleading for the Lady's intervention, the world glitches again, and I am alone in the cave. I don't feel concerned. The glass covering preventing access to the spring has disappeared, and I place my hands underneath, allowing the cool, pure stream to trickle through my fingers. The voice speaks again, sweet and loving and wondrous beyond all measure.

'You have come a long way to seek safety, my lord. Soon you will find it — hope and happiness and a new home.'

Reality un-glitches, and I process out, smiling contentedly through the brain fog, guided by the milling direction of the crowd. We carry on down the riverside, passing the bridge leading to the expansive park-like grounds on the other side. Close in, some small-scale arches protect hundreds of candles that flicker like dancing fireflies even in the daylight, carrying people's hopes and prayers for intercedence upwards in their smoke. Overlooking it all from the rear end of the park is a stately manor, a guarding, watchful presence, surveying all that it owns.

It seems to call me home. It seems to *be* home.

On my left are the baths, carved back into the very rock face itself. A wooden sunshade protrudes several metres out from the stone, providing shelter to the waiting pilgrims, who hope submergence will wash away their sins and carry away their sicknesses. None of them seem to notice as the central door, solid burnished metal that shines like Perseus' shield, swings wide open to reveal the Lady waiting for me as she stands ankle-deep in a shimmering pool.

She beckons me in, a loving, welcoming smile on her perfect face as I walk past her and lie back in her waters, cocooning myself in their embrace. I let them carry me away into darkness and nothingness.

When I come back to something resembling consciousness, I feel...wonderful. Like the weight of centuries has lifted from my shoulders, an Atlas-style burden thrown down, and my heart feels light, filled with joy and peace. When the Lady, *my* Lady, walks out from behind the curtain, I fall to my knees in rapturous joy to catch sight of her, of her beatific smile. She walks forward, and the world narrows to just the closing distance, and her footsteps bring her to me, bring me into her presence. Her voluminous white robes swirl around her, eddying on currents in the air that no one can see or feel, and in her hand is an ivory staff, the hollow centre wound through with more material of the same colour, although I find my eyes slide off it. A natural reaction. I am in the presence of perfection incarnated. Her accessories are as unworthy of my attention as I am of hers.

She lays a gentle hand under my chin and lifts my head so that I dare to match vision with her. Tears of privilege and wonder pour from the ducts, an entirely unworthy tribute.

'You have sought for respite so long; through ages and aching and aid always offered, never gained. The pain is such a weight, the searching and suffering and shouldering of burden after burden with never a time to simply put it all down. You have wanted a chance to believe once more, to believe and breathe and be at ease once and for all. Outside, there is another future filled with darkness and despair and desolation of your poor pure soul. I offer you a protection, a place of peace if you will take it.'

I look up in reverence at this perfect creature, so benevolent and merciful, and I want to throw myself forward in willingness, in acceptance of her bountiful generosity.

The world shudders, and grey monochrome bubbles like the inverse of a photo negative catching flame, then reality seems to split in two along the grey-scale blossoming out. For a moment, an older woman replaces the Lady, her head bound in a giant white dreadlock. She says, 'There is always a price.'

The separation calms, the picture fading away, leaving only the harrowing sight of the Lady, the wonderful Lady, shock and hurt written on her elegiac expression. I realise in horror that the words I heard actually came from my mouth. She marshals herself though, recomposing her features, and when she smiles again at me, it is the first touch of sun on a flower that was curled up on itself for an eternal winter, that it might dream to unfurl a first petal.

'The price is less than what I offer: the protection and perfection and privilege of being both in my company and by my side, my companion for the time you have. I need certain things to maintain. The tasting and taking of *talent* that is so weighty and tiresome is a gift for us both. Wouldn't you like to give me a gift, young Cathar?'

I want to. I want to more than I have ever desired anything. I want to please this miraculous being, to show myself worthy of her approval, of her gracious blessing, to win her favour and affection. Anything is worth sacrificing –*anything*– to be at her right-hand even for a moment.

'And will you give it to me? Willingly and wilfully and without hesitation or doubt?"

'I will, my Lady,' I breathe, and I give myself up to the haze flooding my awareness as all my conscious thoughts fade away into the greyness, and all that remains is her ruby-red lips and the elation brought on by the smile I put upon them.

CHAPTER TWENTY-FOUR
MONTSEGUR, 5 MARCH 1244

I refuse to give up all hope despite the situation.

'We still have some days left, you say?' I ask the guard. He nods.

'Aye, until the sixteenth. All those who will renounce their faith then will walk away. The rest will burn.'

Susane lets out an audible sigh of relief. 'Then all can be saved! They can easily recant later a few words said now.'

I shake my head sadly. 'Unfortunately not. Any Perfect who denies their beliefs even to save their skin will break their Consolamentum. They damn their souls to nothingness, to oblivion upon death and undo the Perfection of those they have saved since then. 'Tis no light course of action.'

The guards nod, their grips easing at my words. It looks like such in-depth knowledge is enough to convince them as to the genuine nature of my faith.

'Aye, Good Man,' the halberd-bearer says. 'They are laying plans right now what course of action to take, but no Perfect will recant.' He stops, looking somewhat shy, a colouring coming to his cheeks. 'I have asked to be given the Consolamentum myself.'

'Me too,' one of his comrades says eagerly, but the other holds himself back. It looks like the example of the Good People inside hasn't swayed every soldier to martyrdom.

'Can you take me in to see them? Who leads them at this time?' I ask.

'Guilhabert de Castres nominally,' one replies as he turns and unbolts the gate. Looking back, he catches my quizzical gaze. 'He has retired mostly into prayer for this latter part of the invasion, and since the surrender, has issued not a word. The Lady Esclarmonde speaks now for the Perfects.'

I breathe a sigh of relief. Guilhabert is a good man but impractical and unaware of either danger or duplicity in his fellow humans. Pierre-Roger will do a fine job of insisting on military discipline, but any further decision making requires a better mixture of incisiveness with sanctity than Guilhabert can offer. Lady Esclarmonde is much better equipped in that department.

They usher us into the crowded central hall. There is little space to manoeuvre. With the French forces having actively assaulted the castle with impunity, those normally resident outside were forced within its protective walls. We avoid the central courtyard, which is likely a menagerie of unsettled and unhappy animals, replete with the resultant waste product produced in such circumstances.

Along the rear wall are the Perfects. Mostly they kneel in obvious prayer, their eyes closed, communing internally. Some offer solace to those who are as lost and unsure as the livestock. One stands sharp and proud, her eyes bright despite the bags beneath that speak of endless sleepless nights. She has ever been described as plain by those who know her not and stunning by those who have gained the grace of her company.

Her poise and self-control speaks loud when her eyes widen but a fraction after alighting on mine. Still, she finishes her conversation with a tarnished-armoured knight, his bobbing head and twisting hands speaking of his earnestness. I wonder how much of that comes from having time proximate to the Lady Esclarmonde.

I make my way across the room, not wearing the black robes, though I have my cord wrapped around my fist for all to see who care to look. I lift it to let her know I come as neither betrayer nor backslider. She gives me a terse nod, though her companion does not notice her attention's division. I wait patiently to the side, Susane guarding my back. I feel no concern about overhearing a private confession. The noise in the room is a muddling, burbling hubbub that makes close and quiet conversations inaudible to any but those intimately involved.

When she finally frees herself from the ministrations necessary, she walks coolly over to join me. 'You look well...for a dead man, Good Brother.' There is a question, not quite an accusation but a definite requirement of clarification before showing any pleasure at my mysterious reappearance.

'The Good God moves in mysterious ways, milady,' I say. It will never be enough to satisfy her, and I know it. Still, I don't feel safe beginning a more detailed discussion of my strange and preternatural recent escapes here, background chatter or no.

'Indeed, he does, Paul. Still, it is upon us to see his signs where they are wrought upon this Evil God damned world. I will know more about your being here. Same as I will know why now, so long after the fall of Lavaur and alone of those Good People present then, it is you who comes calling. At a strange hour for visitations too.'

'He's not alone,' Susane says, making me start. I didn't think her close enough to have overheard our words nor invested enough to care at their exclusion of her.

The intent is a sting to the mannered lady, daughter of the old Lord of Foix, sister to the next, aunt to the current. 'My pardon, lady.' Esclarmonde bows and spreads her hand in an inviting gesture. 'Welcome to our halls, and may the Good God allow your enjoyment of our hospitality, such as rests with so little time ahead.'

Susane matches the bow and tone; one would believe her as nobly born as Esclarmonde. 'I thank you for both your welcome and the respite offered at your hearth. May your god grant you strength in these dark hours, the equal of both your manners and your grace.'

I interrupt. The introductions are satisfactory, enough to appease etiquette. Now I will see my fellow Good People saved afore our charming conversing eats up all the time that remains. 'Is there somewhere we might talk in private, milady?'

She nods and leads us away, weaving through knights and families, farmers and Perfects, nodding, smiling, reassuring with a passing touch before we head out a side door and into a small library. It seems positively spartan in its ordering and content after my time in residence with Isaac.

Esclarmonde pushes the heavy oak door firmly to, then whirls to face me. 'Privacy we have now, Paul. I know not if you come to gloat or drive a knife into my belly, but as I burn in but a few days, I'll take the risk. Come now, I'll have some answers.'

I hold my hands up. 'Peace, Good Lady. I come as neither assassin nor assailant. I remain the man I ever was.'

'The Good Man you ever were?' It is an incisive question, picking up on the unspoken absent word and probing for more.

I sigh, unsure myself. 'I cannot answer that. I am no longer Perfect, that much I know. Yet, I believe in our faith still, and I come for no other reason but to offer succour if I can.'

'There is a story that requires telling here, if I'm the judge.'

I hesitate. Still, I am here to ask for her trust. I do not feel that I can request that if I hide my fall from her. So I tell her. Of Nicetas' betrayal, the mysterious Bogomil priest who turned out to be a dark mage. Of the harvesting of our fellow Good People. The infernal horror I felt bubbling behind reality as he corrupted the Holy Grail. That bastard Catholic, Arnaud Almeric's own papally approved magic, and my battle of will with Nicetas. The breaking of the Grail and my death. My vengeance against Almeric, murdering him with poison, and my apprenticeship to Isaac. I realise I'm taking a risk, indeed a double one. I am revealing my deepest secrets and sins to Esclarmonde and to Susane at the same time. There is no other option, though, if I'm to persuade her to follow me off this mountain.

The Lady says nothing during my telling, simply listens intently. 'So,' I finish, 'I have come with some hope of redeeming myself. I may not be Perfect, not anymore. If I should die and not come back... When that happens, when I die finally, I shall be dust, I know, condemned to nothingness. I believe in the creed though. Before then, I would see our faith safe and out there once again in the world. I offer a way out, an escape for the Perfects who rest, to give chance to rebuild once more.'

Still, the Lady says nothing. For a moment I think she believes me not, that I have lost her with my fanciful sounding tale. Then she sighs. 'I did not think it would be you, Paul. What a strange way the Good God has of showing us his will.'

Then she stands, and I watch agape as she glows with a white power that radiates out and fills the room. As it fades away, she smiles kindly at me. 'You are not the only one to have had recent encounters with strange and eerie forces, Paul.'

It appears I am not indeed.

Chapter Twenty-Five

LOURDES, 10 APRIL, PRESENT DAY

Lost in a talent-induced fugue.
Sadly, I fear for more
nefarious reasons than when that
hypnotist made me run around,
clucking like a chicken on stage.
Naked. Arsehole.

I remember nothing of the next period. That's not strictly true. I have no clear memories, but there are sensations, impressions that linger. The most powerful is the sense of contentment, of peace and wellbeing, as if Ahab has slain his White Whale and found an end to his obsessions and drive, arriving back to land, never to roam again. I am happier than I have ever been, than I ever could be again, and there is a narcotic-like feel to it. It is an unending high without the moments of doubt and descent towards the gaping mouth of madness at its absence. She is never absent because even when we are not in the same room, I am in her domain, in her grasp, in her service, and her being permeates everything, myself included. I walk on cloud nine, my brain wrapped in pink cotton candy, and all is as it should be, as I could ever have hoped for it to be.

It turns out I am Sleeping Beauty in this story, although without the creepiness and personal violation involved by the prince in the original. I feel lips brush against mine, lips that aren't hers, and although my initial reaction is to be filled with horror and disgust at the thought of my unintended betrayal, rapidly I feel the fog lifting and the gears of conscious thought, which came to a grinding halt, slowly turn once more. I blink and see the woman who kissed me.

Sharp-eared and of a beauty akin to the Lady, albeit without the supercharged aspect she has (a charge provided by magic, I realise as the wheels behind my eyes start to tick around again little by little.) Behind her is a human woman, her eyes scanning all directions as she stands in readiness for whatever might come our way, strong and stoic and as deadly as she is beautiful if I am to judge. A man lingers further back, a thin, gangly figure compared to the grace of the other two. I don't know him as well as I do the women — the thought of which is quite astonishing because it carries with it the implication that I know the other two. *This* thought leads to the blindsiding realisation that I know one of them intimately. The fact that they have names and that I know their names as well knocks that previous thought completely off balance. It is only when I realise just how much of a twat the one with the chin tattoo is going to call me for my actions leading up to this moment, that I feel like I am getting back to being myself properly.

'How did you get in here?' I ask, still trying to shake the last haziness out of my befuddled head.

Then something happens I've never seen before. Aicha hesitates. As she does, there is something in her eyes, a quick flash of emotion that could be a deep, weighty sadness or, in anyone else, might be fear. Then it is gone, the sardonic expression locked in place, and the warrior is back.

'I made a deal with the White Lady of the Pyrenees,' she answers nonchalantly, as though saying, 'I bought two pints of lager and a packet of crisps.'

I fight incredibly hard to stop my jaw from disconnecting as it hits the floor. 'First, how? Second, what? Third, any other single word question that might help clarify what you actually did?'

'First question, I used my favour with the Nain Rouge. Called him out.'

Ah. Genius. Of course. The Nain Rouge — a nasty little unseelie fae, a maliciously murdersome trickster, who tried to trap me in a pocket dimension to gain unfettered access to Toulouse to play his nasty little games. I beat his game, and Aicha burnt down his home. He owed us a favour each because she hadn't done it with him still inside. Each of us holds a gruesome keepsake — one of his fingers. When burned in the mountains, it will summon him to our side. Apparently, Aicha used hers to get him to find the White Lady of the Pyrenees for her. Then she struck a bargain with that mysterious creature. Makes sense. I can't think of many forces powerful enough to break through the Lady of Lourdes' barrier. The White Lady of the Pyrenees though? She ticks that box.

'Got him to find her and get me a pow wow. Not the first time our paths have crossed. As for the second...' Her eyes narrow. 'I said *I* made a deal with her, not me and you and your was-dead fae wife and Bill...'

'Gil,' Gil inserts hopefully.

'... who shall forevermore be known as Bill for interrupting and correcting me. Details don't matter. It was enough to get all three of us in and break the enchantment on you. Counteragent required lip-to-lip by someone who loves you. Wasn't gonna be me, and Bob doesn't know you that well.'

I can't argue with that and nod my thanks to Susane. I'll worry about the whole "someone who loves you" part of it when my head isn't already messed up by a wish-granting faerie witch. Speaking of...

'I know how she's granting wishes!' I am excited to actually contribute something to the conversation. As my memories of recent times start to extricate themselves from the cotton wool her *talent* wrapped them in, the source of her power –or that aspect of her power at least– makes itself eminently clear. The "thingery-me-bobbing" of "bounded bonery" as Franc called it. I also realise she's not going to do us any favours. That we're going to have to take what we want. Before she takes everything she wants from us, leaving us as emptied out shells.

Aicha arches her eyebrow at me. 'Let me guess. Magic?'

'I mean, well, yes, but specifically how she manages it. It's her staff!'

'Is that how she hypnotised you, Paul?'

'Yes!'

'With her powerful rod? Denial. River. Egypt.'

I groan. 'Yes, thank you, Moses. How about we get the staff? Then how do we get back out again?' I ask.

'That is less likely — difficult and dangerous and almost certainly dead-ly,' a voice purrs from the doorway.

With the glamour broken, I can see Melusine properly for the first time. Not that it changes that much outside of returning my ability for independent critical thought. She is entirely desirable whether or not she has someone bespelled. She has that timeless hourglass figure beloved of the fifties pin-ups and cinematic villains (because, of course, if a woman's sexuality isn't commercialised, then she isn't to be trusted, according to the patriarchy). Her white robes are a masterpiece of seductive design work, covering all the parts that need to be covered to remain decent (by patri-archal standards once again, of course) while simultaneously accentuating them, drawing the attention in with each subtle positional shift. Her fae heritage is clearer, yet somehow less disturbing than is the case with Susane. Perhaps it is the change wrought on my former wife, the shift away from humanity that creates a dissonance for me between what I see and what her dying wrote into my heart with each knife wound I found on her shredded corpse. Melusine looks entirely correct in her ethereality and wears it just as comfortably as her robe.

Then there is the staff. The "thingery-me-bobbing" made of "bounded bonery" as Franc described it. It's the sort of design work that would make a metal-dragon's-claw-ring-wearing, point-capped-teeth goth kid leave some potentially embarrassing marks on their underwear. Bones wound in impossibly twisted forms create a caging tube. It looks like a combination of femurs, radii, and ulnae shaped around and across each other. Through the centre of it runs what looks like a complete human spine, and on the top is what I initially took for a fractured globe made of pale-yellow pebbles. After some further inspection, I realise it is the carpal bones of a hand grouped together as they would normally be, and then held in place to the top of the spinal column by various finger bones gripping downwards vice-like. The orb at the top is clamped in place by them like a diamond in an engagement ring. At the other end, the tail of the spine pokes out of the bottom of the bone-cage arrangement, and I think that the triangular coccyx looks worked, honed to a sharp, stabbing edge. And the whole assemblage is absolutely screamingly powerful, oozing *talent*.

'I don't suppose you'd consider just giving that to us, would you?' I ask, nodding my chin at the staff. The resultant peals of laughter are not a sign of a positive response to my request, I suspect.

'Give you my Staff of Power? Do you know how long I spent gathering the required parts for this, searching and selecting and shaping them together, to grant wishes for given magic? Even then, I had to feed it my sister's heart, still beating and bloodied and broken to bring it to fruition.'

I keep edging my fingers into certain, very familiar shapes, trying to ready myself for go time, but something's wrong. The sweat forming on my brow is not a good sign. At all. I keep her talking, at least for the moment.

'Okay, so I can get that you need to feed *talent* to it to get the wishes. I mean, the design alone hardly screams "flower and fuzzy feeling magic", does it? It's very metal, by the way.'

The fae lady looks baffled — momentarily. 'It is bone, Cathar, not metal.'

Aicha whooshes her hand backwards over her head, and I decide explaining "being metal" isn't a conversation that is going to successfully distract her for long or will get us any useful information, so I plough on.

'Don't worry about that turn of phrase that you probably don't hear from too many geriatric Catholic pilgrims. What I don't get is, why then do you keep some people? I didn't seem to be about to be let go any time soon, yet you dumped Jean out on the street without a second thought.'

The Lady turns her head to me, a puzzled, regretful expression on her face. 'I cannot grant my own wishes. To keep me company and make the demands I desire, I need a champion, companion, and consort. I am not avaricious; I only ever need one.'

Wow. Saved from a slow death to act as a rechargeable battery and wish slave for a monogamous faerie creature. Not my idea of a retirement plan. That also, sadly, answers the lingering question I had about Ahmad. I didn't expect him to have any powers left if he still lived here somewhere, but I hoped he might somehow be around. I guess she drained him dry eventually. Without his *talent*, he'd age like any normal human, and it's been nearly a hundred and fifty years since he started investigating. Anger builds at the thought of the eminent scholar stolen away from a world he would have helped as much as he could. I can't help thinking that he would've achieved much more than I did if he had gone north to seek information from Bernadette, and I'd been the one ensnared in the seductive spider's silk that Melusine had spun across this town.

'What about the others who visit? The miraculous healings of the lame and desperate?'

She pulls herself straight and huffs indignantly. 'Do you consider me entirely selfish, Cathar? I am always happy to take and trade and transfer power to my staff in exchange for a simple wish.'

Aicha coughs into her hand. It is a loud throaty cough. A loud throaty cough that mysteriously sounds a lot like someone saying, '*Bullshit*'.

Melusine swivels to face her, her features puckering in like someone stapled lemon slices to her tastebuds. That she still looks like the epitome of womanhood perfected should tell you exactly how good looking she is.

'Do you have something to add or alter in my account, Druze?' she says, and I am not at all surprised by the haughtiness that permeates her sentence. It seems to be the go-to mode of communication with anyone the fae consider below them. Set Faezers to snub, so to speak.

Aicha looks around as though searching for another immortal Druze warrior who just drew the attention of someone who could probably classify as a demi-goddess. 'Oh, sorry, were you talking to me? Did you not hear me before? Bullshit.'

'Are you accusing me of lying, Berber?'

'Oh, pulling the race card. Okay, weird lizard-slash-human-slash-pointy-eared-twat thing. Not accusing you of lying. Accusing you of not telling the whole truth. I'm sure it does wonders for your minor solar-system-sized ego to grant passing fancies to plebeian humans now and again. Sure, it also keeps you topped up on the *talent* front. Fucksake, you've got me alliterating now as well. Don't think that's everything though, is it, Wankerbell?'

Melusine rocks backwards as though Aicha slapped her across the face. The expression of shock and horror would have been hilarious if I wasn't struggling so badly, and if she didn't possibly have the power to swat us all like blood-drunk mosquitoes.

'Did she just allege or accuse me of actual onanism with a *bell*?' she asks me, aghast.

I chuckle. Looks like she isn't a fan of J M Barrie or Disney then. I think about how to translate it into sufficiently antiquated language so she'll understand. 'Wankerbell is a play on words of a famous faerie character. She's calling you an addle-pate, in effect. Slightly beside the point. She does that to most people.' And still I'm trying to make something magical happen. Still nothing. The air resists my movements, and I'm trying not to focus on what that might mean. *Keep it together, Paul. Eyes on the prize while she remains distracted.*

Aicha holds up her hand in objection. 'Not true. I do it to people I like or people I really, really don't. Only seem to end up in the company of one or the other… Mostly the other.' She turns a momentary brilliant smile on Melusine. 'Guess which camp you fall into?' Her features lock down into their expressionless norm again. 'Now, again, not the only benefit, is it?'

I can see the exchange has bewildered the half-fae, but I'd lay money, due to her outraged response, that she is as incapable of lying as a full-blooded fae is. 'My benefits are mine own, not for detailing or discussion or debate.'

Aicha nods thoughtfully. 'Fair point. Let me guess then. People who get miraculously healed, they're very grateful. Grateful to their god. Grateful to the Lady. Probably mainly to the Lady who did the actual healing. Lot of them probably just ask for help from the Lady. Thank the Lady. *Pray to the Lady.* Bet a lot of them stop thinking so much about their god or about which Lady. Lot of potential power for someone who gets charged up that way, am I right?'

Displeasure forms in Melusine's face, the creeping heat building there, simmering anger soon to reach a roiling boil. I breathe a slight sigh of relief when I finally feel my hand slip through the air itself and into my etheric storage.

'You are a rude thing, little Druze, and I think it is time that I –'

'Yeah, fuck what you think,' Aicha says as the dagger she palmed is already speeding up across the space between them, aimed straight between the Lady's eyes. Looks like it's go time, after all.

CHAPTER TWENTY-SIX

LOURDES, 10 APRIL, PRESENT DAY

House of Flying Daggers? Michelle Yeoh's got nothing on Aicha.

The blade flies as straight and as true as any that Aicha has ever let fly, glowing as her *talent* imbues it with greater velocity, accelerating it at lightning speed across the room before burying itself into Melusine's head. For a moment, I dare to hope it is going to be that easy. Then the Lady's eyes swivel upwards and a vaguely put-upon frown creases her lips. Guess not.

'How rude,' she mutters. The knife's penetrated, but it isn't the hilt-deep, brain perforating "say goodbye to your ability for conscious thought" penetration I expected. Melusine's attention turns back to Aicha, and a poisonous smile smooths out the frown. It is a thoroughly unpleasant expression. That she still looks stunning when wearing it is feeling like a bit of a piss-take, to be honest.

Melusine reaches up to where the knife is sticking out from her forehead, reminiscent of the pump handle on a beer tap. She flicks her head in my direction, but her eyes never leaves Aicha's.

'Do you know he made me a pledge, a promise — a position taken by my side in exchange for a tiny traded titbit.'

'Right, first, way to give a guy a complex,' I interrupt. 'My, ahem, magic, isn't under-endowed, thank you very much. Second, you had me glamoured!'

She inclines her head slightly as though it is the pivot point of a scale weighing the balance of what I said. 'Of sorts, there is a truth of trace amounts in your telling. However, you remember when you made your pledge? There was a loosening, a lessening, a lifting of my charms prior to your promise. Somewhere, at least, in your tired, trapped, torn-up heart, you wanted to give up, to be exonerated of the loads you've chosen to bear.'

She shrugs, a fluid, graceful gesture to show unimportance, though whether of what she is saying or of us or of the entire world outside of her is impossible to say. 'Regardless of whether you feel it was choice, coercion, or a combination of both, there are rules, rubrics, regulations upon my curse. And when a man who promised himself to me breaks his solemn vow, it empowers me after to do this.'

I don't know if you've ever seen the old sci-fi TV series from the eighties called *V*. It was brilliantly done, super creepy, and had a famous scene, where one of the apparently benevolent alien visitors tore off their human-like facial covering to reveal a freaky space reptilian lurking underneath. There were a bunch of loonies watching, like David Icke, who seemed to take that as an instruction manual for what was actually happening in the world and why society was so messed up (some people really struggle with subtleties like metaphors, I guess). Of course, if all the royal families of Europe *are* actual descendants of Melusine and possess any of her abilities, the conspiracy nuts thinking giant shapeshifting lizards are running the world might have a point after all. *Hmm...*

Ahem.

Going back to Melusine, if we didn't already establish that she has zero awareness of any sort of societal or cultural movement that has taken place since she established herself in Lourdes, I'd be tempted to believe she acted as a consultant on the show.

She digs her perfectly manicured fingernails into the fissured flesh around the knife blade and sloughs off any illusion of humanity entirely by tearing her face in half, her fleshy exterior lifting cleanly away from vermillion scales revealed underneath. Her outer layer effortlessly cleaves in two, following a seamless line directly down the middle of her body, like a stripper shedding a quick release Velcro system for instantaneous nudity and maximum impact. I think the likelihood of the revealed dragon wanting to give us a lap dance is pretty unlikely. Plus, having a two-tonne lizard sit on your groin isn't likely to do wonders for the family jewels. Or your life expectancy.

The room is palatial in scale, and that is a good thing as otherwise, she'd have crushed us during her transformation. It makes me realise, though, that she probably had all the rooms built (or, considering the legends, simply magicked into existence) on a scale that would allow her free movement in her dragon form, which stretches to at least six metres. Her wings, hard ridged bone structure stressing scaled plate patterning, remain thankfully folded. I suspect there are some razor edges to the impossible aerofoils, but unfurling them will hinder her movements. Aicha drew the major part of Melusine's attention just prior to the transformation and is now face to snout with the creature. Gil sensibly pulled himself back towards the wall, out of the (probably literal) line of fire on her right side. I stand on the opposite side with Susane, and I push her backwards simultaneously, both to put her out of danger and to free up my area of movement. I pull my sword out, ignoring the molasses-like sensation as it comes free. I don't know whether Melusine can still talk in her dragon form, but I take the whole burying a blade in her head and her transforming into a giant fuck-off lizard as signalling the end of pleasantries.

The best plan seems to be to take advantage of Aicha drawing her ire and attention. Sidling round towards her hind end as quietly as I possibly can, I attempt to plunge my sword into an adductor so finely toned it'd make fitness instructors the world over weep into their protein shakes and doubtless create the Scaly Fiery Death Machine Trim'n'Tone program in tribute. That Melusine is still physically perfect, even if the structure is now an armour-plated lizard rather than a magical seductress, is still bloody annoying. But then again, dragons often are.

What dragons aren't, as a rule of thumb, is very sociable creatures. Hoarders never play well with others, and just because you are a gargantuan flying serpent doesn't change that fact. What they are, however, almost exclusively, is exceptionally vain, taking the idea of the serpentine, blowing it up to inconceivable proportions (and if ever there was a doubt that magic was an integral part of some creatures, the impossibility of dragons in terms of flight and scale is inarguable proof), and covering it in the most beautiful and perfect scale armour imaginable.

There are exceptions. The Tarrasque is not a pretty sight. That might go some way to explaining why he's such a complete and utter arsehole, although he's such an unbearable prick that I don't really want to even look for any excuses for him. I suppose Lou Carcoilh probably fits into the general category as well, but he's a unique case. Thankfully.

Melusine takes the idea of dragons, the image of reptilian perfection, and hones it even further. She is awesome in the sense of awe-inspiring and breathtaking in the reflective sheen of her flawlessly arranged scales that ripple gracefully even as she roars in fury when I slide my sword between two of them and into her thigh until it scrapes the bone. I know a lot about dragons from having fought a few of them over time, and I've put in enough study to know where their weak points are and just what angle one needs to strike from in order to penetrate past their defences. I might have got eaten a few times finding that all out, but it was worth it. Education is a wonderful thing.

Sadly, a significant "but" needs to be appended to the above sentence. Knowledge is, indubitably, power, but when it comes to shoving a sharp pointy thing through striated muscle capable of launching a two-tonne bestial equivalent of a flying armoured tank (complete with requisite flamethrower), then power is also power, as in rippling pectoral style brute force. My years of martial arts training often allow me to compensate while the bodies I wear catch up to where my spirit believes it is in terms of physical fitness. Piercing fibrous tissue so densely packed that it will make Schwarzenegger in his heyday give it all up and concentrate on growing a beer gut instead is not an easy task at the best of times, and I only picked up this current body a few days ago. The finely honed edging of the blade helps me out, but I can only get so far in, and I'm not about to perform some spectacular debilitating cut, taking that leg out of action for the rest of the fight. I've basically managed the equivalent of walking up to you and jabbing quite a large toothpick hard into your thigh — painful, yes; incapacitating, no. And she reacts much as I imagine you would were I to appear out of nowhere right now and perforate your leg with a cocktail stick. She slaps me. Hard.

Now I say slap because that's certainly what it feels like. In reality, I'm not convinced you can count being hoofed backwards into a wall so hard that you leave a Tom and Jerry style imprint in the plasterwork by a dragon's hind limb as a slap, but I'm pretty sure that the intent is the same. I think about standing back up but realise that being able to do anything other than wheeze like an asthmatic antiquarian hound over cracked ribs and probably some internal bleeding is a prerequisite for such a plan of action. I settle for slumping against the wall I just slid down, just for the time being, of course. Just until I remember how to breathe again.

Meanwhile, I'm stuck in a ring-side seat for the upcoming Aicha and Melusine Show, which is going to be bloody spectacular and spectacularly bloody. I'm pretty good with a sword and a witty riposte — in an Insult Sword Fighting "I am rubber, you are glue" kind of way. Aicha is a whole 'nother level of badassery with a blade. If you think about it, a dragon's talons are basically the equivalent of giving Wolverine's adamantium claws to the Hulk. Seeing as how they're all longer than my arm, it places an opponent in a similar situation to facing off against ten telepathically linked master swordsmen who've all been chugging down Dr Jekyll's secret sauce just for kicks. Add to that the rows of torso-sized incisors powered by jaws strong enough to snap an aircraft carrier in half (trust me, I've seen it happen), and the odds for a one-on-one battle with swords are infinitesimally small. All those knights who used to claim they went three rounds to emerge victorious wearing full battle armour were lying toerags who either sliced up a large snake or stood a long way back while they (or a paid associate) used the magical equivalent of a thermonuclear device to blow the dragon into lots of much, much smaller dragon pieces. Life expectancy is minimal in direct combat. Unless, of course, you're Aicha.

You can describe her movements as balletic...if Jackie Chan had trained her in ballet. She dances around the claws, their scissoring movements making me understand exactly what Lewis Carroll meant by blades going snicker-snack. Melusine doesn't leave with Aicha's head, though; the Druze is always just *somewhere else* as the weaving lethal digits spring forward — positioning herself aside or around or even underneath one as she parries another that comes shooting out of nowhere. She is an effortless blur, poised in the centre, her state meditative as she flows from position to position. She is a zen bushido master, schooling a creature that should have been able to tear her in two, deflecting with a wakizashi that she drew to partner with the katana that she's testing Melusine with constantly, probing and searching for pathways through the living razor-wire writ large of talons and teeth. Astoundingly, she seems to find some, and although the fight isn't going entirely her way (she is still doing the lion's share of evasion, and despite how effortless she makes it seem, the start of sweat glistens on her brow), most of the patches of dark ichor-like substances on the floor seem to be from places where Aicha penetrated under plates and scored deep gouges in the flesh underneath.

I need to get myself back up and in the fight, so I heave myself up through the pain that paints my peripheral vision a worrying red and threatens to make everything else fade to grey. I've been trying to heal, trying to get my ribs to reform enough to stop doing hole puncher impressions on my lungs. Though I'm not convinced it worked, not enough, not as it should, I stagger to my feet, ready to go reclaim my sword and join in the hoedown.

But I guess you don't get to survive more than a thousand years as a shapeshifting reptilian fae creature swanning around with the nobility of a society famed for their penchant regarding burning woman for knowing such dangerous things as how to count or how to say no without being pretty damn sharp. Melusine divides her finger forces and performs a pincer movement with her right claw while sneaking her left behind Aicha, slashing at her tendons.

Aicha twirls, bringing her katana behind her into a guard position, blocking the talons, but the momentum commits her to moving and, for a moment, both her feet are off the ground.

It is in that moment, in that split second as she spins, that Melusine's claw equivalent of a little finger –which is still about as long and as wide as my right leg– flicks backwards in a quick but casual movement, disembowelling Aicha, tearing her guts out to drape across her wicked nail as though having just unpicked a problematic knot in a piece of thread.

It is a death blow to most anyone. It is a minor inconvenience to Aicha, but she is still out of the fight for the moment.

I stagger-run forward, haul my sword out of the dragon's thigh, and start sizing up a more opportune attack route than "stick it in the nearest bit of flesh to me".

Me extricating the blade was probably quite uncomfortable for her (one can only hope) given her head swishes backwards to peer at me with an incoherent rage. The look of malignant concentration suggests she is working out exactly how to remedy the annoying problem of me as quickly as possible. Yay me.

She kicks out at me with a side lunge of the same leg she caught me with before, which brings up inappropriate mental images of dragons doing aerobics. I'd chuckle if I didn't have to throw myself sideways to avoid being decapitated. Apparently, she's decided that I actually merit using her sharper physical implements instead of just a casual back kick. Truly, my parents would be proud had they not been dead for over eight hundred years.

Smacking into the cold marble surface goes down as well as a karaoke rendition of NWA's 'Fuck The Police' at a five year old's birthday party. Not that I've ever done that. There's no video evidence, and the defence rests its case. Basically, the parents — I mean the ribs, are not best pleased, and that sneaky grey-out keeps trying to take over my vision whenever I get momentarily distracted. I manage to turn the collision with the floor into a shoulder roll that avoids me getting pinned to it like a medal of bravery by the following talon.

I'm not winning, regardless of my tiger blood status, but I've done what I needed to. I bought Aicha some time, and there's a howl of pained wrath from Melusine as she whips her head back round to look at the scale that my magnificent friend carved like a slice of salami off the side of her neck. The dragon redoubles her previous efforts against the Druze warrior, her claws blurring as the ringing of steel against keratin becomes so rapid it sounds like a Victorian matron furiously ringing a dinner bell to summon unhurried tykes to the table.

The transformed fae is a study in multi-tasking; despite attacking independently with her ten frontal claws, she's also fending me off with her hind leg, and by "fending off", I mean coming dangerously close to making a Paul pancake at any moment, while I lumber around like a brain-drunk zombie, gracelessly avoiding limb loss by haphazard luck as much as any form of athletic ability. Somehow, despite what I suspect is a medium grade concussion to accompany my snapped ribs, I wonder why she isn't employing some smarter tactics considering she pulled a beautiful switch'n'bait on Aicha before to make a friendship bracelet of her innards. Having me harry her from the side, even as haphazardly as I'm currently managing, is a massive disadvantage and keeps her attention divided. It's allowing Aicha to get in a whole host of effective nicks and cuts that cumulatively could eventually cause even a dragon problems. If she drives Aicha in my direction and pivots herself simultaneously, she'd have no problem eradicating me rapidly, which would allow her to give Aicha her undivided, murderous attention. There's no way I hamstrung her with my foolhardy thigh poke, so there has to be another reason for it. She's unwilling or unable to move the main part of her bulk from its current position. Why?

I have a sudden thought. 'Aich,' I yell as I come within millimetres of performing my world-famous one-off squashed-raspberry impersonation.

'Kinda busy,' she replies, leaning into a short sword block, using the leverage to pivot and drive her blade-tip into the joint of the same digit, albeit sadly not enough to actually sever the claw.

'There were three in the bed,' I shout, doing my drunken master playing dodgeball impression again.

'Don't want to know about your love life ever, *saabi*. Especially not now.'

'No, c'mon, *laguna*. The children's song. There were three in a bed. What did the little one say?'

She springs backwards, performing a twisting half-somersault over a claw from the other hand that tried to sneak up and goose her. As she lands, she rolls in my direction, handspringing back to her feet with an annoying amount of poise and grace, setting her to the dragon's left side. As the creature's neck swivels to follow her, she feints to its right, setting up enough of a counter-motion as Melusine tries to rapidly change direction that her front breast lifts slightly up off the floor.

I'm never sure if it's just that Aicha has entirely too much confidence in my ideas or even more in her fighting ability, but as she tacks back from the feint, she releases the wakizashi from her left hand and throws it straight at the bottom of the exposed breast.

The beast rears up as the whetted short sword hits a sweet spot between two scales and sticks. This is nothing compared to how much Melusine moves when Aicha follows it up by launching what is effectively a flying kick straight onto the hilt of the blade, pushing it up to the grip.

The dragon roars and scrambles back a step, pulling up and away, both to reduce ease of access to the wakizashi and to instinctively make herself bigger, more frightening to the irksome little prey that doesn't understand that its role is to curl up in abject terror and wait to be devoured rather than baring its teeth and biting back. I immediately see why she's been staying prone and trying to take us down from a stationary position. Her staff lies underneath her. By rights, she should have crushed anything below her bulky form to powder, so either the magic within the staff is protecting it or this isn't the first time she's done this and has previously worked out a posture that keeps it safe from her flattening mass. Or most likely both.

If I throw myself at the staff though, I am likely to get squished well before I can roll away. There is only one option. I'm going to throw my sword.

Now when people throw their swords in films, it's some writer who's working on the principle that sword just equals oversized knife, so, assuming that someone is Conan strong, they can just treat it in the same manner, pinning an exasperating foe to a wall by tossing it end over end and scoring a perfect bullseye on their midsection. You will be shocked –shocked!– to hear that in real life, this doesn't work at all. Hell, even tossing knives that aren't made to be thrown is incredibly difficult. Swords are balanced entirely differently, and while you might get lucky and knock them out with a pommel hit, your sword is just as likely to go skittering off sideways or smash into the floor with resultant damage to its beautiful, worked edge. However, a sword like mine, effectively a standard long sword that was the choice of nobles and knights for a fairly large proportion of European history, can be thrown if you use the right technique.

I flick my wrist upwards and release my sword simultaneously, following its upward trajectory with my hand as I reverse my grip direction, catching it at shoulder height, my hand wrapping round the pommel like a javelin. Then I launch it in the same continuous movement directly at the staff. It's a manoeuvre I once practised endlessly but haven't needed for a very long time, so I'm immensely relieved when the tip catches underneath one of the twisted bone guards and carries the staff out from underneath

Melusine. The sword and staff clatter together against the opposite wall, right by Gil's feet.

Stooping, he scoops up the staff, looking at it somewhat wonderingly before turning back to the battle. Everyone stops. Everything grinds to a halt, and four sets of eyes, three human and one reptilian, turn to fix on the slender human who has suddenly just gained a wishing staff.

Almost instantaneously, the dragon is gone, and Melusine is back in her Lady aspect. Blood besmirches her white garb, but she still looks beyond magnificent, the epitome of feminine beauty. She throws out her *will* at Aicha and I. Susane, who kept back during the entire fight, actually drops to one knee, her head bowed as though trying to remain in place against a whirling gale. I grit my teeth and lean in, but there's little in the tank to resist except my innate stubbornness and centuries of magical experience.

Aicha is the most charged up of us *talent*-wise, and Melusine knows it. She focuses her attention and *will* on the biggest threat, but Aicha is giving as good as she gets. We've ended up in the magical equivalent of a Mexican stand-off. None of us can move, including Melusine. The only one not affected is Gil, and she turns the full-beam, blinding headlamps of her smile and attention on the little rabbit.

'There are precedents in tomes and tales and tellings of moments when young heroes find objects of power arriving in their hands just in time to save the day and the fair maiden.' The fae queen actually batts her eyelashes as she says this, a coquettish blush reaching her cheeks. 'Come forward, my new lord.'

Gil's eyes fix on her, and he half-steps, half-stumbles forward, somnambulistic in his movements.

'Don't do it, kid. *Urk,*' I say as the magical pressure assaulting me concentrates itself on my windpipe, meaning I have to use all my remaining energy to protect that one spot so my throat doesn't cave in.

Aicha is far too busy matching *will* for *will* with Melusine. Powerful as Aicha is, Melusine has the edge on her, and if she starts getting distracted by trying to talk, chances are high that Melusine will be free in a moment to take back her staff by force and strike us all down at the same time.

Gil carries on, hesitantly advancing, showing no sign of having noticed me, and the Lady's smile grows ever brighter, ever more captivating as she whispers promises to him.

'Together we shall rule, my lord. You shall wield my staff; you shall stand as my prince, my protector, my paramour. I shall be your most subservient wife, passive and perfect and passionate in our chambers to bring you pleasure beyond all mortal's ken. Come and stand by my side, and you will rise like Charlemagne, like Arthur — a heroic ruler, regent, royalty ready to carve out your legend.'

The young man comes level with Melusine, standing in front of her with her staff grasped horizontally across his right palm as the Lady coos her promises seductively, drawing him in through this natural element of her *talent* that requires no expenditure on her part. She is siren-like, and her song is a part of her very being.

'You will make the wishes, selected and shaped and said into being. Wish away these nuisances, these little buzzing bothersome beasties, and we can enjoy all that we can make together in the privacy of our bedroom. What more could you wish for, my lord?'

Gil looks up into her eyes, and the smile that spreads across his face is almost as dazzling as hers. I despair. I have no idea how well my reincarnating magic will stand up against a super-powered faerie wish nor whether it might cancel out the effects of the Aab-Al-Hayat on Aicha. I am certain that Susane won't survive it, and I weep over coughing half-gasps as I struggle to breathe and grieve simultaneously.

The boy leans forwards, his eyes locked on to Melusine, and she closes her eyes, her lips puckered, a gentle sigh fleeing as she waits to be embraced by her new suitor. Instead, Gil inclines himself to be next to her head and speaks gently into her ear.

'I wish you would die.'

Then he plunges the sharpened coccyx tip of the staff into the side of the Lady's neck.

CHAPTER TWENTY-SEVEN

LOURDES, 10 APRIL, PRESENT DAY

I don't think Melusine saw that coming. She's looking a bit green around the Gils.

The Lady's eyes fly open, and the colour drains from her face as she opens and closes her mouth, unable to comprehend what has happened or shape the thoughts into words to express the realisation that her ending has just been woven. The pressure of *will* holding us all in place pops like a soap bubble prodded by an intrigued toddler, and I am delighted to rediscover how to breathe easily. Well, as easily as it's possible to breathe with several cracked or broken ribs, at least one of my lungs possibly punctured or else filling up with blood, and my throat sore from the strangulating pressure. It is still considerably more possible to do than it was a moment prior.

Melusine sinks to her knees, and she looks with horror and something akin to awe at the young man who resisted her magic and overcame her mesmeric charm.

'How?' she gasps, the first drops of blood trickling from the corner of her lips, red paint dribbling its way down her pale porcelain skin.

Gil shrugs as though slaying mythological demi-gods is an everyday occurrence for him. 'First, you aren't my type, Lady. Not even slightly, so the offer of your bed, nah, not for me. Second –' He leans forward, back to the position where he murmured her death to her. 'I already have a lord, and I already made him a willing gift of my *talent*. I chose my service. You have nothing to offer me. Nothing that will see him live anyhow.'

Where the blood marks rivulets down her chin, the skin starts to darken. Then all her veins follow suit, the blood inside turning to black sludge, unable to flow like the waters that once marked her renewed claim to power. She draws a shuddering breath, still desperate to understand how the impossible occurred even as she comes to her own personal closure.

'You aren't the first...man who prefers the company of other men that I've drawn...to my side...' she gasps, a gurgling creeping into the timbre of her voice that suggests the end is drawing in.

Aicha steps forward. 'I've a thought about that. Last time you were running this whole femme fatale, Mrs Robinson flex, society was different. Always been an equal amount of same-sex orientated people. Back then, though, men wanted to be straight. Wanted to have babies. Wanted powerful dynasties and bloodlines.'

Gil laughs, a bitter touch to its tone. 'I never wanted to be straight. And I was desperate to escape my family and their nutty dynastic drive. I certainly don't want to emulate them.'

I nod thoughtfully. 'I think you're on to something, Aich. There was nothing in the dream you sold that would appeal to Gil on any aspect, whether sexual or political. Combine that with him already being pledged and having given up his *talent* previously, and he is outside of your control. Glad he came along for the ride,' I say and tip him a wink that brings a fresh-faced grin to his face.

I don't know how he is holding on to any of the charming innocence considering he's just killed an uber-powerful magical being and has been living on the streets under Franc's watch for the Good God knows how long. I suspect his life is so isolated and so incredibly miserable that even the insanity of kicking about with us on one of our terrifying, death-defying adventures isn't enough to change who he fundamentally is.

Melusine is wheezing now, close to the end, but she raises one still flawless finger and beckons me closer. I approach warily; she wouldn't be the first enemy I tangled with who decided to take me down with them. I pick up my sword as I go, then bend down to hear what she has to say. As I do so, I am astounded to see a single tear rolling down her cheek as an intensity of sadness overtakes her, comparative to a whirlpool that will suck you down into its tumultuous depths. She reaches out a wavering hand and strokes my cheek tenderly.

'Poor Cathar,' she says, her voice reedy and quavering, almost drowned out by the door-creak breaths she's fighting to get in and out. 'I would have kept you safe. Talentless, yes, but safe. There's so much misery to come, so much hurt and heartbreak. I'm sorry...sad...sorrowful...that I couldn't...keep...you...safe...'

The wheezing inhalations ease, and her eyes slide closed. I feel her body about to mimic their action, so I catch her and lower her to the ground, head-fucked by her dying statement. It came totally out of left field and I don't know what to think about any of it. I don't get much of a chance to anyhow, though, because Susane lifts her hand and throws an entire world of *will* that she's apparently been keeping under wraps at my *talent*-depleted team.

Gil goes flying head over heels and cracks his head on the floor before lying still. I'm not sure if he is alive or dead, but I'm not in any state to check because I'm not doing much better. The *will* forces me backwards away from Melusine's body, but I huddle down, leaning into her power, trying to keep myself from being thrown like a rag doll myself. Aicha is holding her own, but she just battled a god-like fae to a *will* standoff after being eviscerated in a sword battle with a fucking dragon, so she's running on fumes too. There is no way she's about to be driven to her knees in a battle of *will* by my apparently treacherous ex-wife, but she isn't about to break the gale force assault that is battering against her to go and stab Susane repeatedly in the face, as I know she really, really wants to do right now.

Susane turns to look at me, although she never lets her attention waver from her *will* as she regards me with a mixture of shame and regret. 'I'm sorry, Paul,' she says, and she sounds like she means it. I can't give a monkey. I am sick to death of people I love coming back from the dead apparently with the sole purpose of fucking me over.

'What is this, Suse?' I ask, anger and confusion and pain having a no-holds barred throwdown for who is going to be most prevalent in my tone, with anger just edging it after a brutal headlock and kick in the balls. 'A double cross by the Mother? A personal attempt to buy safety for yourself from the Seelie Court? I thought you came back for me! Why do this after all of that?'

'I did come back for someone, Paul,' she replies sadly. 'But I didn't come back for you.'

It is hard to say if it is the words or a sudden movement of a floating piece of my rib that makes my heart go *ouch*.

'So there was somebody else? Were they already around when you died that first time?' A sudden thought strikes me in the same place that rib pierced me, making my shoulders cave in. 'Was that who killed you?' I rasp. 'Did they know about your fae rebirth?'

Susane's eyes soften as her heart bleeds tears behind them. 'He was around then, of sorts. I'm sorry. It's all very complicated, but probably easier if I let him explain himself.' She turns to look at the doorway. 'He's just arrived.'

A man walks in through the entrance, totally unaffected by everything going on. As I look closer, I realise he isn't a man but a fae, although with traits that are human-like enough that I suspect he was a Cagot prior to his elvish second life. He is a handsome devil, cascading black curls striking against a pale skin I suspect was bleached on his resurrection, doubtless of a more Mediterranean complexion before. He carries a swagger to his step, as though supremely confident in himself. Mind you, with all the other magic users in the room currently occupied or distinctly dead, he probably has reason to be. His clothes are nondescript, a plain black T-shirt and jeans with walking shoes, looking as though he dressed down to make blending into a crowd easier. It makes the one defining piece of his attire even more striking — a large silver or white gold ring with a signet shaped into a Jolly Roger — a skull and crossbones with what looks like rubies implanted in the eye sockets. Perhaps he was a pirate before his death or else just thinks it makes him look like a roughneck.

'Christ,' Aicha says through teeth gritted in continued effort. 'It's Captain Fook.'

The man doesn't even seem to register what she said. All of his attention is entirely focused on me. He regards me with an intensity that makes me wonder if we've met before. Perhaps I spilled my drink on him back in the seventeenth century, and this was all a long con setup to get revenge. Considering recent events, that sounds plausible. I realise I am rambling mentally, trying to distract myself from just how uncomfortable I feel under the man's regard. If I wasn't already sweating from trying to stay conscious in the face of the potential onset of organ failure, I would have started to sweat now without a doubt. This carries on for as long as I can stand it. I crack first.

'What?' I ask petulantly. Today has already been shitty, the last couple of weeks shittier, and this is lining up to be the shittiest possible icing on the world's biggest shit-cake.

He starts, as though he forgot that I am alive, that I can interact with him, and then he smiles, a broad, friendly, welcoming open-armed embrace of a smile that makes no sense at all...until it does.

'Hello, Father,' he says. He may well have said something else as equally world-shattering afterwards, but I sadly miss it due to me momentarily blacking out.

Chapter Twenty-Eight
MONTSEGUR, 5 MARCH 1244

I am still reeling from Esclarmonde's casual display of her own *talent*. 'What is the story behind this, my Good Lady?' I ask dumbfounded.

She gives the slightest headshake. 'Not mine to tell or at least not in detail. Know only this. I cannot leave this place. Nor can the Good People here gathered. Or at least not many. There are three I will send out with you. They will carry certain texts and treasures with you. It was...advised that someone would offer an avenue of escape. It was also told in most clear terms that the Good God would not wish for us to take it. Indeed, it would serve his purpose for us to remain. I have spoken to those of the faith still here. All will remain. I insisted on the youngest trio to accompany you. They assured me that was as it should be.'

I shake my head in disbelief. 'They'll kill all of you!'

She smiles, sadness in her eyes, unclear whether for me or herself. 'Only the Perfects, Paul, though many will convert. Still, is death ever the end, my friend? And even if it is, are not some things worth dying for?'

I try to push thoughts of my own adventures recounted to her aside, but the parallels are undeniable. 'Is there nothing I can do to persuade you?'

'Nothing, Paul. Good Man, I name you still. Help those who will flee to go. Know I can tell you nothing else, save one thing.'

She leans forward, her words a whisper in my ear for my hearing alone. 'She said to tell you I shall see you again afore the end of it all. I wonder what she meant by that. I look forward to finding out.'

She kisses my cheek, gentle as a breeze's caress of a sapling's branches, and then leans back. 'Now it is time for me to find your new company for leaving, then to minister to my people for the time that remains.'

She turns to leave, but I seize her wrist. 'Who?' I cry, frustrated and hurting afresh at the thought of losing almost all of those left of my people. 'Who is she?'

Esclarmonde just shakes her head gently and pulls her arm from my grasp. Then she turns on her heels and heads back into the Great Hall. I sink into a reading chair, hard-backed and plain-built. I've failed. Of two hundred Cathars, I will save three? I am naught but a poorly laid joke, a half-shaped punchline by all accounts.

The touch on my wrist this time startles me out of my miserable reverie. Susane is crouched in front of me, looking me direct in my eyes, a softness there she never spared for me previously. 'You have not failed, Paul. Would you put so little value in the three who will leave? This was a choice made by your people. Do not deny its worth by comparing it solely to the size of those left behind. You came here to help the Perfects. They have told you the help that they wish. Just because it isn't the help you wanted to give does not mean it has no value.'

'I came here to save them,' I say bitterly.

'I think you came here to redeem yourself,' she replies, her tone untouched by my dark state. 'Perhaps there are other ways to do such, Good Man. Or perhaps you do not need to, except to find peace with yourself again.'

She leans in and touches her forehead to mine, communing with my pain and grief, offering silent understanding. Then she leaves me to come to terms with what occurred and what will be my last time among an assembly of Perfects. The last great gathering of Good People that the world will ever see.

We make our way back down the mountain in a petty silence stained by my black mood. I cannot bring myself to talk to the three young Perfects who accompany us, their black robes freshly dyed and their leather cords newly tanned. It is Susane who takes care of them, guiding their steps and ensuring they neither trip nor fall in the treacherous tunnels.

When we get to the bottom, Susane ushers them out ahead of us. As I approach the cave exit, the ringing in my ears would have deafened me if I wasn't so astounded by the pain when she slaps me clean across the face.

'You can have a moment of grief, Paul,' she says, as furious now as she was gentle in the library. 'You may not make others pay more than they can ever possibly afford to appease your self-imposed misery. This is not the man I believed I guided. This is not the friend I made.'

Her words are a sharper slap than her open hand was. She is, of course, entirely right. I draw myself up and nod. 'My apologies, Susane.'

'Not to me, foolish boy. To those three scared young men who followed in your irksome wake all the way down as they left everyone they know to die, back above them, while you strode on ahead, wrapped up in your own black cloud, so sure your misery was of more import than anyone else's suffering.'

I can't argue at all. I draw breath to apologise again, check myself, and head outside to apologise to the poor lads I have shown neither respect nor understanding, bowing my acknowledgment of Susane's superior wisdom to her as I pass. Her returning nod and self-aware smile tells me she already knew the truth of it whether or not I acknowledged it.

We trek back to Mirepoix as fast as possible, although we need to make camp for the night. I've shaken off my ill humour — or at the very least, have effectively disguised it under layers of bonhomie, and the young Good Men open up as we sit around the campfire. Their eager breathless discussions of theology, of the true path of a Good Christian, seem virtuous to the point of naivety in the face of their status as the last remaining Perfects. I feel *old*, far more than my fourscore or so years. It is as though I have lived so many lives already. The thought of the countless ones that might lie ahead seems a heavy weight to carry. Though the thought of becoming nothing, of ceasing to exist entirely holds no attraction to it either. It is only when the young Perfects stumble on their words and lapse into silence, shooting glances my way, that I realise I have allowed my dour mood to show once more. I excuse myself from the fire and their company, claiming calls of nature and then a desire for sleep.

I go far enough to remove myself entirely from their company and allow them a return to their eager theologising. I sit down in the shadows. I only notice Susane's presence when she sits beside me.

'You are both a deaf and daft mooncalf, Good Man. Still, you can learn. 'Tis more than I'd say for many and a note to your credit. Good to have one at least, eh?' She nudges me with her elbow, scuffing at the dirt with her foot as she does so.

'I can only give credit to my teachers, who remain as ineffable as they are humble.' I nudge her back, and we both chuckle softly.

'What will you do now, Paul?' she asks.

'I'll see them equipped and send them where they can find refuge for the time being, though I'm not sure where genuine welcome will await them anymore.' I sigh, unbearably sad at how the creed once so dominant in the Languedoc has ended up persecuted to the point of eradication. 'I will do my best, though, to bring honour to those who have given such excellent instruction. Then I shall return.'

'To Montpellier?' she asks, frowning.

'To Montsegur. I will pay witness to the end of the Perfects, our present charges excluded. They will not be seeking heretics amongst onlookers. I shall stand and behold their passing, and I shall try not to weep too long or deep at the bloody waste of it all.'

She rubs my shoulder companionably. 'We all have our duties to bear, my friend. What will you do after?'

I feel my heart lift to be named as such by her. 'Then I shall return to Montpellier. I owe Isaac a century of study. Well, I owe him much more than that. Still, that is what we have agreed for now. I suspect I shall have much more to learn even at the end of that time period. What of yourself?'

'As I said — duties to bear. Our community is disparate, set apart. They sorely need guidance. I have a lot of travelling and establishing myself amongst them to do, just as my mother did and still does. One of us out there to guide. One of us here to guard the land. Our responsibilities do not allow us all that we would wish for.'

I sit quietly for a while. 'What would you wish for, Susane?'

She hesitates, still nudging at the sticks and leaves with her toe point. 'Too much that I cannot speak of. Even to you, Paul.' She looks up, her eyes bright, with a wild, irrepressible grin on her face. Then she springs forward and presses her lips to mine. The shock sends lightning sparks through my whole body. When she pulls away, I am entirely incapable of thought or speech.

'Tell you what, Good Man. I have no plan to be dying anytime soon. Go get your training finished. Find your peace and your redemption. Then come and find me in your two or three hundred years when it is done. Maybe we will be confident enough of our responsibilities to choose some things we would truly wish for at that point.'

I am nowhere near close to regaining my tongue, but I make a promise to myself here and now. When my apprenticeship is done, when I have mastered my *talent*, and I am a Power in my own account, I will come and seek out Susane, Princess of the Cagots.

I will dream of this moment now, and then many times in the intervening centuries. I have no doubt of that.

CHAPTER TWENTY-NINE

LOURDES, 10 APRIL, PRESENT DAY

Where are all the Good Men dead? In the heart or in the head? Both, possibly. They certainly feel pretty empty right now.

When I come back round, not much has changed, except that the fae claiming to be my son is over where Gil lies. He leans down to pick up Melusine's staff, which he regards with the studious eye of an antiques dealer, establishing the veracity of some forgotten treasure retrieved from a family loft. He nods, satisfied, and turns back towards Susane. That same broad smile breaks across his face again as he sees me waking up.

'Ah, good. Not got much time to stop and all that, eh, but wanted to catch you quickly before popping off. Terribly sorry to relieve you of this, Father, but I am afraid I am in dire need, and needs must when the devil does what he does, and all that.'

I look from him to Susane and back again, though when I speak, I am really addressing her. 'Are you sure? How is this possible?'

'It's him,' she says. 'He snuck a message to me in the fae realm by passing it on to a Cagot on her deathbed. I found a reason to get sent across to

Earth again, volunteering to shepherd a newly reborn Cagot across, and took a detour to find him where he'd told me to. He's my flesh and blood, Paul. I have no doubts at all.'

'As for the how,' the fae, my son apparently, interrupts smoothly, striding back towards Susane. 'I haven't got time to get into all the details; places to go, people to visit and all that, what, but suffice to say, I was still alive when poor Mama was sliced up, and I was close enough to term to cling on, so to speak. Too pressed to regale you with all the nitty-gritty, et cetera, et cetera, but I survived and was kept in the bastard's service until I killed him. Put together all the details, found out about Mama. Hey, presto, here we are! Thought about reaching out to you, of course, but you were always terribly busy, and I have my own little... Well, I suppose you could call it a quest of sorts, pardon the turn of phrase. Anyhow, I knew we'd have a smidge of a difference of opinion on this one, nobody's fault, both likely to think ourselves in the right, road to hell and great intentions and all that, hah, what? Anyhow, can't stop, must dash, catch up properly next time, eh, old boy?'

Just like that, he dismisses me from his attention. It is like I cease to exist, certainly that I cease to matter. He turns towards Susane. 'Come now, Mama. Time for us to leave, eh?'

'But, son,' she starts, a strange hesitance in her tone from a woman who's just been foolhardy enough to assault and make a lifelong enemy out of Aicha Kandicha. 'He could still be useful. He's your father. Bring him onboard. He could come with us.'

The tone of my son changes entirely. There was a foppish carelessness to his speech before, lifted straight out of the roaring twenties. That disappears, and there is a cold steel to his voice. 'We discussed that, and the conversation is closed. I said, we are leaving.'

Susane shrinks back into herself as he speaks, and I wonder what she's been through to make her react in that way when I've never seen her back down from anyone or anything before. Maybe it results from regaining our child, torn from her. Perhaps she is terrified that if she disagrees, he'll disappear all over again, snatched from her a second time. It is plausible, but I am not convinced. There is something of the tremulous smile of the wife nursing a black eye that came from falling down the stairs. Repeatedly. It sets my teeth on edge and raises up my hackles even though she just stabbed me in the back. She looks across at me helplessly but just nods and then walks to the doorway. They are about to leave, but he turns back to look at me one last time.

'One last thought, old chap. That dastardly Franc fellow that you seem all cosy and in cahoots with, enemies of my baddies, and all that, what. Not quite the decent sort he proports to be. Perhaps a tad less honest than he comes over as, so to speak, eh? Should you be interested in such conjecture, perhaps desire a little corroboration and all that, I'd advise a wee trip over to Canigou. Course, quite a way away, time of the essence, and all that, what. But if one were to find the old blighter's home in Toulouse while he was absent, might well find a shortcut, in a manner of speaking, that might be easier when he's not there to keep it covered up. Have a bit of a poke around, look for a hidey hole, all magically concealed, et cetera, et cetera, not much of an ask for the likes of you, I'm sure, and you might well find something that piques your interest, old fellow. Ta ta.'

He lazily waves his hand over his shoulder in farewell and casts a su-percharged ward across the doorway as he does so. Then the two of them disappear from sight, Susane's *will* now gone.

Aicha rushes forwards, looking to see if she can tear the ward apart with brute force, but she is too low on energy to pull off such a thing. She sizes up to blow a hole in the nearest wall, but tendrils of the ward have wriggled their way through, penetrating the concrete so that any sudden structural change in them will cause the ward to explode. Aicha will survive it, and I'll pop back up in another body like the immortal bad penny I am, but Gil won't, and considering he just saved our bacon, I'm not about to throw him to the wolves even to get answers to the shit tonne of questions that have just taken up residence in my brain like a swarm of enraged wasps hopped up on methamphetamine-laced sugar water.

She turns to me, visibly frustrated. 'Come on, Paul. Give me a hand, fucksake.'

I sigh and pull myself wearily to my feet. I can see Gil is still breathing, although we need to go over and inspect him properly soon because he is still unconscious. Regarding what I want to say to Aicha though, that is no bad thing.

I pick up my sword and use it like a walking pole to limp over to her. 'Aich, we've got additional problems. Look.'

I raise my blade and concentrate on imbuing it with my *talent*. Normally it would roar to life, covered in a raging green balefire that is both super useful for battling supernatural foes and looks cool as fuck. Now there is almost nothing. At the very tip, a tiny green spark pops in and out of existence, flickering and vanishing as I practically collapse from the effort.

Aicha's eyes widen. 'Paul, are you... Did she...?'

I nod wearily. 'She took most of my magic. I'm running at about, ooh, shizzard level of power right now. Won't interfere with my reincarnation, far as I can tell, but I'm the magical equivalent of a wet fart in a paper bag otherwise.' I laugh harshly. 'Irony is, it was probably my nicked *talent* that powered up the staff for Gil's killing blow. Boo ya.'

'Shit,' she says. 'Explains why you were so fucking useless in that fight. I mean, even more fucking useless than you are normally. Says a lot.'

'Thanks, *laguna*.'

'Any time, *saabi*.'

There doesn't seem anything else worth saying for the time being, so Aicha helps me back over to Gil's side. The impact hurt him, no question, but not fatally. Healing magic's never been a speciality for either of us, seeing as how one of us regenerates instantly and the other just purloins another body when needed. Still, Aicha has enough know-how to get Gil properly stabilised and keep my current physical frame going, at least for the meantime.

Sitting on the floor, I hug my knees while Aicha finishes tending to Gil. I sigh, beyond pissed off at how much of a clusterfuck this whole situation has turned into.

'The girl's doomed. So's Franc.'

Aicha looks up at me sharply. 'Did your best. Think you paid a high enough price for the effort too.'

I shrug. I'll get properly depressed about my new state of magical abilities at the bottom of a bottle — or five — of whisky once we get out of here. For now, it's beside the point.

I turn to Gil. 'First, good work, dude. That was seriously impressive. Fuck what Melusine said; that was some proper heroics.'

Gil bobs his head, trying to smile but not really managing it. 'I did what needed doing, is all. Is Franc really doomed?' There is a pleading tone to his voice that makes me understand that he really wants to save Franc, not just to save his own skin but because he actually likes the slimy river monster. I nod my head wearily.

'As far as I can see. Is there any way I can speak to him? No point delaying the bad news, eh?'

Gil looks heartbroken, but he musters up his determination, biting his lip as he nods. He concentrates hard, and in an instant, his eyes turn that eerie milky white that signals Franc is in residence.

He cranes his neck about, taking in the scene at hand. 'Well, well, little Undyer, did your dutyings and no mistakery, upon my oath. The Lady Melusine seems mellowed by the chippings and choppings of blade and *talentry*. Fine work, fine work, indeed, boyo.' He looks around again, peering and searching. 'But where is her staffery, all bonings and banings of man and mage?'

I take a deep breath. Beating around the bush isn't going to prolong either of the two lives we came here to save. 'I'm sorry, Franc. We got bushwhacked. Double crossed. Susane did a number on us and took the staff.'

Franc bares Gil's teeth, fixing them in a furious grimace that shouldn't be possible with his dental arrangement. 'Vile faelings, all truths that tells lyings more stronger than an honest mistruthery.' He spits on the floor and looks glumly at the dead body of the Lady Melusine. 'No doubtings they did their harvestings of her vital vittles' and all, little lordling.'

I look at him, confused. 'Harvested her? No? Why would they?'

Franc raises his head slowly to look at me, disbelief and hope warring in his expression. 'They took naught from her carcass, no quick snipperies and lift away, all gone in bags and byeses?'

The urgency in his tone is enough to stir me to my feet, over to the body to check that the fae (I still can't think of him as my son, not yet. Too much, too soon) didn't help himself to some organs or offal when I took a momentary shock-induced nap.

'She looks intact, apart from the gaping stab wound in her neck, Franc. Why?'

Franc gives his watery, gurgling chuckle, which sounds so wrong coming from Gil's mouth. 'Then all is not lost, wrackedy ruinations and wreckery, my little lordling. No indeed. Her heart, all grist and pithings, wizenry as 'tis, will provide the necessatations of healer as required, all givings and gainings of *talentry* that's gone a-waltzing away, upon my oath. A quick snatchery of bitings, chomps and chews and swallowings down gulletry, and right as rainings and pourings she'll be, will she not?'

I decipher the word salad in my head and take a sharp breath. If what he says is true, eating Melusine's heart will restore the girl's magic. A sudden thought strikes me. I narrow my eyes at the possessed boy. 'How do you know all this, Franc?'

He gives an innocent shrug, as though surprised by my question. 'Why, 'tis only the same workerings as she did pull, all savageries and stabbings, upon my dear motherling's form. She is my auntling herself, is she not?'

I groan. 'That would have seemed like useful knowledge to give us previously, Franc! Why didn't you tell us that?'

He shrugs again. 'Never askings did you make, Undyer. Can't be knowings all the whys and whereforery of your seekings if you don't actual seek, can I now?'

'Franc, you are spectacularly useless sometimes. Listen, the Mother is already waiting with her child in Narbonne. I'm going to get there as soon as I've carved the heart from a dead fae-dragon hybrid, which was never a sentence I expected to say. You need to be there before me, but do not engage in conversation with the Mother if you don't want to get murdered before I arrive. You are going to renounce any claim on the girl, publicly, and we'll see if the Mother keeps her word should the heart actually heal the child. I'll be about an hour and a half behind you. I'll let the Mother know we're on our way, and we better hope she can hold on that long. You may get lucky one more time yet.'

'I'll be crossing my digitry and be taking my leavings, both of Toulouse and your good self for now, boyo. Adieu until Narbonne, Undyer, and my thankings and appreciatery of all your doings until now.'

The unnatural blankness evaporates from Gil's eyes as Franc leaves him, and the youngster re-joins us. I guess Franc is taking the whole situation seriously after all — that is the first time he's thanked me. Ever.

Aicha gives a triumphant hiss, and I feel the wards that are blocking us in the room drop. She took the time to unpick them carefully rather than just blowing them up. I feel like a proud father whose little girl is suddenly all grown up. I'll never, ever recount that image to her, though, as she'll probably beat me into an even bloodier pulp than Melusine did.

I clap Gil on the shoulder. 'You've done amazing work today. You've been a real asset, but you came damn close to dying too, and you're a long way from fully better. There's unpleasant, bloody work to be done here before we can leave, and you've more than done your part. Take a rest, even a little snooze in the car, whilst we finish up here.'

He nods gratefully, and Aicha passes him the car keys. He winces as he takes his first step, but he masks it quickly and keeps himself steady and upright as he walks out of the room. I am more than a little impressed by the kid. He can be almost invisible, likely by result of nature and nurture, but he has a core of steel running through him, something that refuses to allow him to be broken ever again. I am not sure I would have handled the situation anywhere near as well as he did were it my turn to be that age all over again.

As soon as he is out of sight, Aicha turns to me. 'Right. Why did you want him gone, Paul?'

I hold up my hands, palms out, asking for patience. 'Something's ringing some bells with me and not happy, celebratory church bells either. I need to speak to Isaac first though.'

He picks up on the third ring. 'Paul, you're still alive!' He sounds as delighted about it as I am. It's nice to have people who actually care about you and aren't actively plotting to stab you in the back.

'Only just,' I say honestly. 'It came damn close, but we're all okay. I haven't got time to go into it all right now. The game is most definitely afoot. First thing, did you work out the protection for Franc's people?'

'We're close, my boy. Not there yet though.' There is a pensive edge to his voice. 'Does that mean you failed to get what you needed?'

'Yes and no. Just please keep going as a safety measure. I need to finish and clean up here, then I'm going to drive to the hand-off at Narbonne, which'll take me a bit over three hours, I reckon, depending on traffic. Aicha's about to leave right now with Franc's lad. We need to get cracking, but I've got another question. Remember what you said about Melusine's sister being holed up in a mountain in the Pyrenees? What was her name? Which mountain?'

'Her name was Palatyne or Palestine depending on what legend you read, but there was a general agreement that she lived in Mount Canigou, between Andorra and Perpignan. Why?'

A chill runs down my spine. I don't trust the fae claiming kinship with me; there is something cold about him, a lack of humanity that I suspect was there long before he became a fae. His casual warning about Franc rings true though, and as desperate as I am to get to Narbonne and get this finished so that I can start hunting the pair of them down, I can't ignore what he said, not with the corroboration I've just received from Isaac.

'I'll not distract you any longer,' I say, ignoring his question. "Zac, Jak, please crack on. Get that protection working. We're running out of time, and I think we might need it yet.'

'All right, lad, we're on it. I want the proper rundown on whatever you miscreants have been up to without us afterwards though. Deal?'

'Deal, man. Was always going to be the case. We've just got to deal with the matter at hand first.'

'Take care of yourself, my boy. Get back safe, okay? Don't burn through too many bodies en route either.'

'Yes, Dad,' I reply, only half-jokingly, and hang up the phone.

Aicha was following the conversation and is unsurprisingly already ahead of me in terms of what the plan is. 'Assume you want me to get back to Toulouse and find Franc's hiding place that Robin Goodfellatio was talking about? What about him and the woman?'

I have a feeling that Aicha won't be saying Susanne's name anytime soon, not until she has her in a position for a very heated conversation. Heated as in red-hot pokers. Possibly a blowtorch too.

'They come next. We'll find them, Aicha. I want to know what they're up to and why they need that staff just as much as you do. Trust me. We've got to get the situation here dealt with first though.'

'Save the cheerleader, save the world stuff, eh, *saabi*?'

'You got it, *laguna*. Now go. I've got some unpleasant amateur butchery to perform, then need to cleanse this place without killing all the priests and pilgrims in the vicinity. I'll not be far behind you, okay?'

She nods, and I turn to consider my forthcoming real-world version of the 'Operation!' game, when I feel her hand on my arm. Turning back, I see something I never wanted to see in her kohl-black eyes. Pity for me.

'You know you could take the heart for yourself, Paul? It'll give you your magic back. Might well need it before the game is over.'

I smile, letting my love and friendship shine through for this amazing woman who's had my back more than I could ever have hoped. 'I know, Aich. You know I can't do that though, right?'

She ducks her head in acknowledgement. 'You should though. Had to try.'

'Noted. Get going, Aich. Smoke me a kipper. I'll be back in time for breakfast.'

She groans. 'I've had enough *Red Dwarf* dealing with that fucknuts of a Nain Rouge again. Stay safe, Paul. See you on the flip-side.'

She stoops to pick up her wakizashi, flicking the tar-like blood from the blade and sheathing it in a continuous movement, and leaves me to perform heart surgery on the dead woman who ate my magic so I can give it to a young girl who will one day be a major rival to me.

Sometimes, being a good guy sucks donkey dick.

Chapter Thirty

Lourdes, 10 April, PRESENT DAY

Half-dead is better than all-dead, right? Definitely better than undead. Take your wins where you can.

I am distinctly grumpy by the time I've hot-wired a car, an older model Renault Megane in a dark shade of paint I'm not even bothering to identify. When I sent Aicha off, I didn't realise just how under-powered I now am. Disposing of the body was easy once I stole a hammer and chisel from a maintenance shed. Once I sliced off extraneous layers of the body's upper torso, smashed my way through the rib cage and then carved the cold fleshy oval out of the chest cavity, the rest of the body disintegrated into dust. Sadly, the various blood and gore spilled during the battle and the retrieval of the heart stuck around, and I didn't have the *talent* resources to just magic it all away. Instead, I had to scrub the place as clean as possible with a fucking bucket and mop, which considering the first pass turned the water a deep pink, had not been swift. I did the best I could and then threw a weak *don't look here* across the doorway. It'll be enough to keep the unTalented away, and I don't have time to worry about magical looters at this moment. If they get there ahead of us getting back, then we'll have words with whoever it was at a later date. I've lost enough time, and I have a date with a powerful witch, a dying, rebellious daughter, and a cursed river monster. Such setups aren't as much fun in real life as they are in fairy tales.

The drive is honestly a bit of a blur. I am far from well, and staying conscious requires continuous effort. If I let myself get distracted, chances are I'll drive straight into oncoming traffic. French drivers are scary enough at the best of times with tailgating and inappropriate overtaking. Ignoring the whole potential "killing an innocent driver and their passenger(s)" thing, even if I wake up in a new body rather than just lie there until an ambulance arrives, it'll be a huge delay I can't afford, and I have no idea if the heart will survive such an impact. It'd be ridiculous to have battled to the death, only to lose out to a head-on collision.

I keep the window rolled down, a mix of nineties jungle on, the fast-pounding beats intermingling with a ragga vibe enough to keep my heartbeat up and my eyes open. Even when my phone vibrates with Aicha calling, I ignore it. I don't dare take my eyes off the road to answer it, and if I pull over, I am not sure I'll be able to get going again without falling asleep. A Whatsapp message symbol flashes up on the screen from her, but I keep driving and hope that 'Warning' by Firefox & 4-Tree coming on is an augery for my opponents and not for me.

It's only when I drive a bit further that I realise I could've connected to the car's Bluetooth.

No, wait...

Hell, I don't even know if the car has Bluetooth. I went old school and grabbed a CD out of my etheric storage before leaving Lourdes. I learned my lesson about keeping entertainment as close at hand as I do deadly weapons.

I shake my head. It doesn't matter. Aicha left me a message to listen to later.

When I pull up outside the Horreum in Narbonne, I listen to said message. Then I watch the video Aicha sent me on my phone.

Exhausting my extensive knowledge of swear words, I scream them into the ether with gusto and aplomb. Broken, still bleeding, and pissed off beyond belief, I get out of the car and hand the keys to one of the Sistren who has closed off the parking space for me. I limp past the "CLOSED FOR REPAIRS" sign hanging on the palisade-like iron gate that fences the lush greenery of the portico beyond. I've no time to stop and admire how well tended the small garden is though. Legs dragging, I head in and down to the Horreum below.

The name makes the place sound like a dungeon or haunted house show, but actually a *horreum* in Latin just means a public warehouse, somewhere to store goods or grain. Nobody knows what else the Romans stored in this one in Narbonne when they made the city their capital of the newly conquered Gaul during their whistle-stop tour taking over the known world, but whatever it was, it was a massive miscalculation. There are very few people, if any, still around from that period who were engaged with the world. Still, back when I was first around, less than a thousand years after the Roman Empire crumbled in fire and infamy, no one who had been in the area at the time would talk about what had happened. Whatever it was, something had turned the whole of Narbonne into a magical null zone, and the epicentre was this very storage space.

The null zone makes Narbonne simultaneously incredibly useful and potentially very dangerous. It won't dispel whatever magic is resident in Melusine's heart though. Aicha won't stop healing. Franc won't stop dying. Yet. Magic carried into the zone still exists. It just won't work when used in there. New weavings will falter and fail, swallowed down by the zone.

The light stone walls are brightly lit by a well installed modern lighting system aiming to highlight the unique, original features, but it does little to eradicate the claustrophobic sensation that the low-slung arched ceiling creates. Nowadays it might be a tourist attraction, but originally, this place was primarily about functionality. A few carved stone details are still visible because even in the most functional of places, the Romans appreciated the importance of artwork: reliefs of amphorae, matching up to a selection stacked artistically on display in one alcove; images of bulls, horses, and other livestock previously stored above the Horreum; faces half-dissolved by the march of time and the paths of hundreds of thousands of fingers tracing their outlines in passing.

In a side room lit with a sliver of natural light from an elevated and grated window slit, Franc sits, propped up against a couple of kegs intended for atmosphere but working equally well as leaning posts for gargantuan troll-like creatures. How he got down into the tunnels isn't clear. He probably had to crawl on his hands and knees. Mind you, considering how deathly ill he looks, he probably can't move about any other way anymore.

My heart sinks simultaneously as my anger rises at seeing him because he hasn't come alone. There is a group of his "lads and lasses", pretty much evenly split between the sexes, either tending to him, wiping his forehead, pressing water on him and the like, or else sprawled out, their backs pressed against the stone walls, not looking in much better form than their master. I'd say there are a dozen of them, but I don't have time to count. When Franc sees me, he tries to push himself up on one elbow, opening his mouth, though whether to smile or speak I don't know and don't care. I hold up my hand to silence him.

'You shut it. Not a word. We'll talk once I've dealt with the Mother and her daughter.'

I turn my back on him without waiting for his reply and haul myself off down the tunnels. I find the team from Bordeaux in another side room, a few turnings further down. The Mother has come more prepared than Franc, having brought a high-backed chair that must be considerably more portable than it looks because it's nearly as intricate as her immovable throne back at the Theatre. Next to it is something halfway between a medical bed and a cradle, on which lies her daughter, her head cradled in her mother's lap. The witch queen sits straight-backed on the bed rather than her throne, stroking her daughter's tangled hair in rhythm to the falling of her tears.

She looks up sharply at my arrival. 'There is a way?' she asks, urgency in her tone.

'There were two, actually,' I say caustically. 'Which is a fucking good thing because your "agent", your "eyes and ears", pulled a double cross on us and stole the one that we had all fucking bled and nearly died to recover!'

There is a moment of prolonged silence. Then...

'What?' The Mother of the Sistren of Bordeaux asks, and that 'what?' carries in it the promise of a hunt, a capture, and a slow and painful dismemberment of Susane if the Mother's ears did not deceive her.

I feel unbelievably tired suddenly. Tired of being let down and hurt by people I loved and thought long dead. Tired of doing ridiculous acts to save undeserving shit stains like Franc. Tired of seeing people suffer and lose and die over and over again because that is what life is. A continual cycle of loss until you drop off the end, and if you never drop off, then you just get to watch it turn around again and again, feeding hopes and dreams into the meat grinder of death and disappointment. I am not sure, but I have a terrible sinking feeling that I just transformed into a New Romantic.

'She set me up. Another fae was working with her.' I hold back the information about his claim to be my son. Once this is all over, we might remain uneasy allies, but we aren't ever going to be friends. Giving her that sort of information without good cause? Not smart in my book.

'They waited until we'd defeated Melusine,' I continue, watching the silent, contained, wrath-of-God level ire rising in the Mother's eyes. 'Then she smacked us all with a shit tonne of magic, far more than she ever had when she was a human, I should hasten to point out. Not enough to eradicate us but enough to hold us in stalemate whilst her buddy waltzed in and relieved us of the artefact that would have saved your daughter's life. Luckily, when we got old shitface next door on a long-distance call, he knew of another way we could manage it, luckily without having to fight another fae queen dragon-shifter with siren-like powers to the death. Would have loved a bit more info on that.'

'There was not much...' she begins.

'That you could tell,' I interrupt. 'We picked that up last frustrating conversation ago. Anyway, according to the Bizarro-world Swamp Thing next door, this will do the trick of restoring her *talent*.' I take great pleasure in offering her the dripping paper bag. The witch takes it and peers in, completely unfazed.

'To be consumed, I assume?' she asks urgently.

'I'd say so. Though I'd wait till you leave the Zone, obviously. Not the most fun time family meal you're ever likely to have with your daughter, but hey, at least it means you *get to have* another family meal with your daughter.'

She nods, and for all the anger in her eyes about Susane's actions, there is a genuine joy and gratitude in them when she meets mine.

'There have been sacrifices made, above and beyond what could have been expected,' she says, and I wonder exactly how much she can *see*, how much she knows.

'We will not forget this, and we owe you a service that may be called upon at a future date. Meanwhile, we name you Friend of the Sistren, and we will help protect your territory for as long as it takes you to... recover.' Yep, she definitely knows. On the plus side, she is prepared to help safeguard my territory, at least temporarily. And apparently, we are going to be friends after all. I'd be full of warm fuzzies if there was space left alongside the internal bleeding.

'Appreciate it, Mother,' I say, too exhausted by what happened and what is still to come to stand too much on ceremony.

'Also know that there will be no rest until the *traitor is found*,' she hisses through gritted teeth, and I know they will pursue Susane to the ends of the Earth. But that's between her and her fuck-up in the first place. She owes me, and nobody is going to harm either of them until I find out exactly what the fuck is going on, who that fuckhead is, if he's really... if it's possible...

I can't even bear to finish the thought, so I concentrate on the business at hand. 'I want her and the fae she's with,' I say. 'Alive, as well. If you capture them before I get my hands on them and deliver them both to me, we can count our favours as squared. Sound fair?'

She nods imperiously. 'There is cause for accord. Now, time draws short, and a leave must be taken. Stay here. Once the Zone has been left and the cure is confirmed, there will be a call, and the curse on that monster will be lifted.'

I nod, and she lifts her daughter carefully, putting her head down on a pillow arranged against the end of the medical bed/cradle. Several of the coven sweep in to carry the bed and the girl together, and the Mother stands. As she passes, she clamps a hand down on my shoulder.

'Sit and rest a while first, Cathar,' she murmurs in my ear. 'The end is not yet upon you, but perhaps the beginning is passed. There is much more pain and darkness ahead before the tunnel's light is reached. Take a moment's peace when you can, and the blessing of the Mother be upon you now and always, Good Man.'

I let my head dip as that is all the energy I have left to acknowledge her words, then go and slump in her Porta-Throne as she disappears up the corridor, following the processional train of attendants carrying a poor, lost girl back up out of the underworld to feel the touch of the sun's rays once more.

I settle down, a broken-staffed, broken-bodied Prospero sinking into the chair. Everything hurts. I just need a moment to get my breath back, to get my bearings and ready myself for what comes next. Just a moment to rest my eyes, is all. Only a moment.

CHAPTER THIRTY-ONE
MONTSEGUR, 16 MARCH 1244

Two hundred and ten. Two hundred and ten people — Good Men and Women, old Perfects in worn black robes, new converts having just taken the consolamentum the night previous, fresh out of their armour and into borrowed garb. Friends I avoided after my failed appeal to Esclarmonde, and strangers who deserved so much better than this fate. Two hundred and ten walk out of the gates of Montsegur, a good half of those who were besieged for over a year, and process down the path and onto the waiting fires. Two hundred and ten Good People burn, and I am there to witness the largest human bonfire ever made and the end of our faith.

I want most of all to make sure that there is no Nicetas-style trickery — fake fires, illusions to allow them to be spirited away and harvested for their energy. I cannot interfere, but I will make sure that they receive the martyrdom they chose. They stride with their heads high towards the constructed pyre, with Esclarmonde at their head. She turns despite the *do not look here* I cast over myself, and she smiles beatifically at me. I can see her peace, her acceptance, and I see that she is trying to reassure me even as she walks to her death. I weep openly, ashamed even if none can see me, apart from her.

I watch them burn, those two hundred and ten, and the tears never stop. They never scream or beg, not even as they fall. There is a purity to this moment such as I have never witnessed. Esclarmonde is the last with her eyes open, always watching me. Her white light builds, brightening and strengthening until she is a star plucked from the heavens and thrust into the middle of the flames' heart, until I can look no more, having to shield my eyes. When I look again, she has disappeared, and the last of the Perfects are gone from this life. I hope they have escaped the wheel upon which the Evil God has trapped us. I hope they find peace at last.

Afterwards, I hear many stories of the white light, of Esclarmonde having turned into a dove and flying to rest on one of the mountaintops. I do not know if there is any truth in any of that or whether it is a reaction of those sensitive to *talent* on seeing her upon that final bonfire. I can only hope there is truth in what she has to say. I can only hope that I will get to see her again before the end.

Chapter Thirty-Two

Narbonne, 10 April, Present Day

Apparently we won. So why do I feel like such a spectacular loser? Oh yes. Because of what I've got to deal with next.

I wake up to the demanding vibrations of my phone. Blearily staring at it as I fight to engage the hand-eye coordination to move the slide button sufficiently to answer, I see I've missed two calls already. Guess I've done more than rest my eyes. I'd love to say that I feel better for the power nap, but I feel like I've been kicked clean in the chest by an over-powered dragon capable of bench-pressing a truck. Weird, that.

I finally emerge victorious from the back-and-forth battle with the answer button. 'Hello?' I say, trying to shake the cobwebs from my head that cling on tenaciously in the face of my half-hearted spring-cleaning attempt.

'There is...progress. Signs of success. It is acceptable. There is a completion of the agreement, Cathar.' The voice of the Mother of the Sistren is all business again, factual and actual, no amity in it. Guess we are just casual friends rather than bosom buddies, after all.

'I'm pleased,' I say, and I am. It guts me enough to have given up my opportunity to restore my *talent*. It would have really pissed me off if it didn't work for the girl, if I squandered the chance unnecessarily.

'The curse will be lifted. It will be gone once the monster leaves the Null Zone.' There is a pause. 'That means that the creature will be as he is until he crosses the border. There is time still for a decision to be made.'

I nod — pointless as she can't see me, but I am not in the best form of my life right at this moment. Sue me. 'Yeah, I think it's about time I had a little tête-à-tête with old Franc. Safe travels back, Mother.'

'There is no safety for your journeys to come, Cathar, but I wish you luck and success in all you aim to achieve. Never forget that you are a Good Man.'

The line clicks off, and I stare at the screen.

'Wow, talk about ending a conversation on a downer,' I mutter to myself and then pop my phone back in my pocket. 'Time to go have a chat with a river dickhead.'

I drag myself up out of the comfy, comfy chair that whispers sweet nothings about sliding back into its warm embrace, and I hobble back towards the other side room where Franc and his gang of miscreants wait.

Before I go in, I take a moment to ready myself. There'll be no more limping, no more evidence of me being close to burning out and keeling over. I'll show no weakness in the conversation that the two of us need to have next.

I saunter into the room, my hands in my pockets. 'Franc! You tricksy old seadog, you. How are you feeling? Still a bit under the weather? Bit run-down? Ah, I understand. Not been in tiptop form myself, not shipshape and Bristol fashion, to keep the nautical theme going. Still, sometimes we're up, sometimes we're down, just have to roll with the punches. Still,

I've got some good news and some bad news. Good news is, the curse is going to be lifted! You aren't going to die from the Sistren's magic.'

I walk over to him, the friendly grin I paint onto my face unable to hide the savagery lurking behind the mask. Franc shrinks back, his blank eyes wide as I pull my sword out of my etheric storage and wave his boys and girls to back away.

'Bad news is, old boy, that you're going to die by *my* hand instead.' I kick the arm he leans on out from under him, taking grim delight at his cry of pain as I fix my sword point to his grapefruit-sized Adam's apple.

'What, again, the betrayalings and breakery of word and honour, upon my oath?' Franc starts but cuts off as I press hard enough to reveal a drop of blood that could be black or a dark shade of green so close to it as really makes no difference. I am just delighted to see the fucker bleed.

'Don't,' I say, emphasising my intent by pushing it a little deeper in. 'Don't you dare fucking talk to me about honour and oaths, you slimy, toad-fucking, oath-breaking twatfish.'

I turn my attention away, to look at the young men and women he brought with him, undoubtedly to act as a human shield in just such a situation. 'You're all loyal to old Franc here, eh? Got yourselves a good deal in terms of the misery the streets can throw at you, hey? Sign on the dotted line, and Franc'll take care of you. Did he ever tell you how final that care could be? No? Then why don't I let you see?'

I pull up the video Aicha sent me with one hand on my phone and click it to full screen before showing it to the scared urchins. Neither Franc nor I can see it, but neither of us need to. The video is in his home.

Aicha narrates during the video. 'Looks like we've found the portal, *saabi*. Tracking down his base wasn't hard without him here to obfuscate. I'm pretty sure this leads straight to Canigou.'

Franc goes entirely white, even the sickly green pallor that normally underlines his unhealthy complexion disappearing. 'No,' he murmurs over the pressure on his throat. 'No, please, my lord, please.'

'Please what, Franc? Please don't find out your sordid little secret, you piece of fuck? Too late for that.'

He doesn't seem to notice. It's hard to be sure where someone is looking when they don't have any pupils, but I am pretty sure his attention is on the group opposite, whose eyes are all glued to the screen.

'Please don't be showing them those imageries, my lord. Please. Not my lovely lads and lasses. Please, Undyer. Please.'

The words fall on deaf ears. I remain inured to his pleas. I've already seen the video. It seems only right that those who believe he'll protect them see it too.

The sound of echoing steps from a stone corridor carry over from the speakers, and Franc pales further when he hears Gil say, 'It's getting colder here, a lot colder than you'd expect the mountains to be at this time of year.'

Franc starts whining. 'No, Lord Cathar, no. Please tells us you didn't let my lovely, my loveliest go down into the darkery there? No, my lord, no, no, no...'

He carries on moaning, but my attention is on the young homeless folk in front of me. I know what is coming up. Part of me feels bad for making them witness what is in the video, but there is another part of me, a vindictive, vengeful part that wants to share the misery considering the price I paid to save the wretch I'm holding at sword's length.

'It's damnably dark, Ms Aicha,' Gil says and then there is a gasp as she lights up the place with a werelight. Most of the watching audience can't immediately identify what they are seeing on the screen, but one sharp-eyed lass starts whimpering, her eyes widening in horror. As the others clock on, there are many who turn green, retching or vomiting, crying in dismay and disgust at what they're seeing. Franc is still snivelling where I have him pinned, mumbling denials or pleas for a mercy he would never show. I turn my loathing regard on him now.

'A fucking cold room, Franc. Hanging joints, salted ribs — fuck, salted whole torsos. Livers and kidneys and hearts, *is it not,* you piece of shit? Guess munching on internal organs runs in the fucking family.' I boot him, kicking him clean in the temple and sending him sprawling, my rage getting the better of me. Besides, I don't need to hold him threatened to keep from being mobbed. None of his lads and lasses are springing to his defence now.

'Bones, Franc. So many fucking bones. Gnawed on bones, like the fucking savage beast that you are.' I plant my foot into his side, driving the air from his chest. I'm wearing boots, but I am driven so hard by my rage I reckon I still break a toe or two, though I pay the pain no mind.

'Bones cracked and marrow sucked. Hands with each finger bitten down to nubs, like a fucking kid's snack, put down and left to finish later. Eyeballs, Franc. Fucking eyeballs...' I gulp, trying to stop myself from crying, feeling the stinging of the tears so close to the surface. 'Eyeballs chomped in two. And the heads still left, kept with the orbs plucked out of them, some of them cracked open like fucking coconuts where you spooned the brains out. *They were fucking kids, Franc!*' I scream, and I kick him again and again and again, screaming uncontrollably, the horror and the fury and the terrible, terrible guilt that I allowed this to happen, eating away at my self-control and self-image. I strike him without stopping, frenziedly beating away at the bastard who made me complicit in so much death of so many innocents.

He curls up in a ball, squealing and trying to protect himself, to deflect my blows with his hands or arms, succeeding sometimes, failing others. As long as I land the strikes on him, I don't really care where they hit. I just want to feel him break. Like that video broke something inside of me.

Eventually, I wear myself out. It doesn't take as long as it would have normally. Physically, I am already ruined. It was only the nervous energy of wrath dancing on the edge of madness that kept me upright and capable of doing damage as long as I did. Eventually, I sink down too. Tears and sputum stream down my face as I gulp for air through my pain and misery. I keep my sword to hand though, still ready to land the killing blow, still holding back for now.

'Why, Franc?' I ask eventually, when the stitch in my side eases up enough to allow me to speak. 'Why, you utter bastard? I thought you could live on their misery? You made a deal with them.'

'Yessssss!' Franc hisses, his head lifting to show a weird luminescent glow to his albumen eyes. 'We made dealings and dutyings and promiseries and pledgings, and they broke them, they did! Always a few, always a few who makes all swearings and solemnries and then goes hopsy daisy, mind changerings and wanting to go back to whereforing they'd come from, the homes and hearthings they'd run from, when they'd come hoppity skippering into old Franc's arms. Decidings that their word was meaningless. Well, if our words are meaningless, then you are meaningless, less meant for mealings. They gave themselves, then wanted to quick splittings and be gone. No, once we makes our dealery then you are mine. I was clear to them at the start, mines is mine under my protectorings, long as they stay true to their word. I only broke those who were quick with their own breakerings. They were mine, manling. *They were mine!*'

The monster roars the last words. I choke in some more air and spit in his face.

'You're a fucking monster, Franc.'

He spits too, a visceral pile of blood to the side, then chuckles and licks my spittle off as it runs down to his lips. 'I am indeed, my little lord, am I not? I am indeed.'

We both sit there, physically wrecked, mentally shattered, all illusions stripped away, a rare moment of honesty between two entirely unnatural beings who should have died a long time ago. My sword is still ready, but it is Franc who breaks the silence.

'Well, what now, little manling? Will it be lopserings and choppery and off with his head? There'll be a tripsing and a traipsing of many a lovely lad and lass along that darkery pathway to keep old Franc company to go look-seeing what's on the other side of that most final of veilings. Might not go crickedy crunch on their bones and organry afterwards, but will be you who kills them, same as old Franc might have, for their promiseries and oathings. Mind, there were always more corresponderings and similarity between us than you were ever wanted to be recognising, all head turnery away from the parallelings, Undyer. Now there are choosings and pickings to be made.' He stops and sighs, suddenly seeming unfathomably old, a dated relic from the past's bad dreams. 'And always the pricery, is it not? Always payings to be made.'

I echo his sigh. 'Yeah, Franc. There are always prices to pay for the choices we make.'

We sit in silence again, and it is me who breaks it this time. 'I can't let you go, Franc. Can't let you do this again. Obviously, you are never coming back to Toulouse, but I can't let you start this up somewhere else, make a new load of minions and a new walk-in freezer.'

The monster perks up. 'I could make promisings, my lord, promisings and oatheries upon my power, to never do such snackings again, not ever. I could go far, far away, on sailings and swimmings, never to be a troubling for you and yours again, upon my oath!'

I don't reply for a moment. Normally, such an oath would be more than sufficient. Problem is, I feel sure he already broke the oath-sworn agreement we made all those years ago with the killings, but I am too tired. Too tired to go watch the memories to verify it even if I could trust Franc enough to head into my mind palace. But also too tired of all the killing, the fighting, the petty feuding between supposed Powers where nothing ever gets better for anyone who gets caught in the middle. Only more death and misery to be shared around like gifts to an Oprah Winfrey audience. You get some, you get some, everybody gets some. Nobody gets out. Nobody wins.

'What do you want in return, Franc?' I ask wearily, heartsick at my words but seeing no other resolution. I won't cause the deaths of any more innocents caught in the middle of supernatural struggles.

'Your oathings given, my lord,' he says quickly, a hopeful note in his tone. 'Your oathings to not come a-hunting poor Franc, no killings now nor later neither, when you're all sad-sacked and guilt-bitten, no lookings and scryery to track me down. A parting of ways and whirrings, clean and complete and a finalry of finishings that leaves us both alive and alone, is it not?'

I weigh it all up, as much as my damaged mind and soul can manage before I eventually nod. 'My oath on that, Franc. Free them all, and I'll leave you be and neither hunt nor harry you if you give your oath never to kill or maim another human and to be gone far, far away from Toulouse, from France, from my goddamn sight.'

'My oathings in return, my little lord,' he says and spits in his clawed hand. We shake, and I feel I've given up the last of my humanity in that act. It is like growing up finally and realising that adulthood is just a progression of appalling options, each worse than the rest, and all of them with terrible, terrible prices to pay. For the first time in a hundred lives, in eight hundred years since I said goodbye to the black robes of the Perfect and embraced my magic, I want to lay my head in my mother's lap, and for her to tell me that everything is going to be okay, that it is all just a bad dream. I wish I could remember what her voice sounded like so that I can imagine those words coming from her lips. I'd have to remember what her lips looked like though. I wonder what she would have thought of me shaking hands with a monster that eats kids who backtrack on their mistake in pledging themselves to him. I wonder if she'd have been able to tell me that everything was going to be okay after seeing that. I wonder if she'd even have been able to look at me.

'Get out of here, Franc,' I say, weary to the bone. 'The curse will lift as soon as you clear the Null Zone.'

'My thankings and gratitude, my Lord Undyer. I shall always hold as a treasure most glittery and of enormous valuings our friendship –'

I am on him in a moment, lifting his massive frame up and pinning him against the wall. Not with magic, no, but with all that pent up anger — at him, at myself, at the way this entire episode has played out. 'We are *not* friends, you fucking piece of shit,' I hiss, my teeth grinding as I speak, as though I might pulverise the very idea of it into dust. 'We are not friends. We never were, and we never will be. You walk away now, Franc, and you keep walking far, far away from me and mine. If I ever see you again, I will kill you and damn the consequences. Walk, now.'

I push him towards the doorway, and he stumbles, landing on one knee. Some of his people rush to support him, although I notice that more still hang back. He raises his head, and his teeth are bared, points that are clearly made for rending flesh out on display. His eyes are a-glow, and I don't doubt that this little display is taking all his remaining energy. Just as mine did. Anger is a powerful driving force. So is stupidity.

'Fine, little manling,' he says as he hauls himself to his feet, leaning heavily on two of his lads who flank him. 'I want none of your amities or alliances neither, upon my oath.' He sneers, pushing away the young men on either side of him, refusing to be seen to need aid, to be vulnerable. 'Not the only typery to be ready to offer out alliancings and camaraderie. There'll be others who'll value to have my truthings a-whispered in their ear-lugs, will they not? Perhaps such truthings as I might know about your fine self, my Lord Undyer.' The sneer is practically a grimace as he spits on the ground between us.

'Just get out of here, Franc. Don't ever let me see you again.'

He turns, pulling himself upright, albeit bent double to pass in the cramped vertical space, only to stop short and start backing up into the room again. At first, I can't understand why. Then I see the point of a katana pressed directly into his forehead, forcing him back.

Aicha strides in, her sword handle half twisted and wrist-locked, compelling Franc into his rearward shuffle. He is bent forward, folded at the waist, his head lifted, though I can't see if his eyes are locked onto the blade or the Druze warrior whose own eyes blaze with righteous fury and a thirst for vengeance.

'You are not leaving, monster,' she says as he continues to back up.

'Aich, this is done. We've made a deal,' I say, trying to catch her eye, to show her Franc's people nearby. She isn't looking anywhere but at the whimpering brute she has caught on the point of her blade.

'You made a deal, *saabi*. Not me. Not going to happen either, a deal between me and him.'

'Aicha, listen to me. This isn't what I want.'

She half-cocks her head, sparrow-like. 'Not sure about that, Paul. Not sure it isn't what you need.'

'Aicha, I don't want these people to die. Listen to me, Aicha. Listen. I don't want this. Not like this, not now. Aicha...'

My words make no difference, no change to her emotionless expression, where only her eyes speak of her desire to rain down bloody murder on the villain in front of her. Franc can see there is no change made, no chance gained even as I start edging towards her, my hands raised, still trying to get her attention, trying to get her to back down. A grin, that disturbing, joyful grin that splits his face from ear to ear as though unhinging his face's lower half, springs up, and he bows as deep as he can. It is deeper than I'd have expected considering he is already almost bent double, and he sweeps his hat off his head as he does so, his eyes never leaving hers.

'Well then, dusk born and walking, 'tis to be yourself who sings my lullaby, eye-closery and sweet dreamings, is it not? Long I've dreamed of our choraling and saltations, a skip-sway-turn and glory in the steelings' clanks. Will you allow me the honour of calling up my watery death, that we may bring our fol-a-diddles in matching clashery?'

'No,' Aicha replies and pivots her wrist as she draws her blade back towards her left shoulder. Then she reverses the manoeuvre, and as fast as I can scream at her to '*Stop!*'...

She decapitates Franc, his head bouncing off his body and rolling to rest at her feet, the unnatural blankness of his eyes finally matching the rest of his lifeless expression.

Franc's people, his lovely lads and lasses, the poor young fools he convinced would be safe under his watchful eye, fall to their knees in sync with the river monster's torso pitching forward, smashing into the ground with the weight of all his sins and all their deaths. Blood bubbles out of their noses, their mouths, their eyes just as the blood pours out from Franc's neck, pooling around his severed head and Aicha's boots. I rush to the nearest of them and try futilely to stem the bleeding, to push the tiny fragment of *talent* I still have into the boy and heal him, but he is haemorrhaging massively, blood leaking from every orifice. He vomits a crimson pool too wide and deep to hold any hope at my feet and is gone. I know without looking, all the others who re-pledged their loyalty to him are too.

I sink to my knees, not caring about the gore I am kneeling in, stroking the boy's hair, clutching him to my chest as I weep. He was nineteen, twenty at the most, full of the wrong decisions of youthful indiscretion, but he should have had the possibility of redemption and learning that growing older can provide. The sword slice snatched that away from him. So much potential erased, his life-thread cut as cleanly as Franc's neck.

I feel Aicha's approach. She stops a metre away, silent and waiting. She knows I have a lot to say...eventually. Even if I feel like there are no words for how I feel right now.

'I told you no,' I say. 'I said no, and you still did it.'

She cocks her head. 'Am I your servant then, *saabi*? At your command?'

'You've never been that. But I thought you were my friend.'

'Always. Always have been.'

I raise my eyes, my vision hazed by the tears filling them faster than blinking can force them down my cheeks. 'Then why did you do this? Why?'

She shrugs, apparently casually, though I can see a certain stiffness, a certain tension to her seemingly relaxed poise. 'Had to be done.' Then she sighs and crouches down to look at me properly, to look me in the eye. 'Paul, you are my friend. You helped me. A lot. Could see my suffering. My hurt. You've never been very good at looking at your own though. When I –' She pauses momentarily. 'Went hunting, I wasn't planning on coming back. Not for a long time, anyhow. Not for good. We would've stayed in touch as friends, but that would've been all. Instead, I was told you would end up being important. That you would need help. That you had spent so long looking for the good, learning to see all the shades of grey. Sometimes you forget that black and white still exists. Sometimes wrongs need righting. Sometimes that means a price to pay.'

'*That wasn't your price to pay*!' I scream at her. I drop my head, still sobbing into the young lad's hair.

'No. It was theirs. The choices they made. I didn't make them. We did our best. Couldn't let him go free to start all over again. How many more would he have claimed? How many more would have died? They paid for their choices. I stand ready to pay for mine. Always.'

'What about the others?' I whisper, not raising my head, not able to look at her again as I ask about all the others I was trying to protect when I bargained again with Franc.

'Isaac and Jakob worked it out. They tied it to your magic in Toulouse. Everyone in the city is safe. They're free now.'

'And those outside the city, Aich? How many aren't in the city boundary? How many did he have spying in other cities or running errands? Hell, how many did he have in the suburbs or nearby towns, extending his area of influence?'

I force myself to raise my head, to meet her impassive gaze head on with the heat of my grief. 'How many died, Aicha? How many dead because of our actions?'

She shrugs again. 'I do not know, *saabi*. We can find out together if you wish. Give their families closure...'

I shake my head. 'There is no we, no us anymore. We're done. Right now, I haven't got time to find out the total price of your actions, Kandicha. I need to go after Susane, after my son. I've not the time to give them peace, so I'll carry their restless spirits with me for now. Just another price to pay, I guess. Get out of here.'

She hesitates again, and I refuse to let myself see the hurt and pain hidden deep in her micro-expressions that nobody else will ever know her well enough to notice. I am too deep in my suffering to bear to see hers.

'Get out!' I shout at her as I bawl my eyes out over the dead and the suffering of eight hundred years. I cry for what seems like a long time, although I couldn't have told you whether it was minutes or hours, only that it felt as elongated as every extended second I've lived during my unnatural allotted time on this planet. When I finally lift my head again, Aicha Kandicha is gone.

I don't know how long I kneel in that room before I stagger up and out, back towards the car. I'll call the Mother on the way out. She can send a clean-up team to cleanse the Horreum. Then I'll call Isaac and Jakob, fill them in on what happened, and we can start trying to solve this whole bloody mess I've found myself in since the shit wizard got his hands on me. Maybe once this is all finished, once I've found Susane and the fae who claims to be my son, once I've found out if Almeric is also still alive and destroyed him if necessary, maybe then I'll finally be able to rest. For now, though, I have two practically impossible tasks to accomplish, and I'll be doing them without the two things I value most in the world.

I'll be doing them without my *talent* and without Aicha Kandicha.

It makes the practically impossible, absolutely impossible. I'm not about to let that stop me from trying though.

AFTERWORD

S o there we are at the end of another adventure, and things are surely at their darkest. Or are they? You'll have to join me for book three, *imPerfect Fae*, to find out exactly how much trouble Paul can actually get himself into without Aicha along to "wipe his arse for him", as she puts it.

Thank you, everyone, for coming along with me on these trips into my insane imagination. It really is wonderful and revelatory just how many people have clicked with my particular brand of madness and demanded tickets to ride on my crazy train, even though it's clearly about to go plunging off the rails at any moment. Probably into a ravine. Filled with ravenous crocodiles. Armed with space lasers.

I've loved adding Gil to Team Bonhomme. He's going to need a while to recuperate from all the madness he's been dragged through, but we'll see him again. In the meantime, there's a short story about his origins that you can grab by signing up for my newsletter here.

Book info regarding the background history and characters:

The fall of Montsegur really did happen like that. The last hurrah of the Cathar faith extinguished in a march to the pyre. While a few stragglers hung on, the movement died in the flames at the foot of the pog.

The Cagot were a real group who genuinely existed, with evidence of them prior to the tenth century right up until the First World War. All the details I gave are true. They really were excluded from every single activity, not allowed to work with metal, not allowed into churches. And to this day no one knows why. They had no ethnic differences, no religious or cultural peculiarities. I came across them searching for a second Israelite graveyard down by Hastingues, having been directed to one at La Bastide Clairence by the B&B owner. While the graveyard itself was less spectacular than the one at Bidache, it was just across from the church graveyard, separated only by a small path, showing how integrated the Jewish community were with the population there. I went for a wander around the church, which was stunningly beautiful, and was baffled to come across what was described as a Cagot door, used to allow the Cagot community to come and accept communion as they weren't allowed to enter the church. I started my research and discovered this baffling, inexplicable history. Them being half-fae seems entirely plausible compared to any other reason anyone has ever given.

The story of Lourdes and Bernadette is true, and as strange as it sounds. It took some persuading for the Catholic Church to declare it a miracle. Now it's a very profitable moneymaker for them. Robert-Houdin was real as well, the father of modern stage magic, and the guy Houdini named himself after. The story of him being used by Louis Napoleon to pacify the Algerians with his "magic" is absolutely true. Ahmad Al-Buni was a real person — not only a sorcerer but a genius mathematician — and his book, *Shams al-Ma'arif*, is still regarded as one of the, if not *the*, definitive grimoire on Islamic magic.

The Grand Theatre in Bordeaux's construction story was told to me by their staff, along with the tale of them finding the ruins of a temple when the work actually started. I've not found supporting evidence for that particular story, but then, I wouldn't. The Mother would never allow it.

The Horreum at Narbonne is really there and can be visited. Narbonne was the capital of France during Roman times, and the warehouse is definitely worth a visit. Don't try casting magic there though. It won't work no matter how hard you try.

L'O'Bohem exists and will always occupy a special place in my heart. It was the first open mic I found when we moved to Toulouse, and the bar was so cool, so completely unpretentious, filled with unique characters, that I fell in love with it. They opened it up during Covid times for me to use to film the music video for my song, 'No Way Out', and I've always loved the vibe of the place. It's a pleasure to have put the bar into my book. I discovered La Chapelle during Covid as well, as it was one of the places taking donations of food and clothing to distribute to refugees through the city. It's an incredible place, and they do amazing work.

My thanks as always to my family for putting up with me, and my children for not exploding with all that curiosity when I won't let them read my books for obvious reasons. To my editor Miranda for, as always, not so much smoothing off the rough edges as sculpting them to perfection. Nick Jones for the stunning cover art — good having you along for the adventure, homey. My beta readers Becca, Becky, and Lauretta — I don't know what I'd do without your input; it's priceless. Heather G Harris and all the rest of the Clean Fantasy writer group for their endless advice and wisdom to a newcomer fumbling his way through the path towards publication. My parents and siblings for always supporting me and never murdering me, however tempted they may have been at various times along the path to me reaching adulthood. Everyone else I've forgotten to mention but who have been there with me on this crazy road. I hope this book stands in tribute to those steps we've walked together.

Now turn the page to read the first chapter of *imPerfect Fae*, where Paul is being typically Paul-like and seeking resolution for his myriad problems. By getting absolutely shit-faced...

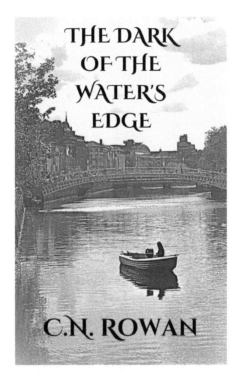

THE DARK
OF THE
WATER'S
EDGE

C.N. ROWAN

"The waters had called to him. He felt a safety there, a kinship with the swirling depths that had been corralled into straightened paths by man's domineering force but that remained wild as an element, untameable and incorruptible.

It wasn't tame though. He'd had to remind himself of that more than once."

Find out how Gil first came to Toulouse, and how he met Franc, in this exclusive short story.

Available for free by joining my mailing list here.-

https://freebook.cnrowan.com/darkwater

TURN THE PAGE FOR THE FIRST CHAPTER OF THE IMPER-
FECT CATHAR BOOK 3

'IMPERFECT FAE'

TOULOUSE, 15 APRIL, PRESENT DAY

I drink, therefore I am. Descartes said that to me after I took him on a four-day bender. Inspired all his later work.

The best thing about having your magic eaten? Getting shit-face drunk after.

Magic and alcohol don't mix, really. Not in the "I drink this, then sniff that, and next thing I know, I've got five new tattoos and I'm trying to chew a police officer's leg off" kind of way but in the "magic is too damn powerful, so booze can't mess with your synapses seriously unless you start mainlining methylated spirits" sense. I am really, really enjoying finally getting smashed off a few simple pints though. It allows me to forget just how much of a shitshow the rest of my life has devolved into.

Whenever the booze haze I've been wrapping myself up in for the last four or five days (a sense of time is the first thing I let go of, swiftly followed by decorum) starts wearing thin, I quickly find myself drowning in all the misery I seem to have encountered recently, mainly brought upon by myself. How did it all go so badly wrong? Let me count the ways...

First, my dead wife, best friend, and son all turned out to be surprisingly ambulatory and sadly not in a *Walking Dead* sense. Shows how crappy everything is going for me when zombified loved ones would be the better option. Instead, my best friend, who I thought died saving my life, reappeared hundreds of years after that event, having spent all of that time planning my downfall as a side event to destroying the world. Then my murdered wife showed up, now no longer even human, in service to a powerful coven of witches who ordered her to watch over me because the river monster I dumbly made a deal with in my grief while mourning said wife (because you know, she was supposed to be dead) decided to eat the magic of one of their daughters. I thought we were sorting some stuff out –me and my dead wife, not me and the river monster, I hasten to add– finally getting some of that closure, but nope. She double-crossed me at the worst possible time, revealing she had even more secrets when surprise, she turned out to be in cahoots with our son – who I believed had been ripped from her belly to be used in some messed up ritual as she lay dying. And what exactly was that "worst possible time", you ask?

After I killed a fucking demi-goddess. But not before she'd eaten my magic. Not my best day ever. Not in the bloody top ten.

Then I had to go kill the scum-sucking, murderous river monster I shared my territory, the city of Toulouse, with. Except I couldn't kill Franc because it would have also murdered all the homeless he kept tethered to him with his *talent* as insurance against such an act.

Ah, but no worries!

I bring my tumbler of whisky to my lips and basically inhale its contents, remembering the rest of my sorry tale.

No worries because Aicha Kandicha, my *ex*-BFF and a ninth-century Moroccan princess turned cold-blooded killer, wasn't okay with us striking a deal that would see Franc leaving my area only to start eating kids somewhere else. So she cut off his head, damning who knows how many poor souls to death. Those in Toulouse were safe, but I watched dozens outside of his protection die just like Franc did. And we'll never know how many more he had outside the city boundaries.

'Damn you, Aicha,' I mutter as I turn the empty glass upside down, wondering where the hell all my alcohol went. 'I begged you not to do it, but you did it anyway. You did it anyway...'

And so our friendship is done.

Pulling the glass to my chest, I hold it close. 'Whisky,' I murmur, 'you're my only friend...'

I'm slumped across a bar. I think. I don't even know which bar. Honestly? I don't know if it even is a bar. I might well be sat at a table in the park. Or on a bench. Or the pavement. I've spent a fair bit of time perfecting my slumping action on each of those recently. I am approaching mastery. Just a little more alcohol, and I'll have it down pat. I search for the drink I'm sure I have somewhere at hand.

Sadly, it seems to have decided to take a stroll when my attention was elsewhere. Tricky little buggers, drinks. Moment you turn your back, they've either gone for a walk, or they're in need of topping up all over again. Sneaky fuckers.

Something cuts through the alcohol haze wrapped around my head. A noise – a blocked, muffled sort of noise that I've heard before. That means something. Something I need to be aware of. Need to do something about.

Blearily, I push myself up into a sitting position. Apparently, I'm not at a bar, after all, but on the damp wooden deck of a canal barge. Oops. Simple mistake to make.

The noise comes again, which is unreasonable of it because I'm still trying to get the world to calm down and stop whirlygigging like a Wurlitzer after the regrettable decision to move. Squinting my ears as hard as I can, I try to focus on it, on why it seems so familiar.

Ah. Realisation comes and burns just the tiniest touch of the alcohol away. Not a lot – not enough to bring me even close to sober. But enough to get me on my feet and moving, half-vaulting, half-tumbling over the barge's gate and down onto the towpath. Without falling into the canal, which is a real and present danger. But right now, I'm more interested in being dangerous.

Because what I heard was the noise of fear. Of a woman's fear. Muffled by a heavy hand.

It says something of how shit the world we live in is that it's a sound I've heard often enough over the centuries to recognise immediately even through the heaviest of booze clouds. Half-sobs masked by weighted grasping fingers as men look to take, as always, what isn't theirs. By force and a malicious greed that soils us all as a species.

Not while I've got anything to say about it.

There. In the shadows of a closed-up squat factory, the concrete façade picked out with splintered boarding and shattered glass. I can pick out shapes. The way they're moving makes me fairly sure they're people. Mind you, everything else is dancing around constantly; the pavement keeps trying to move away from my foot each time I put it down, and I'm having to concentrate really hard not to go arse over tit every single step.

As I stagger towards them, I start to distinguish features enough to be able to perform a rudimentary headcount. Three. Or four. One of them might be a bollard. Or he might be kneeling. I can't tell at this distance –and this level of drunkenness– if any of them are male. But I'm prepared to lay money on it for all of them. All except their intended victim.

As the sound told me, they're restraining her. One of the fucking shameful excuses for a human being has his pork-sausage fingers half-shoved into her mouth, keeping her quiet enough while his friends root through her belongings. I've got no idea if they're going to be satisfied with stealing her valuables or if this is just the warm-up, the amuse-bouche before the main course.

Either way, I'm not standing for it. I mean, I literally *am* standing for it, in the sense that it was the only thing capable of dragging me back to my feet, unsteady and swaying though I may be.

But this is my city. And shit like this? Gets dealt a smackdown.

'Oi! You sorry sad sack bunch of wankers!' is what I try to yell at them. Unfortunately, I chose far too many words starting with S, so most of what came out basically sounds like a snake having a stroke. The 'wankers!' is clear at least. And enough to get their attention.

Good. Let's fucking rumble. I step forward, bringing my fists up to a classic pugilistic guard...

Which is enough to completely off-balance my body as it was previously relying on my hands to keep its wobbling under control, like a tight-rope walker's pole. Now that they're not splayed to the side but are pulled up tight in front of my face, my foot skids off sideways and I go splashing face-first into a small pool of foul-smelling water.

Nope. Not water. The Good God damn it.

By the wheezing chuckles emanating from the group, I've not struck them paralysed with fear by my menacing entrance.

Right. Never mind. Take two.

I drag myself back up, only buckling once, kneeling back in the puddle because, obviously, having my top half soaked in stale piss isn't enough.

Normally I don't use magic on the Talentless. But these guys are fucking scum. And I'm properly annoyed now.

'Right. You fucking asked for it,' I slur and launch myself into what might just pass for a run. Albeit more where I lean in the direction I want to go and rely on my legs to work fast enough to stop me from faceplanting back onto the concrete.

And as I gather up speed, I pull on my *talent,* drawing it to me, ready to set the fuckers on fire, ready to make them burn like a fucking Bastille Day fireworks display. As I near, I stretch my hands forward and push my power out...

'Oh, do you think he's one of those street magicians? You know, like Dynamo?' The rough timbre carries vague curiosity tinged with boredom. Not the vocal reaction I generally look for.

'Yeah, I saw that too! Little poof of flames. Whaddya reckon? Bit of black powder up his sleeve?' A second voice sounds even less impressed than the first one.

Oh. Right. I'm not packing the big guns magically now. Not even a Super Soaker. Fuck. Forgot about that.

Never mind. I've got hundreds of years of street fighting and martial arts experience at my fingertips. I don't need magic for a bunch of shitheels like these.

I'm leading the charge now with my right shoulder, and Bored Goon Number One's voice definitely came from my right. My vision's blurring like the world's shittest shakicam home movie, but I don't need to see. I've got training. *Instinct.* I place my foot, and miraculously it plants, solid. Using that, I pivot, twisting from the waist, bringing a spinning back fist crashing round...

And missing the bastard by a country mile, smashing straight into the brick wall behind him.

I hear the pop, but the pain's too diffuse and blinding for me to work out exactly how many knuckles I broke.

I'm quickly distracted from that anyhow. By the fist crushing my cheek-bone.

My neck doesn't snap –I can tell that because I'm not dead or severely paralysed– but my pain receptors aren't convinced because they're screaming blue murder. Or, at the very least, aquamarine murder. The left side of my face is on fire, but the right side doesn't get left out for long because I hit the floor hard, grazing most of the top layer of skin off as I go.

Not my most graceful entry into a fight ever, it would be fair to say.

I might not be sure how much damage I took to my neck, but there's no question at all to the amount I take to my ribs when a heavy shoe crunches down on my chest; it breaks at least one rib. Instinctively, I curl in on myself.

And now I'm a prone target.

The kicks rain down, shot after shot to my sides, then my back as I roll around like a shell-beached turtle.

Getting my arse handed to me by a bunch of Talentless thugs. Fuck my life.

Of course, I may be drunk. Scratch that. I am drunk, and those first few blows basically put me out of action. But I'm not completely done. And even without my magic, even pissed out of my skull, if I didn't manage to break my own hand on that wall, I'd stand a decent chance against these goons.

So instinct does what it needs to. A foot flashes past my peripheral vision, and my hands lash out of their own accord. I've got a grip. But I've used both my arms to get it.

Ah, fuck it.

I open my mouth and bite down hard, squeezing my jaw together. Then I twist and tear my head backwards.

Considering the mouthful I spit out, I reckon someone's going to have difficulty standing up for a while. Intact calf muscles are useful for that sort of thing, and I've just gouged a steak-sized chunk out with my teeth.

Screams and swearing erupt, and there's a momentary lull in arriving beatings as everyone tries to work out what the fuck just happened. I use it to get back to one knee. Ah ha, you fucktoboggans. Now we'll see what's really up.

Except I feel a swift punch to my side, a jab that seems to keep going, not bothering with practicalities like stopping on contact with solid flesh. And a familiar pain, as sharp as whatever caused it, comes screaming up through my insides as I topple forward.

I've just been stabbed.

Oh, they got me good. I can't tell what they've punctured and perforated yet, but more than one organ I reckon. My lungs are struggling, but that might be the shock. Or one might be ruptured by the blade. Both are possible.

It's funny. I'm already soaking – in booze, in the stale piss I slipped in. But I can still feel the difference, can still feel how much blood pumps out of the hole. The warmth spreads along my side, then my back as I perform a rolling slump over, and there's a lot of it.

I'm a dead man. Just a matter of time.

Through the greying blurs that make up my vision now, there's only one bit of good news. The shithead who stabbed me is standing over me, his blade wavering. Probably the first time he's ever taken a life. Wait till my body disintegrates. That's really going to shit him up for a minute before the magic kicks in, and he forgets all about it. His mate, who's now half a calf muscle down, is sat on the floor, bawling and snivelling, which warms my soul, and the third of their trio is trying to wrap what looks like an Armani jacket around the gushing hole I made in his leg to stem the bleeding enough for them to get out of here.

And there's no sign of the woman. She managed to hightail it out of here while they were distracted with murdering me.

Good. That makes it all worth it.

That's as much as I'm allowed to see. The smeghead who stabbed me's regained a little of his shaken confidence, at least so I gather by his sudden snapped off kick to my jaw. His heart's not fully in it –it can't be; I don't lose any teeth– but it's enough for me to end up kissing the concrete again, my eyes closed.

Lying in my own blood. Stinking of piss. Killed by some mortal hoodlums. I think I might have reached a new low.

Ah well. Won't be alive for much longer now. The Good God knows I'm going to need a drink again after this particular humiliation. I wonder if they'll do a runner, leave me to bleed out. Or whether they might gather some collective strength, goad each other on, and stab me again to finish the job.

In the end, the answer is neither. Because although my eyes are closed and absolutely determined not to open, I hear a familiar voice. One I've been avoiding since I got back to the city a week ago and went on a bender instead of letting him know about the shit-heap of a situation I'd just got back from.

'You stupid sods. This is what you were taught is right, is it? To terrorise women? To kill brave but *bloody stupid* –' Okay, that part is definitely addressed at me. ' –drunks who try to do the right thing? Fine. You'll all remember this. Every single night, you'll have this scene come back in a dream. And that woman? She'll wear the face of any woman who's ever mattered to you. See your mother, your sister, your one true love who got away. See them cower and scream in terror from your actions and feel that shame because you gave them that feeling. You planted that trauma in their heart and marred them with it. Carry that forever and may you never get a night's peace ever again. Now get out of my bloody sight before I forget I'm a pacifist.'

I manage to crack my eyes open a tad, and the area is bathed in a silvery light, like the moon decided to pop down to have a guided tour around the streets of Toulouse. Except it's not from a celestial body.

It's from a celestial being. An angel. It's the light of Nithael radiating out of my mentor –who's also the nearest thing I've had to a father in the past eight hundred years– Isaac.

Boy, am I in trouble now.

'Well, this is a right bloody mess you've made here, lad.' Yep. That's a distinctly pissed-off tone right there in his voice.

'I might have got a bit pissed, 'Zac.' That's a valid excuse, right?

'I think that might count as the bloody understatement of the year, lad. Getting jumped by a trio of Talentless hoodlums? What the bloody hell is going on?'

Two bloodys in one sentence. Isaac is definitely pissed. Mind you, there's a clear answer to his question. 'Well, right now, 'Zac, what's going on is I'm dying.'

'Ah, damn it.' I feel him crouch down to check on me. His arm comes behind my shoulder, lifting me up, cradling me to him as my life leaks out all over his crumpled shirt. My vision clears enough to allow me to focus on his face. More lined than mine, he looks to be in his early forties, but his tight brown curls and sparkling eyes combined with his kindly demeanour garner attention wherever he goes in that "sexy college professor" sort of way. Not that he cares. Or even notices.

'I'm a mess, 'Zac. Best just to let me die. Come back afresh.'

'Except I've spent a week trying to track you down, lad.' There's the recrimination again. 'I'm not eager to go hunting again.'

I shake my head, which turns out to be a bad idea considering the swelling forming around my neck. I wince. 'I'll ring you straight away, promise. Sorry.'

Gently, he levers me up into a sitting position, holding me on either shoulder so he can look me in the eye. He purses his lips, then nods. 'All right, lad. You better bloody do.'

Then he lifts a hand away and clips me hard round the back of the head.

'Ow! Fucksake, 'Zac, what was that for? I'm fucking dying here! Literally!'

'Well, one, for making me so bloody worried for a whole bloody week. And two, because you're going to get out of having a bloody hangover that you full well bloody deserve, so you can have a ringing head right now instead! And maybe it'll remind you to bloody ring me as soon as you come to, you bloody idiot.'

As my vision fades to black and my life fades away, I can only think one thing.

Six bloodys. In one paragraph.

Isaac is seriously pissed off.

ABOUT THE AUTHOR

It's been a strange, unbelievable journey to arrive at the point where these books are going to be released into the wild, like rare, near-extinct animals being returned to their natural habitat, already wondering where they're going to nick cigarettes from on the plains of Africa, the way they used to from the zookeeper's overalls. C.N. Rowan ("Call me C.N., Mr. Rowan was my father") came originally from Leicester, England. Somehow escaping its terrible, terrible clutches (only joking, he's a proud Midlander really), he has wound up living in the South-West of France for his sins. Only, not for his sins. Otherwise, he'd have ended up living somewhere really dreadful. Like Leicester. (Again – joking, he really does love Leicester. He knows Leicester can take a joke. Unlike some of those other cities. Looking at you, Slough.) With multiple weird strings to his bow, all of which are made of tooth-floss and liable to snap if you tried to use them to do anything as adventurous as shooting an arrow, he's done all sorts of odd things, from running a hiphop record label (including featuring himself as rapper) to hustling disability living aids on the mean streets of Syston. He's particularly proud of the work he's done managing and recording several French hiphop acts, and is currently awaiting confirmation of wild rumours he might get a Gold Disc for a song he recorded and mixed.

He'd always love to hear from you so please drop him an email here - chris@cnrowan.com

f   facebook.com/cnrowan

a   amazon.com/author/cnrowan

g   goodreads.com/author/show/23093361.C_N_Rowan

⊙   instagram.com/cnrowanauthor

ALSO BY C.N. ROWAN

The imPerfect Cathar Series

imPerfect Magic

imPerfect Curse

imPerfect Fae
(release 6th July 23)

imPerfect Bones
(release 7th August 23)

imPerfect Hunt
(release 4th September 23)

imPerfect Gods
(release 2nd October 23)

An imPerfect Trap (prequel novella to imPerfect Magic)

Milton Keynes UK
Ingram Content Group UK Ltd.
UKHW011109280823
427620UK00004B/490